Praise for

REMEMBER MIA

"As riveting as *Gone Girl*, but with an even sharper emotional edge, this story of a missing seven-month-old baby and the mother who has no recollection of the events surrounding her daughter's disappearance will pull you in from the very first page. The fast-paced plot, psychological intrigue, and engrossing twists will have you flipping pages faster and faster as Estelle's memories are gradually uncovered and piece by jagged piece the puzzle comes together."

—Kelly Jones, author of *Lost and Found in Prague*

"*Remember Mia* is a twisty, gripping read—beautifully written and impossible to put down."

—Meg Gardiner, Edgar® Award–winning author

REMEMBER MIA

ALEXANDRA BURT

BERKLEY BOOKS, NEW YORK

BERKLEY

An imprint of Penguin Random House LLC
375 Hudson Street, New York, New York 10014

This book is an original publication of the Berkley Publishing Group.

Library of Congress Cataloging-in-Publication Data

Burt, Alexandra.
Remember Mia / Alexandra Burt.
pages cm
ISBN 978-0-425-27840-6 (paperback)
1. Mothers and daughters Fiction.   2. Missing children—Fiction.   I. Title.
PS3602.U7694R46 2015
813'.6—dc23
2015002916

PUBLISHING HISTORY
Berkley trade paperback edition / July 2015

PRINTED IN THE UNITED STATES OF AMERICA

10 9 8 7 6 5 4 3 2 1

Cover art: *Steps* © by Frederick Bass/Getty Images.
Cover design by Diana Kolsky.
Interior text design by Kelly Lipovich.

Penguin
Random
House

For all mothers, especially mine.
For all daughters, especially mine.

PART 1

I can't explain *myself*, I'm afraid, Sir . . . because I'm not myself, you see.

Lewis Carroll, Alice's Adventures in Wonderland

MISSING: SEVEN-MONTH-OLD INFANT
DISAPPEARS FROM CRIB

Brooklyn, NY—The New York City Police Department is asking for the public's help in locating 7-month-old Mia Connor.

The parents and the NYPD are pleading with the public for any assistance in the investigation and are asking Brooklyn residents in the North Dandry neighborhood to come forward if they witnessed any suspicious behavior on the night and early morning of the 30th.

Mia Connor was last seen by her mother, Estelle Paradise, 27, around midnight when she laid her down to sleep. The mother discovered the child was missing when she woke up the next morning. The father was out of town when the infant disappeared.

"It's very frustrating," said Eric Rodriguez, spokesperson for the NYPD, when he appeared briefly at a news conference on Friday. "We're hoping somebody will come forward and give us the information allowing us to locate the child."

Immediately call the TIPS hotline if you have any information about the infant's whereabouts. All calls are strictly confidential.

Mia Connor has brown eyes and blond hair, is 25 inches tall, and weighs 14 pounds. The day of her disappearance she wore white one-piece pajamas with a cupcake print. She has two bottom teeth.

CHAPTER 1

"Mrs. Paradise?"

A voice sounds out of nowhere. My thoughts are sluggish, as if I'm running underwater. I try and try but I'm not getting anywhere.

"Not stable. Eighty over sixty. And falling."

Oh God, I'm still alive.

I move my legs, they respond, barely, but they respond. Light prowls its way into my eyes. I hear dogs barking, high-pitched. They pant, their tags clatter.

"You've been in a car accident."

My face is hot, my thoughts vague, like dusty boxes in obscure and dark attic spaces. I know immediately something is amiss.

"Oh my God, look at her head."

A siren sounds, it stutters for a second, then turns into a steady torment.

I want to tell them . . . I open my mouth, my lips begin to form the words, but the burning sensation in my head becomes unbearable. My chest is on fire, and ringing in my left ear numbs the entire side of my face. *Let me die*, I want to tell them. But the only sound I hear is of crude hands tearing fragile fabric.

"Step back. Clear."

My body explodes, jerks upward.

This isn't part of the plan.

My vision is blurred and hazy. I make out a woman in baby blue scrubs, a nurse, slipping a plastic tube over my head, and immediately two prongs hiss cold air into my nostrils. She pumps a lever and the bed jerks upward, then another lever triggers a motor raising the headboard until my upper body is resting almost vertically.

My world becomes clearer. The nurse's hair is in a ponytail and the pockets of her cardigan sag. I watch her dispose of tubing and wrappers, and the closing of the trash can's metal lid sounds final, evoking a feeling I can't quite place, a vague sense of loss, like a pickpocket making off with my loose change, disappearing into the crowd that is my strange memory.

A male voice sounds out of nowhere.

"I need to place a PICC line."

The overly gentle voice belongs to a man in a white coat. He talks to me as if I'm a child in need of comfort.

"Just relax, you won't feel a thing."

Relax and I won't feel a thing? What a concept. I lift my arms and pain shoots from my shoulder into my neck. I tell myself not to do that again anytime soon.

The white coat rubs the back of my hand. The alcohol wipe leaves an icy trail and jerks me further from my lulled state. I watch the doctor insert a long needle into my vein. A forgotten cotton wipe rests in the folds of the waffle-weave blanket, in its center a bright red bloody mark, like a scarlet letter.

There's a spark of memory, it ignites but then fizzles, like a wet match. I refuse to be pulled away, I follow the crimson, attach myself to the memory that started out like a creak on the stairs, but then the monsters appear.

First I remember the darkness.

Then I remember the blood.

My baby. Oh God, Mia.

The memory of the blood lingers. There're flashes of red exploding like lightning in the sky; one moment they're illuminating everything around me; the next they are gone, bathing my world in darkness. Then the bloody images fade and vanish, leaving a black jittering line on the screen.

Squeaking rubber soles on linoleum circle me and I feel a pat on my shoulder.

This isn't real. A random vision, just a vision. It doesn't mean anything.

A nurse gently squeezes my shoulder and I open my eyes.

"Mrs. Paradise." The nurse's voice is soft, almost apologetic. "I'm sorry, but I have orders to wake you every couple of hours."

"Blood," I say, and squint my eyes, attempting to force the image to return to me. "I don't understand where all this blood's coming from." Was that my voice? It can't be mine, it sounds nothing like me.

"Blood? What blood?" The nurse looks at my immaculately taped PICC line. "Are you bleeding?"

I turn toward the window. It's dark outside. The entire room appears in the window's reflection, like an imprint, a not-quite-true copy of reality.

"Oh God," I say, and my high-pitched voice sounds like a screeching microphone. "Where's my daughter?"

She just cocks her head and then busies herself straightening the blanket. "Let me get the doctor for you," she says and leaves the room.

CHAPTER 2

Voices enter my consciousness like a slow drift of clouds, merging with the scent of pancakes, syrup, toast, and coffee, making my stomach churn.

A gentle hand touches my arm, then a voice. "Mrs. Paradise? I'm Dr. Baker."

I judge only his age—he is young—as if my brain does not allow me to appraise him further. Have I met him before? I don't know. Everything about me, my body and my senses, is faulty. When did I become so forgetful, so scatterbrained?

He wears a white coat with his name stitched on the pocket: *Dr. Jeremy Baker.* He retrieves a pen from his coat and shines a light into my eyes. There's an explosion so painful I clench my eyelids shut. I turn my head away from him, reach up, and feel the left side of my head. Now I understand why the world around me is muffled; my entire head is bandaged.

"You're at County Medical. An ambulance brought you to the emergency room about . . ." He pauses and looks at his wristwatch. I wonder why the time matters. Is he counting the hours, does he want to be exact? ". . . three days ago, on the fifth."

Three days. And I don't remember a single minute. *Ask him, go ahead, ask him.* "Where's my daughter?"

"You were in a car accident. You have a head injury and you've been in a medically induced coma."

He didn't answer my question. He talks to me as if I'm a child, incapable of comprehending more elaborate sentences. *Accident? I don't remember any accident.*

"They found you in your car in a ravine. You have a concussion, fractured ribs, and multiple contusions around your lower extremities. You also had a critical head injury when they brought you in. Your brain was swollen, which was the reason for the induced coma."

I don't remember any accident. What about Jack? Yes, Mia's with Jack. She must be.

One more time.

"Was my daughter in the car with me?"

"You were alone," he says.

"She's with Jack? Mia's with my husband?"

"Everything's going to be okay."

The blood was just a vision, it wasn't real. She's with Jack, she's safe. Thank God.

Everything is going to be okay, he said.

"We're not sure of any brain damage at this point, but now that you've regained consciousness we'll be able to perform all the necessary tests to figure out what's going on." He motions to the nurse who has been standing next to him. "You lost a lot of blood and we had to administer fluids to stabilize you. The swelling will go down in a few days, but in the meantime we need to make sure you keep your lungs clear of fluids."

He picks up a contraption and holds it up in front of me. "This is a spirometer. The nurse will give you detailed instructions. Basically you keep the red ball suspended as long as you can. Every two hours, please." His last comment is directed toward the nurse.

The gurgling in my chest is uncomfortable and I try not to cough. The pain in my left side must be the fractured ribs. I wonder how I'll be able to stay awake for two hours or wake up every two hours or use this contraption for two hours, or whatever he just said.

"Before I forget . . ." Dr. Baker looks down at me. He is quiet for a while and I wonder if I missed a question. Then he lowers his voice. "Two detectives were here to talk to you. I won't allow any questioning until we've done a few more tests." He nods to the nurse and walks toward the door, then turns around and offers one more trifle of news. "Your husband will be here soon. In the meantime can we call anyone for you? Family? A friend? Anybody?"

I shake my head *no* and immediately regret it. A mallet pounds against my skull from the inside. My head is a giant swollen bulb and the throbbing in my ear manages to distract me from my aching ribs. My lids have a life of their own. I'm nodding off but I have so many questions. I take a deep breath as if I'm preparing to jump off a diving board. It takes everything I have to sound out the words.

"Where did this accident happen?" Why does he look so puzzled? Am I missing more than I'm aware of?

"I'm sorry, but I can't tell you much about the accident," he says. He sounds subdued, as if he's forcing himself to be composed in order to calm me. "All we know is that your car was found upstate at the bottom of a ravine." Pause. "You have a lot of injuries. Some are from the accident. Can you remember what happened?"

I reflect on his words, really think them over. Accident. Ravine. Nothing. Not a thing. There's a large black hole where my memory used to be.

"I can't remember anything," I say.

His brows furrow. "You mean . . . the accident?"

The accident. He talks about *the* accident as if I remember. I want to tell him to x-ray my head, and that he'll find a dark shadow within my skull where my memory once was.

I'm getting the hang of this. Before I say something, I concentrate, think of the question and repeat it in my head, take a deep breath, then I speak.

"You don't understand. I don't remember *the* accident and I don't remember anything *before* the accident."

"Do you remember wanting to harm yourself?"

"Harm myself?" *I would remember that, wouldn't I? Why am I so forgetful?*

"Either that or you were shot."

Was I shot or did I harm myself? What kind of question is he asking me?

I turn my head as far to the left as possible, catching a glimpse of the outstretched leg of a police officer sitting by the door, out in the hallway. I wonder what that's all about.

Dr. Baker looks over his shoulder and then faces me again. He steps closer and lowers his voice. "You don't remember." He states it matter-of-factly, no longer a question, but a realization.

"I don't know what I don't know," I say. That's kind of funny, when I think about it. I giggle and his brows furrow again. I'm getting frustrated. We're going in circles. It's difficult to stay awake.

Then he tells me about my voice. How it is "monotone" and that I have "a reduction in range and intensity of emotions," and that my reactions are "flat and blunted." I don't understand what he's telling me. Should I smile more, be more cheerful? I want to ask him but then I hear a word that puts it all to rest.

"Amnesia," he says. "We're not sure about the cause yet. Retrograde, maybe posttraumatic. Maybe even trauma-related."

When you hear *amnesia* from a man in a white coat, it's serious. Final. *I forgot* sounds casual—*oh, I'm forgetful.* I have amnesia, I'm not forgetful after all. What's next? Is he going to ask me what year it is? Who the president is? If I remember my birth date?

"*Retrograde* means you don't recall events that happened *just before* the onset of the memory loss. *Posttraumatic* is a cognitive impairment and memory loss can stretch back hours or days, sometimes even longer. Eventually you'll recall the distant past but you may never recover what happened just prior to your accident. Amnesia can't be diagnosed with an X-ray, like a broken bone. We've done an MRI test and a CAT scan. Both tests came back inconclusive. Basically there's no definitive proof of brain damage at this point, but absence of proof is not proof of absence. There could be microscopic damages, and the MRI and the CAT scan are just not sophisticated enough to detect those. Nerve fiber damage doesn't show up on either test."

I remain silent, not sure if I should ask anything else, not sure if I even understood him at all. All I grasp is that he can't tell me anything definitive, so what's the point?

"There's the possibility that you suffer from dissociative amnesia. Trauma would cause you to block out certain information associated with the event. There's no test for that, either. You'd have to see a psychiatrist or a psychologist. But we're getting ahead of ourselves. The neurologist will order some more tests. Like I said, time will tell."

I take a deep breath. He's relaying medical facts to me but I just can't shake the feeling that there's something he is not telling me.

"They found me where again?"

"In a ravine, in Dover, upstate. You were transferred here from Dover Medical Center."

Dover? Dover. Nothing. I'm blank.

"I've never been to Dover."

"That's where they found you—you just don't remember." He slips the pen back in his coat pocket. "You were lucky," he adds. He holds up his index finger and thumb, indicating the extent of the luck I had. "The bullet was this far from doing serious damage. Really lucky. Remember that."

Bullet. I was shot or I harmed myself. *Lucky. That depends on whom you ask*, I think to myself. *Remember that.* How funny. My hand moves up to my ear, almost like a reflex. "You said there's damage to my ear. What happened to it?"

He pauses ever so slightly. "Gone. Completely gone. The area was infected and we had to make a decision." He watches me intently. "It could have been worse. Like I said, you were lucky."

"That's some luck," I say, but when I think about my ear, I don't really care.

"There's reconstructive surgery."

"What's there now? I mean, is there a hole?"

"There's a small opening draining fluids, other than that, there's a flap of skin stretched over the wound."

An opening that drains fluids. I'm oddly untouched by the fact that a flap of skin is stretched over a hole in my head where my ear used to be. I have amnesia. I forgot to lock my car. I lost my umbrella. My ear is gone. It's all the same: insignificant.

"And you call that lucky?"

"You're alive, that's what counts."

There's that buzzing sound again and then his voice goes from loud to muffled, as if someone's turned a volume dial.

"What about my ear?"

He looks at me, perplexed.

"I remember you told me it was gone." *Completely gone* were the words he used. "I mean my hearing, what about my hearing? Everything sounds muffled."

"We did an electrophysiological hearing test while you were unconscious." He grabs my file from the nightstand and opens it.

He flips through the pages. "You've lost some audio capacity, but nothing major. We'll order more tests, depending on the next CAT scan. We just have to wait it out."

I look at the police officer's leg outside my door, and I wonder if he's protecting me or if he's protecting someone from me.

"I remembered something." The words come spilling out and take on a life of their own. "I need to know if what I see . . . I . . . I think I remember bits and pieces, but it's not like a memory, it's more like fragments." It's like flipping through a photo album not knowing if it's mine or someone else's life. *Blood. So much blood.*

"You may not be able to remember minute by minute, but you'll be able to generally connect the dots at some point. It's a Humpty Dumpty kind of a situation; maybe you won't be able to put it all back together."

"I'm very tired," I say and feel relieved. All the king's horses and all the king's men. Wild horses. I make a decision. The blood was just an illusion. A figment.

"Let the nurse know if there's anybody you want us to call. Don't forget the spirometer—every two hours . . ."

He points at something behind me. "Behind you is a PCA pump. It delivers small amounts of pain medication. If you need more"—he puts a small box with a red button in my hand—"just push the red button and you'll get one additional dose of morphine. The safety feature only allows for a maximum amount during a certain timed interval. Any questions?"

I have learned my lesson from earlier and barely shake my head.

I watch him leave the room and immediately a nurse enters and I concentrate on her explaining the yellow contraption to me. I'm supposed to breathe into the tubing until a ball moves up, and I have to breathe continuously to try to keep the ball suspended as long as possible.

I have amnesia. My ear is gone. I feel . . . I feel as if I'm not connecting like I should. I should yell and scream, raise bloody hell, but Dr. Baker's explanations of my lack of emotions, "blunted affect" he called it, seems logical. Logic I can handle; it's the emotions that remain elusive.

There's something they're not telling me. Maybe because they don't subject injured people—especially those who've been shot, who lost an ear, who were *that close*—to any additional bad news. That must be it. Maybe the police will tell me, or Jack, once he gets here. They already told me I've been robbed of hours of my life, how much worse can it get?

I hold the spirometer in my right hand. I blow into the tube and allow my mind to go blank while I watch the red ball go up. It lingers for whatever amount of time I manage to keep it suspended. I pinch my eyes shut to will the ball to maintain its suspension. Suddenly bits and pieces of images come into focus as if they are captured on the back of my eyelids. My mind explodes. It disintegrates, breaks into tiny particles.

Mia isn't with Jack. She's gone.

The realization occurs so abruptly and is so powerful that the wires connected to my chest seem to tremble and the machines behind me pick up on it. The beeps speed up like the hooves of a horse, walking, then trotting, then breaking into a full-blown gallop. Mia's disappearance is a fact, yet it is disconnected from whatever consequences it entails—there's a part I can't connect with. An empty crib. Missing clothes, her missing bottles and diapers, everything was gone. I looked for her and couldn't find her. I went to the police and then there's a dark hole.

Like a jigsaw puzzle, I study the pieces, connect them, tear them apart, and start all over again. I remember going to the police precinct but after that it gets blurry—hazy, like a childhood memory. My mind plays a game of "telephone," thoughts relaying messages, then retelling them skewed. Easily misinterpreted, embellished, unreliable.

Every time I watch the spirometer ball move upward, more

images form: a bathroom stall, a mop, a stairwell, pigeons, the smell of fresh paint. Then a picture fades in, as if someone has turned up a light dimmer: fragments of celestial bodies; a sun, a moon, and stars. So many stars.

Why was I in Dover? Where is my daughter and why is no one talking about her?

As I lie in the hospital bed, I am aware of time passing, a fleeting glimpse of light outside, day turning into night, and back into day. I long for . . . a tidbit of my childhood, a morsel of memory, of how my mother cared for me when I was sick, in bed with the flu or some childhood disease, like measles or chicken pox. But then I recall having been a robust child, a child who was hardy and resistant to viruses, to strep throats and pink eyes.

I don't know what to tell Jack once he shows up. He will question me. Jack will ask me about the day Mia disappeared. About the morning I found her crib empty. Amnesia is just another shortcoming on a long list of my other countless inadequacies. Shortfall after shortfall.

I must be insane, for the only explanation I can come up with is of my daughter and my ear, together in the same place. And above them, floating suspended like a mobile, the sun, the moon, and the stars. Bright as bright can be, surrounded by darkness. A chaotic universe illuminated by heavenly bodies.

I rest my hands on my lap. My body stills, comes to a halt. I was in an accident. I was shot or tried to harm myself. My ear is gone. There's a hole that's draining fluids.

I don't care about any of that. Mia's gone. I can't even bear the thought of her. I want the pain to stop yet her image remains. I raise my finger to push the red PCA button, longing for the lulled state the medicine provides. I hesitate, then I put the box down. I have to think, start somewhere. The empty crib. The dots. I have to connect the dots.

CHAPTER 3

Every single night I relived my daughter's birth: her first gasp triggered by the cold birthing room, that gasp turning into a deep breath, then a desperate cry escaping her lips, her attempt at negotiating the inevitable transition between my womb and the outside world.

And every morning I realized that her actual cries reached deep into my dreams, and I woke up feeling like a million tiny bombs were exploding inside my head. Then my muscle memory kicked in. *Wake up, get up, feed her, change her, bathe her, rock her, hold her. Feeding and changing and bathing and rocking and holding.*

I had stopped keeping track of time, the date, or even the days of the week. I was unaware of whatever events might be gripping the rest of the world and I hadn't picked up a book or a magazine in months. My life was reduced to a process of consolidating motor tasks into memory, looplike days and repetitive responsibilities performed without any conscious effort.

As I rose from the couch, the world spun and then stilled. I listened for the echoes of Mia's colicky morning cries, by then six months after her birth, hundredfold replicas of her initial primal emergence that visited me in my dreams. Lately her cries had been reaching me time-delayed, distorted almost, as if communicating a certain distance between us.

That morning, I listened, yet the house remained silent.

Barefoot down the hallway I went and paused by her door, still ajar. The watchband had left an imprint as if I had been tied up all night. It was just before nine and I'd been asleep for an unprecedented six hours. Usually by this time, Mia was attempting to pull herself up by the bars of the crib, her eyes rimmed with tears and rage.

A fleeting sense of normalcy enveloped me, a make-believe image of a round-cheeked child pressed against the mattress manifested itself, an elfin body heavy with peaceful sleep.

Mia's door was cracked just as I had left it hours ago. Opening it wide enough to pass through, I entered the room. Something jabbed at me, made my heart stumble.

The Tinker Bell mobile overhead, unbalanced and lopsided, somehow imperfect and disturbed. The room, barely lit by the sunlight spilling through the window, soundless. Her crib in front of the window, empty and silent. Abandoned. Not so much as an imprint of her body on the sheets.

My molars pulsated as I inspected the windows and rattled the cast-iron bars. I searched the entire apartment, rechecked every window twice. Not a trace of her.

I ran to the front door. The locks were intact, the metal still scratched, the paint still chipped, signs of my clumsy attempt to install a dead bolt. All locks were engaged and everything was where and how it was supposed to be. Except Mia.

There was no proof that anyone had been here—no footprints on the floor, no items left behind—nothing was disturbed, yet this

peculiar energy hovered around me. The apartment seemed physically untouched, but felt ransacked at the same time.

I realized the contradiction of the moment: Mia was gone, yet
there was no evidence, no clue, that someone had taken her. No
shards on the floor, no gaping doors, no curtains blowing in the
breeze of a window left ajar. No haphazardly bunched-up sheet,
no pacifier, no toy discarded on the floor.

9-1-1.

I ran to the kitchen, yanked the receiver off the wall mount,
and stopped dead in my tracks. The dish rack was empty. No
bottle, no collar, no nipple. No formula can, no measuring cup.

I rushed to the trash. Surely her soiled diapers must still be in
there. The can was empty, even the plastic liner was gone.

I ripped open the fridge. All the prefilled formula bottles I had
prepared the night before were missing.

Back in her room, the shelves of the changing table, usually stacked
with diapers and blankets, were empty. The closet door was wide
open, not a hanger dangling, not a shoe left on the closet floor.

I pulled the dresser drawers open. All her clothes were gone.
Every single drawer of the dresser bare. Not a button or a tag
tucked in a corner. The basket on top of the dresser, where I kept
the diapers and the ointment, was empty. Nothing but empty
pieces of furniture.

I checked every inch of her room, every drawer, every corner
of her closet. My heart dropped into my intestines. Not only was
Mia gone, but so was every trace of her.

The 70th Precinct on Lawrence Avenue in Brooklyn was a five-minute
walk from North Dandry. As I passed through the building's glass
doors, the front desk clerk lifted his index finger, indicating he was
talking on the phone, and then pointed at the earpiece.

A janitor pushed a neon yellow bucket and a scraggly mop across the floor. He wore blue overalls and clear booties over his white sneakers. I watched him as he wheeled the bucket across the floor, mopping in circular motions, dipping the mop in the wringer and squeezing out the water.

I studied my reflection in the glass door and saw a woman rocking back and forth with the movement of the mop, cotton strings slithering over the linoleum floor, *wipe, dip, wring, wipe, dip, wring.*

Footsteps jerked me back into reality. Behind me, simultaneously a door opened and a phone rang. A detective in slacks and a light blue shirt, his tie tucked into his waistband, walked up to the counter. He held a short, skinny man by his tattooed upper arm. The man was almost catatonic. The detective gave him a shove to move him along, making the man's chest hit the edge of the counter. He had a crooked smile on his face and seemed indifferent, as if he had been through this too many times to care.

"Get an officer to take him to booking," the detective said to the clerk. "I don't want to see his face again until he's sobered up."

"I need to speak to someone." My voice was loud, so loud it made the clerk look up from the phone. "Please, I need help."

"Just a minute," the detective said. "I'll be with you as soon as I can." He was too far away for me to make out his name on the tag clipped to his shirt pocket. He seemed young, maybe too young. Will he understand me, is he a father, has he worked with missing children? I wonder if I should ask for a more experienced detective.

"I need to talk to someone," I repeated, even louder than before.

He stepped closer, reluctantly. "How can I help you?"

Words sped through my mind, then images of locks emerged, doors secured with bolts, hasps, and locksets.

HELP, I screamed in my mind. I opened my mouth but no words emerged. I swallowed hard, the gulp in my throat echoing through the silent precinct hallways. I wanted to confess to whatever it was I had done, *must have done*, for no one disappears through locked doors or walls.

Nausea overcame me. I welcomed the strangled retching, wanted to let go of the words, the confession. I refused to fight the heaviness in my throat. Saliva collected in my mouth and instinctively I pinched my nose to keep the vomit from ejecting through my nostrils.

He stepped backward, as if I were a contagious leper. "There's a bathroom right over there." The detective pointed toward a door less than ten feet away.

I convulsed with spasms and on all fours I knelt in the stall. Ripples shook my body, my cold skin was covered in a layer of sweat. Eventually I managed to get to my feet, and as I studied my reflection in the mirror, I rummaged through my mind for an explanation, never lifting my gaze off the stranger that stared back at me. I felt fury for the woman in the mirror, a woman with unwashed hair, her eyes sunken in and sad, the woman who had replaced the real me.

Back in the hallway, the detective was waiting for me. "Ma'am?" He seemed impatient, as if dealing with someone who had no real police business after all.

I didn't know what to tell the detective anymore. Had someone walked through brick walls, had some ill-fated Houdini act occurred while I was sleeping? When a magician pulls an endless scarf out of a hat, everybody knows it's a simple trick, but this was real. And I didn't know if I was a victim or if I was guilty. A crime has been committed. But what kind of crime?

I don't know where my daughter is.

An all-encompassing statement, implicating everything possible but not implying anything specific. No fault, no crime, no blame. Just a fact.

I don't know where my daughter is.

I couldn't fathom a single logical way of explaining how Mia had disappeared.

Say it, I kept telling myself, *say it. JUST SAY IT*. I pushed myself to speak but the woman I had become didn't comply. There was nothing anyone could do for her.

No one can help me. No one can help me. No one can help me.

Like an oath, I repeated it three times, hoping the reiteration would conjure up some sort of sense and logic.

As I looked past the detective, down the hallway, the tattooed man from earlier darted for the front door. The detective's eyes followed him and then he ran after him. The tattooed man, unsteady on his feet, had reached the glass door by the time the detective got ahold of him.

I focused on the floor and the tiny specks in the blue linoleum. I felt my knees weakening, I had to keep moving, keep the blood circulating through my body.

No one can help me.

I exited the precinct and kept on walking. I felt numb inside, anesthetized, yet somehow purged, ready to accept the facts. The numbness dissolved long enough to allow the gravity of what I must have done to sink in. As I passed a store window, out of the corner of my eye I saw a woman studying her hands as if she hadn't seen them in a long time.

In that brief yet gruesome moment of clarity I realized those hands might just be the hands of a monster.

CHAPTER 4

"I came straight from the airport. I can't even wrap my mind around this. What the hell happened?"

He whispers, yet his words pierce through me. His comment feels familiar. Not the words, but the feeling it evokes. I've been belittled so many times. So many faux pas committed by me—little ones first, then major ones.

My hands shake, then my whole body trembles. Whether with fear or anger, I don't know. I fix my gaze on Jack's anxious face and search his features for some sort of empathy, but he's all business; his suit, his posture, his demeanor.

"Someone took her, Jack."

"What do you mean 'someone took her'? Where were you?" He slides his briefcase across the nightstand, sending a plastic cup tumbling over the edge and to the ground. "What the hell is going on?"

"Jack, I—"

"I leave for a couple of weeks and you get in an accident in . . . Dover? What did you do there? That's hours from here!"

He swipes his hand through the air as if to dismiss me when

I open my mouth. "Who loses a baby, Estelle? Who? Tell me who loses a baby?"

I press my lips together. I don't dare make eye contact with him.

"Why did you take her to Dover?"

The beeping and buzzing of machines behind me is the only sound in the room.

"I didn't, Jack, that's the thing. I don't know why I was even there."

"I was questioned by the police—no wait, *questioned* isn't the right word . . ." His face twitches, then he steps closer. He lifts his index finger as if to scold me like a child. "I was *interrogated*. I was detained at the airport, taken to the police station, and interrogated like a common criminal. Just what did you tell them?"

"I didn't tell them anything. Just that you were out of town and—"

"And what?"

"Nothing else. What do you mean? I have nothing to tell them."

"They sure had a lot of questions. I was treated like a suspect."

"They always suspect the parents first, you know that."

"I've never been so humiliated in my life. Once my boss gets wind of this . . ." He doesn't finish the sentence. "Where is she? Tell me where she is."

"She's missing, Jack!" I'm alarmed by the distance in his eyes. I want to cry but that would only make him angrier. All this time with Jack has paid off—I've learned to hold back my tears.

"I know she's missing, they're searching for her. I want to know how it happened. Tell me everything. I talked to the police and the doctors, but I want to hear it from you."

I start with how I found the empty crib. How it was a Sunday and none of the workers were in the house. How I called Lieberman but he was out of town, just like every weekend. How nothing made sense. How I went to the police. He doesn't say, *It's going to be okay* or *We'll sort it out.* He just says, "Go on."

When I'm done, he shakes his head. "I should've never left town.

Never. You fooled me. You told me you were okay and I believed you. Did you leave her somewhere? Tell me where you left her."

Jack's got it all figured out, like always. In his world you ask questions and get answers, but this isn't a courtroom and I couldn't tell him what had happened if I wanted to.

"Jack—"

"You promised me, *promised me*, you were okay, and now look what you've done."

"I'm sorry, Jack. I'm so sorry."

"Sorry isn't going to cut it. My daughter is gone. *Gone*. Did that sink in yet?"

"I don't know, Jack, *I don't know*."

"You don't know where you left her?"

"No, I didn't leave her *anywhere*. I don't know where she is."

"Did you leave her with a sitter? Did you leave her at an over-night day care? Maybe—"

"No, no, there was no sitter. No day care."

"I should've known something was going to happen. I never should've . . ." He doesn't finish the sentence.

Remember, a change of scenery would do me good, you said. It would be like starting over, you said. I believed you, Jack. I thought I could leave the other woman, the one who had taken over my life, I could leave her behind. But she followed me.

"None of this makes any sense." Suddenly his face relaxes. "You've been acting strangely ever since you had Mia. Either I worked too much or I slept too late. Nothing was ever right. I'm starting to think this was your plan all along."

"My plan? What plan?"

"Yeah, you land a lawyer, get married, have a baby, divorce him, and get alimony and child support. *That* plan."

"You're the jackpot and I'm the gold digger? We're broke, remember? You took this job in Chicago because we are broke."

"I'm just trying to understand what happened. I've done nothing but support you. What happened to you, Estelle? Did you wake up one day and just say to yourself, *Fuck Jack, fuck Mia, fuck everything*? Just like that? I've done everything you wanted me to do, given you everything you've ever wanted. Now it's time to do something for me."

I just look at him.

"Tell me the truth. We can still fix this."

"I was in an accident. I have amnesia. I don't know what happened." My voice is monotone, like a robot repeating a prerecorded statement.

"Let's assume you really don't remember, let's entertain that for a minute, but explain to me how you don't call me. Explain that to me. I'm her father—how do you not call me? Was this another one of your crazy moments?"

"My crazy moments?"

"One of those moments when you go off the deep end. When you can't hold the baby, when you can't stop crying, when you follow me to my office, when you go through my stuff, when you can't pick up the phone, can't dial 9-1-1! One of those moments. Do I need to go on?"

Everything in his world is either black or white. The scary thing is that I have to agree with him, I'm not good for anything. I tried to be a good mother, I tried to do what mothers do. I wish I could make him understand how hard I tried.

"Everything okay in here?" We turn toward the door, where a nurse stands, holding an empty tray.

"Sorry," Jack says and I nod in agreement. "We'll keep it down. Everything's all right."

Jack doesn't like to be told how loud he can speak. He lowers his voice but the look in his eyes makes up for the contained rage.

"There's a cop sitting outside. Do you get how serious this is?"

I nod.

"Any idea why he's here?" He doesn't wait for my answer and lowers his voice to a whisper. "It's not for your protection."

"What are you saying?" I ask and can't keep my voice from shaking.

"You need a criminal defense lawyer."

I cringe at the word *criminal*.

"Jack, I'm not a criminal. I don't remember what happened. I'm beside myself!" Is it possible for a nonexistent ear to throb? I know my outbursts only reiterate the fact that, in his eyes, I've lost my mind. I know I must look like a deer right before the bumper makes contact.

"I woke up and she was gone. Everything was gone. That's *all* I remember."

"Something must have happened. Did she cry and you got upset? Did you do something to her?"

I try to sit up but the pain in my ribs is excruciating.

"Look at me." Jack steps closer and he grabs my chin, turning my head toward him. "Look me in the eyes and tell me what happened."

"Do you think I'd hurt our daughter?"

The candor of my question startles him. His eyes widen, but immediately he catches himself and lowers his voice back down to a whisper. "I'm not saying you hurt her. All I'm saying is that I blame you for what happened." Jack opens his briefcase. "One more thing," he adds.

There is always one more thing with Jack.

"I'm not sure if you're getting this, but there's a possibility you'll spend the rest of your life behind bars or strapped to a gurney if you don't remember what happened. Now is the time to grasp the severity of your situation." He pinches his lips into a straight line and adds, "I've talked to the doctors at length, and if I can convince the DA, I'll get you into a clinic with a doctor who specializes in memory recovery."

I stare at him, and then I lower my eyes.

"Where's this clinic?" I ask.

"Here in New York. The doctor, some foreigner from the Middle East, specializes in trauma-related memory loss." His shoulders relax but even his expensive suit can't hide the fact that suddenly he looks like a deflated balloon. "I need you to sign a voluntary admission to a psychiatric facility for an unspecified length of time."

I attempt to organize my thoughts into separate, manageable portions. It barely seems possible. *Memory recovery.* I imagine wires hooked up to my brain, truth serums, and my retina relaying images to computer screens. *A psychiatric facility. Unspecified amount of time.* I'm agreeing to go to a loony bin and I won't be able to check out.

"I don't belong in a psych ward. I'm not crazy."

Jack cocks his head and raises his brows as if he has caught a kid in a lie.

"In your eyes I'm just this lunatic, right? Why don't you just say it? You think I'm crazy, don't you?"

"Not crazy in a certifiable sense, not crazy as in failing a psych exam, but I believe that you need help and that this clinic might just be your only chance. And most of all, it's Mia's only chance." His voice is soft now, almost seductive. "I don't think you have any other choice. This is it."

I force my legs off the side of the bed. My rubbery socks search for the sticky linoleum floor. I feel suspended, unable to find the ground. The second the pen rests at the end of my name, I feel an overwhelming urge to take it in my fist and scratch out my signature until the paper is torn to shreds.

Jack grabs the pen and pulls it from between my fingers and checks his watch.

"That doctor will help me remember and we'll find Mia. We'll find out what happened, right, Jack?"

He closes his briefcase and leaves the room before I can even get my feet on the ground.

CHAPTER 5

One day after I finished college, I told myself, *Take one year and figure out what you want to do with your life*. I was waiting for a sign, some sort of higher intervention one might refer to as palm-reader stuff. I'd walk down 57th Street and tell myself the next billboard that catches my eye, the next car graphic, tote bag, or flyer blowing my way was going to be the answer.

At the time, I worked at a health insurance call center, where I met a woman who at first glance seemed out of place. Delilah, middle-aged, short, and heavyset, was covered in tattoos she hid amazingly well under white oversized blouses and cardigans. She was far removed from the twenty-somethings filling up the cubicles around us. Every time she pushed back her cardigan sleeves, a gesture signaling a difficult customer, a tattoo on her forearm emerged: *Dead Men Tell No Tales*.

"You keep looking at my tattoo," she said one day from the cubicle next to mine, and muted her headset.

"Quite a message," I replied.

"Kind of a funny story," she said.

"Dead men tell no tales? How funny can that story be?" I asked.

Delilah told me she'd been a prison guard for twenty-five years. With every passing year her people skills and faith in humanity took a turn for the worse. Her husband left her and she had no relationship with her five children—they weren't even speaking to her. As a matter of self-preservation, she decided to spend the rest of her working career in customer service. "Forces me to work on myself every day," she said and switched to a noncommittal voice accepting the next call in the queue.

The concept intrigued me and I wondered about my own character shortcomings. I'd never sought lasting friendships, never seemed to truly connect to anyone else, and I had basically remained a loner all my life. I wondered if I just needed to meet new people or maybe the right people, or just put myself out there so I'd fit in somewhere. I quit my job at the call center that very day.

Two days later I found a job as a hostess at La Luna, a bar and grill in Manhattan, mostly frequented by judges, DAs, defense lawyers, prosecutors, and armies of executives working in the surrounding buildings. La Luna's neighborhood on Lexington and 50th was a hodgepodge of restaurants and bars, office buildings, law offices, and an occasional Starbucks to break up the monotony.

Weeks later, I saw a man standing in line, waiting to be seated. He wasn't stunningly attractive and there wasn't anything unusual about him that caught my eye, but still I couldn't wait for him to get to the front of the line.

"Jack Connor," he said and straightened his tie. He was expecting a party of two to join him and wanted me to give him the best table in the house. I liked the way he looked into my eyes and weighed his words before he spoke.

He followed me to a table at the far end of the restaurant, looked around, and pointed at a table by the front window. "I think I'd prefer that one."

That's how I met Jack. Me challenging myself, him telling me what I offered him wasn't good enough. Later Jack read my name off the tag on my blouse, his voice a soft baritone.

"Estelle Paradise."

Over the years, I had heard many jokes regarding my name and I was prepared for one then but none came. Jack was lanky and wholesome, but the dark circles under his eyes spoke of long hours and work beyond his physical capacity. I realized that his left eyebrow was noticeably raised and had a much more pronounced curve, as if the world was under his constant scrutiny.

"You keep looking at my eye," he said.

"I don't mean to, I'm sorry." I blushed and turned away. There was something slightly off about his face and his facial expression seemed to be in a constant state of disapproval.

"Hypertropia," he said and wiggled his brows. "It's a muscle imbalance, the visual axis of one eye is higher than the other. It's hereditary. I wore glasses when I was younger but short of surgery one eye will always be slightly higher than the other."

The very next day he dropped by for a drink. He sat at the bar and watched me as I walked the floor.

"You know what you should do?" Jack asked that day.

"What's that?" I held a stack of menus like a shield between us.

"Check to see the progression of the tables instead of just marking the occupied tables at your station."

"And why would I do that?"

He looked at me, puzzled. "To see if the tables are on dessert or if they've paid their checks. It expedites the operation."

"I'll keep that in mind," I said and laughed, trying not to focus on his eye again.

"Would you go out on a date with me?" Jack's voice shook slightly, enough to be noticeable if you paid close attention.

"We're not allowed to go on dates with patrons," I lied and brushed invisible crumbs off my blouse. No one cared whom we dated; the waitress and hostess turnaround was staggering.

His eyes remained on my chest, and then he got up and downed his drink. "If I stop coming here, will you go out with me then?"

"Don't hold your breath," I said.

A month later, we went on our first date. I wore my best dress, black, sleeveless, while he wore khakis and a blue unbuttoned shirt. A movie and then dinner, during which we both had too much to drink. In my tipsy stupor I must have told him about my rent being late because he offered to pay for the next month. "Come on," he said, "let me do something for you."

That line got to me. Any other night the comment wouldn't have. After all, I was used to getting by and had always been able to muddle through, but money was tight, and I was struggling to keep up with my student loan payments. Jack's comment later was "Liberal arts? No degree at all is better than a liberal arts degree," and so I was stuck in a hostess position while all the waitress slots, popular for their high tips, were filled. I had yet to gain any additional insight into what I wanted to do with my life and I wondered if Delilah had told me a story altogether.

That night, Jack's shirt smelled of starch and I wondered how his lips would feel on mine. My mouth on his mouth. A taste of what life could be if I let him do something for me.

On our second date, during which I expected reality to set in and expose how different we really were, Jack put his coat around my shoulders as the temperature dropped on our walk to the restaurant. The itchy wool and the smooth lining was every cliché of every romantic movie I had ever seen. The guy who put his coat around the girl's shoulders is the good guy, good guys give you their coat, and bad guys take your clothes off. During dinner, I told him about my dating rules.

"Thirty days, no making out, no sex." It was more or less my way of evoking a response regarding his intentions, but Jack, unshakable, undeterred Jack, didn't flinch.

"I've got my own rule. It's more like one hundred and eighty days, but okay. I accept," he said and added, "So, we're officially dating?"

"Whose side are you on?" I asked while we passed the MetLife Building. "Careerwise," I added and moved my body closer to his as we walked hand in hand. "I've always wondered how lawyers figure out if they prefer being a defense lawyer or a prosecutor. Seems like two very different sides of the law to me."

"You just pick a side," he said and furrowed his brow as if my question made no sense at all.

When I asked him what he wanted to do years from now, he said, "I'm looking to become assistant DA. From there, district DA, then judge."

"And then you'll run for public office, like mayor or something?" I joked.

"Mayor?" He paused. "Probably not. I don't do well with crowds and public speaking. Supreme Court maybe. They submit their rulings in writing. Seems like the perfect fit."

Jack was arrogant, but at the same time his overconfidence was harmless and refreshing and made me want to know more about him.

"Defenders probably see the good in everyone," I said. "Prosecutors expect everyone to be a criminal. Don't you have to take a stand in your heart?"

"My heart? That's a very emotional way of looking at the world."

"Tell me about growing up," I said, wanting to change the subject.

Jack named his childhood experiences like he was reading a grocery list. "New Jersey, public schools, wrestling team, single mom." He paused slightly, then continued. "An only child, sort of. My mother was an employee at the New York Public Library. We struggled, to say the least. My mother was a saint, she never even raised her voice at me."

"You were *sort of* an only child?"

Jack then told me how his father, Earl, had left his mother when he was still in diapers. Earl, a big-rig driver who spent a majority of the year on the road, met another woman, a beauty salon owner named Elsa. He gave up his trucker job, something he had refused Jack's mom for years, and started driving a city bus instead. He didn't disappear from Jack's life. No, he did something much worse.

"I ran into my father in school, in front of the principal's office. I hadn't seen him in years, couldn't even remember the last time he'd spoken to me. For some odd reason that only a ten-year-old can comprehend, I felt he had come for me. Just when I was about to run into his arms, I heard the principal's voice over the PA system. *George Connor, please come to the front office.* That was the day I learned of my half brother, George. And that we lived close enough to go to school together. Five blocks, to be exact."

I didn't know what to say so I asked him about his mom. He let out a breath that sounded like a groan. "In a way, she killed herself," he said, and I could tell it was an emotional subject for him. "She started working three jobs, trying to send me to private school after the whole incident with my brother. She wasn't feeling well for a long time, and when she finally went to the doctor, it was too late. She had ignored all the signs for too long and was diagnosed with colon cancer. Eventually she had surgery but they just stitched her back up, there was nothing they could do. The cancer had spread to her brain and her liver."

I thought about my own family and how my mother didn't seem to feel any guilt pursuing her photography career. I remembered all the nights without dinner on the table and the door to the darkroom locked. Many years after my parents had passed, I still couldn't make up my mind if I should feel cheated out of her attention or happy she had a career of her own.

That night, we broke the thirty-days-no-sex rule and made

love for the first time. It was a chaotic mess: him fidgeting with the condom wrapper and me not knowing where to put my legs. When I woke up the next morning, Jack was sitting in bed, furiously writing in a notebook.

"Are you writing me a poem?" I asked jokingly.

"A speech," he said. Jack had been selected to deliver the keynote speech for an annual function sponsored by the New York City Bar Association for over eight hundred law students. For the next two weeks he outlined the speech, then revised it just to start all over again. The night of the event I watched him deliver the speech and didn't see a hint of anxiety. He spoke with confidence, made eye contact, and told anecdotes and jokes. Something wasn't right, there wasn't even a hint of anxiety in his voice or his demeanor. Later I found out that speaking in front of crowds wasn't his only problem.

On our way to the reception room, Jack excused himself, his forehead covered in sweat. People were asking for him, wanting to meet the bright young attorney who had delivered such an inspiring and confident speech. I waited in front of the restroom, then checked the coatroom and behind the stage, but Jack had all but disappeared. His cell went to voice mail and I finally decided to hail a cab and go home. I found him vomiting behind a porta-potty in a construction zone in the parking lot.

Jack mumbled something about an upset stomach. "Go in and let my boss know I have a stomach virus," he said in one uninterrupted breath and then continued to dry heave. It wasn't just a fear of speaking in front of crowds but having to mingle with people that did him in.

"A slight bout of anxiety. Not a big deal, I'm working on it," he confessed later. "I prefer a courtroom to a cocktail party. So what?"

A few months later, I told Jack I might be pregnant. There was a long silence followed by an unsure smile.

"Let's get married," he said while we waited for the test results.

"Don't do this because of what your father did, Jack," I said and wished I hadn't said it out loud. Jack's face seemed to melt, his eyes turned big, wounded almost. He recovered quickly and smiled at me again, this time with his lawyerly confidence in place.

"What my father did is irrelevant. I don't allow other people's shortcomings to affect my life decisions. And most of all"—his voice became gentle and he held my face and kissed me—"it feels right. It just does."

By the time the faint pink line appeared in the result window, we were engaged. Neither one of us was sure if it was the right decision but I trusted Jack to make the decision right. I pushed my doubts away and, like shells on a beach, I collected my feelings; there was excitement and joy and an immediate attempt to make a switch from pregnancy to baby, from *I'm pregnant* to *I'm going to be a mother*, and everything about that seemed to leave me raw, like sunburned skin. The fact that I felt inadequate, even at that moment, would emerge again and again in the months that followed.

We went to the courthouse and married in front of the justice of the peace. There was no stretch limousine, no heaving the bridal bouquet into a group of shrieking bridesmaids, no festivities, no honeymoon, no father-in-law telling Jack to take good care of his daughter, no family to toast the bride and groom. Jack wasn't big on celebrations and it was all the same to me. I decided to keep my maiden name and Jack didn't put up a fight.

The courthouse clerk took a photo of us, the only one we have of our wedding day. Jack wore a black suit and a dark blue tie. I was in a cotton dress, white, versatile, appropriate for many occasions. In the picture Jack's got his arm around my shoulder, allowing me to lean into him. Behind us on the wall, a blueprint of the original courthouse layout, the light-colored lines on the blue background reminiscent of prints on my father's study wall. In the left corner of the photo, even though I tried to crop it out later, on the hallway courthouse bench, Jack's briefcase photobombing us from the edge of the picture.

We always meant to find a special frame for the wedding photo, but it was to remain in its original frame. Plain black wood. And then we never really thought about it anymore.

On the day of the twenty-weeks anatomy scan, we were ushered into a small examination room. I glanced at the screen mounted above the keyboard.

"Hi, I'm Debra." A woman in a spotless pink uniform entered. "Before we get started," she said and vigorously pushed buttons on the keyboard, "would you like to know the sex of your baby?"

The sex of our baby. I looked down at myself, anxiously scanning the small bump protruding from my abdomen. So far I was hardly showing, and the notion that there was a human inside of me, however small, seemed inconceivable, let alone that it was a boy or a girl.

"Yes, we'd like to know," Jack said.

The truth was that I hadn't decided if I wanted to know the sex and the fact that he answered for me made me furious. Furious that he was speaking on my behalf. But I knew that if I was to question him later, he'd just come up with an example of what I had said to make him believe that I wanted to know, that it was a good idea, that we had agreed, and knowing the sex was the right thing to do.

The nurse looked at me and I nodded and managed a smile. She got up and turned off the lights. The room was warm and intimate, and the dark allowed me to blink away the tears that had formed in my eyes.

"I apologize, this is going to be cold," Debra said as she

squeezed gel on my belly, making me shiver. Jack reached for my hand and together we stared at what looked like a triangular slice on a pitch-black background.

"Here we go," Debra said and put the head of the wand on my abdomen. "That's the spine," she said and pushed harder to get a better picture.

My baby's spine, tiny little bones in a perfect line, was a lovely string of pearls. My throat closed up and I stared at the image in awe. Debra pushed another button and the image went fuzzy. I blinked quickly so I wouldn't miss anything.

The nurse adjusted the wand and a face came into being. It seemed spooky at first, like a skull mask, but it was the most beautiful face I had ever seen. The lips seemed to pucker, the chin was slightly recessed. I could hardly breathe at the thought that there was a human being inches below my skin.

I heard the nurse's voice from far away, pointing out all the major organs.

Larynx is fine, cross section of the brain, kidneys, liver, lungs, heart.

When she said *heart*, Jack squeezed my hand. Hard.

Much to his dismay, I had read obsessively on the development of the fetus in utero. I was fascinated by a story of a doctor who performed fetal heart surgery on a woman with an ectopic pregnancy. The article described the intact and fully transparent embryonic sac, and the image of a tiny human, no larger than an inch, swimming in amniotic fluid, its head bowed and legs flexed upward.

I wasn't even in my second trimester then, and I knew every congenital heart disease by name, *aortic valve stenosis, ventricular septal defect, anomalous pulmonary venous return,* and had asked for extensive testing to be done, but my obstetrician had declined.

"There is no reason whatsoever to suspect your baby has any

kind of hereditary malformation or defect." Dr. Bowers had taken off his glasses and looked at me as if I were a child asking for a trip to Disneyland.

"Both you and your husband are healthy and it's just not justifiable," the doctor had said.

Even before Dr. Bowers had declined to do any more tests, Jack had long refused to accompany me to any new appointments, had even gone so far as to forbid me to see another specialist. Jack also refused to engage in conversations about the articles I read, and so I tried to silence the worry in my head, kept it in a safe place along with the anxiety and the panic.

The nurse had just told us the baby was fine, the ultrasound was perfect, but I was so nervous that suddenly the baby started doing summersaults inside of me.

"A perfectly healthy baby, did you hear that?" Jack said and stroked my cheek.

"And now the sex of the baby," the nurse said and dug deep into my abdomen, "if the baby is willing to give up the information, that is. Girl parts look like three lines, boy parts, well, pretty much like you expect them to look. Unfortunately baby's legs are pulled up and we can't see anything."

"I see it, right there, it's a girl." I pointed at the lines I thought were the unmistakable signs of a vulva.

"Don't get carried away, you'll be in for a rude awakening if you interpret it yourself," Jack said and furrowed his brow. His hand tightened around my hand as if he was trying to squash my enthusiasm.

The nurse smiled at him. I understood; it was hard not to smile at a father-to-be, hard not to feel privileged to share these moments with expecting parents.

"A girl," I said.

"She's right, you might as well buy all pink." Debra's voice reached me from afar. "I'll print that profile shot for you."

A flurry of images popped into my head: bows and dresses, tea sets and dollhouses, braids and ponytails, and nail polish. All my worries had magically disappeared, like footsteps in the sand erased by a single ocean wave, one minute there, then gone.

After thirty-two hours of labor, "normal for a first-time mom" according to Dr. Bowers, I was exhausted and all I wanted was for the pain to stop and to close my eyes. After four hours of unsuccessful pushing, he suggested a cesarean section.

When Mia finally came into the world, she was purple and limp. The doctor suctioned her throat and, after what seemed like an eternity, put her on my chest. Wrapped in a flannel blanket, she rested in my arms, and we looked at each other. Even though I had prepared for childbirth, had done Lamaze and infant care and CPR classes, had watched countless births on TV, natural and cesarean, and imagined it a hundred times, the moment still took me by surprise. She was so beautiful and fragile, and I felt an overwhelming sense of trepidation, as if I might break her.

The fact that she was healthy was the biggest miracle to me. The whole "ten fingers, ten toes" thing didn't make a lot of sense to me. What about her heart, her brain, her lungs? When I asked the nurse for the Apgar score, she looked at me puzzled. "She's a beautiful baby, perfect in every way, everything is fine."

What does she know? What I held in my arms was the product of cell division and multiplication, a process that had begun at a furious rate only minutes after conception. Cells had traveled down the fallopian tube to the uterus. By the end of the first week, a single cell had transformed into millions and into a body big enough to be seen without a microscope. Cells had formed muscles, the circulatory system, the skeleton, the kidneys and the reproductive organs, the nervous system, senses, and skin. And the heart had begun beating after three weeks. And now she was here and I was unable to go back and make right what rogue cells had potentially done wrong.

But then I looked into Mia's eyes, steel gray and unable to focus, seemingly out of line and slightly crossed, the puffiness of her eyelids making it almost impossible for her to open them wide, and I knew that she needed me and that I was put on this earth to protect her, and for a short moment in time I didn't worry about anything at all.

CHAPTER 6

I hear a forceful knock on the door. By the time I open my eyes, two men in suits have entered the room and introduce themselves as Detective Walter Daniel and Detective Sydney Cameron. Detective Daniel is a large middle-aged man. His bulky body renders him soft, especially around his eyes. He takes out a small notepad with a flip cover and stands beside my bed, ready to take notes.

I start with the day I moved to North Dandry and Jack went to Chicago. I tell them about the locks I had installed, which causes Detective Daniel to nod approvingly. When I catch myself rambling, I slow down, tell myself I must consider carefully what I'm going to say next. When I finish my story with leaving the police precinct, Detective Daniel motions to the younger detective, whose name I can no longer remember. The younger detective, very short with feminine hands, gets up and leaves the room. Detective Daniel pulls up a chair and sits next to my bed.

My head is pounding and I feel like I'm hooked up to a bag of caffeine. I'm trying to remember, and at the same time I'm trying not to say too much. I've been watching his face closely and as my story has progressed, his demeanor has changed; first he stopped smiling, his brows rose intermittently, then they furrowed. Then his face went blank.

When I tell him I don't know where my daughter is, he stops taking notes and doesn't seem to get the urgency. *Kidnapped* is the word I use.

He sits there and just looks at me. Looks at me as if I were a child telling a tale of monsters under the bed. I realize he doesn't believe me, and then it hits me like a brick; there's no urgency in his behavior, no AMBER Alert, no press conference, no urgent phone calls, no commands given to uniformed officers. That's what's supposed to happen, but he just stares at me. Does he not believe me? I *must* make him believe me.

"I locked the doors! No one could've come in—I'm sure of that. I know I should've . . . but I wasn't . . . I never left the door unlocked! I checked every night."

"They're looking for your daughter as we speak." He closes the cover of his notepad and slides the pen in his suit pocket. He lifts himself off the chair, sighs heavily, and pinches his lips as his kneecaps make a cracking sound. "What do you think happened?"

I close my eyes and take a deep breath. The odor of disinfectant is overwhelming and the headache that started behind my eyes has moved to the back of my head.

"Please, somebody must have seen something. I can't remember anything but I know I've never been in Dover. I'm bad at reading maps, I wouldn't know how to get there. I don't think I'd just drive up there for no reason. It's all very confusing."

"Maybe you just drove and you decided to stop there. It may not have been your destination. Just a place to stop."

"Stop for what?"

He ignores my question. "We'll need a photograph of your daughter."

"Hundreds. I have hundreds of pictures of her. At my house. They are in a black camera bag, on memory cards."

"We found those." He pauses ever so slightly, then continues. "We need a recent portrait, you know, with her face. A likeness of her that people can recognize."

I must think about this carefully. "It's hard pointing a camera at her. The flash startled her and I haven't taken any portraits, not lately. She's been so fussy, I didn't want her to . . ." I must be vigilant. Speak slowly. I must make sense. I must convince him. "I don't have any recent photos of her. She's only seven months old. The doctors said, they told me she . . . she . . . she's a colicky baby. The doctors told us there was nothing wrong with her. Just a colic. It was going to pass any day."

"How old did you say she is?"

"Seven months."

"Babies are colicky at that age? I have three kids. I can't say I took care of them, but my youngest was colicky. They usually grow out of that pretty quickly." His brows are raised. So are his suspicions. "Did you take her to a doctor?"

Pacifier, warm baths, soft blankets. Burp the baby. Hold the baby. Rock the baby. Walk the baby, drive with the baby. Soothe the baby.

"They did a couple of tests for reflux disorders. She gained weight, never had a fever. He said she was fine and to wait it out." They also told me if I ever felt that I couldn't cope, to go to the nearest emergency room, but I don't mention that part to the detective.

"All right," he says and scribbles something in his notepad. "How about DNA—a brush maybe? Or a bottle she drank out of? Or a handprint or a footprint? You know, those kits you buy at a department store, where you use clay and take an impression of a foot or a hand?"

I shake my head.

"A hairbrush? A toothbrush? You know those little plastic things you attach to your finger and brush their teeth?"

I shake my head.

"A diaper? There must be a dirty diaper somewhere?"

Again I shake my head. "It all disappeared." I say it so softly that I don't know if he heard me.

"It disappeared," he repeats as if I just told him the day of the week.

Why isn't he alarmed?

"Yes, everything disappeared, her clothes, her bottles. All of it, everything's gone. Her closet was empty, her diapers were missing, her formula. Everything."

"We are aware of that fact. So you're telling me that someone took her and that person also took all her things? That's a very odd crime." He tucks the notebook in his pocket as if the ramblings of a madwoman are no longer significant enough to be written down, and then crosses his arms in front of his chest. "If the doors were locked all night and were still locked the morning you found the empty crib, there must be another explanation. I have to be honest with you, that doesn't make sense at all."

My story not making any sense is a cruel statement. "I know how it sounds, but that's all I can tell you."

Daniel's face relaxes, he leans forward. "I can only find her if I know where to look." He pauses and then adds, "Where should I look for her?" His voice is gentle as if he is trying to convince a child to tell the truth.

"What are you trying to say? That I know where she is and I'm not telling?"

"You knew she was gone and you didn't tell."

He's right. I don't know how to respond to that.

"If you know where she is, you have to tell me," he continues. "She's so little, helpless, she is cold, hungry. She's all alone out there."

I pinch my lips to keep the tears in check. I don't want to cry in front of him. Whenever I cried in front of Jack it made everything worse.

"Did you ever feel you were capable of hurting your baby?"

Was I capable of hurting her? I shake my head for I dare not speak out loud. There they are, the images emerge as if the detective hit a button, and they splatter against the wall like photographs from a slide projector: Clenched fists, legs pulled up to the stomach, a baby's tearless rage directed toward me. My love for her powerless, incapable of easing her pain.

"Did she cry a lot?" he asks.

"She was a colicky baby, you know, very fussy . . . but I would never hurt her. She was my life."

Something in his eyes twitches, then he nods as if I said something he expected to hear.

He abruptly turns around and leaves the room, as if everything I just told him is meaningless. Then I realize I spoke of Mia in the past tense.

NO NEW DETAILS RELEASED
OF SEVEN-MONTH-OLD MISSING FROM CRIB

Brooklyn, NY—After a frantic search for the infant missing from her crib in Brooklyn on early Sunday, October 1st, no new details have been released.

According to Eric Rodriguez, spokesperson for the NYPD, police have no idea how a kidnapper may have gained entry to the home. "At this moment we have no suspect description. We have no vehicle plates to trigger an AMBER Alert. There are no eyewitnesses and the entire surrounding area has been searched by officers, including a K9 unit," Rodriguez said. "We are following several leads but we know nothing for sure yet."

"Many child abductions involve one of the parents, but we have both the parents here. So that puts us on a little higher state of alert," Detective Robert Wilczek said.

A source told CTAB-TV that the child's disappearance was especially concerning given the fact that the mother didn't report the abduction immediately.

Police are urging anyone with information to call the TIPS hotline.

CHAPTER 7

Mia Paradise Connor and I were released from the hospital five days after the delivery. Jack went back to work, took over the night feedings on the weekends, and I slept, ate, and showered whenever possible.

I was in awe with what I had created. I stared at Mia, her plump cheeks, her little bird mouth twitching in her sleep. I bathed her and patted her dry, gently rubbing lavender lotion all over her. By then she was far from the puffy-eyed, bowlegged newborn; her curvy legs had straightened, her cone-shaped skull had rounded out, and her flaky skin was now pink and spongy.

When she became more aware of her surroundings, she studied my face, trying to memorize it, as if I was all the comfort and love she needed. She'd wake up in my arms, open her eyes, frantically search for my likeness, immediately settling down when she recognized me.

Mia's cries were distinct; one seemed to complain about a minor discomfort, like a sock too tight, a jacket too warm. There was the tired cry, fussy, drawn out, telling me she was ready to take a nap. Then there was a more relentless cry that seemed to signal hunger, nothing a bottle couldn't fix. And then, at about three months old, another cry emerged. An abrupt cry, a cry that seemed to signal pain, as if she were stuck with a needle. She suddenly shunned containment, something that had calmed her before, and protested every time I swaddled her. It seemed as if her bones became rigid and every time I wrapped her in a blanket she clenched her fists, arched her back, and her muscles tensed.

Need to make a fussy baby feel safe? How about the age-old tradition of mimicking the condition in the mother's womb? All you need is a blanket and a clever folding technique.

Her abrupt cry was not a mere request, but an urgent demand to fix whatever bothered her. And from then on she put more energy in her demands, cried more loudly, fed more voraciously, and protested more forcefully. If I didn't respond to her needs immediately, she'd fall apart, come undone. I wondered if she felt deeply and therefore reacted with such fierce power when her needs were being ignored. I went into overdrive to respond immediately, became obsessive in trying to prevent her from getting upset, and in return she extracted every bit of energy from me. I willingly complied, but still, she wanted more.

I gave her all I had, yet something had gone amiss, had gone awry. I was somehow removed from the person who had adored the moments with a baby in her arms, as if I had left that person behind and another one had emerged, a person neither one of us recognized. I woke up just as tired as I had gone to sleep and blamed it on not getting enough rest. But then I did the math, and with Jack doing the weekend feedings, staying up late caring for Mia, I was able to get six hours of sleep a night, at least four times a week. I went on with my life, took care of Mia, breast-fed, sang to her, gave her baths, but something felt horribly wrong. What had happened to the euphoric love I initially felt? Why wasn't I happy anymore? Where had the magic gone?

Every morning I woke up and reality closed in on me. I was granted a peaceful second or two, but then a dank layer of sadness wrapped itself around me. I felt as if I was playing a role and never was that more apparent than when I met other moms at the park. They seemed more cheerful, happy, and content to be mothers than I ever was or ever could be. I wanted to adopt their stories as mine, to pretend to be one of them, all the while accepting my lack of enthusiasm as a personal character flaw. I decided to make up for it in other ways.

I snapped. My Leica X2, small enough to operate with one hand, was my new obsession. I snapped Mia from every possible angle. Perspectives of feet, toes tucked under, spread apart, soft tiny nails, bending easily. Her elfin hands grasping small objects. Ears folded like rose petals, moving up and down as she drank from my breast, pink lips curling around the nipple.

One day during breast-feeding, Mia dozed off and unlatched. She had long unlocked her lips, but her tongue still made clicking sounds. As she was asleep, she was malleable, her legs soft, as if there were no bones inside of her. Wobbly Jell-O met my lips as I kissed her, they seemed to sink into her. I reached for my Leica, snapped images of blue veins running across her eyelids, too small for even a thread to fit inside of them. There was a larger vein by her temple, like a widening channel of a river nearing the sea, its currents waiting to be met by the tides. I snapped close-ups of breast milk running down her cheek, toward her ear, cataloging every tiny amount of milk that had just fallen short of reaching its intended destination. I took shots of my engorged and leaking breasts, drops of nourishment trailing from my cracked and sore nipples.

And then, out of the blue, the camera flash irritated her, sent her into a frenzy. She started crying and wouldn't stop, as if my attempts to capture her likeness had suddenly repulsed her. I rocked her, allowed her head to rest on my chest. Nothing consoled her, not my songs, my gentle voice, not my nipple, nothing. And from then on she cried every time I fed her.

I sang to her, *Sleep, baby, sleep, your father tends the sheep, your mother shakes the dreamland tree, and from it fall sweet dreams for thee. Sleep, baby, sleep.*

My way of making up for my shortcomings as a less-than-mediocre mother was going from doctor to doctor, and the same diagnosis was thrown at me as if I ought to know what to do with it: *Colic. Otherwise healthy. Cause unknown. No obvious reason.*

While her constant state of crying seemed acceptable to Jack, he became increasingly worried about the bills, specialist co-pays, and out-of-network doctors. "Colic," he said. "They all tell you the same thing. A lot of babies are colicky. It'll be gone before we know it."

"I want to take her to another hospital. Maybe there are some more tests they can do? If I can't get a referral, we'll just pay out of pocket."

At the mention of money, the pity in Jack's eyes faded. He stiffened, ever so slightly, but I saw how his spine straightened, his eyes narrowed. I was afraid to mention that my credit cards were maxed out.

"Give it another month or two," he added on his way out the door. "She'll be fine."

I nodded, even more exhausted than I had been minutes earlier, as if that were even possible. Two months, that's sixty days and sixty nights.

"You know you're nuts, don't you?" Jack said and slammed the door shut.

One morning, a Saturday, too early to get up and too late to fall back asleep, I reached beside me and found Jack's side of the bed abandoned.

I heard a voice that almost made me panic, a high-pitched babble voice unknown to me. I got up and went to Mia's room. There was Jack, holding Mia under her armpits, a five-month-old grouchy bundle of anxieties with fingers moving around like an orchestra conductor.

"Why won't you sleep?" Jack said.

Then he switched over to that whiny, high-pitched voice. *I don't want to. I want to be awake so I can look around.*

"How come you can talk?" Jack pretended to be confused.

I can do anything, Daddy. Jack, mimicking a conversation, impersonating Mia, switching from his regular tone to a squeaky voice.

"Why won't you settle down, little girl? Something on your mind?" Jack's facial expression was sheer concern.

Mia's arms were flailing, her legs kicking.

Nothing wrong with me, Daddy.

"I knew there's nothing wrong with you. You've been fed, you've been changed, you've been burped. No need to be fussy." Jack then rocked her gently in the cradle of his arm, the crook of his elbow a perfect fit.

"There you go, princess. That's better, isn't it?"

Much better, Daddy.

"Just relax, go back to sleep. Mommy doesn't like it when you cry so much."

But I'm just a baby.

"I keep telling her that but she's just not listening."

Life turned into a blur of bottles, diapers, and crying. I'd go one, sometimes two days without closing my eyes. When I did manage to sleep, I crashed. And then I woke up with a start, from comatose to alert, as if someone had grabbed my shoulder and shaken me awake.

Zombielike I shopped for baby clothes, loaded the cart, walked the aisles, and bought multiples of everything: booties, outfits, socks. I purchased everything that promised relief from her crying: rosemary-scented sachets, calming lotion, and alarm clocks with waterfall recordings, white noise boxes, and a bear with taped womb sounds. Regardless of how much I bought, I never felt as if I could give her what she needed. I could buy entire stores and yet my attempts didn't amount to anything. Because deep down inside I was a fake.

One day, with another collection of bags in hand, I went home. Jack was in his office, talking on the phone, holding Mia in his arms. She looked peaceful and calm, her face relaxed, her lips loose. The moment I reached for her, her face tensed, her lips curled downward as if to say *How dare you approach me.* I immediately let go of her as if my fingers had touched hot stone.

"Every time I pick her up, she cries. She hates me. What am I doing wrong?"

"How do you come up with that kind of stuff?"

"But she cries when I hold her. I must be doing something wrong."

"You're not doing anything wrong. Relax, she's just a baby," Jack said.

I told Jack that I constantly worried about someone hurting her, her suffocating on a pillow or blanket, choking on something. Jack told me to stop imagining the worst.

"Don't overthink everything," he said, "and don't be so tense all the time." As if taking it in stride was going to make it better. In his world, everything was fine. In his world, children didn't die of SIDS, didn't choke on marbles, didn't succumb to high fevers, didn't suffocate on their vomit. Didn't have mysterious illnesses that went undiagnosed until it was too late.

There was this animal inside of me, created while she was in my womb, born on the same day Mia was born. At first, it had quivered ever so slightly, then it stirred, agitated at times, but I was able to pacify it by keeping watch. Then it started to thrash and I felt powerless. I went there. I went there all the time and then I stayed there. The thought of impending doom loomed over me, tethered like a wild creature with a rope, making it impossible for me to get away. And nothing could convince me otherwise. I didn't want to hold her, because as long as she was in Jack's arms, she was his responsibility, as if I could pass my duty like a baton to him. On his watch, she'd be fine.

That day in his office, Jack handed Mia to me, one hand under her head, the other supporting her legs, her body wrapped tightly in the blanket.

"I have to go to work. I'll be back in a few hours." He presented the bundle as if she were an offering.

Suddenly images of a sacrificial goat slaughtered on a mossy stone altar flashed across my mind. I could almost feel the sticky blood between my fingers. I saw a radiant light the size of a baby's pupil glowing beneath the soft spot on her head. There was a demon trapped beneath that spot, a demon that made her reject me, made her cry and wail every time I touched her. If I could get to that spot, create a tiny hole, the demon could escape, and we could both find peace.

I remained still, didn't dare reach out for Mia. Jack looked at me, bewildered, his lips curled into a half smile as he tried to gain control.

I grabbed the scissors from the pencil holder and left his office. In the hallway powder room, as the scissors rested on the edge of the sink, I pumped antibacterial foam into my palms. I studied my reflection in the mirror and tried to come up with some sort of courage to tell him about the darkness and the shadows that had become my life. A life reduced to a small pinhole, depicting the entire world misshapen and distorted. Through this tiny hole, I saw blood, I saw the cold stone of an altar, covered with sharp instruments, jagged and spiky and able to drill their way through soft fontanel tissue. A sharp instrument, like a pair of scissors, resting on the edge of the sink.

The nursery was fecund with smells: powder, oil, lotion, chamomile and rosemary, and dirty diapers. Jack had scolded me many times not to let them pile up.

The mobile above her crib—a colorful array of butterflies, june bugs, blossoms, and Tinker Bell in its center—moved gently in the breeze of the ceiling fan. The blinds were drawn, the curtains closed. The rocker sat silently next to her crib, covered in white linen, its footstool soiled with black shoe polish streaks from Jack's shoes.

I emptied the shopping bags, one by one, placed every item in baskets on the white shelf, convinced that as long as I kept her room in order, I could also keep the chaos at bay. I took out the clothes and reached for the scissors to cut off the tags.

The cold metal rested in my hand. Before I even cut off a single tag, Jack walked in, Mia in his arms. She was quiet and her eyes scanned aimlessly about. Then she focused on the ceiling fan. Jack placed Mia's body against my chest, and kissed me on the forehead.

"I have to go to work, I'm already running late."

I needed him to stay home, but I didn't know how to ask for it. Jack gently brushed Mia's cheek with the back of his index finger. Her lips opened and the pacifier popped out of her mouth as if giving way to the pressure inside of her. Her lips searched for their comfort and came up empty. Her face contorted.

The front door slammed shut. Jack was gone and so was Mia's composure.

I held her inches away from my body, as if distance between us could soothe her, take the edge off her discontent with my presence. She broke out in a wail, its volume increasing with every passing second. I turned to place her on the changing table when my eyes caught a glimpse of a shiny silver object. The light and the turning blades of the fan created ghostly shadows that prompted me to pick up the scissors and cradle them in my palm.

Her body seemed to be vibrating, her crimson face determined to ignore the need to fill her lungs with air.

I willed myself to ignore the scissors, but they seemed to pulsate as if they had a life of their own. I pinched my eyes shut, yet the scissors floated up and toward me, first only inches, and then farther up, turning their sharp points toward Mia's skull, determined to release the glowing demon underneath its connective tissue.

I gently placed Mia in her crib. As I pulled my hands up from under her body, I prayed that she would survive. Despite me.

That day, I knew I was capable of anything, capable of silencing her cries. That's when I knew her life was at stake. And I screamed and for the first time the volume of my screams topped hers.

Jack's "few hours" always turned into a full twelve-hour work-day. As I pressed my forehead against the window, waiting for his return, I tried to recall how long he had been avoiding all physical contact. When was the last time he had hugged or kissed me, and for how long had he been secretive? Jack was becoming more and more detached, icy even, barely talking to me. Working late was no longer an exception but a rule and his distance added more insecurities to my already frazzled thoughts.

I watched Jack exiting a sleek black town car. When he walked through the front door, his eyes were two seas of silent reproach.

"Sorry, I'm late," he said, meaning *If you had picked up the dry cleaning, I'd have been on time. And with all the time you have, why isn't dinner ready and why is the house still a mess?*

"Took me forever to get a cab," he added.

His briefcase was already open, his BlackBerry in his hand.

"A cab?" Hadn't I just seen him exiting a town car?

We stared at each other for a moment, then I lowered my gaze. I knew I had changed physically, I could see it in Jack's eyes every time he looked at me. I weighed about as much as I did in high school, maybe even less. My facial features seemed to have corroded and I had aged a decade in the past two months. Before Mia, I had a haircut every couple of months. I used to go to the gym, yoga, Pilates, you name it. I never seemed to have any energy anymore.

"You said you'd be back in a couple of hours."

"What the hell, really?" Jack said. "Can you tell me what you want from me? I just want to understand because I can't see how making money is not the right thing."

I tried to work out what to say. How could I explain when my head felt so cluttered and fragile? For a fraction of a second he looked like a little boy about to listen to a parent preach, and I saw how afraid he was that I was going to say something else, would question him further, something neither one of us had the energy for. I wanted to ask him why he'd tell me he took a cab when he got out of a town car, and if he was having an affair, but I wasn't sure I really cared. His distance paled in comparison to whatever crazy I had living inside of me.

Hey, honey, welcome home! Guess what, there's a demon trapped inside of our daughter's head, and with every passing minute it's getting harder to resist the temptation of jamming a sharp object into her fontanel.

"She cried all day, Jack. I don't know what to do anymore."

It's because of the demon.

"Did you take her out?"

You haven't left the house in days.

"All she does is cry. Why would I take her out?"

The demon is making her cry. If I can get to the demon, everything will be okay.

"Well, what *did* you do?"

I didn't answer.

Help me, Jack, help me. I'm afraid of hurting her.

"She doesn't cry all the time, Estelle. She's not crying right now, is she? She cries sometimes, all babies do, that's how they communicate." He plopped on the couch and opened his briefcase. "I have work to do; let's talk later, okay?" Jack absentmindedly jabbed chopsticks at Chinese leftovers while hacking away on his BlackBerry.

"It's okay," I said more to myself than to Jack. I stared out the window, my reflection nothing but a distorted body in a sea of darkness.

Jack's mood tended to improve the sleepier he became. Later, in bed, he caught me staring at the ceiling. He asked, his voice now soft and gentle, what I was thinking about.

"Dark, horrible thoughts," I answered but kept my voice light and cheerful. "Demons, mainly."

He brushed my words off with a halfhearted smile. "Well then . . . as long as it's nothing serious. You can always get a sitter a couple of times a week. I'll help out as much as I can."

"Sure," I said. Our conversations were nothing but a distorted reality we both chose to accept. There was nothing he could do for me.

"Well, then let's not dwell on it."

"Yeah, let's not," I said and felt a cold fist tightening around my heart.

"I'm sorry about earlier. How was your day?" Jack said, flipped over, and pulled the blanket over his shoulders.

"Just the usual."

Let me see. The thought of tomorrow being just like today makes me want to jump off a bridge. I feel as if I'm at the bottom of a dark well with my feet submerged in murky ankle-deep water, toad cadavers floating atop the slimy water's surface, spiderwebs full of dried-up cocooned bugs and beetles. And that's before I look closely.

Jack's breathing was slow and steady. I didn't have to look at him to know that he was asleep.

But it really didn't matter because even if he was awake, he couldn't bear half of what I had living inside of me. And regardless of what people say, you can't see the stars from the bottom of a well.

CHAPTER 8

parked in front of Jack's building and watched the traffic lights change and cars float by. When the security guard made his rounds, I took the elevator up to the fifth floor and found all the offices dark, except Jack's.

As I listened to the contorted voices drifting toward me through Jack's office door, I imagined what hands were doing, where tongues slithered like snakes, what pieces of clothing were draped over office chairs or bunched around ankles like turtlenecks, what the room smelled like. I observed myself in the glass door panel and was dumbfounded by the woman I had become. No longer a woman, really, but a crone, in baggy clothes and stringy hair with a chilly, triumphant cackle. I knew I was helpless, for the crone's powers were infinite.

Seconds after I began pounding the door with my fists, Jack ripped it open, looked at me, with surprise at first, then his eyes turned into rage. I didn't speak, just turned and ran. I reached my car, shaking, unable to think, but I managed to drive home. When I pulled into the driveway, I was surprised I had made it there.

Aashi, the sitter, was asleep on the couch in Mia's room. A medical student from India, chronically sleep deprived yet easygoing and patient with Mia's colicky behavior, she smelled of cardamom and anise and her upper lip appeared darker than the rest of her face. My hand still hovered over her shoulder when she opened her eyes.

"Mrs. Connor, she didn't wake up at all. I fed her around ten, and she fell back asleep right away," she whispered and brushed a blanket of black hair from her face, her colorful bangles dancing on her wrist.

"She must have been really tired," I said. "We spent all day at the park, all that fresh air . . ." What sounded like a pleasant outing had been nothing more than a screaming baby in a stroller who eventually fell asleep out of sheer exhaustion.

I looked over at Mia, picture perfect in her crib, her face angelic and placid while only hours earlier she had thrashed her hands toward my face, her mouth a gaping wound.

Aashi left and I wandered around the apartment, unable to settle. I found myself in front of Jack's office. I didn't want to snoop but my behavior at his office—now nothing more than a moment of lunacy—demanded an explanation and I had nothing to give him. Nothing but a sea of irrationality. Jack was going to ask questions, he'd want to know what had possessed me to do what I had done. I needed a logical reason, proof of his infidelity, proof that he couldn't be trusted any longer. I had to find a picture, a letter, a photograph, anything tangible beyond a random accusation that would justify my outburst.

I stood in the doorway, taking in the shelves and filing cabinets. I had no idea what I was even looking for. Jack had started paying all the bills after Mia was born, handled all the paperwork, and I was glad he did. There wasn't another chore I could manage, especially not anything that involved deadlines. But maybe his taking over the finances was just a way of increasing control over the woman who had floundered. It was ironic that the differences that brought us together—Jack's sense of purpose and his attraction to my carefree attitude toward life and, as he saw it, unpredictability—were the very things that were also driving us apart. That and the fact that I was an absolute failure as a mother.

The floorboards creaked as I entered the office and a familiar aroma of leather greeted me. Like an observer I stood beside myself, watched a woman scan fake paneling between rows of books, pushing at conspicuous spots, looking around, expecting an antique oil painting to fall off the wall, an envelope yellowed by age dropping to the ground, containing some clandestine content. The woman's fingers slipped, almost snapping her nails off, as she tried to pull open a locked drawer. I watched her, running her fingertips alongside the bottom of the desk's surface, pushing here and there, lifting keyboard, mouse pad, and desk organizer, but reality greeted her harshly: no hidden drawers, no secret compartments, just a piece of contemporary office furniture. The woman jerked back into reality when the phone rang.

I backed away from the desk. The chair fell to the floor. *Thud.* The phone continuously nagged to be picked up.

Ring. Ring.

Its pesky urgency was replaced by an infant's faint gurgle echoing through the house. The baby monitor's light display on Jack's desk indicated the volume of Mia's cries: six out of ten. Then the lights alternated from the middle scale all the way to the top. The phone went silent and so did the baby monitor. The phone rang again, slicing the air with determination. I ignored Mia's cries emanating from the baby monitor and wiped the tears that were running down my neck, trailing inside my sweater. I looked at the clock on the wall. It was midnight.

The gurgling baby monitor turned into a whimper, the whimper into a howl, and the howl into a full-blown bellow. The lights remained at the very top of the display window, until one last gurgle drifted off into the distance. Then there was silence.

I left the study and went through the bedroom into Jack's

walk-in closet. A masterpiece of built-in shelves constructed of maple wood and hardware of brushed steel, next to mine, separated by a wall, both accessible by individual doors. Jack's dress shirts, arranged by color, immaculately pressed, aligned on one wall, his shoes along the other. I looked up at the top row of storage shelves, reachable only with the attached rolling ladder.

Reluctantly I passed the full-length mirror, a shadow of Jack appearing, checking his designer suit, belt, and shoes, playing a cruel trick on me.

As I stepped closer, a figure stared back at me. The woman was a stranger, a mere visitor who looked at me in anger. I considered her, even tried to force a winsome smile on her, yet her opaque eyes seemed empty, like doll's eyes. Not one of those pretty dolls with an elaborate dress and curly hair, no, less than that, really more like a rag doll with crooked button eyes attached by only a wisp of thread. A thief of a woman, so powerful and potent that she made off with my prized possessions, my composure, my sanity, my joy, and the part of me that was a mother. Unable to lift my gaze off her, a familiar yet lesser twin almost, an inferior replica of myself, we stared at each other, contemplating if we'd met each other but I couldn't place her and she wasn't sure of me, either.

That night, in Jack's closet, surrounded by immaculately pressed shirts and shoes shined to perfection, I fell apart into millions of little pieces. The walls closed in, wrapped themselves around me. I felt threatened by my own skin, by the cars driving by, the honking cabs, and the sirens. The ticking clock—I could clearly hear the ticking all the way from the other end of the apartment—held a message for me that I was unable to decipher. No longer was there a difference between the mundane and the bizarre. I saw the world through a magnifying glass, and my mind was about to explode and spatter whatever was left of my lucidity all over Jack's starched shirts and polished shoes. I was a bloated corpse and I needed relief. I needed to make sense. But was sense something one can make?

White noise on full blast. A voice escaped the subdued grain of the maple shelves, and unlike mine, it made sense.

The box, it said. *Where is the box?*

The box that didn't fit with the rest of the items in the closet?

Yes, that one.

The box that was old and torn, which I noticed every time I hung up his clean clothes, that he moved from the overhead storage one week to a lower shelf the next?

Yes, the old yellowed photo box with reinforced metal holes, rectangular and flat, larger than a shoe box.

Am I supposed to look for it and open it?

Yes, look for it. Then open it.

I pulled the ladder to the far corner of the shelf, its metal balls sliding along the tracks, humming like a swarm of hornets. I kicked off my shoes and climbed up.

There it was. A quite unremarkable and ordinary cardboard box. I managed to climb down the ladder without dropping it, sat it on the floor, and knelt next to it.

The box was cumbersome to open; the lid had to be lifted on both ends simultaneously. I recognized the castle logo in the lower right-hand corner: Rosenfeld, Manhattan—one of the largest wedding gown stores in New York, maybe even the country. I parted the tissue paper. Photos with scalloped edges, tinged yellow by time, depicting people unknown to me. A little boy in a blue coat, a woman standing next to him, leaning on him, her arm around his shoulders.

A property deed. Jack had mentioned that he had flipped properties while in law school but I didn't know he owned a house. A deed for a brownstone on North Dandry in Brooklyn.

Before I could make sense of the deed, I came across a black pouch, heavy in my hand. I felt the shape of a gun through the velvety fabric. I removed the revolver from the pouch and cradled it in my hand. It seemed old-fashioned, but I really knew next to nothing about guns and therefore I pointed it away from me and randomly pushed the cylinder. It swung to the right. It was empty.

Below the black pouch was a concealed-handgun license card, laminated, with Jack's information. I never knew Jack owned a gun, let alone had a license to carry, but it seemed logical for a lawyer to have one. Tucked in the corner was a full box with bullets.

I grabbed a few and lined them up in my palm. They were cold and made a gentle clinking sound when they touched. I filled up the chamber, engaged the cylinder, and allowed my finger to gingerly touch the trigger. The gun I could stomach—lawyers owning guns isn't unheard of—what was hard to believe was the fact that it had been there all along and I never knew.

I turned the gun toward my face and looked down the hole. It soothed me somehow, and as I wondered what it would be like to put the cold barrel in my mouth, I heard the ticking of a wristwatch. Then the crinkly plastic sound of a diaper demanded my attention, a whiff of baby powder along with the stench of deceit, a combination that had the power to silently command me. I looked up.

There was Jack, standing in the closet, Mia sleeping in his arms. There I was, gun in hand. He stared at me, his eyes blank. I hid my hands behind my back and for a second I wanted to kick the box to make it slide under his dress shirts, the Berber carpet allowing it to glide like a ghost to a secret hiding place. I needn't have worried; Jack was focused on the usual.

"Didn't you hear her cry?" Icicles around his every word. Again, I wasn't vigilant enough. Again, I failed to be the mother I should have been.

There were words Jack never said, words Jack never used, yet I had heard him say them over and over again—*flawed, unfit. A bad mother, a bad wife. Faulty and imperfect.* I had no business being there. I had no business being at his office earlier, in his closet now, his house in general, his life, period. I had no business being the mother of his child.

"What's this?" I said, holding up the deed in front of him while hiding the gun behind my back. I was surprised by the strength of my voice. Everything was wrong. Jack, Mia, the ticking clock, the gun, the photographs, the property deed. "We're not as broke as you're making us out to be. While we've been struggling, you owned a house worth what . . . a million? Were you ever going to tell me? What other secrets do you have?"

His posture wilted, he looked like a little boy: small, softened, less confident. "It's a property I tried to flip but haven't been able to find a buyer for."

I stared at him, suddenly realizing that I knew next to nothing about him.

"It's just an investment property, it's in shambles. What did you want me to do? Worry you even more? You're doing a great job at that already."

"I'm your wife, I think I ought to know everything about our finances."

"There weren't any problems until you started with your obsessions, all those doctor visits while you were pregnant, all those tests you insisted on, all those specialists you consulted, over nothing. It was nothing until you made it into something."

"So it's nothing to you? Or is it something you didn't want me to know about?"

"I didn't say that. We are broke, if you care to know." He raised his voice then; I felt him dropping the façade, becoming real. "We have perfectly adequate health insurance. But you insisted on all those specialists that weren't covered. And I get it, you know I get it. You were worried. But you didn't stop there, either, did you? Even after Mia was born, you continued . . ."

I could tell he was looking for words, looking to put a name to my madness. Am I even mad? Was there such a thing as a little bit crazy? A lick of mad? I worried about Mia. I still do. Every waking minute.

"You've been feeding that dragon ever since, haven't you?"

I chuckled. Nice analogy. *Feeding the dragon? But what about our daughter? I knew what he was going to say. But what kind—*

"You started taking a perfectly healthy baby from doctor to doctor. And that's not normal."

Normal? What kind of mother would I be, Jack, if I didn't try to help my child? What kind of mother would I be?

"There's something wrong with her. She cries too much. Don't you get that?" My accusation seemed to trigger additional resentment on his part and, as always, Mia's excessive crying was just a figment of my imagination.

"There's nothing wrong with her, *nothing*. The fact that you can't handle a baby doesn't mean there's something wrong with *her*. You've been taking Mia from doctor to doctor and they all tell you the same thing. A colic, she'll grow out of it. You can't continue to insist on all these tests that make no sense. I've been allowing you to do this for the longest time but I need you to stop this madness."

Jack stared at me for a long time. Then he took a step back. His voice was calm but his neck was covered in blotches.

"I don't know what to do but I can't allow you to go on like this."

Jack's mind was not prepared to wrap itself around such an unwelcome emotion as this: *he didn't know what do.* Jack was too rational to accept chaos. He had been trying to put me back together but now he realized he was finally out of options.

His decision to get married because I was pregnant had backfired on him. Not only was I not keeping up my end of the bargain, but at the same time I kept him from fulfilling his. There was work to be done, lots of work. An infinite workload of case files, preparing witnesses, and interviews. And even though he was exhausted, I knew that the pressures of his job felt perversely comfortable to him compared to what awaited him at home every night. I threw my head back and burst into an overly animated gesture of joy.

"This whole marriage was a mistake. Come on, Jack, this is your way out." You shattered into a couple of pieces, Jack put you back together again. Even four, six, or ten, with enough glue he could make you right. When *I* shattered, the pieces were too many to count. It wasn't even a matter of how many, but how much. Like sand. Uncountable. And when Jack felt backed into a corner, he reacted.

He walked toward me as if to grab me. "Just listen to yourself . . . you're irrational. You follow me to work, you come to my office, embarrass me? I don't know what's going on, but you need help."

I just stared at him as I watched him pause just long enough to shake his head. Then his voice turned to ice.

"I find you here, in my closet, while Mia is screaming her head off. Does that strike you as rational?"

Mia stirred, her little hands reaching for something invisible, sounds of distress escaping her lips. Jack's eyes were darting left and right. When he finally spoke, his voice was down to a whisper.

"I no longer trust you with my daughter. This stops tonight." He kept switching Mia from one arm to the other while she was growing visibly upset. Tears started to well up in her eyes and short of a bottle nothing was going to calm her down. "Estelle, this can't go on any longer. Why can't you just—"

"Just what? Be normal? Is that what you want me to be? Normal?"

He stood there, didn't say a word. His face was empty, I had hit the nail on the head. A normal woman is all he wanted. And I was everything but. Cha-ching, *you lose, Jack.*

"You need to get help," he said. "I'm taking off tomorrow and we'll go see somebody. You need professional help."

I stood there, waiting until he left the closet, cautious not to turn my back on him. I went to the kitchen and, while the bottle warmed in the microwave, I slid the gun in the back of the junk drawer.

I fed Mia, put her in her crib, and went into the study, where Jack was perched over a case file. He looked as if nothing had happened at all. When he saw me, his demeanor changed. He seemed agitated. I sat in a chair in front of his desk and crossed my legs. I managed a smile and hoped my face didn't seem too contorted. I wanted to appease him, to seem as sane as possible.

"There's something we need to talk about," Jack said.

I took in a deep breath, then I exhaled. "This is when you're going to tell me about your girlfriend, the one from your office?"

"There's no girlfriend. I . . . I wanted to tell you when the moment was right, but hell, no moment is right lately." He paused for a second, "The woman at my office was Victoria Littlefield."

The name sounded familiar but I couldn't quite place it.

"She's from the DA's office and we were discussing a position." He got up, stepped closer, and lowered his voice to a whisper. "Until you barged in like a maniac, that is. I can't even blame her that she didn't offer me the job once she found out I have a lunatic for a wife. This job is all I ever wanted. Ten years from now I could be DA. But that doesn't matter anymore now, does it?"

His eyes communicated what he didn't say out loud. That the way I acted earlier was the wrecking ball that tore a gaping hole into the walls of our already-fragile marriage. And his career.

"You've no idea what I've been going through," he said. "Sometimes I drive an hour out of my way just to get gas. That hour in the car, by myself, is the closest I've come to normalcy in months."

I held back the tears. He was a trapped man. A man trapped by a woman who didn't measure up.

"I know you do more, you have more responsibility with the baby, but I get up in the middle of the night and feed her, and I still go to work the next day. And it's not like I'm just shuffling paperwork. I can't come home every time you call. I've been working my entire career for this DA job and you . . ." He paused, deflated. "It stops tonight. Tomorrow you're going to see a doctor."

———

When I arrived at the clinic, Jack was waiting by the door, looking impeccable in his suit, dark gray, Hugo Boss—his favorite, stylish and simple, he wore it, as usual, with a white shirt and a gray tie. I was late and Jack looked irritated. I could tell by the way he raised an eyebrow as I walked up. When he spotted me, his forehead wrinkled, furrows so deep I hadn't noticed before. I felt guilty. After all, Jack's time was precious.

"Sorry I'm late." I raised my face but all he did was lightly brush his lips across my cheek.

Jack was all business during our appointment. His lint-free suit, his starched shirt, all signs that he'd made a success of his life. He told the doctor how I was obsessing over "minute details" and how I didn't want to "accept colic as a diagnosis" and how he'd been able to "hold things together" all by himself.

I watched him steal a glance at me while he spoke, probably wondering how we arrived at this implausible moment when all he'd ever done was "provide and support." All he ever did was be there for me, and here I was, frazzled and sunken in.

Dr. Wells took one look at me, got out his prescription pad, and scribbled on it. "If nothing's happening, we'll just adjust the dosage." Then he told me to come back after a month so I could tell him all about the improvement. "Once the baby sleeps through the night, life will be different. Some new mothers need adjusting. Give it some time."

I realized he wasn't a psychiatrist or therapist, just a family practitioner. Because specialists cost co-pays, and "Dr. Wells is capable of prescribing an antidepressant."

You poor sap, a bit of time and a good night's sleep is what I need?

"Right," I said, smiled, and cradled my purse. It was heavy. Inside was Jack's gun, vibrating joyously.

On our way home, in the car, Jack seemed appeased. In his world you solved a problem by coming up with a remedy and the fact that the bottle of pills in my purse was going to make everything okay was just the way he knew the world to be. An orange bottle with three refills and his life was back to normal.

"Tell me you're going to be okay." His voice was soft, fragile almost. "Please take the medication and just get on with it."

"It?"

"Life, get on with life. Take the baby out, meet other moms in parks, I don't know, whatever moms do."

I was tired of him selling me his logic like a snake oil salesman offering a cure for ulcers. It was laughable. Mingle with other moms and a pill a day will take my sorrows away.

"It's not complicated if you really think about it." He put his arm around me at a light, pulling me toward him. "You overanalyze everything, that's what your problem is. It's not about being perfect. It's about changing a diaper, warming up a bottle."

His embrace felt staged. I looked out the car window, focusing on a tree almost as tall as the building behind it. I wondered if the roots of a tree were really as deep as a tree was high. It seemed impossible almost, a terrifying and secret part of the city, invisible to its inhabitants.

The pills gave me strange dreams. I hardly slept and I was so tired I could care less about anything but pretending to be okay. When I told Jack I wanted to stop the medication, he frowned.

"But I can't sleep and my hair's falling out," I complained.

He glanced at my hairline. *Are you sure?* his eyes seemed to say as if he watched me attempting to fit a round shape in a square hole.

"Those are not side effects according to this," Jack said and flipped over the medication flyer. "Dry mouth, skin rash, nausea, vomiting, and shallow breathing. Hair loss is not one of them. Maybe you should take some vitamins."

"What about numb hands and feet?"

"Go to a gym, one that has child care. Maybe you're not moving enough."

What about the fact that I'm just acting like I'm okay, I wanted to ask. *What about being a con? Is that a side effect?*

And I had to promise Jack I'd continue the medication. Thirty days later I wanted to believe that I was better, but fear was still everywhere—in my head, my throat, my chest. It wrapped itself around my heart, my stomach. I feared something terrible was about to happen, the most terrible thing you can imagine. Jack's promise to cut back at work never materialized, and when a week later, he actually did come home early from work, he was cheery. With the slightest curve at the corner of his mouth he handed me a box of Chinese takeout.

"Your favorite," he said.

"You've been doing a lot better," he said. "Don't you think so?" he asked but didn't wait for my response. He spoke of money and credit, and that the financial problems with the property weren't going away. He couldn't be in that amount of debt and having a foreclosure hanging over his head wasn't going to get him that DA job. And that he'd come up with a plan.

"A plan," I said. "What kind of plan?"

"We've run out of options and I made a decision," he said. His words flew by, hardly reached me. "Here's the deal," he said. "The economy is in shambles, huge salaries for associates at big law firms are no longer, but there's money to be made in foreign exchange deals, equity, and debt. There's a company in Chicago," he said.

"We're moving?" I asked.

"Kind of," he said. "The brownstone, the property with the huge mortgage, that's part of my plan. Renters won't put up with the noise of the construction. With the money I make in Chicago we can pay the mortgage, finish the renovations, and in a year at the most we'll be able to either sell it or rent it."

He looked at me with his eyes blazing as if he'd just solved all our problems. He was smart, I knew that, I loved that about him, but he was also shrewd. Driven. He was hardwired to get what he wanted, and whatever Jack wanted, Jack was going to get.

"I can't believe I didn't think of this sooner," he said. "Legal staffing is the new thing now; it cuts down on expensive billable hours. Outsourcing saves money with legal support work expenses. We'll be out of this financial hole in no time," he said.

"I've accepted a job. Walter Ashcroft, a legal staffing firm in Chicago," he said. "And I'll be moving to Chicago. I've arranged for you to stay in the brownstone in Brooklyn."

Jack wasn't a bad man. I was neither seeing him with rose-colored glasses nor was I overly critical. He used to be gentle with me and he had good intentions. He had hope, no, more than hope, faith even. He decided moving me into the brownstone in Brooklyn was the solution, a brownstone that was, even according to his own words, in shambles. Birds of a feather, I thought. Shambles.

I needed him to be there in case I wasn't getting better, but I didn't know how to ask for that, and so two months later I was in my car on the way to North Dandry while Jack was at the airport waiting for his flight to Chicago.

"I can't say I like it but I don't see any other way right now," he said when I called him from the car on my way to North Dandry. "The project manager is living in the upper apartment while he's supervising the construction on the other two units. His name is Lieberman. If you need anything and I'm not available, call him. You won't have to lift a finger. The movers will unload and unpack. It'll be the easiest move you've ever made."

"I don't need anyone to check up on me, Jack."

"I'm just saying if you need anything, call him. I'll be gone for three weeks, four tops, after that I'll come home for a weekend. I told you that last week, remember?"

Was he trying to tell me that I was senile?

"I'll fly home as often as possible, I promise, depending on the workload. Plus I want to be there when Mia crawls for the first time."

"I'll record it so you don't miss it," I said and was amazed at how rational and normal I sounded. The night before we had watched Mia, six months old then, prop herself up with her hands. She was able to roll from her back to her stomach and vice versa but my fears of SIDS were as strong as ever. She still wasn't sleeping through the night and preferred the bottle to solid food.

I heard muffled voices and the sound of Jack switching his cell from one ear to the other, then a metal detector alerting and a voice telling someone to step aside. I imagined Jack, his arms raised, the handheld metal detector following the contours of his body.

"I'm at the gate. Take your meds, okay?"

"Sure." I knew Jack had been counting the pills and only stopped after I had phoned in the refills.

I swerved to the right and hit the curb. It took me only a few seconds and the car was back under control.

"Bye. I'll call you, okay?"

I didn't answer, hung up the phone, and threw it on the passenger seat. I may have sounded all right to Jack but I felt like a lunatic. If I looked in the rearview mirror and saw a foil beanie on my head, I wouldn't be surprised.

I spotted the NORTH DANDRY sign and pulled up to the curb. I killed the engine and looked at the brownstone. As I turned around, I realized Mia's contorted body was hanging over the side of the seat, her head turned at an odd angle. She had fallen asleep. And I had failed to buckle her seat belt.

NEW DETAILS RELEASED: MOTHER
OF ABDUCTED INFANT WAS FOUND UPSTATE
ONE WEEK AFTER THE DISAPPEARANCE

Brooklyn, NY—Police have released new details in the abduction of 7-month-old Mia Connor. According to an unnamed source, the mother, Estelle Paradise, was found in a ravine near Dover, NY, about three hours from NYC. She was found days after the actual disappearance of the infant. Estelle Paradise had critical injuries to her head and her torso and was treated for hypothermia and other serious accident-related injuries.

A man walking his dogs made the discovery. "They just took off," he said about the two chocolate Labradors, "like hounds from hell. There was no holding them back. Usually I whistle and they come, but they ran down the ravine. I thought I'd lost them, then I heard the barking."

The ravine locals refer to as "Echo Ravine" makes an 80-foot drop to the riverbed below. Officials said it took six hours to remove the injured mother from the ravine due to the steepness of the embankment. The Dover Fire Department assisted with the rescue.

The mother was first taken to a Dover hospital and later transported to a hospital in New York City. The mother's condition has been upgraded from serious to fair. No official source has commented on her exact injuries.

No further information regarding the abduction of Mia Connor has been released.

CHAPTER 9

"Detectives." Dr. Baker nods at them on his way out. "Thirty minutes tops. If her vitals make somersaults, I'll put my foot down."

The detectives wait until Dr. Baker has left the room.

"My name is Detective Wilczek. I'll be heading the investigation. You remember Detective Daniel?" He points at the middle-aged rotund man. "We appreciate you talking to us, Mrs. Paradise," he says and pulls out a notebook. Wilczek is in his forties, buzz cut, thin, and wiry. His nails are bitten to the quick.

Dr. Baker has removed the morphine pump and I try to ignore the pain behind my left eye.

"I'd like to go over everything again, if you don't mind. I understand you must be getting tired of repeating the same thing over and over, but I prefer to hear it from you."

My routine, Jack's job in Chicago, the days leading up to her disappearance, the morning I found her crib empty. While Wilczek takes notes, he never interrupts me. When he doesn't take notes, he twists the narrow wedding band on his left hand with his thumb.

"Tell me about the locks. Why did you have those locks installed?"

I found a window left open, a door ajar, and crooked blinds. Nothing major, yet worrisome, and I couldn't convince myself that it was "just the wind." Because reason was like a ghost, one minute there and gone the next. Vanished. It was as if reason were able to dissolve into the very air itself. I wondered if someone had rigged the house with secret entrances and passageways like some creepy old mansion. I even occasionally found my eyes scanning the walls and floors for telltale signs of intruders, but of course there were none.

"I wanted to be safe."

"Did you feel threatened in any way? Did anyone make a threat toward you?"

"No, nothing like that. I was basically living there by myself most of the time; it was just a precaution."

"Nothing odd happened in the days before your daughter disappeared?"

Once, there was an imprint in my bed, the sheets crumpled, as if a supernatural visitor had taken the liberty of resting there in my absence. Then one day I came home and the mirror seemed off-kilter. Was I imagining it, is my view of the world skewed somehow? My first thought was *There's someone here*. But the house was empty. So I dismissed it.

"Not that I remember," I say.

"Who had access to the apartment?"

I think about it for a while. "Jack. The movers. The man who installed the locks." Suddenly my pulse quickens. "The man who installed the locks . . . he was odd, he looked at me the entire time."

"We dusted the entire apartment for prints. The ones on the door are from the gentleman who installed the locks. We checked out his alibi and he's been eliminated. He takes care of his elderly parents. There are prints from your husband, mainly on the furniture. Some other prints on furniture checked out as the movers." Wilczek's voice turns composed, almost kind. "Were there any strange phone calls? Anyone watching you? Anything out of the ordinary? Even something insignificant might be a very important fact."

The coffee table had been moved, haphazardly pushed aside. There were visible dents in the rug, as if my mother's spirit, annoyed by my lack of furniture placement, had come to properly rearrange my table. I dismissed it as if I was accepting a warped and disturbed home.

"Nothing out of the ordinary," I say.

And then: "Tell me again why you didn't call 9-1-1?"

"I had the phone in my hand, dialing the number, and then I saw that her bottles were gone. Her clothes, everything. I didn't understand what had happened."

"So you did what?"

"I looked for her, everywhere. In my car. In alleys, around the neighborhood, everywhere. I asked a homeless woman on the corner if she'd seen anything. I even looked in Dumpsters." I catch myself but it's too late. The word *Dumpster* echoes in my mind. It just didn't sound right. *I looked for my daughter in Dumpsters.* Why did I even say that? Why would I even entertain the possibility of my daughter thrown away among trash and garbage?

"You went up and down the street you say. Did you ask for help?" Wilczek's voice remains calm.

I shake my head.

"How about the workers in the house?"

"It was a Sunday, everybody was gone."

"How about your neighbor?" He checks his notes. "Lieberman, the other person living in the building, right? Did you ask him for help?"

"He visits his sister on the weekends. He leaves on Friday

afternoons. I called him a few times but I couldn't even leave a message."

"What did you think happened to your daughter?"

I fold over my blanket like an accordion, its waffle-weave pattern a shadowlike illusion that seems crooked, and I'm looking for order among chaos.

Focus on his question.

"I didn't have any idea."

"Did you call your husband?"

"No." I lower my head and wonder where I'd be right now if I had called Jack right away. Jack would have called the police, he would have rushed home, and he would have known what to do because Jack always knows what to do. Not calling him was just another one of my blunders. "He had just left and started his new job. I knew it would be hard for him to call every day and he was due to come home in a week or two for a few days."

Wilczek leans forward, adjusting his tie. "Why didn't you ask him for help? He's a lawyer, he's got resources and connections other parents of abducted children only dream of."

"I . . . no . . . I was confused. I thought many things."

"Did he call you at all after he'd left New York?"

"Yes, we talked. Not at length, no, just how are you, how's the baby, everything okay, how's the house coming along, that sort of thing."

"Tell us why you bleached your entire house."

I bleached my house? Oh yeah, that. I remember the bleach. I was on the brink of something that felt like horror. Yes, *horror* is the right word. I had to occupy myself. I felt soothed by the acid burning in my nose and eyes, the struggle to breathe as if someone had his hands around my lungs, the wheezing and coughing I welcomed. When I returned to North Dandry, after I had left the precinct, a stench hit me, a fusion of coffee grounds and dead air behind windows that had gone unopened for days, maybe even weeks. And then I saw the filth; the grimy drain and the moldy ring around the faucet. I went to work among buckets, rags, and steel wool. When one toothbrush wore down, I got another from the bathroom drawer. I dipped the bristles in bleach and scoured the grout between the floor tiles, ran ice cubes through the disposal. I cleaned room after room, removing objects from shelves, mopping, wiping, scouring. As my hands started to burn and my cuticles all but dissolved, I realized that this mission was designed to make something right, something that I wasn't sure I had wronged to begin with. I cleaned with bleach, yes I did. Detective Wilczek wants to know why, and who could blame him, I know what he's insinuating.

The detective waits for an answer but I have no logical explanation for him and so I remain silent. I look out the window as if to find the answer in the distance.

"I need you to explain why you left the precinct without reporting the disappearance. Picking up the phone and then not reporting her missing after you realize her things have disappeared is one thing. But then you decide you need to talk to the police after all. You walk to the station but you don't ask for help. You must understand that this doesn't make sense. There's no intruder, no break-in. Just a missing baby and a mother who can't remember anything."

"Dr. Baker told you I have amnesia, right?"

"Mrs. Paradise"—Wilczek scoots his chair closer, his eyes appear soft—"children don't just disappear out of locked apartments. They don't disappear without a trace. Are you telling me that someone walked through walls and made away with a closet full of clothes and a dozen baby bottles? Boxes of diapers? And all that while you were sleeping?"

I have to agree with him. It sounds like a melodramatic soap opera.

"You missed a doctor's appointment," Wilczek continues. "Some sort of scheduled vaccination. You've been to all previous appointments, but not that one. Why didn't you go?"

"I forgot." I didn't go to her scheduled vaccination appointment? I would never just miss a vaccination, there must have been a reason. Something irks me but I can't put my finger on it.

"The day care said you never returned with her shot records."

"The day care needed the complete shot records to enroll her, and since I missed the vaccination appointment, there was no reason to go back. And it wasn't child care, really, just a couple of hours here and there."

"Did you reschedule the appointment?"

"I was going to but then she . . ." I pinch my lips shut. I need to be alone, I need to think this through, everything's unclear, too vague to put in words.

"She what?"

"She disappeared."

Wilczek lowers his head and studies his notebook.

"Tell me about the homeless woman."

"There was a homeless woman on the corner, I'd seen her before, and I thought if she'd been there all night, she might have . . ." It dawns on me that if he knows about her, he's undoubtedly spoken to her. "You talked to her? What did she tell you?"

I watch his eyes fly over the notes in his little book. "I don't want to go by what other people tell me when I can hear it from you."

"She was confused. She had a dog with her. That's all I remember."

"Tell me about the car seat," Wilczek says.

I hear a beeping sound behind me, speeding up. Then it hits me: I left a car seat on the curb and I gave the homeless woman my suitcase. I shake my head in disbelief. My heart is beating in my throat. How stupid and how random. Why did I do that?

"I don't know what to tell you." I try to sound calm but I can feel the tears gathering behind my eyes. My heart is beating fast and my head is shaking from side to side. Anxiety tremors, according to Dr. Baker. "As far as I understand it, the way it was explained to me, I have amnesia. The accident caused me to forget what happened the days before. My memory only goes so far."

"So there's something you're not telling me?"

"That's what I'm trying to explain to you. I don't know what I'm not telling you. I can't possibly know what I don't know." The comment makes me smile. I catch myself but it's too late.

"Time's up." Dr. Baker pokes his head in the room and shuts down the interview. When the door closes behind him, Wilczek gets up to leave.

"Did you find any blood?" The words escape before I can rein them back in. *Careful. Be more careful.*

"Blood? What kind of blood?" Detective Wilczek's facial expression is blank.

Are there different kinds of blood? Blood is blood. *Don't say that out loud.*

"I'm just wondering if there was *any* blood."

"We're waiting on forensics," he says. "But like I said, all that bleach . . . Call me if you can think of anything else. We'll talk again soon."

I nod and close my eyes.

Minutes later, I stand up, unsteady at first, then I get the hang of it. I slide my feet more than lift them off the ground, which makes walking easier. I reach for the doorknob. I can't resist the urge and peek out the door down the hallway and wonder what would happen if I just started walking. My guard leans forward ever so slightly when he detects movement.

A baby's wails travel down the hallways, straight through the open door, aiming directly into my auditory cortex, hitting it like an arrow pierces a bull's-eye.

I slam the door shut. I lean against it as if I'm attempting to keep the acoustic waves at bay. I run my fingers through my hair, upward, and hold my head, gently at first, then I pull my hair as hard as I can. My scalp starts to pulsate but the pain drowns out the baby's wails. If I could cut off my other ear to deafen the cries, I would.

Mia is gone and I'm the suspect.

And as I sit on the floor in my hospital room, I see myself not so much for what I am, but for what I'm not.

I'm not a tearful mother whose eyes are red and swollen, begging the kidnapper to return her child. Dr. Baker called it "blunted affect," a lack of emotional reactivity, a sign of trauma, maybe even brain injury. I wish he was here right now to watch what this crying baby is doing to me. I'm not a pleading mother. Instead I say things that I find suspicious myself, I smile when I have no reason for happiness. I ask questions when clearly I don't remember. I can only imagine what the detectives are thinking right about now.

I've seen distraught mothers on TV, mothers who clutch their kid's beloved stuffed animal, mothers who promise they'll never stop looking. The fathers behind them, arms wrapped around them, families gathered in support of them, wiping tears, trying to hold in their emotions. I've seen mothers on front pages, eyes glazed over, the Valium doing its job of delaying the anguish for at least a few hours. The agony in the parents' eyes is painful for the onlookers, even translates through television sets—it is unrestrained, unedited, and raw.

And then there are the monsters. Monsters lying about the disappearance of their children, tearful pleas to phantom carjackers, Munchausen syndrome lunatics running into emergency rooms, cradling dead or near-dead babies. Newborns stuffed in trash receptacles after being born in Walmart bathrooms. With their umbilical cords still attached.

Jack's words *We can still fix this* echo in my mind. Did I do something that needs fixing? I remember the scissors and sharp objects near her. And how the cord of the lamp by her crib made me nervous. I never carried her in my arms walking down steep stairwells, always had her safely tucked away in a car seat. Sharp edges and blunt corners, heights atop stairs seemed tempting.

I have a suspicion. I won't tell anyone, but I whisper it to myself.

CHAPTER 10

I met the property manager in front of the brownstone on North Dandry. Jack had hired Yolanda Drake of Hudson Bay Property to oversee the renovations of the brownstone. She started talking the moment I got out of the car.

"Sometimes properties are . . ." Yolanda paused and searched her mind for the right word. "Cursed," she finally said and lifted her index finger.

"Cursed? Isn't that a bit over the top?" I narrowed my eyes in disbelief and gently straightened Mia's head, as not to wake her. I couldn't believe that I had forgotten to strap her in.

"No, 'cursed' *is* the right word. The contractor ran out of money, the subcontractors quit, workers stole materials from the jobsite, and no one got the appropriate permits. You name it, it went wrong with 517. I've never had a property that had so many problems. The contractors have been ordered to fulfill the contracts but they have to be supervised. No one is very happy at this moment, especially your husband."

I tried to look enthusiastic about the gossip she was so willingly sharing with me and nodded in agreement.

"The property should have sold or rented months ago and everybody is getting impatient. Brilliant idea to have someone on site at all times to make sure everything goes smoothly. David Lieberman's quite proficient and he keeps the workers in line. Lieberman reports to me, I report to your husband."

Suddenly a sound startled me. It started off as a murmur, then turned into a loud crash, making me flinch. A cloud of dust emerged from a huge green metal container connected to a bright yellow construction chute in front of 517. Within seconds we were covered in a cloud of construction dust.

"Is there a provisional date of completion?" That's what Jack had called it. A provisional date of completion, meaning the moment when renters wouldn't be bothered by the noise. I wondered how Jack thought my living there in the meantime would be a good idea, even remotely.

"We're playing it by ear. Contractors are never on time."

"My husband told me it was a matter of a couple of months."

Yolanda Drake shifted her considerable weight from one foot to the other and raised her eyebrows. "Anything is possible, I guess," she said and handed me the key. "It's all yours," she added and wiped her hand on her pencil skirt.

My eyes followed her until she disappeared around the corner. The key to 517 felt warm to the touch. I glanced back at the car. Mia was peacefully asleep in the car seat, calmed by the humming engine from the ride over here.

I switched on the baby monitors and left one on the passenger seat and tucked the second one safely away in my purse. I cracked all windows half an inch and turned off the engine. The temperature was a comfortable sixty degrees, the sky overcast. The tinted windows hardly allowed any visibility into the car's interior.

Apartment A1 was located on the first floor. I calculated I could get to the car in less than thirty seconds if Mia started to cry. I was reluctant to wake her, knowing it would result in another crying fit, making me think how hard it must be on her to respond to life with such violent protest. Every nap was hope on my part, hope that she'd wake up and be calmer, more content.

I walked up the steps to the front door. It opened before I could fully insert the key. In front of me stood a man in steel-toed boots covered in wood shavings like coconut flakes on a cake. He stood on the threshold, the rim of the yellow hard hat shielding his eyes. He lifted his head and his eyes skimmed over me. He continued down the steps and turned to the left. I watched him as he walked away, down the sidewalk and up the block. His stride was wide, his torso upright.

I entered the building. I stood still just long enough to take in the scent of fresh paint and a faint odor of disinfectant. A1 in cursive gold letters on the door straight ahead. To the left was a large opening taped shut with heavy-duty tarp to keep the dust and debris out.

A hair-raising shriek made me reach for the baby monitor. The green display sat idle, a faint sound of white noise in the background. Then a whining sound turned into a throaty grind. I shut the monitor off, then back on. Nothing but white noise. When I inserted the key into the lock and pushed open the door, I realized the sound was coming from behind the tarp: carpenters sawing wood, framing walls, or working on the hardwood floors.

The two-thousand-square-foot apartment's floors were solid cherrywood, native to upstate New York. The distance from the front to the back was an impressive forty feet. The hallway led through two parlor doors into the living room, which took up the entire back of the building. There were two rooms on the left; the kitchen and the dining room, eventually leading into the parlor. There were three rooms on the right; the first one the bathroom, the other two bedrooms.

My footsteps echoed through the rooms and the light flooding through the windows was harsh and uncomfortable. The walls were bleak, painted in an abrasive white. I inspected the doors and windows. A double-cylinder dead bolt on the front door, a type of auxiliary lock that required a key to project or retract the dead bolt from either side. There was also a mortise lock, usually found in older buildings, making any attempt to break in practically impossible.

Suddenly the monitor unleashed violent static and then went silent again. I manually switched over to the second channel. Again, nothing but white noise. I switched back to the initial channel and heard a man's voice. Before I reached the car, baby monitor in hand, the monitor changed to a gentle buzz, then to a protest, and finally an eruption. Mia's stuttering gasps interrupted by attempts to fill her lungs with air.

I dug into my purse for the car key, and when I looked up, the man with the steel-toed boots, whom I'd seen earlier, stared at me. His eyes went from the car—echoing with screams—back to me, to the monitor in my hand. My cell phone rang and the moving company confirmed the address. When I turned back around, he had gone.

———————

A week later, I stood by the window, parted the curtain with my hands, and looked out into the fall night. It was almost dark and the streets were deserted except for a few people taking their dogs for a last pit stop before they'd curl up on couches or on kitchen floors. Leaves tumbled about like discarded paper, following their destinies into storm drains, iron window grates, and curbside puddles.

I pulled the curtain, layered it midway where the panels met, and shut out the dark. Night falling on New York City was not my favorite time of day. The outside noises—the traffic, the hurried voices, and the screaming children in the school courtyard across the street—never completely stopped but slowed down like a clock that needed winding.

Later, I jerked up from a half-sleep state, a buzz echoing in my head. I listened but it was quiet. I shut my eyes again. Three more buzzes sounded and I realized it must be the doorbell. I peeked through the hole but all I could make out was a shadowy outline of a man.

"Yes?" I said through the closed door.

"Mrs. Paradise?"

"Yes?"

"David Lieberman."

At first, the name meant nothing to me, and then I remembered Jack and the property manager mentioning the name of the upstairs tenant who was overseeing the renovations. I had a feeling he wasn't going to go away unless I talked to him.

"Just a minute," I said, ignoring Mia wailing in her crib. I opened the door, chain still engaged, and looked at him through a crack in the door.

"How's the pressure?" Lieberman checked his hands and proceeded to clean the fingernails of one hand with the nails of the other.

"What?" I wanted to tell him to leave me alone but he'd probably tell Jack, and Jack would call and scold me for being rude. After all, according to Jack, Lieberman was here to help.

"The pressure. The water pressure."

"I'm sorry?"

"The water pressure." He emphasized every syllable, as if I was either incapable of understanding English or partially deaf.

"What about it?"

He cocked his head. "Someone's crying in there," he said.

"What can I do for you?" I said, ignoring his comment.

"If you pick her up, she'll stop crying. I've been listening to her all day." He gave me a stare. "Not that the walls are particularly thin in this building, but noise travels."

"What about the water pressure?" I tried to keep my face expressionless.

"Have you taken a shower lately?" he asked and looked me up and down through the crack in the door: my greasy hair, my wrinkled shirt, and the pants I'd been wearing for a week. "There's a problem with the plumbing, they are working on the pipes."

"I hadn't noticed."

"She isn't going to stop crying until you pick her up." His neck craned to see what was going on behind me.

I started to think that my expressionless face might be a mistake. "Let me call you after I check, okay?" I closed the door and on my way to the nursery, I caught a glimpse of myself in the mirror. I looked emaciated, my cheeks sunken and my eyes black holes surrounded by dark circles. I couldn't even remember the last time I had taken a shower.

A couple of hours later the buzzer went off again. This time I opened the door and stood in the doorway. I had all but forgotten about the plumbing and the water pressure.

"The pressure seems fine," I lied, "but I can't tell a difference, to be honest with you."

"Would you mind if I checked?"

I didn't say anything.

"I met your husband a couple of times." He hesitated ever so slightly, then added, "He asked me to check on you."

"I don't need to be checked on."

"Maybe that came out wrong. He wants me to help you if you have any issues. Plumbing, electric, whatever you need, just tell me. I'm either next door or upstairs. Except on the weekends, I'm never here on the weekends. I visit my sister upstate. But during the week, Monday morning until Friday afternoon, I'm all yours." He smiled at me, then cocked his head. "You didn't call me and I realized you didn't have my number." He stepped closer and handed me a piece of paper. I got a whiff of sawdust and oil.

"I'm not sure what my husband told you, but the moving company gave me a list of plumbers and electricians."

Lieberman nodded. "Do you have any idea how long it takes to get a plumber to show up? You have more important things to worry about," he said and raised his eyebrows.

Mia was fussing in the background. "Right," I said and grabbed the door.

"I'm around nail guns and saws all day. It can get pretty loud and the ringing in the ears sometimes takes hours to go away," he said and tapped his right ear with his hand. He smiled without showing teeth and took his New York Yankees hat off. "I go home at the end of the day and then I hear the baby cry through the ceiling. That's all I'm saying. Must be hard, all by yourself."

He looked even younger with his hat off.

"I'll check the pressure again and I'll call you. Promise."

"Okay then. If I don't hear from you, I'll just come back," he said and laughed.

I offered him a smile that was friendly without being encouraging. Before I shut the door, I heard the tarp move and for a second the construction noise increased. Then the tarp closed and all was quiet again.

A couple of blocks from North Dandry, a Child's Play offered child care services by the hour.

"Here's a copy of our policies. The by-the-hour group drop-off times are flexible. The other groups adhere to a curriculum and you have to talk to the individual caregiver regarding the drop-off times." A middle-aged woman in ice cream cone–littered scrubs handed me a stack of papers from behind the counter.

We toured the facility. Behind a two-way glass wall two staffers in pink scrubs sat in padded gliders, each one rocking a baby in her arms.

"Her immunization record must be up to date," she said and pushed her glasses back to the bridge of her nose. "There's a list of shot records required by law in your paperwork. Take it to the pediatrician and have them look it over. It's pretty standard."

We passed the window of the toddler room, where about two dozen children, in groups of three or four, were lying on the floor curling their bodies into the shape of each letter of the alphabet.

A woman in purple scrubs joined us. After she introduced herself as the director, she glanced down at Mia thrashing her arms and legs. "Anything out of the ordinary we need to know?" she asked while Mia was catching her breath between two wails.

"She's just a bit fussy today," I said and struggled to pop the pacifier back in Mia's mouth.

"Don't forget her shot record—we can't enroll her unless the paperwork is complete," the lady in purple reminded me. I signed the required paperwork and handed her a check for the application fee.

After I left the day care, I thought about things that seemed to be out of place lately: a formula bottle I thought I had left on the counter was now in the fridge, baby clothes I had left draped over the crib ended up in the hamper, windows left ajar, and dirty diapers I'd left around the house wound up in the trash. It was probably my imagination; it wasn't as if Jack was catching a flight from Chicago to New York, secretly checking in on me, moving things around. "Mommy brain" they call it, I kept telling myself, assuming that the part of my brain that used to be involved in planning and foresight was taken over by the baby's schedule. It was probably the unfamiliar surroundings but I didn't need another worry.

Mia was asleep in her stroller when I entered a hardware store just a couple of blocks from North Dandry. The sales clerk at Taylor Hardware, Security & Lock wore an apron with the name *LARRY* stitched in cursive across the pocket, almost illegible in all capital letters, and a slightly more complicated name would have been impossible to decipher. Larry climbed ladders and pulled boxes from the very top shelves while I listened patiently to his explanations, taking mental note of possible lock choices, all the while looking into Larry's watery eyes stuck behind his enormous glasses.

"What kind of locks you have now?" he asked and pushed his glasses up on the bridge of his nose, leaving fingerprints on the lenses.

"A latch set with a keyhole on the outside and a thumb turn on the inside. There's also a chain door guard." Mia started to stir in the stroller and I knew it was only a matter of minutes until she'd break out in a full-blown howl.

"Are you looking for additional security? Like a dead bolt or something?"

"There's no such thing as too much security." Mia started to fuss and her hands began to flail. I rocked the stroller back and forth, knowing that picking her up wouldn't do any good. I hoped I'd make it through the lock purchase without Larry giving me any advice on how to console a screaming baby. Mia seemed more content being left in her stroller than in my arms, as if my embrace was the most uncomfortable state of being.

Larry's eyes were huge behind the lenses as he rose his voice to top Mia's crying.

"How about an old-fashioned alarm system sounding like sirens and hell rolled all into one?" he said. "The security company will dispatch a car within minutes. We've got a special going on, twenty percent off and free installation."

"I don't want to alert anyone, I just want to be able to lock my doors and keep them that way." I kept rolling the stroller back and forth, trying to stop Mia's crying.

"An alarm system is—"

"Just tell me what else you have that I can install myself." I checked my watch. Larry took the gesture as impatience on my part and started pulling cardboard boxes and metal parts off the shelf behind him.

"And I need tools," I added. "Like a screwdriver and a hand-held drill."

"She's got a set of lungs on her." He looked down at Mia, whose face had turned red, her mouth a gaping well of fury.

"Just give me what I asked for. Don't forget the tools."

He wasn't offended by my rudeness. "Are you sure you can manage? I'll talk to the boss and we throw in a free installation. If you live in the neighborhood, that is."

"Not too far," I said and checked my watch again.

"I'll install the locks myself if you're interested." He stepped closer, and when I reached for the boxes, he didn't let go immediately. "Seriously, I will. We have a special going on."

After he rang me up at the register, I left the store, knowing his eyes were following me as I walked by the glass storefront. I had seen the disappointment on his face when I paid in cash. I knew he wanted to look at my credit card and remember my name, even look me up later. Or ask for my driver's license to find out my address.

Back home, I went to work but realized quickly that I was in way over my head. I couldn't even hold the drill steady nor could I identify the exact spot where the screws were supposed to go.

Two hours later the metal door to my apartment was scratched and dented. I studied the parts I had bought at the hardware store. I read the back of the boxes until the words no longer made sense. The bolt throw seemed too long and I couldn't find the steel insert. One of the locks contained a free-turning cylinder but the screws were too short to reach the wood studding beyond the doorframe. I was frustrated, sweaty, and discouraged; my knuckles were bruised.

The hardware store address and phone number were printed on the top of the receipt, and I hoped Larry's offer for a free installation was still good. I called the hardware store and asked for him. I heard paperwork being shuffled, and the bell above the door jangling. Eventually Larry came to the phone. I explained who I was and what I'd bought, and asked if the free-installation offer was still valid.

"Yeah, about that," Larry said, and I heard the sound of the register open and shut. "I was wondering how those locks worked out for you. I can come by after work and take a look. What's your address again?"

"Five-seventeen North Dandry, apartment A1. There's a lot of construction going on and I was going to ask one of the workers, but . . . anyway . . . I don't want to disturb them."

"Like I said, it'll be after hours. It's just something we do out of courtesy for our customers."

We agreed on a time and hung up. If Larry got the job done quickly, neither Lieberman nor Jack would ever find out that I had locks installed. After I hung up the phone with Larry, a faint whine crept toward me from Mia's room. There was no shower in my near future but at least the installation of the locks seemed certain. After I fed and changed Mia, I stood with her in my arms, looking out the window facing the street. The windows still had their original cast-iron bars and unless someone took a metal saw to them, they seemed very sturdy and safe.

Larry appeared with his tool belt fitting snuggly around his waist, his belly drooping over in the front. He carefully laid out all the locks on the foyer tile.

"Locks have personality, you know," he said.

"Well, they weren't speaking to me," I said and passed Mia from one hip to the other.

She let out a sudden screech that prompted Larry to drop the electric drill. It left a jagged crack in the ceramic tile.

"Darn it," Larry said and inspected the damage. "Little one scared me. I'll replace that for you free of charge."

I didn't care for him to come back. "Don't worry about the tile. I'll have that fixed. There's lots of tiles stacked in the hallway."

Whatever I hadn't managed to do a couple of hours earlier took him all of twenty minutes.

"Anything else I can do for you?" Larry asked and took his time returning tools into his red Craftsman box. "While I'm here. I'm handy with a lot of stuff." He winked at me and with the back of his hand wiped the sweat off his forehead. "If you don't mind, call my boss and tell him about my work. It's almost Christmas, which means bonus time."

I promised I would and that I'd call him if I needed anything else, and shut the door quickly. It was dented, the paint scratched, but I thought that I had all the locks I needed to keep us safe. Now, even if he had a key, Jack wouldn't be able to just barge in unannounced. And I wouldn't have to second-guess my mental state every time something seemed out of place.

Later that night, I walked across the room to the fireplace and poked the logs until the flames grew into a joyous blaze. I sat in front of the fireplace, yoga-style, and raised my palms until the heat of the flames became unbearable. I looked around the sparsely decorated room, which consisted of a couch, a chair, and an old table.

Jack's architect had decided to convert the brownstone into four separate units in order to take advantage of the rising real estate values. One unit was occupied by Lieberman and another by me. The two units next door were still under construction. I envisioned how this building must have been a century ago. Opulence lingered just beneath the coat of wear and tear. Single living rooms replaced double parlors, kitchens became smaller but more efficient, and entry foyers disappeared completely. The parlor doors had lost their shine and the marble mantels had long been replaced. The ceiling plaster-work was still intact but showed patches here and there. All interior doors and wood moldings showed deterioration and fatigue, but the allure was in just that: the beauty of imperfection. I wondered how every little scratch or scrape had gotten there. The rooms were spacious, their ceilings an imposing fourteen feet. The sleek mahogany doors were the most distinctive feature of the apartment.

The ceiling work of the house was machine-made, rather than handmade, and of papier-mâché or stucco, rather than plaster. The combination of luxury, faded glory, and ornate shabbiness gave the apartment a kind of magical charm. Since the first story's floor plan was the exact mirror image of the second floor, four identical apartments had been created by using the former grand entrance as the hallway and separating two units by a simple wall.

While the left side of the house, apartments 2A and 2B, was still under construction, the right side of the house, 1A and 1B, had been completed almost nine months ago.

Mrs. Drake, in our initial meeting, had explained the legal ramifications. I hadn't understood most of it, but figured that the completion of the two unfinished apartments was behind schedule due to the lawsuit that Jack had filed against the contractors. The settlement stipulated that the contractors now had to complete the left part of the building within a certain time frame.

The blaze in the fireplace had eased and the shadows flickering across the walls were subtle, almost comforting. I fell asleep as the rainbow-colored craze of flames turned into a tamed orange glow, exhausting itself.

The next morning—four empty bottles on the couch proof of the number of night feedings—I took two aspirin for my headache. I waited for the buzzing in my head to ease, for my thoughts to stop spinning.

The doorbell buzzed, followed by Mia crying. I went to her room, picked her up, and to my surprise she settled down the second the bottle hit her lips.

Through the peephole I saw a shadow passing by the door. Later, after Mia had gone back to sleep, just as I was pulling her door shut, the doorbell buzzed again. This time I just yanked the door open. It was David Lieberman. He bowed his head and took off his hat.

"I need to measure the pressure. Looks like we have to flush the pipes."

"I thought it was all taken care of," I said and realized that my headache had stopped. "Kitchen or bathroom?"

"Kitchen. The pipe connections in this building are a maze."

"So just turn on the water and check for what?"

"May I?" Lieberman put his hand on the door. Then he paused. "What happened here?" he asked, gently stroking the door's surface with his fingertips, the tips caressing every groove and dent.

"I had some locks installed."

"You had some locks installed." Lieberman seemed puzzled, rubbing the chipped paint. "Low pressure is just inconvenient but high pressure can do a lot of damage," he said and held up some sort of gauge device.

Mia was fussing in her crib. I could hear her getting more impatient, the intervals between her protests getting shorter, her objections louder and more urgent by the minute.

I opened the door and stepped aside. He went straight to the kitchen and screwed the gauge to the faucet. I mumbled an apology and went to Mia's room to change her diaper.

I put her on the changing table, leaned over her, gently cooing, hoping she'd cooperate. The toy I handed her flew to the ground. Mia was delighted to be free of the diaper, stretching her limbs, enjoying how her legs moved without a wad of diaper between them. She was all joy and play until it was time to put on a clean diaper. I distracted her as much as possible, but her body tensed and her legs stiffened to the point that it was tedious to pull the diaper through her legs to fasten the tabs. When I was finally done, I found Lieberman still under the kitchen sink.

"Shouldn't a plumber take a look at this?" I distinctly remembered that he said he was just supervising the contractors. He stood by the sink and turned on the faucet. It barely trickled and the pipes emitted a humming noise, then the walls around us seemed to vibrate and I felt a tremor under my feet.

"I'm going to have to turn the water main off." He pointed at Mia in my arms. "You'll have to use bottled water in the meantime."

"How long is this going to take?" He hadn't even laid out his tools yet, and I wondered what he'd been doing the entire time I had changed the diaper and dressed Mia. I felt a tinge of impatience.

"I'll take care of the pipes," he said and grabbed a wrench off the counter. "You just go and get some water." He pointed at my purse on the counter.

I wasn't in the mood to get dressed and run to a store to purchase water, but I put Mia in her stroller and grabbed my purse, happy to get away from the noise of groaning pipes and not having to deal with Lieberman in general.

As I passed by my usual market, Mia was still crying and I decided to continue farther down the block to the next corner market. Minutes later it started to sprinkle and I covered the stroller with a blanket. By the time I entered the market, Mia was asleep. The clerk was framed by porn magazines in plastic pouches and probably had a shotgun stashed close by.

I grabbed a gallon of water and made my way to the counter. I sat the gallon on the counter. When I reached in my purse, there was no wallet. I rummaged senselessly through the compartments filled with tissues and receipts as the clerk looked at me sideways. I mumbled an apology and quickly left the market.

When I returned to North Dandry, Lieberman had left. The

second I set foot in the kitchen I spotted my wallet on the kitchen counter under a stack of mail and papers. Next to it sat a bottle of water. I shook my head, scolding myself for being so scatterbrained.

I opened the fridge door. I felt a sinking feeling of despair as I stared at an array of bottles filled with baby formula.

I didn't even attempt to construct an elaborate rationalization as to why I couldn't remember what I had done mere hours ago. Between the wallet, the water, and the formula, I realized that at some point I had to admit to myself that the word *forgetful* was no longer accurate and that *brain on fire* was more like it.

I tried to forget my absentmindedness but something remained with me. A nagging voice in the back of my mind that whispered *What are you going to misplace next?*

TIMELINE OF MIA CONNOR ABDUCTION

Brooklyn, NY—The case of seven-month-old Mia Connor is gripping the nation. Nothing short of a tragedy, the facts of Mia Connor's disappearance seem to be pointing in a disturbing direction.

In the days before the disappearance, Mia's mother, Estelle Paradise, had locks and bolts installed by a local hardware store. According to a store clerk from Taylor Hardware, Security & Lock, she wanted to "keep people out." He described her as "preoccupied, a bit on the edge," then added, "and she never tended to the baby. She was crying the entire time."

On September 30th Estelle Paradise, 27, is seen on surveillance tapes attempting to purchase a gallon of water. She never pays for the water but storms out of the convenience store, leaving the water behind. On October 1st Estelle Paradise finds her daughter's crib empty. She doesn't notify the authorities.

According to surveillance tapes, she enters the 70th Police Precinct in Brooklyn on Sunday and is seen vomiting in the precinct hallway after exiting a bathroom. She then leaves without talking to the detective, who remembers her as "disheveled and worn-out."

Estelle Paradise is found on October 4th at the bottom of a ravine in Dover, NY, with life-threatening injuries. Among other items a gun was found in the car.

She is transferred to County Medical in Brooklyn on October 5th. Upon her arrival she is listed in serious condition. The next day her husband, and father of Mia, Jack Connor, 38, arrives at County Medical. According to an unnamed source, an arraignment can be anticipated within two weeks, depending on the mother's recuperation. She is listed in fair condition.

PART 2

"Begin at the beginning," the King said, very gravely, "and go on till you come to the end: then stop."

Lewis Carroll, Alice's Adventures in Wonderland

BREAKING NEWS: NO ARRAIGNMENT IMMINENT FOR ESTELLE PARADISE, MOTHER OF MISSING 7-MONTH-OLD MIA CONNOR

Brooklyn, NY—At this time no formal charges will be brought against Estelle Paradise, mother of missing infant Mia Connor.

On Monday morning the courthouse was abuzz with anticipation of the appearance of Estelle Paradise for a possible arraignment. Legal sources predicted that in the absence of a body charges ranging from second-degree murder to aggravated manslaughter were most likely.

In a staggering turn of events, the statement of the DA caught everyone off guard.

DA Barrymore read the very short statement in front of the media that had gathered hours before. "Estelle Paradise is at an undisclosed location awaiting psychiatric care. No formal charges will be filed at this point. This is an ongoing investigation and we cannot comment any further. I will not be taking any questions."

When DA Barrymore walked away from the microphone, the media broke out in a frenzy. Phone calls to the DA's office from multiple news outlets have not been returned.

CHAPTER 11

As we cross into Queens, I catch a glimpse of Creedmoor sitting silently on a hill overlooking the East River. Jack's subdued, almost as if he's in a trance. We ride in silence until he jerks the steering wheel to the right and almost sends my stomach over the edge. I dig my heels into the floor mats because there's only one thing Jack hates more than a woman's tears, and that's vomit on his charcoal Corinthian leather seats. The car slides as if suspended on a bed of marbles and comes to an abrupt halt.

I watch him as he hides his face behind his cupped hands. Suddenly he's slouched over, his shoulders are bobbing, and his hands are rubbing his eyes. When he starts shaking his head, I realize Jack's crying. He looks up at me and I'm amazed.

I remain removed from his pain, maybe because I've been alone with mine for so long that I don't seem to know how to comfort him. I stare at the tears emerging from his eyes and random facts pop into my head—happy tears emerge from the right eye, the first tear from the left eye signals pain, but I don't remember if that's true or a myth—but either way, Jack doesn't look right crying. I take deep breaths to calm my stomach, at the same time I try to figure out what's going on with him. Before I can even think of a reason, Jack's composure resurfaces and his outburst is over just as quickly as it began. When he finally speaks, his voice is so low I can hardly understand him.

"My entire life I knew how to deal with other people's problems and then this happens and I'm just fucking lost."

He goes on to tell me how he hasn't been sleeping, how he's just muddling through, and how all of this is tearing him up, and how I'm not the woman he married—*that* woman was dependable and capable—and how he's been wondering if *that* woman will ever come back, and how it doesn't really matter because nothing will ever be the same. And how he is torn—he never says just what he is torn about—and he can't keep wondering about the truth day in and day out. That living like this isn't a life at all, and that there's nothing brave about fighting all the time, and he's no longer got the strength for both of us, and now all he's got left is the love for his daughter. And that she is so small and fragile and never did anything to harm anyone and everything is just a mess and he can't cope any longer but he will do everything in his power to bring her home. And then: "I don't know what it is you did or didn't do, Estelle, I just can't wrap my mind around it and that's why I have to step back."

Stepping back. I can't fathom what stepping back entails, but I feel something taking hold, something sinister and rather final, but I'm behind with my thoughts and I'm not sure what's going on, and therefore I just sit and listen and look at him, hoping my facial expression is sympathetic and attentive. I want to be supportive and I hope I am but I have no way of knowing. I'm in a peaceful state of not caring about his pain and I want to remain there, if possible.

"I've met guilty people, innocent people, people who I didn't know if they were guilty or not, and everyone has the right to counsel and a defense, and that's what being a lawyer's all about, that's what this entire legal system is all about. But this is nothing like that at all, this is personal, this is my daughter."

His words are a constant refrain of tiptoeing around what he really wants to say. His emotional quandary is the love for his daughter—and I give him that, he's got his priorities straight—but I wish he would just say it, just say *I don't know if you're guilty or not*. That's what it all comes down to.

And then he goes on about how he didn't do anything to deserve this, all he ever did was protect her and care for her and provide for her, and he needs to concentrate on what's important and he can't do that when he's around me. I space out, not on purpose, it's just something that happens, and once I jerk back into reality, I'm not sure if I missed anything significant. He uses words like *doubt* and *responsibility*, they roll off his tongue, and *apprehension* and *contempt*, and my mind shrieks yet I can't interpret any of the words buzzing around in my head, can't get them in the right order to make sense of them. I try to focus, come up with a coherent state-ment, anything that reassures him that I'm worthy of his trust. I want to scream at him that all *I* ever wanted was to protect her, and that *I'm* no different than he is, that *I* don't deserve this, either, and for fuck's sake, what does *stepping back* even mean?

And for a split second I have a moment of clarity and I under-stand that he's failed me, that he's to blame for this, that he didn't live up to his responsibilities, that I at least tried while he just . . . just gave up on me. That Mia wasn't safe because I wasn't well, and that he abandoned me and therefore he abandoned both of us a long time ago.

But I don't tell him any of this because we've talked too much about how I feel, and I know he's done talking about my pain. It's all about him now and why he's come to the conclusion to . . . what was it again? To *step back*.

"I'm sorry," he says and his voice cracks. "I can't think about what happened to my daughter and love you at the same time."

I look at myself in the side-view mirror. He's right, as always, Jack is right, there's no telling what I did. I can't be trusted. I want to come up with some sort of consolation for him, I want to tell him that I understand and that he needs to concentrate on finding our daughter, I want to say something coherent, something supportive, and I think I can get there, I trust myself enough that I can console him somehow. The right words must be in my vocabulary.

"Sometimes I imagine her dead," I say and stare straight ahead. I hear my own voice, so small and meek, and I know I have failed him, yet again.

Later, after Jack drops me off at the Creedmoor intake office, as the nurse bends over to pick up my suitcase, I realize Jack's left without my noticing. It isn't until that moment that I wonder how many things in Jack's life are failures and I can't think of a single one, except me. Jack cannot connect with failure, it's that simple. And I decide to abandon hope and just let it be. Jack's out there and I'm in here and we both have to cope. Apart from each other. It's easy for me to imagine him gone, I know what it means when someone is gone, comes up missing, stolen, kidnapped, whatever. Whatever.

I remember feeling those feelings and thinking those thoughts yet they tell me another story. I later hear that I screamed, that I scratched orderlies, my nails digging deep into their arms, leaving bloody trails. That's when I remember the photograph in my father's study, the Riverside Church, built about the same time as Creedmoor. I imagine how Riverside, Lego-like, ascended brick by brick toward the heavens while Creedmoor's castle, wrought of brick and stone, slithered its way across the meadows on this magnificent estate. Creedmoor is my life now and I'm going to live it, for what else am I to do?

Later, a nurse stabs a needle in my arm and then I just lie in bed and stare at the clock above the door. The nurse hurries out of the room as if something is chasing her and she doesn't want it to catch her. I don't blame her. I feel the same way.

———

One hour later, I sit on a leather couch opposite a large glass window. From the couch, I can see the smokestacks of an old factory assembled of bricks the color of coagulated blood.

I swear that one of the stacks—the one located slightly off to the left—is leaning, like the Tower of Pisa. Even though it does not draw any tourists—no one takes family photographs in front of it, and no one sips coffee in a nearby café—it is my favorite smokestack.

The crooked stack seems like an intruder in a landscape of otherwise right angles and man-made harmony. Its wretchedness is familiar to me and I imagine myself extending a hand through the window, up the hill, tilting the warped stack back to its precise vertical existence. I want to make everything all right for the stack; I want to save it from its troubled life, want to deliver it from its outcast status among the other stacks pointing straight into the sky.

A man enters the office and introduces himself as Dr. Solska Ari. A balding man in his fifties, with rosy cheeks and perfectly capped teeth, impeccably groomed, smelling of starch and shoe polish. His glasses sit low on the bridge of his nose. It's not until we shake hands that I realize he's a man of average height yet he has the aura of a giant.

Our first session is filled with small talk and educational memory lessons. He doesn't take notes, but runs a digital recorder.

"Let me tell you about my first case as a psychiatrist," he says and stares off into the distance. "A woman ate an egg and suddenly, out of the blue, her memory was erased. I couldn't get what happened to her out of my mind. What caused her memory to not function properly?

"Short of brain damage, nothing is lost, the brain doesn't

forget. Your memories are tucked away in drawers, and sometimes those drawers are locked. Locked by emotional distress, stress hormones. Historically people who suffered from amnesia were believed to not want to remember. Brain researchers hung up on the hardware portion believe they can't remember. I'm somewhere in between; I believe it's a combination of both."

As I listen, I realize that his most striking characteristic is his placid nature. Tireless in patience and attention, he's a reverse gravedigger of some sort, unearthing what is underground. I want to believe he can help me find my daughter, I want to one day look back on this moment and remember him as the man who gave me back my memory, my child, my life.

At the end of the session, he asks me what went through my mind when I was told I had amnesia.

"Confused," I say, "a lot of confusion. The implications were endless."

"I understand your daughter's life is potentially at stake. Time is of the essence and I need you to understand that there's a lot of work ahead of us," he says and adds, "and I have to ask you for your trust."

I raise my eyebrows. Trust. Just trust me and everything is going to be all right, is that what he's asking me? Is it as simple and as complicated as that?

"Did the egg lady ever remember? It couldn't have been about the egg, right?" I ask and offer an ironical smile.

"Of course it wasn't," he says and adjusts his impeccably knotted tie. "Nothing is that simple and it was never about the egg. I'll make you a deal: we find out what happened to your daughter and I'll tell you all about the lady who ate the egg."

The next day, at the beginning of our second session, Dr. Ari asks me about the most peaceful place I can imagine. "Like a refuge, a hiding place, where you feel safe."

"I'm not sure . . ." I say and look at him, puzzled.

"Have you ever paid attention to your breathing when you feel relaxed?"

His question seems silly to me. "Can't say I have," I answer and wonder if imagining myself on a beach is what he's looking for.

"In the middle of a very stressful situation we usually wish for a safe place," he says. "Have you ever wished to be somewhere else during such a moment?"

Every day I want to be somewhere else, I think but don't say anything.

"Imagine a safe place. Give it a try."

I know what he wants to hear and immediately I come up with several options; "A beach, a park bench, beside a waterfall, something like that?"

"No good," he says and bounces a pen on his desk. "Those are no good."

"I don't know," I say. "You asked. That's what I came up with. Why's it no good?"

"Stereotypes, nothing but stereotypes. Like wanting to travel around the world. Who wants to travel and never belong? Always on the move. That's just something people say. No one really means that. I want you to think about this." He pauses and throws the pen on the desk. "You've never been to a safe place, you say?"

I shrug my shoulders.

His eyes light up. "How about getting there? Think of a mode of transportation that takes you to a safe and peaceful place. You don't need to know the specific place, let's imagine your journey there. Nothing you anticipated, something that just happened, a voyage of sorts. Let me give you an example." He takes off his glasses and leans back in his chair. "Long time ago, in a country far from here, as a young boy, I used to spend the weekends at my grandmother's house. I remember her bed being high above the ground, I seemed to sleep almost in the clouds. Of course, I was young and short and Daadi's bed was just high, but it seemed that way to me then. I had a lot of nightmares as a young boy, but whenever I slept at Daadi's house, I didn't wake up at night, there were no monsters. Her bed was magic, in a kid sort of way, but magic nevertheless."

"I thought you said a mode of transportation. I don't get it."

"It transported me to my good dreams. I don't remember the dreams anymore, but I had a lot of them in her bed. It seemed nothing on earth could touch me there, nothing could hold me back. And every morning I woke up to the smell of *nashta*. And she was singing while preparing it." His eyes turn glassy, as if he's far away. But just as quickly he snaps out of it, furrows his brows, and his eyes now demand my own little memory of childhood peace.

"Your peaceful place is your grandmother's bed, I get it. Unfortunately I can't compete with that," I say. "No grandma and no *nashta* in my past." I think about his story and try to remember all the places I'd been as a child. But all I remember is getting sick in cars, on boats, even in buses.

"I love to ride elevators." I'm surprised when I hear the words coming out of my mouth. I realize it's actually true, there's something about the humming, the feeling in my stomach, the door opening and closing, and then I am where I wanted to be. Just by the push of a button.

Dr. Ari's eyebrows relax; he looks pleased.

"An elevator it is. Describe your favorite elevator. Then enter."

I close my eyes. "Two shiny panels meet in the middle, silver panels. The doors slide open and I get in."

Dr. Ari's voice is soothing. "It's comfortable and spacious. The lights are low, it's almost dark. You can go anywhere you want to go. No one controls the elevator but you. Walk in, turn around, and face the panel by the side of the door. The panel is rectangular. The buttons are round, lit, and embedded in the panel. They start at number ten and go all the way to number one."

I imagine the panel. I push a button. The doors close silently.

I'm safe and contained in this dark box. As the elevator descends, I have a moving sensation in my stomach, then the forces balance themselves, and right before the elevator stops, the force lessens and, again, I experience a floating feeling.

"Perfect," Dr. Ari says and smiles. "I want this elevator to be a place of peace and control. Anytime you feel anxious, I want you to step in and go to a lower floor. The farther down you go, the more relaxed you'll become."

"And what's it for? The exercise, I mean?"

"When humans get stressed or experience fear, our bodies exhibit a very primal response. You've probably heard of the fight-or-flight response. When facing a threat, our bodies respond with very distinct signs; a change in blood pressure, breathing, heart rate, temperature, muscle tension, just to name a few."

"Right," I say and imagine saber-toothed tigers pursuing a zebra.

"Our body is basically getting ready to fight or run away," Dr. Ari continues. "I want you to face your fears, force your body into a 'relaxation response.' Once you manage to relax, over time, you will develop a heightened state of awareness. That's what we're after, being aware."

"Sounds easy enough," I say.

"Not quite. Combating primal responses requires practice. A trained nurse will instruct you later on today."

The more I think about this concept, the less I can imagine any possible scenario that is positive for the zebra. "That means while I'm trying to remember, I won't be afraid and I won't run. I'll tell my body to relax and be alert." Fighting makes no sense when confronted with a saber-toothed tiger and I don't think a zebra can outrun a tiger. Staying put seems like certain death to me.

"That's the plan. You won't avoid, and you won't struggle against it."

"*It* being . . . ?"

"The past."

"Right," I say but I can't help thinking of a tiger sinking its teeth into my neck.

On the morning of our third session a damp blanket of fog has spread over the East River and the familiar smokestacks in the distance are all but disappearing behind its dense layer.

First I hear Dr. Ari's voice coming from afar, and then I comprehend the words. "Tell me about Mia." His voice is low, yet urgent.

I wanted truth serums and potent pills forcing my memories to the surface. I expected to be hypnotized, I imagined a chemical manipulation of my brain. But after two sessions with Dr. Ari I've figured out that I am all there is. Just me, my clouded mind, and Dr. Ari goading me on.

"Tell you about Mia?" I repeat his question to buy some time. I focus on the vague and ghostly smokestacks outside the window, looming a safe distance from this office within the thick cloud of water droplets. I wish the layers of skin that he is trying to peel away were just as safe from him as that old decrepit factory in the distance.

I don't know what happened to my daughter, Mia. I opened drawers, old shoe boxes, and unlocked doors that led to storage spaces under stairs. I climbed into Dumpsters, looked under beds. I searched for her. A daughter is not something one misplaces like a set of keys or a take-out menu. What I know for sure is that one morning I woke up and she had vanished as if she had been swallowed by a hole in the universe. Not so much as an impression of her tiny body left on the sheet-covered mattress. Someone took her without picking the locks or prying the hinges off the doorjambs. She's left a silence behind, a silence so loud it keeps me awake at night.

On a good day, after I've been able to sleep three continuous hours, I imagine her with a nice couple in Arizona, tucked away in loving arms. When I imagine this scene long enough, it feels almost real. On a bad day I see her mutilated and lifeless under a mountain of dirt and pine-needled soil, next to acorn caps and deer droppings somewhere in the woods of upstate New York. The worst days are the ones when I can feel a sticky substance between my fingers and I wonder if I'm the one to blame.

But good days and bad days are not conducive to the truth. What I need is a clear day. A day so clear and pristine, so sparkling and new, that I dare to explore what happened to Mia.

For now, I have to take solace in imagining the abandoned factory with the crooked stack. I envision homeless people sleeping on top of cardboard there, junkies passed out in dark corners under colorful graffiti—their very own billboards on the edge of human society. Old, battered shoes, their counterparts lost forever, with all the missing socks we never seem to find. I can hear feet kicking cheap plastic gin bottles. They take off into the dark like shooting stars, hit the walls, and bounce back just to end up again in the middle of the long dark halls with their windows nailed shut decades ago. After self-inflicted prodding, digging, turning over stones that resisted turning like boulders in front of caves, some-where between mandatory journaling and lights-out, I am ready. I will hunt her last images; I will try to catch the coattails of the truth and hang on to them, even if they pull me straight into hell.

My eyes focus on what's outside the window. We both have been waiting for this moment. He wants to solve the mystery not even New York's finest have been able to crack. His legendary status for restoring the forgetful is at stake. As for myself, if I can't come up with a logical explanation, I will face life in prison. I am lucky in a way, if there is something resembling luck in my position; New York abolished the death penalty years ago. I can always plead insanity, for what mother in her right mind kills her infant daughter? And if I didn't kill her, what woman in her right mind does not know where her daughter is? Either way, my end of the stick is shitty.

"Tell you about Mia?" I can hear my own voice as if it were prerecorded. It sounds nothing like me. "Where do you want me to start?"

Dr. Ari's Adam's apple is bobbing as he swallows. He pushes the chair from his desk and rolls back a couple of feet. He glances at the digital recorder to make sure it is on.

"Start wherever you want."

"I remember . . ." I hear my own voice trembling. I feel shaky, my stomach muscles are tight. I am trying to sit straight, keep my composure. I choose my words wisely, for they have the power to set my world on fire.

I'm trying to make a connection; I'm reaching for a marker, longing to connect the dots. I look down and avoid his eyes. I fold my hands in my lap. I'm surprised by the way this memory has returned to me.

"Go on," he says.

CHAPTER 12

During the day thousands of coal black crows spread out over the Creedmoor estate, but in the afternoons they flock together in smaller groups to gather in their communal roost once dusk nears. All day long their calls create a tremendous noise level but then they settle down and remain quiet during the night. I watch them work in pairs, construct nests with dead branches, pick at their own feet when frustrated, play with acorn caps and sticks. The view of the building from above, a bird expanding its wings like a giant chief crow, might be the reason they gather here.

I discover a nest in the tree in front of my window. By the time I spot it, it's fully constructed—I make out twigs, feathers, leaves, and mud—and I watch the pigeonlike bird lay her first egg. She leaves the nest immediately after and I worry about the egg and what will become of it. The next day she lays another one, just to abandon both of them. My anxiety heightens with every passing hour, but on the third day she returns and starts incubating the eggs, and from that point on she hardly leaves the nest.

Creedmoor is a dinosaur in its own right. It was built in the 1920s; its cutting-edge psychiatric technology mocks the history trapped in its walls after decades of chemically induced seizures and lobotomies. Even electroshock therapy is back in the medical community's good graces, renamed electroconvulsive therapy and performed under anesthesia without adversely influencing treatment effectiveness.

Creedmoor's legacy of long-forgotten architecture claims to have sheltered the likes of Sylvia Plath, Edie Sedgwick, and Ed Gein. Ed Gein gained notoriety in the '50s after authorities discovered he had exhumed corpses from local graveyards and constructed keepsakes from their body parts.

The Kirkbride-style building is a leftover from the early twentieth century, a relic building style considered an ideal sanctuary for the mentally insane. Kirkbride buildings segregate the patients according to gender and severity of symptoms, male patients in one wing, female patients in the other, each wing subdivided with more severe cases on the lower floors while the better-behaved patients are confined to the upper floors.

Not everyone considers Creedmoor the relic it is. I hear investors once had big plans for the building. A conversion into condominiums was imminent, but the project was shut down since the layout was not suited for individual residences. Its corridors were too long, and its rooms too small.

My room, at least for the time being, is my own; I don't have a roommate. My bed frame is made of strong metal pipes, and the linens are soft, worn bare from years of laundering in scalding water.

The breakfast bell sounds at seven on weekdays, on Saturday and Sundays at eight, and the patients descend to the cafeteria at the end of the hallway on the main level. We all have preassigned tables. The table next to mine is the gathering place for a flock of anorexic women. Their condition is obvious: instead of eating, they merely rearrange their food, pick over their plates like seagulls over a garbage heap. Their fingers seem dipped in blue ink and their hair is thin and downy like an infant's, while enamel erosion has claimed their teeth.

My only company during meals is a middle-aged woman, Marge Ruiz. Marge is placid and looks twenty years younger than she is. Her story is similar to mine, I guess one can say; we're both guilty of not speaking up when we were supposed to. Almost as if missing a deadline has sent both of us to the loony bin. Marge decided to keep the death of her mother a secret until the smell alerted the neighbors. She never told her husband or her children about her mother's demise; she continued to visit her corpse for months, bringing fresh eggs, milk, and bread.

Marge's family comes to see her every weekend. They invade the visitors' garden, lounge in lawn chairs on the covered terrace. Marge has five children and twice as many grandchildren. Her family's consolation prize for Marge is a weekly white paper box filled with sugar-topped croissants—*cuernos de azúcar.*

While Marge is surrounded by her family, I spend my time on a lawn chair under a big oak tree in the garden behind the main building. I practice the elevator technique obsessively and eventually I feel myself calming down the moment I imagine elevator doors opening.

I carry my journal with me; I write down every word and every image that pops into my head. Images that defy interpretation I attempt to draw. After a few days pass, I neither recognize the drawings nor am I sure that I even drew them.

Dr. Ari had handed me the journal during our first session. "As many details as possible," he had said, "even if it seems trivial. It may turn out to be significant in the long run. Write down thoughts, images, even your dreams. The patterns and recurring themes speak volumes about what's attempting to resurface. Everything is important. Everything."

I draw random squares in my journal. Four corners, then I go over the outline again and again until the lines fill the entire square. Those are the black boxes that contain the past. By writing and drawing in my journal, I try to force my hands to materialize a thought, to force that black box open. I descend into a state of relaxation and I allow my thoughts to wander, without borders and restraints. I see images, yet I don't know their meaning. The sun, moon, and stars are ever-present heavenly bodies; they never change.

Sometimes, when I sit under the oak in the visitors' garden, I catch a glimpse, a flash of an image. I know it's there, right below the surface. The image floats by me like a cloud, a duplicate of a thought I once had—I'm not sure what else to call it—during which I catch the distorted image of some sort of replica, a copy of a copy, if you will, and I try to latch on to it like a fish to hooked bait. A theme emerges. Fruit. An abundance of fruit. Baskets overflowing—fruit, ripe and fragrant, bursting open. I want to be the fruit, want to will the fruit to deny its breaking point. Their insides luscious, their skins bouncing back as I poke at them. Eventually they burst open and I try to force the fruit—with some sort of mind control—to withstand.

Dr. Ari enjoys when I speak of these visions, he leans in closer, pays attention to my every word. He's of Pakistani descent and somewhat of a legend at Creedmoor. Countless framed official documents grace his office walls: undergraduate degree, medical school, residency, and finally Creedmoor's president and psychiatrist in chief. I wonder if he has a wife, a family. There are no photographs, no children's arts-and-crafts projects on his desk. No hint of his private life.

I like to think of him as a magician unearthing skeletons and bringing them back to life. He smiled when I told him and said, "Thank you. It's not quite as glamorous as excavating vessels from antiquity, but I envy your point of view. Most skeletons refuse to be uncovered. Makes for hard work."

He told me he specializes in RMT, recovered memory therapy. That RMT sometimes, "depending on the case," includes psychotherapy methods like hypnosis, even sedative-hypnotic drugs, age regression, and guided visualization. And that RMT is not considered formal psychotherapy, nor is it used in mainstream psychiatry.

I assume that he stumbled upon the crime-solving part by accident. Marge, also a patient of his, "may or may not have killed her mother," according to Oliver, one of the orderlies. Maybe my case will be another cornerstone of Dr. Ari's already-legendary status.

"We can only operate with the data we are consciously aware of. Everything's there, just covered in a layer of dust. Gaining access to what lies beneath is what it's all about."

During the second week Dr. Ari talks a lot about how memory serves us. "Memory is nothing more than a concept that explains the process of remembering. Imagine you are trying to locate a parked car in a crowded parking lot. You were present at the act of parking the car, yet you're unable to recall its exact location. Your subconscious mind knows its precise position and RMT will allow you to go back to the moment you parked the car."

More than anything, I've been surprised the DA allowed this experiment. But neither the state of New York, the DA, or the Medical Board of Psychiatry has anything to lose. It seems like they've agreed to ignore scientific integrity and allow junk science to give it a whirl. I am well aware that Dr. Ari is operating on the fringes of science, and my constant jokes about RMT standing for "Rogue Medical Tests" have made him smile but haven't cracked his shell of professionalism.

The next day, a Tuesday, when I reach his office, the door is ajar. I enter unprompted and uninvited. I'm immediately aware of his disapproving demeanor. The digital recorder, usually on top of his desk, is still tucked away in a drawer. His white coat is still unbuttoned. I have walked in without his permission, and I have not only breached regulations, but also etiquette and, more important, his rules.

I did so because I am afraid. Last Friday, after I described to him the day my daughter Mia disappeared, he alluded to a new direction in our approach to my therapy. His eyes seemed restless that day, and I have a feeling that today we'll dig deeper, we'll do more than just gently brush away the sand from a shard of an ancient vase. Today we might lift the entire vase out of its sandy grave and, like archaeologists, we will proceed with caution, so as not to break the object into a million pieces.

I sit across from Dr. Ari, who, as a matter of retaliation, ignores me for quite some time. He is not the kind of man who expects an apology and so I don't apologize for my impulsive entry. Eventually we exchange a few banalities and he distractedly flips the pages of my journal. He seems to be rushing along today, his whole demeanor reeks of urgency, and I have a feeling something that I'm not prepared for is about to happen. The official charge by the DA's office is less than two months away and he probably does not want me to be a nut he failed to crack. I wonder what he has left, what else he has tucked away in his pocket. Is there a magic trick that will clear the clouds in my head?

His voice jerks me out of my thoughts. "Do you remember the conversations we had regarding forgetting and the reasons why we forget?"

During my research hours I read up on memory and how our brain copes with the loss of it. I actually find the entire memory business fascinating, but I'm also trying to show off, want him to know that I'm committed, even after our sessions end.

"I recall the decay theory and the interference theory. Memory retrieval—let's assume that the memories made it all the way into long-term memory—fails because the memories have decayed over time or have been subjected to interference."

"Very good. Your memory loss is quite peculiar. There's no physical evidence of brain damage and therefore I cannot say with certainty why you don't remember. The moment we retrieve your memories, we will know the reason why. Not before then. There is no magic pill I can give you, no blood test or MRI that will tell us what causes you not to recollect the past. I hope you know that."

I nod but I know he's not telling the entire truth. There're sedative-hypnotic drugs to help uncover the past stuck in my head but he wants the truth to come out organically, unrestricted, because who'd be able to separate the wheat from the chaff, the truth from drug-induced visions?

"But there's something we can do," he says. Then he throws a huge brick my way. "It's time for a field trip to 517 North Dandry."

I catch the brick and cradle it. It's made of a brown stone; it is a piece of North Dandry, where Mia disappeared. I try to embrace it and make it my own, but it topples me. My heart rate picks up and my head starts pounding. My thoughts race, culminating in one predominant message: *I can't go back there.* I try to remind myself of how inevitable this pain is. I force my breathing to slow, the image of the elevator an ever-present symbol of composure.

Dr. Ari is watching me like a hawk.

"You seem to be feeling better. Why don't we—"

"I can't do this." I fear my voice will start trembling, but I manage to keep it stable.

"Revisiting the place where it all happened will allow you to re-create lost memories," he says. "There's no need to get upset. Just let me explain what we're going to do."

The place where it all happened. Hearing it out loud makes it real. What he means to say is that we're going back to the scene of the crime.

"Memory retrieval is much more likely when we test in the same physical context in which the memory we're trying to uncover originally occurred. The application to re-create the past when it comes to trauma-related amnesia is frowned upon, yet the concept itself is nothing new. We will make an attempt to re-create the same emotion you felt when the memory was born."

Memories are born. Do they die, too?

"You call it 'retrieval,' 'physical context,' and 're-creation,'" I say and gesture quotation marks every time I use one of the words with which he disguises what is really going on. "You want me to stand in her room, look at her crib?" I'm not sure if I can do what he's asking me to do. The thought of going back to where Mia disappeared fills me with a terror that reaches around my heart, wrapping itself around it like a fist.

I stare out the window at the scudding clouds and a concept pops into my head, an article I read in one of the medical journals scattered about the many waiting rooms at Creedmoor. *Takotsubo.* Stress-induced cardiomyopathy. Broken heart syndrome. *Takotsubo* are octopus traps that resemble the shape of the heart in an angiogram. I almost expect the sound of shattering glass and for my heart to explode into pieces.

As if Dr. Ari can read my mind, he gets up, walks around his desk, and stands in front of me, half sitting, half leaning on his desk. He crosses his arms.

"Those memories are potent and powerful, but your daughter's life is at stake, Estelle. We need to try; *you* need to try." His voice is urgent now and so are his eyes.

I want to be cooperative and I want to find the truth, like him. But what I want most of all is to not have a breaking point. Like the fruit in my dreams I try not to break open.

The crib.

The locks.

The empty closet.

"How about guided visualization? Can't I just pretend I'm there? Isn't that the same? Maybe we can try that and then . . ."

He shakes his head and I know I've lost the battle.

"Remember I asked for your trust?"

We are beyond guided visualization. We are beyond chatting and are all about doing. There's nothing else to say. No sage will emerge and offer me an ancient remedy, no shaman will throw bones and predict the future, and no crystal ball will tell us the truth. Something inside me refuses to give in but I know I can't deny the truth's power, its thrall mysterious and potent. All I can do is tilt toward the truth and believe in its light. I'm willing to walk on a wire but at the same time I fear I'll plunge into an abyss.

"Do you believe in hell?" I ask.

"Hell in a religious sense?"

"No, hell on earth," I say.

He thinks about it for a while. His eyes wander, then he looks at me. "I'm Muslim," he says. "We believe that hell is guarded by Maalik, the leader of the angels. He tells the wicked that they must remain in hell forever because they abhorred the truth when the truth was brought to them."

"Maalik." I repeat the name, testing its power over me. Nothing. I feel cold inside.

"According to my faith, once the truth is brought to you, don't deny it. Then you have nothing to worry about," he says.

I'm not familiar with Islam or any other faith, I barely know how to pray the Rosary and I haven't been to confession since my communion. Electroshock therapy seems like a walk in the park compared to the hell he has in store for me. His words echo, determined to reach me. *Allow the truth to be brought to you and don't deny it*, is what he said. And I won't have anything to worry about.

"Going back is like paying with a pound of flesh then?" The pound-of-flesh reference strikes me as familiar, something more than just a reference to Shakespeare. My hand moves up to my ear, or rather where my ear used to be.

"When?" I ask, and hope for weeks.

"Soon. We still have a lot to talk about before we go but you'll be ready. That's a promise."

"I guess," I say, and don't mean it.

He looks at his watch. "Tomorrow we'll continue."

Continue. Go on. Marge had asked me the other day how I go on. I didn't answer her for I don't think I'm going on at all. I feel incomplete, as if someone's made off with part of my body, leaving me an empty, tormented vessel. A vessel forever open topped, never again capable of holding it all in. Every hurt, every feeling magnified a thousand times. I have to find a way to go on, a way of living with this pain.

There's a knowledge that has manifested itself without my consent, and that knowledge is hard to swallow. I seem to have acquired it like a wooden nickel, by sleight of hand from some evil trickery. I will never be able to call it the past and bathe in some sunny, brighter future—the past is all there is for me, it's what my life's made out of. Just that, and nothing else.

I remember I used to sing to Mia. I would clear my throat and she'd focus on my eyes, and then smile. The first note always made her cock her head.

Sleep, baby, sleep.

She'd babble along as if attempting to sing with me.

Your father tends the sheep.

There was a frown, a wrinkled forehead.

Your mother shakes the dreamland tree.

Her eyes never left my face, she'd blink, ever so fleeting.

And from it fall sweet dreams for thee.

The singsong tone and exaggerated pitch prompted her to screech.

Sleep, baby, sleep. Sleep, baby, sleep.

When I get up to leave his office that day, I realize that the birthing pain will never cease. Like a shore pounded by waves, the force is perpetual and our cord will never be severed. North Dandry is the scariest place I can imagine but there's no alternative. And so I resign myself for the time being.

And just as I walk out I hear his voice.

"Tomorrow you'll tell me about your family."

The weight of my family's history is not a matter of heaviness; it is almost weightless, like a ghost.

Tell me about your family. Such a simple request, yet such a complicated web.

CHAPTER 13

Someone had shoved a lump of clay into my hand. Even now, so many years later, as I sit in Dr. Ari's office, that lump has remained with me. I fight the urge to look down at my hand. I have forgotten about it at times, but have been reminded frequently, like a pebble in a shoe, its presence rendering me unable to move. I'm struck by the intensity of my feelings, even after all these years.

My mother had delivered a healthy baby girl: Marcia Paradise. I was eleven; my brother, Anthony, almost eighteen. It was a weekday, and we had stayed home from school. Mom and Dad had finally called and said they were on their way home. The previous night I had gone through my bookshelf and closet and selected toys and books for my new sister.

The doorbell rang, but instead of my parents, two police officers and a lady in a beige coat stood on our front stoop. They were matter-of-fact: my parents had been in an accident on their way home from the hospital—"pileup," the officer said, and I didn't know what that meant but didn't dare ask—and did Anthony want to call anybody?

Within hours Aunt Nell, our only relative and Mom's sister, arrived from New Jersey and made the living room couch her home. Her crimson-rimmed eyes were puffy and she had a habit of shredding boxes of Kleenexes that piled up on the coffee table. Nell and my mom, born ten years apart, had the same chestnut hair and nearly identical profiles. Nell's hair was shorter and she seemed like a less refined and polished version of Mom.

I remained quiet, didn't ask any questions, I still wasn't sure what had actually happened. The next morning I opened the newspaper and stared at the picture of the accident. There was an aerial photo taken by a news helicopter, cars piled up like an accordion—hood-bumper-hood-bumper—like endless roadkill on a gray strip artificially painted onto an otherwise green landscape. The roads seemed like a concrete maze of asphalt and steel bridges, some looping above, some ducking under. It was hard to believe that somewhere in there were my parents and my baby sister.

I went into my father's study and retrieved the round magnifying glass he used when studying his antique map collection. My hand shook as it hovered over the newspaper. The harder I tried to make out our white Suburban, the more the pixels began to dance in front of my eyes. It was impossible to see what was left of my family and I wondered if anyone took a photograph of the baby. I waited, for days I waited, expecting someone to pick apart the cars and uncover my parents.

"It's just the three of us now," Nell said the day before the funeral, "and we have to talk about what we're going to do." She sipped her coffee, frowned, and added two more cubes of sugar. "A lot of things are going to change but I want you to know that"—she cleared her throat and eyed the coffee in her cup—"the sooner we make those hard decisions, the better."

I stared at the rings her cup had left on the poplar table, hoping they'd come out with the Old English oil Mom kept under the sink.

"Anthony and I talked earlier and we thought it'd be best if you'd come to Jersey with me, Stella."

"To live?" I asked.

"Right," said Aunt Nell.

"For how long?" I asked.

"That's the thing," Aunt Nell said. "After we go to Jersey, you won't be coming back."

I looked around. "What about the house? All our stuff?"

"Selling the house is the best thing to do." Aunt Nell pushed her cup toward the middle of the table, making the rings worse. "We'll sell it with everything in it."

I thought of the friends I didn't have and the park that was too far to walk to by myself. I suddenly felt a panic I couldn't describe.

Aunt Nell emitted a constant odor of stale smoke and I'd seen her by the open kitchen window with a pack of Virginia Slims in her hand. Every night I went to bed imagining her falling asleep with a slim white cigarette in the living room, burning down the entire house.

"*Waisenkind*," I said and traced the coffee rings on the table with my eyes.

"What?"

"*Waisenkind*. It's a German word, it means 'orphan.' We read about it in school. Children packed their suitcases the night before they were shipped off to the concentration camps. That's what they wrote on the suitcases. With chalk. *Waisenkind*. An orphaned child. I want to pack my suitcase."

"That's macabre and you'll do no such thing." Nell shook her head in disgust.

"But what can I take with me?"

"We'll manage." Aunt Nell smiled and nodded the way grown-ups do when they don't mean what they say.

I looked around the house. The surfaces were dusty, as if the cold ashes from the fireplace had coated the house in soot. I wanted to take the layer and wrap it around me, the first layer to hide my sadness, the subsequent layers to form a coat that would protect me, so no one could touch me on the inside. *Just pretend*, I said to myself, *pretend you're okay.*

Aunt Nell got up and put the cup in the sink. The rings on the table had widened and had soaked into the wood. I doubted they would ever come out.

That night I climbed into the attic and pulled the biggest suitcase I could find from a shelf of dusty boxes. I packed my father's maps, my mother's photographs, a white baby outfit and a pair of baby shoes, the newspaper with the article of the car pileup, and Anthony's science fair award.

Days later, when I opened the suitcase in New Jersey, it was full of clothes. When I asked Nell what she had done with the items, she just shook her head.

"Hanging on to the past is just not very helpful in this situation. We have to make the best of it."

When I started to cry, she said, "This is as hard on me as it is on you. Please don't make a scene."

No one had actually uttered the phrase yet, not Nell, not Anthony, had spoken the words *Your parents are dead.* Somehow my mind accepted their deaths but I could never shake the feeling that I had abandoned them prematurely.

"Every morning I would wake up wondering if it was all a dream. It wasn't like I tried to convince myself they were still alive, it was more me getting used to them being gone, over and over again, and every morning, during the first few seconds after I opened my eyes, it felt as if they were still alive." Every morning they died all over again, every morning I started out with hope and, within seconds, hope died. Every day, all over again.

I pause and look around Dr. Ari's office, a large rectangular space. A door behind his desk leads to what I assume is his private bathroom. I'm aware that I picked the beginning of the story, but why the clay in my hand and the funeral? I hadn't thought of my parents in years, the last time probably in high school, about the time I stopped searching for my mother's face in a crowd, when my heart no longer skipped a beat when I saw a white Suburban.

"Dr. Ari, why am I talking about this? There're no family secrets hidden away in the attic, no bodies buried in the backyard. Why are people always mesmerized with their childhoods?" I keep pulling on my shirt sleeves, they almost reach my fingertips. "I don't have a single recollection of my childhood before the age of ten. Am I *supposed* to remember anything that far back? It seems like there is this point, there's nothing before and everything after. I'm not sure I'm making sense, I guess what I'm trying to understand is if there's a reason why I don't remember my early childhood."

"Not remembering doesn't mean your childhood was bad, but not having bad memories doesn't mean that it was good, either." He seems proud of the comment but confusion must be written all over my face. He crosses his legs and shifts in his chair as if to get comfortable, ready for an extended monologue. "The first years are all about attachment. The kind of adult you are is the most reliable indicator of a positive or negative childhood, more reliable than any memory or the lack thereof." Dr. Ari looks at me as if this is supposed to explain something.

I am perplexed. "Judging by my sitting here, that means what?"

"Thinking about your mother, what is the most—"

"Let's get real, let's just call it what it is. I'm trying to remember if I had anything to do with the disappearance of my daughter. And I'm being kind by choosing those words, I could ask the real question, the one everybody's wanting an answer to." I can feel myself getting upset, my heart is beating hard against my chest and I feel the urge to get up and move around.

"So you don't want to talk about your mother?"

"No, no, you're getting it all wrong. I can't remember my mother, her scent, the touch of her hand, her presence. I remember she was always busy, slightly distant maybe, but what does that mean?"

"Like I said, it means nothing at this point," he says.

"What if I . . ." I stop, I don't know where to go from here.

"Being distant is not hereditary, it's not a genetic mutation, if that's what you're wondering," Dr. Ari says.

"Maybe not in a hereditary way but how about a pattern? Is that possible?"

"We can't draw any conclusions from that. Let me give you an example: The child of a drug addict will deal with the addiction somehow and one way of coping is keeping the drugs a secret. Which leads to keeping more secrets. Think of the behavior of children more like an attempt to cope with their parents' shortcomings."

"It's a shame my mother is not around to answer any questions." I try not to sound sarcastic but I can't help it.

"In my line of work we usually don't confront parents until it is too late. Makes for a one-sided conversation, doesn't it?"

"That's why so many people see shrinks."

Dr. Ari squeezes his lips shut until they disappear and his mouth looks like a slash made by a knife. He begins to tap his leg, then scoots to the front of his chair and leans forward.

"Don't think of me as a shrink. Think of me as, as . . ." He is scanning his mind for the right word, and then his face lights up. "Your midwife, in a way. Think of me as your midwife. I'm here to assist you with birthing the past. Neither compassion nor friendship will help you complete the process. In the days to come you'll ignore me, beg me to make it stop, most certainly you will hate me at some point. Eventually, when you cradle the truth in your arms, you'll realize that I was on your side all along."

You're on my side then? I want to ask him, but I don't. As I think about his words, I realize that the only thing I can ask is for someone to be on my side. That very moment, I decide to trust him and that I will allow him to take me places I would rather not go if I want to find my daughter. Or find out what happened to her. Or find out what I have done to her.

"Tell me about the funeral," Dr. Ari says.

I'm a miner, I descend deeper into the mine shaft and all I have to do is bring gemstones up into the light. If memories are gems, I will continue on, leaving it to Dr. Ari to separate fool's gold from whatever is precious.

The funeral. What a spectacle that was.

———

Standing beside a dark hole in the ground, staring straight ahead, someone shoved a lump of clay into my hand. Three coffins had been propped up—a small one in between two larger ones—and after the undertakers lowered the coffins, one by one, they pulled away the ropes with an indifferent flick of their wrists. The priest was young and his attempt at growing a mustache had resulted in nothing but a few sorry whiskers. His skin was poreless, as if he had been dipped in wax.

Suddenly I remembered Joan Hardaway, a girl who lived on our street and went to school with me. At school, we had heard she was a "cutter" but we didn't grasp what that really meant. All we knew was that she liked to hurt herself. Joan Hardaway was a doughy girl with a flaky scalp and yellow teeth. I saw her legs once, after PE when we changed clothes. Her thighs were covered in red spiderwebs, deliberate etchings like images drawn in the sand, illegible, but spelling out some sort of pain. I remember thinking how odd it was to create more pain in order to forget pain. It seemed illogical then.

Aware of Dr. Ari's questioning eyes I realize that I haven't spoken in a while. The memory of the funeral evokes nausea, just as strongly today as it did fifteen years ago. I must stay focused; I must speak slowly and deliberately, must tell him what happened.

"I threw the lump of clay and it thumped off my sister's coffin and rolled into a flower arrangement." I tell Dr. Ari how I turned into a bystander because being in the picture seemed too painful, as if observing myself reduced the pain somehow, and vividly, I see Anthony and me, standing there, holding hands. By the time they lowered the coffins into the ground, I started crying. I tried to pull away from Anthony but he held on to me, squeezed my hand so hard it hurt.

"No. *No. Wait*," I screamed, followed by a universal gasp among the real bystanders. Women started sobbing in the cluster of mourners, handkerchiefs pressed against their mouths, their eyes wide, and embarrassment in their muffled voices.

"Stella, please, don't." Anthony's voice was pleading. "Stop pulling so hard. Stop pulling my—"

My sobs became louder, the tears made it impossible to see anything, but I knew everybody was looking at me, staring at the little girl who was losing it. I managed to pull my hand out of Anthony's grip and stepped forward.

I had no plans to jump in, I didn't prepare for a leap. I lost my footing when the ground caved in right at the edge, by the mat of artificial grass. I fell and landed, like a shovelful of newly dug earth, on one of the larger coffins. I rolled over and looked up, my shoulder throbbing. The scent of gardenias was overwhelming, the wreaths were sharp, making my skin itch. Dozens of eyes stared down at me, towering, countless hands extending, waiting for my hand to reach out and grasp theirs. I sat on top of the coffin, not sure if it was my mom's or dad's, those eyes staring down at me. I looked past them, up into the sky. Anthony finally lowered himself into the hole and held me up for hands to pull me out.

Hours later everybody had gathered at our home, a house with a cold and ashy fireplace that felt unsympathetic. I sat in an arm-chair turned to face the front door, and the first thing anyone saw when they walked in was a girl with a sullen face and a full plate in her lap. I had filled it with meatballs, potato salad, finger sand-wiches, and stuffed mushrooms. Aunt Nell gave me a look, and I stacked some more sandwiches on top. I sat, plate on my lap, not bothering with a fork or napkin, not planning to eat any of the food at all. I eyed the people spilling through the door. My silent guarding of the door didn't go over well; adults didn't know whether to stroke my hair or hand me a fork. No one greeted me as they entered the house but one middle-aged lady with notice-able upper-lip hair, who I had never met before, kept eyeing me.

"Hello, Sally," she said, and offered her hand. How I wished to be a Sally somewhere, I thought, but didn't correct her nor did I shake her hand. Her dark reddish roots made it seem as if she were bleeding from the part in her hair.

"I'm so sorry for your loss," she added.

"Thank you, Shirley," I said. "Thank you so much."

She looked at me, puzzled, and walked off to talk to Aunt Nell.

The entire time I sat by the door, "Shirley" kept eyeing me sus-piciously. I sat for a long time and watched the stream of mourners reverse itself until finally the house was empty.

Then I grabbed Anthony's hand and pulled him into the study. The walls were covered in black-and-white photographs of buildings, a majority of them industrial. The first one, right by the door, was the Lipstick Building, at 53rd and Third, shaped as if oval hatboxes had been stacked on top of one another. There were also photo-graphs of churches. I recognized the Riverside Church. Bryant Park Hotel. There was Grand Central Terminal, my favorite. Photographs lined the walls like family pictures. My father's interactions with the world were made of stone and steel, slabs and cement.

The shades had been pulled and the big cedar chest in the

corner released a spicy odor, strong and fragrant. Dad kept his historical map collection in that chest. Over the years the maps' wet-rag-in-the-kitchen-sink aroma had changed to the same aromatic odor of the chest. There was also a faint smell of smoke in the air. I had seen Aunt Nell smoke on the front stoop or in the backyard but maybe she had started plopping herself down in my father's chair, propping up her feet, having a cigarette. I had a vision of her, wearing my mother's dress, walking through the house, smoking, and making endless plans we knew nothing about.

Anthony closed the door behind us. The moist spring air played gently with the thin, parchmentlike blueprints and floor plans on my father's mahogany desk. Anthony looked at me and then lowered his head. I detected shame in his posture.

I looked at his face, a face that had changed dramatically over the past week, as if adulthood had come to him overnight. His facial hair so out of place, his body large and more muscular than I'd remembered. He seemed grown up, capable, and I felt small next to him.

"We don't need Aunt Nell, we can take care of ourselves. You're almost eighteen and they'll let you take care of me."

"Stella, I can't."

"Yes, you can. *We* can. Aunt Nell is nothing to us, I can hardly stand to look at her, and I wish she'd pack up and leave. The sooner the better."

"I can't take care of you, I can't. It's not that I don't wa-wa-want to. I ju-just, I . . ." He started to stutter, something he hadn't done in years. But he regained his composure, as if he decided that this childish affliction was uncalled for. His eyes were red and he paced the study, looking for words and a way out. "I'm going to a military academy. I'll be leaving in two months." His words hung between us and sucked the air out of the room. The world was motionless, even the curtains had stopped wafting in the breeze.

My throat was sore, and every time I swallowed I was back in the dream where a blackbird had slipped down my esophagus in slow motion. Just as the pain of the beak ripping holes and tearing flesh lingered, so did the cruelness of his words. My heart pounded as if the blackbird was trapped in my chest, its wings expanding with every minute. I caught a glimpse of why Joan cut herself to get away from pain. If you replace one hurt with another, it seems as if you're in control somehow.

"It won't be as bad as you think," Anthony said, and I felt myself shifting, departing from my body.

The echo of Nell's heeled shoes tapping over the wooden floors came down the hallway toward the study, but then it quieted and I was no longer sure if someone was coming toward us or moving away. Either way, I felt nothing from that point on.

Dr. Ari pushes a box of Kleenex my way. I'm not sobbing, there's just a trail of tears running down my cheeks, my neck, in my mouth, and under my shirt. They taste like the tears I had cried the day of the funeral and I wonder if tears of joy taste any different. The memory of my parents' funeral is strong, yet I don't know why it still has such a fierce hold on me.

I keep my posture upright, attempting to make my pain inconspicuous. I'm not fooling Dr. Ari, the ever-present hawk, spotting pain like prey, descending, striking.

"I'm so very sorry this happened to you," Dr. Ari says.

"I felt safe in my sadness and I told myself it couldn't get worse. My parents were dead, my brother was leaving, and Aunt Nell was picking at what was left of our family and our house, like a vulture pecking away at spilled guts on a road. I had basically reached the lowest point possible. But I was wrong. So wrong."

I look down at my hands, expecting to see that lump of clay. But my hands are empty. We have barely peeled away the outer layer and we both know there are many more layers left to tear away, wounds to be opened deeper until white bone shines through. I am done; I am not going to volunteer any more information.

I hear a voice. It is my own voice, betraying myself.

"Look at me. Just look at me, sitting here, trying to remember something that . . ." I'm searching for words, probing my mind, struggling to interpret the turn my life has taken. "What now? I don't know where to go from here." Maybe I was just a kid who lost her parents and felt alone. Maybe my childhood was tragic, but my despair had started before the funeral, way before everything, maybe even from the moment I was born.

"Dr. Ari, are some people born sad? I don't mean introverted and withdrawn, but depressed? Did I emerge from my mother's womb with a predisposition to . . . whatever it is . . . sadness? Is that possible?"

"There is a genetic vulnerability caused by neurotransmitters and biochemical agents, but there are also developmental events, like the death of your parents. Grief is a very strong childhood stressor."

For the first time I see myself through the eyes of people at the funeral. I was what? Eccentric? It's like looking in a fun house mirror only I'm *not* distorted, I am *that* way, a gloomy girl, sitting at the door, staring at people—that's me.

"To be honest, my glass has always been half empty. Not only as an adult, but as a child.

"I don't remember any specific moment I felt happiness. I don't remember being just over the moon, elated, whatever you want to call it. Happiness is almost something that I can't feel, like I'm not made to pick up on it or something." I point at the digital recorder in front of him. "Like this recorder. It can only record audio, it can't pick up on anything else. You can't record the temperature of the room, you don't know what the weather was like when you listen to the recording later on."

"I beg to differ."

"About what?" I ask.

"That there were no moments of happiness in your life. Maybe you don't remember every single one, but . . ." He pauses and then his face lights up. "When I was a child, my grandmother taught me to play *petteia*, a board game. A simplified chess game, if you will. But you win by majority, not with a certain piece or final move."

"Your grandmother teaching you a board game is happiness?"

"It was not so much the game itself but the fact that she tried to teach me some sort of lesson. I remember that you had to somehow surround your opponent's stones in order to win."

"So she taught you some kind of war strategy, is that what you're trying to tell me?"

"I never saw it as a war strategy, just the fact that patience is always rewarded. But mostly I remember the clicking of the stones on the board. The scent of the tea, the jingling of her jewelry. Her patience while talking me through the moves, explaining the strategy. And she always allowed me to redo a move if it proved crucial. She was a kind and wise woman."

"Do you still know how to play the game?"

"Barely. I don't think I ever really mastered it."

"So . . . the lesson here is?"

"There are moments of joy in everybody's life. Happiness, like sadness, comes wrapped in many layers."

"Just like memories."

"Just like memories," he says.

"I just have to find those moments." I pause for a while and consider the ratio of sadness and happiness in my life. "Sad moments are right on top, but the happy ones seem to hide."

I turn my head toward the wall to my right. A file cabinet takes up the entire wall, small drawers strategically concealing its utilitarian purpose. Smooth-sliding pullout drawers filled with obsolete paper files. Dr. Ari's awards hover in symmetry, under Plexiglas, anchored with invisible wall attachments. He does not believe in signs of weakness in his constructed world, therefore even the frames must pretend they don't need a nail to stay put.

"Anthony probably doesn't even know I'm here."

Dr. Ari raises his eyebrows, then flips over my file, as if handling the folder gives him an illusion of manipulating my known past with his hands.

"That's a conversation we'll have soon." Dr. Ari pulls out his pocket watch as if he doesn't trust the timekeeping abilities of the plastic clock on his desk. "For tomorrow I want you to think of the concept of happiness."

"Can one think of happiness?" I ask.

"A memory is a place you visit, not where you live. Happiness therefore is not a permanent state of being, but more a moment in time. Think of a moment for me?"

Later that night, as I write in my journal, I reflect on Dr. Ari's story of his grandmother. I try to recall happy surroundings and details, more than the feeling of happiness. I try to think of past happy moments as having fallen to pieces and recovering them is just a matter of putting them back together. Then an image pops into my head. The image of a building and its still beauty in stark contrast with the busy atmosphere. In that memory, my father wears a dark blue suit and an overcoat. I wear a dress and black lacquered shoes that pinch my toes. We are in Grand Central Terminal for my tenth birthday and my father has promised me a "well-guarded secret."

"When we leave the terminal," he says, "you'll be one of a chosen few who know about this secret." His voice sounds conspiratorial; all that is missing is a black cloak and a magic wand.

"You're not serious, are you, Dad? You're kidding, right?"

"Estelle, I'm very serious. Do you know who Adolf Hitler was?"

"Of course I know. The dictator of Nazi Germany. I hope this isn't a history lesson."

"No, it's not. It's your birthday after all," he says and chuckles.

"What does Hitler have to do with this secret?"

He lowers his voice, bends down, and whispers in my ear: "What if I told you that he sent spies to sabotage the secret."

"And did they?"

"No. The FBI arrested them."

"The FBI is involved?" This is so much better than anything else I could have imagined.

We reach the Main Concourse and Dad grabs my hand. I look at him and then follow the direction of his eyes upward. We are standing under some sort of astronomical mural. The background is blue, the constellations golden. It covers the ceiling of the entire Main Concourse. I'm getting dizzy looking up. I lower my head and hold on to his hand.

"What's that?" I ask.

"That, my love, is a design by a French painter. How many stars do you think are there?"

I'm feeling queasy. I decide not to look back up and I just guess what I conceive to be a fairly accurate number. "Five hundred."

"Two thousand five hundred stars. It's supposed to be the Mediterranean sky. The larger stars are the constellations."

"What's so special about it and why did the spies try to sabotage it?"

"Oh no, this isn't the secret the spies tried to sabotage. We'll get to that later. I just wanted to show you this because the painter made a mistake without knowing."

"A mistake?" I scan the mural.

"Yes, he used an old antique manuscript. Took them a long time to figure out the reason why he made the mistake. See, they ended up being backward. Back then the cartographers displayed the zodiacs as they appeared from the outside looking in."

"Do you have that manuscript at home?"

He laughs and says, "That would be like having the *Mona Lisa* hanging in our living room. But I have a replica. I'll show it to you when we get home. Let's go."

He tightens his grip around my hand as we walk to the back of the terminal. We reach an old service elevator. He pushes a button and the door opens immediately as if it had been waiting for us. We get in and the elevator descends, screeching and shaking. I love the moment right before the elevator stops and my body feels weightless, as if the entire world pauses for a second.

When we get out, we are in a utilitarian part of the building. The room is huge, its ceiling higher than I expected a ceiling to be underground. One side of the room is covered with boxy metal containers with controls and the other holds old machines that look like colossal clock gears. The floor grates are large and vibrate through my shoes. I feel hot air blowing through the grates, and I hear giant fans underneath me.

"Here we are!" My dad is elated. I feel like I'm letting him down, as if I'm supposed to know the significance of this room. "M42," he adds.

"Right." I don't know what else to say.

"This is a very important part of the terminal. Only a chosen few know about this secret basement. You're standing in M42, the secret sublevel. How about that?"

I look around and I have to admit that the large gears protruding from the ground are very mysterious but I'm still disappointed. "Is this what the spies tried to sabotage?"

He lowers his voice as if he's trying to keep his answer a secret. "If the spies had disabled the converters, they would have shut down the entire terminal during the Second World War. It was so guarded that anybody down here without permission would've ended up in jail. Or shot."

"Okay then."

"Do you know what that means?"

I don't know what to say, and shrug.

"It means that you're standing in a spot that isn't on any map, any blueprint. Every building ever built has a blueprint, every building has to be designed on paper before the builders put brick on top of brick. Walls hold up the roof, floors hold up the walls, that sort of thing, and architects calculate and plan every inch of a building. You're in a room only a few people know about, yet millions pass over it every day. Pretty fascinating, isn't it?"

I ponder it for a while and I'm starting to understand his enthusiasm. "I guess I shouldn't tell anyone about this, right?" I say and add a conspiring wink.

His brow furrows, but only for a moment. Then he smiles at me. "It's our secret. One day, maybe ten or fifteen years from now, there'll be guided tours, TV specials. And then everyone will know about this place." He checks his watch. "But for now, it's our secret. What do you think?"

"It's pretty cool, actually. That we're here when it's still special."

"I think so, too. I knew you'd love this place," he says and hand in hand we walk back to the elevator that takes us back upstairs to the main terminal buzzing with people, insectlike, fulfilling their destinies and a complexity of tasks, demonstrating what a wonder the world really is.

That night, as I lie awake and stare at the ceiling in my room, I try to understand what has happened, not the details or minute particulars of my daughter's whereabouts, but my possible part in the direction my life has taken.

I close my eyes and travel back to my childhood, I feel the chenille bedspread under my fingers and hear the old oak tree scratch the windowpane. The only filter people have is their childhood and as my parents' ghostly apparitions materialize, I concede my parents were physically there for me; they fed me, clothed me, and provided for me.

And then it hits me. My father never pulled me off a ledge, never ran into the street after me to save me from an approaching car. I don't remember receiving any physical affection from my mother but I assume that she sat with me when I was sick as a child, and I'm almost sure she sewed my Halloween costumes.

But once I look for more than the average proof of affection, I come up empty. It all comes down to this: I don't know how to judge my parents' love for me. Life never prompted them to take extraordinary measures, never urged them to declare the depth of their love beyond genetic affection. They cared for me. Beyond that, it was run-of-the-mill obligation. And again, my satchel holds no jewels. Just rocks.

CHAPTER 14

"Tell me about Jack," Dr. Ari says.

We have finally arrived at the chapter named Jack, the man I was to marry only a year after we met. Speaking of him starts to unsettle the ground.

It seemed I went from my parents' house in Bedford to Nell's house in Jersey, and then off to cheap apartments in basements. Last stop before North Dandry was Jack's apartment on William Street.

"Jack used to call me his princess, he was old-fashioned in many ways: flowers, gifts, opening doors, that kind of thing."

I remember Jack's apartment, perched on the thirty-sixth floor of the Gotham Tower Condominium Building, with its unsettling echo between the walls.

"This is a big place," I had said and tried, unsuccessfully, to keep my heels from clattering on the slate floor.

"You say that like it's a bad thing." Jack took off his coat and sat his briefcase on the enameled lava countertop. The gesture was an indication of things to come; when I think of Jack now, I see him either putting on a coat or taking it off, coming or going, but never really being there.

"What's the price of admission?" I asked lightheartedly, eyeing the tin ceiling promising to last a lifetime.

Jack stood by the window, enthralled by the stunning view of the city. "Your soul," he said jokingly, his shadow disturbing the perfect sheen of the hardwood floors.

Dr. Ari watches me fold my arms in front of my chest.

"Jack lied about money from the beginning. I believe he mostly lived off his mother's inheritance or some sort of insurance, he never said. He had flipped some houses during law school, mostly successfully, but there was no way he could've afforded the place he lived in with his salary alone. And after we got married, we had money problems almost immediately and Jack eventually took a job in Chicago. It was a temporary job but it paid well and it would allow us to get out of debt soon or so he said."

Dr. Ari takes off his glasses and polishes the lenses with a cloth he keeps in his desk drawer. Is he ready to look closer or is he just tired of smudges infesting his world? He taps his pen on the folder in front of him, then opens it, shuffles papers around. He wants to make sure he gets it right.

"Mia was six months old and it must've been a difficult decision for your husband to leave you behind in New York, considering the state you were in."

"Women raise children alone every day." *My mother was a saint*, Jack had told me. *She never raised her voice at me. Raised me by herself.*

"Tell me how you were feeling." Dr. Ari reels me back in, not willing to let go of what's on the other end of this rope.

I look around his office, trying to focus on anything that will allow my heartbeat to slow. The pounding in my temples is painful, as if there is something trapped inside of me trying to escape.

I tell him how I was tired, overwhelmed, covered in spit-up. How going out just meant having to put on clothes and fake a smile for the world around me. How my bad days started with watching Jack leave in a dry-cleaned suit and a starchy shirt, smelling of shoe polish and coffee, and how I descended into darkness the moment the door closed behind him. Then Jack came home and I was still alone and I descended even deeper. How I couldn't keep up with Mia's demands, how Jack told me, in so many words, to snap out of it. And how all those months of Jack telling me to get it together had finally paid off and by the time he went to Chicago I had managed to turn myself inside out, like a dirty sock, into a better, more cheerful version of myself.

"Did you ever see a doctor?" Dr. Ari's eyes are observant and concerned.

When I tell him a doctor prescribed antidepressants, he asked if I ever saw a professional, a counselor or psychiatrist, and if I ever attempted therapy.

"Imagining the sound of my own voice made me sick just thinking about it."

I hold myself perfectly still and lower my eyes. I focus on the manila folder in front of Dr. Ari. His hands are folded, resting on top, his manicured nails shiny and perfectly shaped. I wonder what the file holds. Police reports, medical files, photographs, newspaper articles.

"I don't want you to think that it was all doom and gloom. The fact that I created a miracle wasn't lost on me, not for a second. I loved Mia so much I thought my heart was going to explode out of my body. But when she started crying all the time, I believed she wasn't well. And then the days became endless." The last words prompt me to shake my head.

Dr. Ari's eyes have the generic expression reserved for the borderline insane. "Did you feel like a bad mother when you couldn't stop her from crying?"

A rush of heat overtakes me. "I did what the doctors told me to do but nothing worked. It's not that I chose to be incapable, I just thought that . . . I wasn't enough. I felt watched, observed, under a microscope. *Watch the crazy woman who can't take care of her baby.* Wherever I went people gave me advice—do this, do that, don't rock her so hard, rock her more, let her cry it out, hold her—everybody and everywhere, nurses, women at grocery stores, at the park."

Dr. Ari pushes my journal toward me. He pulls a deep breath in and then lets it go, releasing his frustration. It fills the room with heaviness.

"You didn't write in your journal yesterday. Why not?"

His irritation engulfs me like a heavy cloud. I haven't delivered the goods; I haven't kept up my end of the bargain. Lately I think so hard my head hurts, every day, during our sessions, every night when I write in my journal, every waking moment, I think. Even my dreams are constant inquiries, intrusively probing for the truth. There's a wall, and regardless of how hard I try to will myself to see what's on the other side, it never manifests itself. Instead, I get headaches—pounding, dull headaches—right behind my eyes.

"Tell me what you didn't write down."

I raise my voice. "It was nothing, really. A large tree obstructing the view of a building. In my dream the wind moves the branches, makes them sway, but I can barely see past them. The windows are looking at me like eyes, I'm close, so close, but then it all disappears and I'm back where I started."

"In a dream a tree is never just a tree." Dr. Ari tries to coax me back to the path of recollection, littered with pebbles supposed to trigger my memory, so I may continue with the story he longs to hear. He retrieves my journal and studies the last entry.

Dr. Ari explained to me that I needed to verbally state my desire to recall my dreams as I am falling asleep. I've been using a special digital alarm clock that wakes me every ninety minutes starting at three o'clock in the morning, during or immediately after the REM periods of sleep. Last night something changed. The tree in front of the house has been a recurring image for some time but now I was inside for the first time. It was small, only a square room, really. There was a river running by the side of it, moving recklessly, its currents were powerful, almost raging. I was aware of the danger, I could almost feel the pressure the raging waters put on the walls around me. They were straining, screeching, and moaning. I could see water trickling through the cracks in the wall and I knew it was just a matter of time before the door would give way to the power of the flood. It was just a matter of time before the waters would gush forth and the river would pick me up and carry me away. In my dream I was searching for a way out of the house, and when the alarm woke me, I was still searching.

As I nibble on my frayed nails, I remember how it felt, searching frantically, heart pounding, breathing rapid and shallow. Sometimes you remember one thing, and that one thing makes you remember something else, and before you know it, you remember everything.

"What I neglected to write down was that last night I remembered searching for Mia."

Dr. Ari opens the manila folder and flips through the pages. He pulls out the North Dandry blueprint stapled to the property deed. A blueprint of a house, a map of its rooms, hallways, and doors. He unfolds it, and disappears behind it as if he is casually reading the Sunday morning paper. He realizes the words are upside down and he flips it over and continues to study. The waxen paper is strong; its creases resist any fold but the original one.

For a moment I'm mesmerized by the sound of the waxed paper. I wonder if words and pictures imprinted on it alter its vibration. The sound of candy wrappers holds the promise of sweetness, wrapping paper evokes Christmas mornings and birthday wishes fulfilled.

There were other maps once, my father's maps, old and frequently handled. Touching them sounded like the passing of distance itself, parchment and vellum, lightweight and translucent. Made from sheepskin, its animal source outdated compared to the waxed paper floor plan Dr. Ari is holding in his hands. I can almost hear the blueprint of North Dandry starting to vibrate.

Finally Dr. Ari emerges from his paper fortification. He puts the blueprint on his desk. The floor plan is littered with interior walls and hallways, their orientation downward from above. Dr. Ari is looking at God's view of a human attempt to create shelter from his wrath.

"Tell me about searching for her."

What kind of mother would I be if I didn't look for my child?

I tried to force myself to think logically. I had read articles about parents who had left infants in the backseats of cars, in strollers, and even at day cares, forgotten like an umbrella on the subway or a shopping bag at a restaurant.

I stood on the sidewalk and looked left, then right. There was an abandoned red velvet couch on the curb, a cardboard sign— TAKE ME—propped up in the corner.

I shielded my eyes with both hands to see through the tinted windows of my car. Nothing but an empty car seat stared back at me. I hit the unlock button on the keyless remote and the trunk popped open: Mia's old rear-facing baby seat and an empty suitcase. I had switched prematurely to a front-facing seat because Mia seemed calmer when she was able to see me. The suitcase in the trunk was dented; the locking mechanism no longer worked. It was the same suitcase I had taken to Jersey so many years ago.

I closed the trunk with a hefty *thump.* The street noises were familiar, it was Sunday and from the church across the street, Saint Joseph's, organ pipes sustained the tones of an unfamiliar hymn. About a hundred yards farther down the street was the subway entrance. A homeless woman sat by the iron fence leading down-stairs. A small dog cowered on a piece of cardboard next to her, a greasy bandanna wrapped around its neck. When I approached, the dog lifted its head. The woman wore at least three or four layers of clothes. Her eyes were closed but her posture was tense.

"Excuse me," I said and watched one of her eyes open. The dog, a scruffy-looking mutt, growled and got up. The woman put her dirty hand on the dog's back. He lowered himself on the ground but kept an eye on me.

"What d'ya want?" she demanded. The top layer of her clothes was a large black garbage bag with a hole for her head and two for her arms. Next to her sat two plastic bags bursting with every-thing she called her own.

"Have you been sitting here long?" I asked.

She sat in silence.

"Have you seen someone leave my building with a . . ." I hesi-tated. Maybe this wasn't such a good idea after all. I stepped closer and the dog let out a low growl. "A baby," I added and realized immediately how insane I sounded.

"Got some change?" The woman pulled a banana from under-neath her raincoat garbage bag.

"No, no, I don't, I don't have my wallet on me, but I need to know if you saw anyone leave the building down there"—I pointed down the street, toward 517—"kind of where that red couch is. With a baby. Did you see anyone with a baby?"

"I see a lot." She made a sucking noise through her teeth and unpeeled the overripe fruit. Then she looked me up and down. "A baby, you say? Your baby?"

"Yes, she's seven months old, someone took her. Did you see anything?"

"Your baby's gone?" she asked and her toothless gums pinched off a piece of the banana. "Should've kept her close." She smacked her lips, taking another bite. "I have a son," she continued. "You wanna see him? He's always with me." She scanned the sidewalk as if to make sure there weren't any onlookers. The dog gladly took what was left of her banana and began to lick the peel.

"Your son?" I asked.

"My son."

"I don't . . . just . . . I really just need to know if you saw anything."

She reached under her raincoat bag, dug deep within the layers, and pulled out a bundle of dirty rags. She unfolded the fabric, one corner at a time, as if the bundle contained a precious gem. When she lifted the last corner, she smiled a toothless smile. There was a large brown mass nestled between the folds. I swallowed hard. A stench of decay drifted my way.

"I wish I had a home for him," the woman said and stroked a mummified squirrel with her blackened fingertips. "He's in bad shape and these rags ain't no place to keep a child. You have something I can put him in?"

She held up the bundle. An incision ran the length of the squirrel's stomach. I shuddered and turned my head. I fought to stay in control of my stomach but the battle was all but lost.

I walked less than half a block down North Dandry, toward Liberty Street. I turned into an alley to the right, at the back of a deli facing Linden Street, and I vomited. I continued to heave, unable to get the hollow cavity of the squirrel's shell out of my head.

I finally looked around: An array of fruit crates filled with wilted lettuces and shriveled cucumbers on top of dented cans of chickpeas. The stench was horrific. A decaying and almost liquefied head of lettuce sat on top of a food crate filled with cadaverous tomatoes, rusted cans of corn, flattened milk cartons, and a mesh bag of shriveled oranges covered in a bluish-green mold.

Walking back toward 517, I again passed the homeless woman. The dog looked up at me, but this time wagged its tail. The woman's eyes were closed, her head resting on her chest. I walked past her, down North Dandry. I opened the trunk of my car, sat the car seat on the ground, and grabbed the old suitcase. Even as I sat the suitcase down next to her, she remained silent and motionless.

Back at home, I sat on the couch for what felt like hours. It was so quiet, I was keenly aware of my own heartbeat. I tried to occupy my mind with questions like where to look, where I had already looked, where to search next. I pushed fears for Mia's well-being and life aside, as if not entertaining them made them less possible. And then it struck me, a newly formed logic, a possibility I hadn't thought of yet.

This is crazy, all of this is *crazy*. I wasn't any different from the old homeless woman on the corner passing off a hollowed-out squirrel as her son. No one came and took Mia. No one took her clothes and her bottles and her formula. No one walked through walls with her diapers, no one got past the locks and bolts and bars. There was only one logical explanation for this entire scenario: There was no baby. There never had been a baby. Mia was but a figment of my imagination. How else could I explain that everything belonging to my phantom baby was gone? I needed proof, proof that she had really existed. I needed to convince myself that I hadn't completely lost touch with reality.

I got up and went to the bedroom. I took off my shirt and my bra. I stood with my back to the long dressing mirror. I remained still, preparing for a moment of truth. Certainly there would be marks on my body if I had given birth. There should be excess weight around the midsection, soft, flabby skin not quite back to its original state. There should be stretch marks, a *linea nigra*, and darkened nipples.

My sanity depended on what I was going to see in the mirror. I took in a deep breath and turned around. The woman in the mirror was lean, on the verge of being bony. Her cheekbones were pronounced, her skin seemed paper-thin. Her breasts were of normal size. There were no stretch marks, no darkened line down her belly, or enlarged nipples. I followed the contours of my stomach, hesitated at the waistband. I closed my eyes and pulled the elastic down. There it was. Raised and pink. A horizontal surgical scar from a cesarean section. I traced the cord of scar tissue, the palpable bumps, the ridge of sutures, with my fingers.

It was real. I wasn't crazy after all. I couldn't believe that I'd ever doubted Mia existed, and the fact that I stood in front of a mirror checking my body for signs of recent childbearing now seemed ridiculous.

I had expected a thin body, but I was merely skin and bones. What happened? What the hell had happened to me? When did I go from a once-attractive woman to this? A few more weeks and I'd be nothing but skeletal remains.

I wasn't so much surprised by the realization that I hadn't imagined Mia, no, the real surprise was that this bony and emaciated woman, this lunatic in the mirror, was in one piece.

What held her together, I had no idea.

PART 3

It takes all the running you can do, to keep in the same place. If you want to get somewhere else, you must run at least twice as fast as that!

Lewis Carroll, Through the Looking-Glass

CHAPTER 15

Dawn has not yet given way to the morning light when an orderly escorts us to a white van. I sit in the back, Dr. Ari takes a seat to my left, behind the driver's seat. His briefcase rests between us, his right arm on top as if he's guarding a secret between its leather skin and silk fabric lining. We depart down the serpentine driveway and the weeping willows' branches waft in the breeze like the coattails of an eerie congregation.

The orderly, whom I've seen occasionally during mealtimes, wears a leather jacket over his scrubs. His name is Oliver. His fingertips are calloused, and veins like blue rivers travel up and then disappear into the sleeves of his jacket. When the time is right, I will inquire about the rugged condition of his hands, but for now, I watch him operating the radio.

Dr. Ari wears a suit and a trench coat. This is the first time I've seen him not shrouded in a white coat. The radio volume is low yet I recognize Maroon 5's "She Will Be Loved."

The morning's French toast is churning in my stomach, but I

vow to keep in control of my body. Thirty minutes into the ride the queasiness stops but a dull pressure has settled between my eyes, leaving fuzzy outlines of passing cars like laser tracers in the dark.

"What happened to your hair?" Dr. Ari asks.

I lean to the left but can't see myself in the rearview mirror. "I cut it last night."

I try to sound indifferent about my hair but I'm not, I actually hate what I've done to it. Wanting my outside to reflect the change I've been going through on the inside, I attempted to change something about me, something visible, something everybody would notice.

Knowing that today's trip was imminent, I wondered where to turn for higher support and I ran across a website of Catholic saints. Both my parents were Catholics, and even though they weren't practicing, my birth certificate proclaims the same denomination. Saint Anthony, a Franciscan monk with tonsured hair, the patron saint of lost articles and missing persons, cut his hair as a symbol of his renunciation of the world. I felt compelled, for a second, to shave my entire head, but then decided to shorten my hair to symbolize a new beginning. It seemed like some sort of clemency, a freeing myself from past sins, but by now I'm questioning my judgment. Did I think I was offering Saint Anthony a sacrifice to appease him for this day, a day that seems frightening and promising at the same time?

"Does your hair have anything to do with our trip today?" Dr. Ari seems impartial regarding my new look but asks nevertheless.

"I was ready for a change, I guess. That's all." There's this sadness again, it sits somewhere between my heart and my stomach, a feeling I've never been able to describe appropriately. It's more like the sensation of craving cold water as if to calm some sort of deeply seated thirst within me. Starting at the right temple, I run my fingers through my hair. It used to reach way past my shoulders;

now it barely covers where my earlobe would have been, exposing the scar and my missing ear.

I study Oliver's profile. He seems nonchalant about this trip, but I imagine him relieved at a day off from having to administer Valium and fasten straitjackets.

"What do you think, Oliver?" I look at him and I know he is supposed to ignore my attempts to converse with him.

"Change is good," Oliver says and winks at me, causing Dr. Ari to clear his throat.

Dr. Ari doesn't mention the fact that my mangled ear is now clearly visible but I'm sure he will eventually. Impulsive as it was, I wanted the world to see that, regardless of what I've done, something was done to me.

We drive silently for a long while. Dr. Ari hasn't elaborated on specific goals for the day but I hope I can bring a story back to him, lay it at his feet like a slaughtered goat, an offering to the gods of lost memories. At the same time I wonder what Dr. Ari's bag of tricks holds. I keep peering at his briefcase—he seems to be guarding it rather obsessively—and I imagine surgical blades, bone saws, and rubber mallets. I picture Dr. Ari stranded on an island, allowed three items of his choice. I pick for him: a lint remover, a digital recorder, and the Quran. Oliver is harder to pinpoint—a radio perhaps, a dog, and a pack of smokes?

As we get closer to North Dandry, I feel the sensation of a soft and smooth stroller handle between my fingers and I remember how moms used to give me dirty looks as I pushed a crying infant along. By the time we'd passed Drummer's Cove, Mia had always calmed down, the rhythm of the drums, the noisy summer celebrations, and the dancers lulling her to sleep.

Prospect Park appears on the left and North Dandry is just a few blocks to our right. Oliver parks, turns off the engine, and exits the van. I watch a dog walker struggling with three greyhounds.

The leashes are tangled, the dogs' tails tucked beneath their stream-lined bodies, pointing at their deep chests. As the dog walker asserts control over the pack, I hear a clicking sound. Dr. Ari has opened his bag of tricks. He's holding a plastic evidence bag with a blue adhesive closure strip. He breaks the seal and hands me Mia's blanket. The experiment has begun.

Scientific facts tumble around in my mind. Scent, the most powerful trigger of all, activates the olfactory bulb, which is con-nected to the brain's limbic system, therefore calling up memories almost instantaneously. When we experience a scent for the first time, we link it to an event, a person, or a moment. The smell of chlorine is forever embedded in our brain as the memory of swim-ming on summer days or a specific moment like the panic we feel after falling into the pool. Scent is the kind of magic that brings forth a rush of vivid memories, time travel at its finest. I wonder if I'll be able to string my memories like beads on a thread and wear them around my neck, and will greyhounds forever prompt me to recall the beginning of this very experiment?

I close my eyes and take a deep breath. I withdraw from the present, remove myself from the sound of running car engines, car alarms, voices, and I let go.

I hear the rustling and crackling of a plastic bag. Allowing the scent of Mia's blanket to take over my brain, I feel a switch inside of me, a switch I can describe only as a powerful tilt toward another point in time. I take in a mixture of baby powder, fastening tape, moisturizer, synthetic diaper, and fragrance. The odor is faint, yet produces powerful physical and emotional reactions. Whatever I've been keeping at bay unleashes itself like a herd of wild mustangs charging through an open gate. A memory reaches my brain as a scent, yet it's so much more than that. It's the all-encompassing sensation of my daughter Mia. Random scenes rush at me.

A newborn's face rests on my chest. Covered in blood and glop, her skull bruised, her skin a bluish tint. My brain stumbles.

Her frailness surprises me, her alertness keeps me at bay. I am unworthy of her, as if I had no right to bring her into this world.

Nighttime feedings, one after the other. The crying, its urgency yanks at me, tugs at me like a rubber band stretched to its limit. Her wails tighten the rubber band, jerking at it to the point of rupture.

Madness located in my jaw. I pull the pacifier out of her mouth, replace it with a bottle before the crying starts. Like a dog's jaw I sink my teeth into the plastic and hold on with hundreds of pounds of pressure. Her pacifier handles are rimmed with the marks of my teeth.

Madness beneath her fontanel, the soft spot between the bony plates of her skull. A wicked invitation. I wonder how deep my thumb will go and how hard I'd have to push before the crying stops.

Short spans of sanity among the madness, capable of drowning the cries: the running shower, the vacuum, the radio. All three at once are rapture, the holy trinity.

Wanting to hold her and cradle her and look into her eyes, cooing her name and smiling—all those feelings and gestures had become alien to me. I was committed: I changed diapers, I bathed her, I fed her. But nothing came easy. Not my love for her, not my being everything to her. Her neediness thrashed inside of me like a creature, tearing at me from the inside out.

There was Jack. His face aglow, he held her instinctively, his love primal. His eyes adored her. A king protecting his kingdom, aware of the pressure, selfless and courageous. Our happiness depended on him. He accepted this fate; he matured in its light. He was rewarded by joyous crows and capers.

As for me, I wasn't worthy of this crown.

The visions release me like a giant's hand returning me to the backseat of the van. Rain pounds the van roof like rapid machine-gun fire. When did the rain start? When did the skies darken and unleash their wrath on me? My face is wet and I'm shaking. I feel like an open wound.

I grab the handkerchief Dr. Ari offers me and wipe my eyes. The rain stops as suddenly as it started. Dr. Ari, his digital recorder in his hand, the blanket in the other, studies my face. The close proximity of our bodies is awkward and uncomfortable.

I look out the window and see Oliver sitting on a bench under a gazebo, close to the park entrance, wires from his pocket reach his ears. He pets an occasional dog, and his eyes follow a group of girls strolling by. I envy him; how easy it must be to guard instead of being guarded.

He takes something out of his pocket, in the other hand he holds some sort of tool, and he carves and sculpts and chips away as if he's creating some elaborate meerschaum pipe.

I give the door a determined pull and watch it slide open on its suspended tracks. I exit the van.

North Dandry is treelined and straight as a ruler. Brownstone row houses sit in harmony like books on a shelf, all old, all narrow. Their façades range from muted yellows to reds and grays. Farther down, as North Dandry turns into Fullerton, the houses switch from Gothic to Greek and Italian Revival. North Dandry's brownstones blend into a cumulative front of arched windows, large chimneys, cast-iron stair rails and fences. A Norway maple rests silently in front of 517 in its own island of tightly packed soil surrounded by a wrought iron fence amidst an otherwise concrete landscape. I must be mistaken, I could have sworn the tree in front of North Dandry was a hemlock and not a maple.

I look at Dr. Ari, waiting for him to give me instructions. Pulling a set of keys out of his coat pocket, he lowers his glasses onto the tip of his nose and fumbles for a specific key.

His voice is as composed as ever. "The building is vacant," he says and offers me a large gold key between his thumb and his index finger.

Is his plan as easy as it is crazy; just go in and demand the building's memories? What if it has a soul and is angry at me? Could it punish me for what's happened here?

"Unlock the door and enter the apartment. Walk through, touch anything you feel like touching." He nods and steps aside. He lifts his right arm as if welcoming me into his home—my home. "Go ahead."

I take the key from him and walk up the steps to the front door. After I insert the key into the lock and turn it to the right, I push and the door opens.

"Entering 517 North Dandry," Dr. Ari says after he turns on the recorder.

An intrusive odor greets me. The freshly painted hallways are harsh and white, almost blinding. My temples start pulsating the moment I set foot over the threshold. The door to my apartment is unlocked and standing in the hallway feels familiar yet strange at the same time, as if I've traveled through time. Is there going to be a magical scent, a sound, or a taste that's supposed to offer an initial trail?

I notice black powder marks on the doors and remnants of yellow tape. Even though the police have undoubtedly gone through the apartment, the place looks tidy. No hastily opened drawers, no cabinet doors ajar. The only sign of strangers having been here are the blinds stuck halfway, leaving the windows in slight disarray.

As I enter Mia's room, my heartbeat accelerates. I cannot dispute the eerie energy of the empty crib in front of the window. The room looks as if a layer of volcanic ash has descended upon it; the crib slats are covered in black powder, so are the dresser, the changing table, the closet door, and the windows. The crib mattress and the bumper have been removed. The Tinker Bell mobile above her crib dangles, crooked and abandoned.

The night sky projection lamp is missing its dome, a sad turtle without its shell. Someone must have removed it to examine the inside of the lamp. I step closer and look inside: two windup cogs and a battery chamber. The lightbulb is missing. I run my finger along the rim of the opening, remembering how much Mia loved the stars traveling across the walls and the ceiling. A sticker on the rim: KEEP OUT OF REACH OF CHILDREN.

My hand starts trembling and I jerk back when something pecks at my finger. I stare at the crimson forming and realize I have sliced my finger on a tiny shard sticking out of the groove where the dome used to be. I rub my bloody index finger against the tip of my thumb. The blood is warm and sticky, and somehow it has turned a crank and, like a jack-in-the-box, a thought forms, takes shape, bobbles, then rests, finally comes into focus. Its melody is one of thunder rumbling in my head and I witness my mind reassembling the moment the memory was created.

Tears, feet, shards, cuts, blood.

Blood, lots of blood.

Tears forging a soft trail down bloody cheeks.

Naked feet stomping furiously among the shards.

Bloody footprints leaving a path the length of the front crib rail.

Wounded hands and feet, covered in cuts and nicks.

My mind shuts down, unwilling to proceed. I grip the image as if I'm floating in the middle of an ocean clinging to a piece of driftwood. The image returns, the random vision of a figment of my amnesiac imagination, a halfhearted truth then, the very first day I woke up in the hospital.

It wasn't a vision after all. The blood was real.

The assembly continues: the night of the hurricane, the power outage, the smoke detector. The molten bottle parts and pacifier.

I have to go further, I am so close.

I forcefully run all four fingers of my right hand over the rim of the domeless turtle lamp. I press hard and I linger, feel the spiky glass cut my skin. As my flesh splits, the blood forms into thick beads and

I run my fingers over the spiky shards, again and again and again, pressing harder, and harder, and harder.

A glass dome.

KEEP OUT OF REACH OF CHILDREN.

Not a toy. KEEP OUT OF REACH OF CHILDREN.

I wait the memory out, allow it to spiral its circular path like a balloon without its opening tied up, until it lies there, deflated, empty. And then the memory appears in its entirety. Seeing is believing, they say, but feeling is the ultimate truth.

My heartbeat slows and I allow myself to connect the dots. I had left the projection lamp with the glass dome next to her crib. Mia must have grabbed it, pulled it into her crib, and somehow broke the dome. Mia's fingers and feet were covered in tiny nicks but after I cleaned her up she didn't look half as bad as she had while covered in blood. Her vaccination appointment was two days later. I didn't know how to explain the nicks and cuts on her hands to the doctor. That's why I missed the appointment. And consequently without a shot record, there was no day care. And before I could make another appointment, Mia had disappeared.

KEEP OUT OF REACH OF CHILDREN, the sticker had said.

I also remember not knowing half the time how I ended up on the couch or in my bed. Not being able to figure out if Mia was crying or I was merely hearing an echo in my head. And then leaving something clearly dangerous so close to her crib. Not as dangerous as leaving a baby unattended in the tub, no, but a sticker giving me explicit instructions. I couldn't even get that right. And I wonder what else I had neglected to do.

I leave Mia's room and go to my bedroom, where everything is covered in a layer of dust. My clothes are still in the closet, there's an empty glass sitting on the nightstand, its yellow content dried up like honey. The scented candle fragrant with bergamot and despair hangs in the air.

But as I walk through the rooms, I feel as if I'm disturbing the past, my mere presence is upsetting the layer of microscopic particles deposited the day Mia disappeared. I want to leave it undisturbed, to maintain its crime scene status for all eternity, and I wish for supernatural powers so every thumbprint and DNA trace will expose a hint as to what happened within these walls.

I feel tired suddenly. I sit at the foot of the bed and close my eyes. Sitting here, I don't remember her first words (was it something like *ba-ba* or *da-da*?), the first time she sat up (was it on the floor or in her stroller?), the first time she rolled over, held her own bottle. There were smiles, but they didn't fill me with joy. Bottles, diapers, crying, over and over, twenty times over, day by day. I was covered in dust, just like this apartment.

The kitchen still smells of stale coffee, the living room of extinguished fireplace ashes. I'm bombarded with odors more powerful than words, captivating me, odors I can't identify—new-carpet smell maybe, bleach, Pine-Sol—and I feel the urge to leave this place. The tangs and whiffs go topsy-turvy in my mind, and I can't think of anything but escaping the stench of guilt this house holds.

I enter the stairwell and reach for the smooth rail covered in layers of glossy paint. The blood that flowed so freely from my fingertips earlier has coagulated. I hook my fingers around the railing. As I walk farther up I hear a familiar sound: a creak on the third step. The creak remains, echoes in my head, and my hand tightens even harder around the railing. I watch my knuckles emerge from under my skin like white river rocks in a riverbed. Suddenly I'm covered in anguish; it soaks through my clothes, opens the pores of my skin, and seeps all the way to my bones.

This time, I see nothing, not a single image. But I feel everything. I hear a voice from far away but I've no idea where the words are coming from until I recognize them as my own. And I return to the day I walked up these same steps.

"She's gone, she's gone, she's gone, gone," I hear myself cry. "I can't find her anywhere." And then floodgates open. I've returned, been magically transported through time and space. The sound of buses, garbage trucks, and children laughing shoots through me like an arrow. I hear pigeons cooing and a sharp slapping sound of wings.

I remember twisting the doorknob and the attic door swinging open. There was light shining through a windowed door at the end of the attic leading to the rooftop. A mummified pigeon lay in the corner, its feathers devoid of vanes, merely spiky shafts attached to a skeleton.

I felt dizzy. I closed my eyes and my knees hit the floor. I felt the impact, accompanied by crowing pigeons, and a feeling wrapped itself around me like a coat, skintight; I was unable to undo its buttons, the fabric had merged with my skin and there was only one way out.

Don't be misled, I wasn't delusional, I didn't think I could fly. I knew why I climbed up in the attic. I wanted to jump off the roof but darkness came before I could make good on my plan.

When I woke up, my knees were throbbing. As I made an attempt to push myself off the ground, I felt something soft beneath me. I scooped it toward me.

When I inhaled, I sensed a sparkle, but not the sparkle of glitter or fireworks, not the sparkle of glistening snow, a sparkle with the freshness of chamomile and lavender and camphor . . . but at the same time it had warmth, but not the warmth of cinnamon or brown sugar . . . the scent was a combination, a juxtaposed blend, delicate and robust all at the same time, like a worn, soft quilt from your childhood . . . yet daintier than cotton, more refined, but strong at the same time. This scent was pure and grand, and it was all around me.

I opened my eyes. I was holding Mia's blanket. Silver stars stitched in the corner, next to a moon and sun.

Mia's baby blanket was staring at me as if to say *Look harder, don't give up so quickly. What kind of mother are you?*

———

We stand in the kitchen as Dr. Ari eyes my fingertips.

"I have to draw the line when you've hurt yourself like this."

I shrug, looking down at my hands. The bleeding has stopped and the blood has dried to a glossy reddish-brown, giving my skin the appearance of having hand-dyed some sort of garment. Dr. Ari turns on the faucet and wets a handkerchief. I wipe my fingertips, turning the pressed and starched cotton carmine. For the first time since we started our sessions, Dr. Ari feels the need to clarify, to put a name to the madness.

"You found Mia's blanket in the attic. You were not sure about what happened, you even thought that Mia didn't exist. Your postpartum depression had progressed into psychosis."

Where is he going with this? I was a monster. I had stopped loving my baby; I was afraid of what I was capable of. And maybe I had hurt her. But I knew for sure I had failed her.

"You needed help, Estelle. This is nothing mothers can just get over by themselves. You needed medication, therapy, support, and friends. Many mothers imagine hurting their infants, even drowning them, burning them. Understand this, if you don't understand anything else: When mothers imagine hurting their children, their mind doesn't signal a wish. It's the mind's mechanism visualizing the worst outcome so you can counteract. It's the part of your mind that is still functioning, jerking you awake, warning you."

I consider his explanation but I'm torn.

"I remember a pair of scissors by her crib when I was still living with Jack. I had cut off the clothes tags. Every time I saw the scissors, I imagined myself stabbing her. I moved the scissors, stuffed them in the very back of the linen closet. I thought I was a monster." The last words come out in a wail.

The more upset I've become, the calmer Dr. Ari appears. It all makes sense to him but I wish it made sense to me, too.

"Postpartum psychoses require immediate treatment," Dr. Ari says. "You lost touch with reality and you still don't know what was real and what you imagined. The statistics are very clear in that most women who experience postpartum psychosis do not harm themselves or anyone else. They don't want to kill themselves or their children. But their thoughts can become so delusional and irrational that their judgment is impaired. Suicide is rare, infanticide extremely rare. It's even rarer that they kill *and* commit suicide."

I latch on to the word *and*. "Commit suicide *and* kill the infant. I didn't kill myself. But I wanted to. What does that mean?"

"You wanted to kill yourself. But then you found the blanket."

"I looked for her," I say.

"You looked for her?"

"In every closet and under the furniture. I opened every drawer, looked behind every curtain. I went outside and looked in the Dumpster. I walked up and down the street, looked in cars. I want you to know that I looked for her."

"I believe you, I know you looked for her. But we're not done, we have to keep looking."

We leave the building and sit in the van. Dr. Ari pulls a golden watch from his pants pocket. It dangles on a gold chain and attaches to the belt loop of his trousers. The sunlight hits it and sends a blinding ray my way.

Oliver is standing by a food truck. He holds a wrapper in one hand and a cup with a straw in the other. He puts the cup next to him on the bench and lifts his face upward. The sun is bearing down on the van and my eyelids are heavy. The past hour is weighing heavily on me. I'm thirsty, famished.

"Estelle"—Dr. Ari's voice is laden with fatigue—"tell me what you know for sure. Tell me what you know to be the truth. Everything we have spoken about, everything you remembered today, tell me what you know with absolute certainty."

I sit in silence for a while. The first thought that enters my mind is sadness. It's located in my stomach and feels like thirst, but no liquid has ever cured it. Even antidepressants have never limited its reach. Sadness had turned into the carnivore of my life, eating up everything in its path. It's a vortex that pulled everything else downward, toward this moment. I wanted someone to unearth me, hold me up against the light, brush me off with a shirt hem, and consider themselves lucky to have found me.

"I've been sad for a long time."

"And after you had Mia it got worse, didn't it?"

"I love her more than anything in the world. But it was so hard."

"Hormonal changes can be so dramatic that they push mothers from a general anxiety to a more severe disorder. Family members don't pick up on it because mothers appear to be fine for long periods of time."

"I understand what you're telling me, but what now? How does that help me now? Or Mia? She's still gone."

Dr. Ari takes off his glasses and wipes his face with the palm of his hand.

"But you are here. And you have to do everything you possibly can to find out what happened."

"What if I hurt her? What then?"

"Let's not ask that question."

"I should have tried harder," I say and cry again.

"Estelle, you have to be aware of this sadness from here on out. A mild depression in childhood can turn into a full-blown depression after adolescence, and you were certainly predisposed to postpartum depression. Slipping into a psychosis could have been prevented." He clears his throat and I've a feeling he has something else to say. "We're still in the infancy of brain research, we know there's a common mechanism, but its nature is still unknown to us."

"Do we have to come back here again?" I ask and look over at the front door of 517.

"I doubt it. You made great progress today." He looks at me for a long time. "You seem to have something on your mind. Can I answer any questions for you?"

"I don't understand this whole memory thing. The doctors told me I had memory loss because of my injuries and that it might take a long time for my memories to return. And some memories would never return, but the MRI didn't show any brain damage. So what is all this . . . this scent"—I point at the blanket in his hand—"and the moment in there, on the steps, how can it just come back to me? Where were those memories? I don't understand."

"I think it's safe to say that it's impossible to untangle the entire ball of yarn that caused your amnesia. There was trauma, there was postpartum depression, psychosis, your injuries, and whatever other condition might have played a role. In my opinion you suffer mainly from dissociative amnesia. I don't think we need to define it just yet, if at all. Dissociative amnesia is nothing more than a mental interruption or breakdown of your memories. You blocked out information that is too stressful or too dramatic for you to deal with. That's the difference between dissociative and regular amnesia; *dissociative* means that your memories still exist but are deeply buried in your mind. Those memories usually resurface the moment they are triggered by something. Hence the scent trigger." He points at the blanket in the Ziploc bag. "If your brain was damaged in any way, the memory would have been lost forever."

"So, in a way I'm lucky." I remember the doctor in the hospital indicating the tiny sliver of luck I had to be alive. "I'm lucky and this close," I say and hold up my fingers. "Right?"

"That's the spirit," Dr. Ari says and motions to Oliver.

Oliver stands up, stretches, and drops the cup in a nearby trash can. He gets in the van and turns the ignition key. I smell the chemical reaction of his skin's melanin to the UV rays. My stomach contracts violently.

"I'm going to be sick," I say and cover my mouth.

"Here you go," Oliver says and shoves a paper bag at me.

I take deep breaths and he appears next to me out of nowhere, standing in the open van door. I hear the sound of paper tearing and then a citrus scent drifts my way. I watch Oliver hold a wet wipe in front of the AC vent. Then he presses the cold wipe against my forehead.

A lemon scent seems to drown out everything around me, the waft of onions from the hot dog stand, the exhaust from the van, the musty odor from the van's AC, turning into the force of Oliver's hands pressing the wipe to my forehead, allowing me to breathe.

My heart is pounding in my ears, yet suddenly this is a safe place to be.

There's another scent mixing with the lemon, earthy and sweet at the same time. It's almost as sharp as pine, but not quite, more secret and not as obvious, as if the fragrance itself was clandestine, meant only for a chosen few. A scent so pure as if it was cut straight from a hole in the ground, ripped from the earth itself.

CHAPTER 16

Dr. Ari takes in a deep breath and rests his folded hands in his lap. "You found Mia's blanket in the attic. Tell me what you did next."

"I don't know why I'm so . . . so afraid."

Afraid is not the right word. Paralyzed, maybe? No, *paralyzed* means "incapable of movement." Transfixed? Yes, *transfixed*, as in motionless, spellbound in a way. But by what I cannot say. Why do I feel as if I'm a hare mesmerized by the curved talons of an eagle? Something I can't quite put my finger on, a complicit state of silence, an almost Manchurian conspiracy wall I feel I'm not allowed to climb. Like a promise I had made, a promise of silence.

"Fear is an autonomic response, don't allow it to distract you. You can't get to the bottom of it unless you let it run its course. Just accept it, but don't make it more than it is."

He pushes Mia's blanket toward me. My hands move but then hesitate slightly. I grab the blanket and I know that I have to search for all the jagged pieces of the puzzle. I close my eyes and enter the elevator.

I hold the blanket as if it is a relic, a sacred object. It still smells like Dreft and baby lotion, but more than its scent its energy travels through my fingertips, up my arms, and straight into my brain. Clutching the fabric tight, squeezing it like a wet rag, wringing it in an attempt to extract every single drop of water, I return to North Dandry, back to the attic.

I went back downstairs, where I found my door still unlocked and the building silent. There was a ringing in my head and my body was tingling. When I entered the kitchen, I broke out in a sweat. Then it all went dark.

The first thing I became aware of was a melodious tolling of church bells. It surrounded me before I even opened my eyes. I listened for a while and realized it was St. Joseph's across the street, summoning parishioners for Sunday Mass. The second thing I realized was that I had pulled Mia's blanket over my shoulders. It barely covered my upper body but the solace it gave me was boundless.

I remained motionless on the cold tile until the buzzing in my head stopped. I sat up and realized I was covered in dust and feathers and other debris from the attic. As I picked off a plume stuck to my pants, I watched the rainbow-colored feather drift toward a narrow gap between the wall panel and the floor. Its downy barbs quivered in the draft, then it was sucked underneath the panel and it disappeared.

I scooted closer, blanket around my shoulders, and noticed the same persistent breeze that had sucked up the feather. The draft was so strong it made me shiver. I managed to get up off the ground, holding on to the countertop, but it took immense effort to stand up on my feet. My skull was buzzing like a beehive. The draft became stronger and colder, the closer I moved toward the panel.

The apartment's walls, as in so many older row houses, were

covered in wood paneling, mostly for decorative purposes. There
were alcoves, niches, false walls covering windows, doors leading
to brick walls. There was even a door without any hardware,
concealed by paint in the hallway. Neglecting those details probably saved money during the renovation process and I wasn't sure
just how many fake panels there were throughout the apartment.
Maybe the panel the feather had disappeared underneath was one
of those panels, just for show and not insulated properly.

When I tapped my knuckles against the panel's corners, it produced a hollow sound. The baseboards continued on both sides of
the panel but were noticeably missing where the panel met the floor.
Like the draft, I hadn't noticed the missing baseboard before, either,
but I could have sworn they had been uniform all around the walls.
But maybe not. I was no longer sure. I bent down and poked my
fingers under the crack. The draft became even stronger.

Moving around proved more difficult than I imagined. My vision
grew blurry, my legs were wobbly, and my tongue kept clinging to
the roof of my mouth. I managed to reach the cupboard and I
downed three cups of tap water. I had to fight to keep it down and
decided to wait before attempting to eat anything.

When the pigeons outside my window started cooing, a recollection of the attic emerged, nebulous at first, then it came into
stark focus. The notion of my jumping off the roof now seemed
overly dramatic, silly almost, just another moment when illogical
actions seemed rational and well thought out. My daughter had
been in the attic at some point and I wasn't crazy after all.

I tugged at the bottom of the panel where the draft was stron-
gest. Nothing. I yanked the knob attached to the panel. It didn't
budge. I kept yanking, gently at first, then I gave it my all, using
both hands. First the panel creaked and screeched, then it popped
out of its rectangular frame. I fell back, and the panel landed flat
on the kitchen floor.

I found myself staring into a compartment the length of a narrow door, its depth that of a pantry or small coat closet. The floorboards were the original hardwood boards, not porcelain tiles like the rest of the kitchen.

And there it was. The shiny rainbowlike pigeon feather. There was a battlefield of dead insects, countless bugs, some flattened, and sticking to the floor, some on the outer edges still plump and stout, and dusty remnants of construction debris, wood, and drywall. Dust covered the floor like powdered sugar, except for a visible disturbance within the layer. And there were wood shavings and flaky particles.

There was a knob attached, not only to the outside, but also the inside of the panel. I stuck my head into the space. An icy draft descended upon me from the darkness above. A sliding door replaced by a panel? There were no visible motors or electrical wires, no ropes, no pulley mechanisms. It was definitely a remnant of an old dumbwaiter from when the row houses were first built.

The discovery was equivalent to having a couple of large cups of coffee and two aspirin. I was more alert than I had been in days. Logic prevailing, short of walking through walls, this was *the* entrance point into my apartment. I grabbed the opportunity like low-hanging fruit, stepped in, and looked up. The space felt like a small shower enclosure, and lifting my arms was impossible without elbowing the walls around me. Once my eyes got used to the darkness, I made out a rope dangling from above. The breeze was even stronger now and there was a faint sliver of light coming from a source less than eight feet up.

CHAPTER 17

There was no cracking, no wailing, no flushing toilets, no water running upstairs. I knew David Lieberman lived in an apartment above mine with an identical floor plan, while the other two apartments next door were under construction. I had seen some of the workers but never talked to any of them, didn't even know how many there were. The workers wore hard hats and passed me in the hallway carrying boxes of tiles, wood, countertops, and kitchen cabinets. They disposed of the rubble and debris through a bright yellow construction chute leading to a green metal container sitting outside in front of the building. I had seen some of the workers carry boxes outside too large to fit through the chute.

I stepped outside my apartment door and listened for any noises in the hallway. The church bells from across the street earlier reiterated the fact that it was Sunday and the construction site was abandoned, explaining why there was no whistling, no banging, no screeching of saws and other power tools coming from across the hall. The building was eerily quiet.

The construction site was straight across from my door, its entrance covered with a heavy blue tarp. I moved its first layer. Then the second layer. I stuck my hand through and my fingertips bumped against a smooth surface. I parted the tarp's last layer and realized a door had been installed. It was identical to the one leading into my apartment. Metal and fireproof, and it was locked.

I went upstairs, knocked on David Lieberman's door, and waited. I knocked again. No answer. Less than a minute later I stood in my kitchen dialing his number. I heard the phone ringing through the ceiling. The answering machine kicked in and I hung up. I dialed his cell and it picked up on the first ring.

Beep. I'm sorry but the person you called has a voice mail box that has not been set up.

After I hung up the phone, I stepped back into the dumbwaiter. The end of the rope dangled from above, swinging back and forth, its end tied into a large nautical knot. I tugged gently but it didn't budge. I pulled harder. After a few tugs, I used my entire weight to test its strength. I was weak, but I was determined. My slight frame made up for the strength I didn't have. I held on to the knot, locked my elbows, and, inch by inch, moved, with my feet, up the wall. My hands took turns reaching up the rope, moving higher and higher until I was perched at the very top of the dumbwaiter.

I listened for a few seconds but heard only the beating of my own heart. My arm muscles twitched and I felt like a pigeon trapped in a chimney. A sliver of light escaped from the panel in front of me; it was not enough to illuminate the walls around me but sufficient to make out most of my surroundings.

I ignored my sore leg muscles but knew I was going to start spasming under the weight of my body eventually. I felt my way along the bottom crack of the panel, one foot pressed against the wall, the other pushing against the panel. I pulled back my right foot and kicked the panel, which popped out of its frame. I swung back to gain momentum and flung myself into the light. I landed on a cold tiled floor, taking some dust and debris with me. I allowed my muscles to rest, and looked around.

My first thought was one of confusion: had I walked in circles and ended up at the same place? This was my kitchen; same flooring, same cabinets, same everything. My second thought was what wasn't there. No sponge in the kitchen sink, no coffeemaker on the counter, no garbage can, no mail, no newspaper. It was the apartment of someone who either just got here or was about to leave. My third thought was to snoop around.

I started pulling the kitchen drawers open and found all of them empty but one: mismatched silverware and matches, a can opener, a piece of string, and a few pencil nubs. I opened the cabinets: lonely dishes and boxes of cereal neatly lined up.

A cardboard box sat on a cheap folding table and a few more flattened boxes were stacked on the floor. Two metal folding chairs rested against a wall. A tool belt was draped over the pantry door-knob.

I pushed open the bathroom door. There were the usual items— shaving cream, a toothbrush, and a bar of soap on the rim of the sink—and a box of Moldex hearing protection earplugs, still sealed, under the sink. I opened the mirrored cabinet: aspirin, Alka-Seltzer, and nasal decongestant. On the top row sat a terra-cotta army of medicine containers, most of them filled to the brim; only a couple of containers were almost empty. I recognized allergy medication by name, some pain medication.

The bedroom next to the bathroom contained large cardboard boxes marked with colorful moving company stickers that, after I gave them a shove, turned out to be empty.

Lieberman's bedroom, dark and musty, was bare but for an inflatable mattress covered with a crumpled sheet and a flattened pillow. There was a desk without a chair and the desk drawers opened and shut with a screech as if they hadn't been opened in a while. All were empty.

The living room was sparse, the furniture cheap and mismatched. A green threadbare throw rug, a couch with sad cushions and saggy pillows, and a coffee table with glossy magazines. They stuck out like a sore thumb, misplaced in otherwise gloomy surroundings. The magazines were travel-related, titled *Caribbean*, *Islands in the Sun*, another one *Afar*. *Luxury Hotels*, *Adventure Travel*, all of them neatly laid out in a row. A flat-screen TV was mounted to the wall, a dining table pushed under the kitchen counter, an office chair on a plastic mat and a frayed mouse pad completed the bleak picture.

I hit the light switch. The dining room chandelier, too bright for the small area, cast a glaring light on its surroundings. The bookshelf on the wall next to the computer held a collection of leather-bound books on military strategy. The books were in chronological order, drab, colorless, with tatty spines, old and worn as if from a library giveaway. From Genghis Khan to Napoleon, to Waterloo and World War I.

I pulled out the first book of the top row and opened it to the title page. The book smelled stale and grassy, with a hint of acidity. It was titled *Baron de Rais* subtitled *The Trial of Gilles de Laval, Baron de Rais*. I leafed to the introduction and then read the blurb: "The ultimate portrait of the face of evil who has come to personify mankind's greatest fears." I quickly shut the book and shoved it back into its spot and wiped my hands on my thighs.

A lower shelf contained a collection of Fodor's Travel Guides: glossy, cheerful, in alphabetical order. Amsterdam, Bermuda, Cayman Islands, Florence, Paris, Italy, London, St. Thomas, the Black Forest, Spain, Turkey. The books seemed new with their spines intact, as if sitting on a bookstore shelf, waiting to be cracked open.

Life in 1B was dreary overall. There was a utilitarian aspect to the place; no family pictures, no knickknacks. The harsh overhead light made the rooms uncomfortable while an annoying fan clicked away above. Its clacking seemed to urge me to move on, reminding me that I had come here for a reason.

The file cabinet had a magnetic pull on me. I opened the top drawer and it swayed toward me, stopping just short of toppling the entire cabinet. There was an array of uniform folders with plastic tabs, handwritten capital letters, all tilted to the left, in unsteady handwriting. I stared at the tabs of the manila folders and imagined the pages contained within. I thumbed through a few folders, clumsily and not very efficiently. There were instruction manuals for TVs, computer warranty information, and contracts from furniture and computer stores. The last folder's label was blank and it contained a collection of newspaper articles, some original, some photocopied, and some printed. I skimmed through the articles:

BRUISES THAT COVER BODY
OF INFANT MADE BY TASER

FERAL CHILD RESCUED FROM MOBILE HOME

BOY LIVED IN CLOSET FOR EIGHT YEARS

MOM CHARGED AFTER BABY DIES IN HOT CAR

TWINS DIE OF NEGLIGENCE

LOCKED AWAY IN CAGE FOR 10 YEARS

MOM OF 5 HIDDEN FROM SOCIETY,
LIVING IN SQUALOR

REMAINS OF THREE INFANTS
FOUND IN LANDFILL

A thought took shape, it rose like dough, increasing its volume, a dense mass turning into a well-risen realization, yet I punched it down, refused to allow its expansion. I couldn't permit the possible implications to take hold and so I stood rooted to the spot, heart in my throat.

This had *nothing* to do with Mia. *Nothing.* I was oddly captivated by Lieberman's collection of horror: news articles of neglected children he chose, for whatever sick reason, to save.

True, we read these stories every day—hardly a summer went by without a parent forgetting a child in a hot car, infants left unsupervised in cribs while Mom enters a crack house or a casino. *How could she?* we'd ask, but all that remains is a faint memory, if that. *I read about a mother once who . . .*

As I scan the first story, I shudder. This is beyond a mother failing to button her children's coats, a lack of lunch money, or uncooked dinners. Stories that spoke of neglect so terrible that seasoned police officers broke down on the stand once the case went to trial. There were mentions of bite and whip marks, lesions and scabs. Scattered feces, swarms of flies, smashed skulls. Six-year-olds appearing to be half their age with scars covering their entire bodies.

There was a medical article titled "Alarming Brain Scans and the Impact of a Mother's Love," emphasizing that children nurtured by their mothers have larger brain structures, and that developmental delays affect children for the rest of their lives. It explained how parents who mistreat their children were also neglected and concluded that neglect is a vicious cycle. The article closed with a list of numbers to call when one suspects abuse.

Was I that mother to him? The one who neglected her child behind a façade of wealth, passing him on the street with a designer stroller? Did a colicky baby trigger images of cigarette burns and a bloated belly from malnutrition?

Ring.

The sound of the phone startled me. The phone's caller ID

displayed the name of the caller as *Seagram Construction, Inc.* When the answering machine picked up, the caller hung up.

I panicked, wondering if I had left the folders out of order. I scanned from the front to the back; they were at least straight and still alphabetized. I closed the cabinet door and resisted the urge to open it back up again.

Ring.

I felt my stomach twisting into a knot. From the corner of my eye, I caught a green object. Somewhere in my gut there was a faint hint of acknowledgement, its cheerful green apple shade—or was it lime, malachite even—seemed familiar, yet oddly out of place in a room of tans and browns. *Ring.*

The green object was perched on top of the bookcase, shoved back as if someone wanted it hidden from plain view but still wanted to know that it was there.

I approached the shelf.

Ring.

The answering machine picked up.

Please leave a message after the beep.

"Mr. Lieberman, it's Frank from Seagram's Construction. I know you are out of town on the weekends, but I need to do an inspection on the progress early Monday. Call me when you get this."

The phone went silent.

But there she was, like a ghost, fading in and out in her emerald glory. I closed my eyes, then opened them again.

She sat atop the shelf. A plastic figure in a sitting position with a hidden button below her skirt that made her glow-in-the-dark wings wiggle. The centerpiece of Mia's mobile above her crib. My heartbeat made the top of my skull pound. Tinker Bell looked discarded, tossed aside. I reached out to her. My fingertips touched her wings.

Ring.

My hand jerked backward. I held myself still, wishing I could will the phone to stop ringing.

Ring.

I had never looked at her this closely, had never really paid attention to her. A green strapless dress with a petal skirt. Blue eyes, blond hair. Pointy ears.

Ring.

Clear wings on her back. Tinker Bell, the fairy whose body turns fiery red when angered because her fairy size prevents her from holding more than one feeling at a time.

Please leave a message after the beep.

A female voice, sharp, impatient.

"David, are you stuck in traffic or something? You're not answering your cell and I can't leave a message. You need to set up your voice mail."

I grabbed Tinker Bell and, as if someone was chasing me, I ran for the kitchen. I was neither crazy nor delusional, I was not losing my mind. The blanket is one thing. It could have fallen out of the stroller, I could have dropped it by mistake. Dragged up there by who knows what. But this? Had he found Tinker Bell, had he run across her in some random fashion, in a hallway, or even on the street, by my car, or on the steps, he would have discarded her or left her where she was to begin with. But Tinker Bell, in his apartment, left deliberately on top of a shelf?

Am I going off the deep end again? I must focus. I must concentrate and think this through.

Was Lieberman a kidnapper? The man who took my child? The more I thought about it, the more sense it made. I didn't care where the truth was trying to drag me; I was willing to follow. I entered the dumbwaiter and pulled the panel back into its frame by its knob, and, to my surprise, it popped easily back into place. I wrapped the rope around my wrists, my feet securely placed against the walls around me.

Back in my apartment, I dialed Lieberman's cell number, and as expected, it went to voice mail. I needed to find him. If I couldn't find him, I'd have to find the sister he visits on weekends, a woman whose name I didn't even know.

I turned on the computer and searched for any information on David Lieberman. The results contained more than three million hits, ranging from Berkeley School of Law to an endodontic dentist in Oregon, university links, and a blogger of vermin-catching techniques in Australia. The usual social networking sites came up, some university faculty profiles, and hundreds of genealogy hits for names spelled remotely like Lieberman.

I clicked on the image search tool and scrolled through the first ten pages, scanning the photos of the David Liebermans of the world. Nothing jumped out at me and after a while the pictures blended into a sea of eyes, noses, and smiles. I had been at this for hours and I was getting tired.

Finally, on page twenty-plus, a picture of two teenagers caught my eye. The boy in the picture was a version of Lieberman decades ago. I clicked on the photo. It took me to the online archive of the *Millbrook Park Townsman*, a small newspaper in Dutchess County, New York.

Decades of headlines scrolled before my eyes. I concentrated on the bold words. One entry jumped out at me: **House Fire Kills Parents, Spares Children**. No reference to the name Lieberman, yet there had to be a connection, according to my search preferences. Another bold link caught my eye: **Gruesome Discovery Made**. I clicked on the link, which directed me to the full text, and I began reading.

HOUSE FIRE KILLS PARENTS, SPARES CHILDREN

DOVER, New York—A couple died early Friday, July 3rd, 1982, when a fire swept through their home on Sparrow Lane in Oniontown, a part of Dover, NY.

The victims are Gabriel, 48, and Esther Lieberman, 41, according to New York Public Safety spokeswoman

Irene McConnell. The couple's children, David, 17, and Anna, 13, are being treated at Dover County Hospital for smoke inhalation. Anna Lieberman was also treated for minor burns to her hands.

"When we arrived, there was fire blowing out of the windows in the front," said Fire Marshal Donald Helm. The shed in the backyard and an old barn were also consumed by the flames. "The entire town is sad for the two children. It's tragic."

The fire was initially reported by a neighbor. According to Fire Marshal Donald Helm, the couple was trapped in an upstairs bedroom. The windows, according to the children, were hard to open at times. "Why they didn't try to escape into the hallway and down the stairs, we'll never know."

Investigators from the State Fire Marshal's Office were at the scene throughout the day, working to pinpoint the cause. Fire marshals and Dover firefighters searched the rubble in the afternoon, looking for clues.

The minor children are in the care of the State until relatives can be reached. The investigation into the fire is ongoing.

The resemblance to Lieberman as a teenager was uncanny. He hadn't changed much; his acne had healed and he had added some facial hair over the years. David was the attractive one of the two, but had the eyes of an angst-ridden adolescent not wanting to pose for a photograph. David stood back, his body in his sister's shadow. Anna was a rather plain girl, her frizzy hair parted in the middle, her lips full, and her smile open, friendly eyes looking directly in the camera. Or maybe confrontational, I couldn't tell.

A little more browsing and a follow-up article in the same paper came up. According to a state agency spokesperson, David aged out of the foster care system weeks after the fire. Anna stayed in the foster care system for months, until finally a relative was located.

Both our stories were so eerily similar yet a mere coincidence of events unrelated, a synchronicity that defied any possible explanation: my parents dying, an older brother leaving behind a younger sister. In both cases an aunt came and took care of the younger sibling. In Anna's case a Laura Dembry came forward. It took only a few more strokes to find out that Laura Dembry was a member of the Church of Appointed Dominion in Plainview, New York, a hamlet in Nassau County, not too far from the north shore of Long Island. There was no reference made as to where Anna went to live. Details became scarce after that and the Liebermans' online story ended there: orphaned children moving on with their lives. But I knew better, I knew from experience that our own personal shadows followed us through life, and I knew that in the aftermath is where the true tragedies occur. Mine, his, everybody's. Newspaper articles weren't the end of anything.

Our similar fates lingered in the air, thick and heavy, like a blanket of fog. I randomly typed the title of one of the books on the shelf, *Baron de Rais, The Trial of Gilles de Laval,* into the search engine and clicked on the introduction. *Baron de Rais had considerable pleasure in watching the heads of children separated from their bodies . . . sometimes he would ask, when they were dead, which of them had the most beautiful head.*

And I remembered the title of the last book, the one at the end of the long historical timeline, as if it staked claim to the present. *The Prince of Darkness.*

I needed to get help but then I imagined how this would go. How this would unfold if I went to the police. I would return to the precinct and I'd tell them about Mia, Lieberman, and his sister, Anna, about my suspicions—never mind the fact that I was the perfect perpetrator, the mother who had access to the baby, a baby who, mind you, had disappeared days ago. And the newspapers, they would have a field day with the articles. *Since when is it illegal to collect newspaper articles?* Child porn, yes, you mention child porn and you have a case, but articles about child abuse and neglect? I can hear the police question me: *How again is this related? Explain this to us one more time? The man collects newspaper articles? By the way, you look familiar? Do we know you?*

Eventually I'd be unable to answer their questions. I'd fall just short of even comprehending their questions, and then I'd be incapable of calming down and my edgy voice would repeat the same nonsense over and over again, *Tinker Bell, Tinker Bell*, and I might as well be talking to the walls because the story was nothing but a macabre and ill-conceived soap opera, a half-baked, crackpot pipe dream by a woman who repeated the same incoherent story over and over again.

And I would carry on with this conspiracy script and not ever make any kind of sense, and then they'd put me in a cell and order a psych evaluation but—with the state of the budget and it being a Sunday—I'd have to wait until Wednesday afternoon and before I could convince anyone of my sanity, Lieberman and his sister would be God-knows-where.

I squint and pound my temple with my fist. Every time I emerge from the past, I'm shocked. How many times did I want to forget painful memories of my life? And now this, here I am, trying to remember them all. What a joke, and again, the joke's on me.

"Call the police." I can't control the tremor of my raspy voice.

I watch Dr. Ari pick up the phone and ask for Detective Wilczek. My stomach starts contracting and my face must show my inner state because Dr. Ari points at a door behind his desk. In there, I heave and heave until clear liquid comes up. The stench of stomach acid fills my nostrils.

When I sit back down, Dr. Ari is still on the phone. I watch his mouth move, occasionally his brows furrow, then his face darkens. He hangs up the phone.

"They've been looking for Lieberman and his sister all along. Not a trace," he says. "Both of them. Off the face of the earth. It's not a crime to disappear; they are looking to question them but haven't located them yet."

I hardly comprehend the words but I know what they mean. Gone. Everyone's gone. And then I ache and I realize I might have to live in this body for the rest of my life. A body that feels like it's wrapped in jagged little edges of pain. Does this story even sound like the truth? This story of orphaned siblings so similar to my story. Where is the logic, how likely is it that the story I'm telling is real?

It could be the truth. Stranger things have happened. A story told is a powerful thing and retelling it over and over leaves trenches in your mind and before you know it those trenches get deeper. A foxhole turns into a dugout, deep enough to hide in.

Yes, it does sound like the truth.

CHAPTER 18

As I stir my orange Jell-O into mush, Marge and I watch the women, six of them, ranging from eighteen to thirty-something, their wraithlike bodies performing eerie dietary rituals, stabbing forks into tiny pieces of sustenance, and miraculously the tines hold on to the morsels; after the women chew elaborately, they conclude the ceremony by gulping down large cups of water. A majority of the time they merely rearrange dietary food groups into mounds of rejection, always aware of their obsession to deprive themselves of nourishment. The orderlies fiercely patrol the borders during mealtime, especially between our table and the group of women who Marge and I refer to as "Farmers' Delight."

Marge at times is an enigma to me. Dr. Ari is rumored to have a very limited number of cases and mainly oversees other psychiatrists on his staff. What is it about Marge that he chooses to be her psychiatrist? I know Marge struggles with the death of her mother but I'm starting to question if she's not as innocent as she wants me to believe.

I've grown to like her and we've bonded, at least as much as this sojourn allows us, and watching the women is a fun distraction until Marge develops peculiar culinary habits of her own: she stuffs large amounts of food into her mouth and swallows without chewing. Her face is expanding by the day with her sleeve hems cutting into her arms, and her waist is ballooning. She is turning into a globe, her belt cutting her in half like an equator line.

"Are you going to eat that?" Marge points at a slice of white bread on my plate. Watching me turn my Jell-O to mush earlier must have torn her up inside.

Marge keeps eyeing the bread, not in the least bothered by the bite marks. There's no warding off Marge when it comes to food; she seems determined to grow beyond the walls of this institution.

"Let me have my lunch in peace," I say but what really bothers me is the fact that I want to ask her about her mother's death, yet at the same time I'm perplexed by my newfound aversion to secrets and lies.

"Don't get testy, I'm just asking. If you're not going to eat it, let's switch trays." She eyes the leftovers at the Farmers' Delight table and I anticipate dire complications in our near future. Everybody's success is guaranteed; she wants their food, they don't want food at all. A match made in heaven.

"What are you trying to do to yourself? Did you talk to someone about this?" I'm perplexed at her size; her hips expand beyond the chair and even her glasses cut into her temples. I picture the day her eyes will disappear in folds of fat and wonder how long the hospital will allow her to go on. If the anorexic women are not allowed to leave food on their plates, someone, sooner or later, ought to intervene in Marge's bingeing.

"Dr. Ari said they'll start supervising me during meals. But so what? There are ways to get food. There are always ways to get food. You think they'll give me their desserts?" Marge is eyeing the anorexic girls and they are returning the favor. I see one of the girls nod ever so slightly. A deal has been struck.

I have my own theory about why Marge has decided to be the ever-expanding woman: She's killed her mother and now wants her back. She intends to re-create her mother's body within her own skin and she won't quit until someone stops her. I feel for Marge, yet I try to keep some distance because I don't want to get drawn into her web of obsession.

"Hello, ladies." I hear Oliver's voice behind me and Marge's face deflates as her plan has been spoiled for now.

Oliver puts his tray on our table and pulls up a chair. Orderlies don't eat with patients but I welcome the distraction. He smells of disinfectant, lotion, and peppermint.

"Thanks again for the other day," I say, recalling the cool lemon-scented wipe on my forehead.

"Sure," Oliver replies and I'm not sure he knows what I'm referring to. "I'll be eating my meals with you from now on. I hope you don't mind?" he adds and he directs the question toward Marge, who raises her eyebrows. We all know he's here to keep Marge from killing herself with cafeteria chow.

He bites into a cracker and starts peeling the label off the orange. His hair is dark brown, his eyes a deep ocean blue. His eyebrows slope downward and give him a rather solemn expression. He wears a playful smile and kindness seems to be etched into his face. His voice is deep, with a serious undertone. He's probably average anywhere else, but within these walls he's a rock star.

"Why are your hands so . . . beat up? Are you working construction on your days off?" I try to sound nonchalant and casual.

"I build stuff, with wood." He chews and I patiently wait for him to elaborate. "It's called wood turning."

Marge is annoyed by his presence. She has gone through another change; besides the alteration of her ballooning appearance she doesn't hold back anymore. When I met her, she was shy and timid and hardly talked to anybody. Now her words exit her mouth with the same speed she fills up her body with food.

"Wood turning? What's that? Dressers, chests, stuff like that? Why don't you just go and buy furniture? Seems like a waste of time. Just saying . . ." Marge eyes his orange.

"It's nothing like carpentry or building furniture. I make bowls, lidded boxes, vessels, urns, pens—that kind of stuff. Delicate things, whatever requires attention to detail."

"Are you gonna eat that?" Marge asks and points at Oliver's orange.

"I'm going to eat at this table from now on, until further notice. Just to keep an eye on everything."

"Show us something then," Marge says and glances back and forth between the two of us and smiles. "One of those wooden things you make."

Out of Oliver's scrubs pocket appears a rounded object. An acorn, not bigger than a robin's egg, complete with a lid and a stem.

"See, I made this from sandalwood," he says. "I use special tools like this one and carve the details. This is called a gouge edge. For very small details, like the cap."

The tool in his hand, the gouge edge, is a concave-blade miniature chisel with a rounded and troughlike groove at the very tip. Oliver places the gouge on his tray. I pick it up. It's not bigger than a regular-sized pair of tweezers.

"It's perfect for small details." Oliver holds the acorn up by the stem. "This is"—he pauses for dramatic purposes—"an acorn." He holds it gently, as if it might break. "The tool is used to carve small indents, to make it look real. I rubbed wax on the cap to make it darker."

"Looks like a real waste of time to me." Marge gets up and slides her tray over the table and turns her attention to the anorexic girls.

Oliver mumbles something under his breath and starts peeling his orange. "By the way"—he leans closer into me and lowers his voice—"you'll have a visitor soon."

I look at him, puzzled. "A visitor?" I ask. "For me?"

"For you."

"Who?" I think of Jack immediately, then I abandon the thought. Thinking of him makes my stomach feel queasy and I try to concentrate on Oliver.

"I didn't get that part." He pauses. "I'm not supposed to tell you, but I thought it might cheer you up. You haven't had a visitor since you've been here."

A kaleidoscope of faces pops up in my mind: the DA, the detectives, Nell, Jack. I'm unable to shut the images off. I extend my perception outward, take in the sound of the loudspeaker, the loud chatter around us, the clanking of lunch trays, and the screeching of chairs. I try to breathe and relax but my heart rate won't slow and I concentrate on Oliver, his nail puncturing the skin of the orange, his thumb working its way under the peel, finally tearing off a section of the skin.

Marge pushes her chair toward the table with the anorexic girls, talking and giggling and pointing at various food items on their trays.

Oliver gets up and raises his voice. "Ladies, no funny business— you know better than that." He points toward the cafeteria exit. "Lunch is over."

The girls get up in unison and leave their trays behind. I watch Marge making her way to the dirty dish bin. A visitor. My thoughts jumble, pull me in every direction possible. My heart beats too fast to stay seated and so I get up, grab my tray.

"You forgot your stuff," I say, and I hand the gouge and acorn to him while balancing my tray with one hand.

He grabs the gouge and slides it back into his pocket.

"Keep the acorn."

"Keep it?"

"I made it for you," he says.

"You made me an acorn. Any specific reason?"

"You'll see."

"Can I get a hint?"

He cocks his head to the left and says, "You know, I think a hint would ruin it. So I'm going to let you figure it out on your own."

"Because I'm a nutcase, right?"

He chuckles, pulling up his shoulders.

"Okay then," I say and slide the acorn in my pocket.

I exit the cafeteria and make my way to Dr. Ari's office. After I knock on the door, I expect my unscheduled appearance to irritate him, but to my surprise I hear a cheerful "Yes?" As I open the door and walk in, I make sure to remain closer to the door than to his desk. Dr. Ari stands by the window, a lint remover in hand, meticulously stroking his navy blue wool coat. I just stand there and stare at him. I don't know how to ask about the visitor without him probing how I found out, without giving Oliver away.

"Estelle, I was just thinking about you." He pauses and checks his appearance in the mirror. "Your brother Anthony's asked for permission to come and see you."

Anthony Paradise, the last time I saw him, had just turned eighteen. I remember his olive complexion and his green eyes. I'd heard he'd gone to a military academy, a choice I have always been puzzled by. There were scholarships and so many opportunities, but he chose a military academy instead of one of the Ivy League schools that were so keen on recruiting him. After I moved in with Aunt Nell I asked about him constantly, but she was always short on words, and I'm no longer sure what I heard from Nell or what I made up myself.

Oliver is nowhere to be found, and Marge is out hunting and gathering and expanding her frame. I realize that I have no one. No friends. I might as well say it like it is—I've never really had friends. All the relationships I've had were thin and inadequate, almost nonexistent. A faint recollection of memories shared at some point in the distant past, yet no lasting connections, no scrapbooks, no matching jewelry or framed photographs. Not one person I can call and talk to. And even if I had a number to call, what would I say?

Hi, this is Estelle, remember me? I just wanted to catch up, so how have you been? I'm in a psychiatric institution because I seem to have misplaced my infant daughter, some people even believe I had something to do with her disappearance. I just need to sort a few things out and so your name came to mind and I just thought I'd call . . ."

I can't get Anthony off my mind. His impending visit, Dr. Ari's comment *Tomorrow, I'll let you know the time,* makes my heart throb in my ears. I mention my unease to Dr. Ari, I even request anxiety medication, but he denies me chemically induced peace like he denies cutting me slack during our sessions. In here you deal with things, that's all there is to it.

For the rest of the day I concentrate on the familiar sterile and hurried efficiency of Creedmoor, but I find it almost impossible to deal with the constant intrusion of the eerie background music reminding me of what and where I am. The sirens don't sound too often because this isn't an emergency room and patients don't generally arrive by ambulance, but are brought in by family members or social workers. Today, though, the siren sound is higher pitched than usual and I know an ambulance is approaching and the pitch will lower once it retreats. There are the rubber soles squeaking on linoleum, the occasional loudspeaker messages that no one understands, wheels of carts and beds, and even occasional moaning. Sometimes screaming. Never silence. Even my olfactory bulb is being bombarded with the scent of latex and bleach and cooking odors wafting through the hallways from the kitchen.

Then I try to shut out the noise and I manage for the most part by focusing on the scuff marks on the shiny floor and the scraped walls. Just when I think I've managed to stay in control, the sound of IV stand wheels meddles with my attempts and I wonder where one really finds silence at all. An underground mine, maybe, a sound-proof chamber? A monastery where monks adhere to the self-imposed vow of silence? My thoughts go topsy-turvy and my mind is about to explode like an overheated lightbulb.

As I walk the hallways, I keep an eye on the floor, tan with tiny specks of gray, white dots here and there if I look really close. I ignore the conversations of nurses passing me, the orderlies with their clipboards and jingling keys, the loudspeaker with its com-mands: *Doctor scratch scratch, please scratch, at the lobby, scratch.* I hear nurses chat from behind a glass wall down the hallway, farther down the hallway there's laughter, cabinets closing, a phone ringing. The world around me is like shards stuck in my brain and my coping ability, already far from being stellar, keeps declining, clogging up the few thoughts I can keep on an even keel. I wonder if there's a pool in this place, somewhere in the basement, some ancient remnant of water therapy for the insane, so I can immerse myself in water so deep the sound waves are dampened, all signals weakened so the world diminishes altogether.

At midnight I carry an empty water bottle in my hand as an excuse for leaving my room. Water coolers are on each floor and in the stairwells, and no one will question me because no one drinks the tap water at Creedmoor, the rusty waterline stains in toilets speak to the water quality and are a clear warning to avoid its consumption.

The west wing is abandoned and most of the doors, rooms, and offices are locked. This part of Creedmoor is not in use, the funds for the renovation probably somewhere in the deep pockets of a wealthy donor, as Creedmoor's days are numbered.

I hear footsteps, too slow for a nurse or an orderly, maybe the security guard checking whatever he checks in this unoccupied part of the building, and I hide in an alcove.

When the footsteps fade into the distance, I continue my walk. I read the door signs as I pass each room and finally I find what I consider the next best thing to an Olympic-sized pool and I enter the room to my right. I shut the heavy door behind me and remain still in the darkness until my eyes adjust. The room is chilly. I put my hands in my pockets, embracing the acorn Oliver gave me, carved by a tool whose name I have forgotten.

My throat constricts as if someone has wrapped a scarf around my neck, slowly tightening it. There's no furniture; the walls and the floor are tiled, nothing but a small cell with a bed anchored to the floor. There are two wrist restraints and two ankle restraints attached to the floor anchors. There are no hard edges or corners.

I feel loopy, almost high. The bed is as narrow as a twin but it is sturdy, and as I sit on its edge, it does not squeak. We are in a seclusion room, its energy heavy and unyielding. The only light spilling through the skylight is the moon.

I lie down as if in a coffin, tucking my arms beside my body, not wanting to take up any more room in this world than I have to. The mockery of this moment, this bed, this building, my life, the extent to which one has to go to find silence to hear the one voice that is true, which is bound to speak the truth if I drown out everything else, the one voice that I demand to hear.

I don't trust my storytelling. I feel as if I have created a clearer and more believable version of myself and that most of what I have recalled so far are just thoughts removed from reality and maybe, just maybe, that's what my madness is—the blurring of the lines, not knowing where one thing begins and another ends.

Tears stream into my ears, down my neck, and I wipe my eyes with the back of my hands. For one split second the moon fits perfectly into the skylight above me, fills it to the brim, its infallible contour contained in a square shape. I want to melt into the bed below me and the moon above at the same time. I imagine Mia and wonder if I'm to blame for her lifeless body resting somewhere we will never know. Maybe the less I resist the truth the more bearable it will be.

I cry knowing the walls are soundproof and for this one moment, in this room of madness, this place of the demented, I want to find the strength to see this through. How easily I could have taken the tool in the cafeteria, small as it was, its blade capable of doing the job if pointed in the right spot at the right angle. And I wonder what keeps me alive. It dawns on me that self-preservation trumps a death wish every time, and part of my self-preservation is the fact that I have the fury of an animal deprived of its young inside me.

I hold the wooden acorn in my hand and remember Oliver telling me there was something I was to figure out for myself. I behold the acorn in my palm, cup my fingers so it won't roll off and tumble to the ground. Suddenly I feel protective of it, I inspect it, run my fingertip gently along its shiny brown cap and its long, recurving scales that tightly overlap. The body is egg-shaped, smooth, yet I can see tiny cracks along its base.

I ever so gently twist the acorn cap while holding on to the base. It moves and I softly lift the lid off by its stem. I flip the acorn over and onto my palm tumbles an acorn. The real thing hidden inside a wooden vessel. I hold the cap to my nose and inhale. Its scent is soft yet has the sharpness of an herbal undertone. That's what I smelled, that day at the park, after I watched Oliver chipping away at something on the bench. The scent of his hands after he handed me the wipe to cool my forehead.

As I summon my story over the next few weeks, I hope that its edges will sharpen and the shadows will disappear. The truth? Maybe this is what the truth smells like. Sweet and rich, like unsalted butter. Pure and unaltered. Maybe my memory isn't just a story, maybe I'm onto the truth after all.

CHAPTER 19

At four o'clock I wait on a bench by the fountain. Every time I hear footsteps coming down the path and the gravel crunches, my heart skips. I wish I had made him wait for me instead because every car door sounds like a gunshot, making my heart speed up.

I wish I had a picture of Mia. I have nothing, no photo albums, no foot- or handprint, no first outfit, not a single witness to her existence. The only remnants of her life are sealed away in plastic evidence bags, leakproof, tear-and-puncture resistant with an adhesive closure and a chain-of-custody label.

"Stella."

A voice behind me, like a feather stroking my arm. It almost takes me down.

I turn around and there he is; taller than I remember him. It seems like a thief came and took him, then returned him, changed in so many ways. He's grown now, slightly haggard and gaunt, almost past his prime, even at such a young age. He's no longer the kid he was when I last saw him. I had missed him becoming a man, missed his first love, his college years, his first job. He's in his thirties and extremely thin.

Anthony opens his arms and we embrace. He's clean-shaven and smells of cigarette smoke. The weeks at Creedmoor have conditioned me to infer, to allow my emotions to draw pictures, and a kaleidoscope of memories, with bits of mirrors creating colorful patterns, rush at me. Vivid, with clear edges, almost a color print photograph, a Polish bakery where we used to buy Krówki, a toffeelike candy bar, emerges. And a flash of Duke, the neighbor's dog we played with, a Doberman mix who walked with a limp and had one ear sticking up. I push the images aside. A feeling of emptiness overtakes me, a sadness that sits in my gut, a feeling of disgust like I've swallowed a fly.

We sit on the bench. There's a ring on his left hand, a gold band so thin it almost disappears.

"So, how have you been getting on?" His voice is deeper than I remember.

Fifteen years later and he wants to know how I have been getting on.

"Stella."

There, my name again.

"I'm so sorry," he says and cradles my hand in his.

Immediately I turn into the girl I was fifteen years ago. We've been apart but regardless of where we go and how old we are, we will always be who we were to begin with: brother and sister. I don't remember much of the house I grew up in anymore, but I recall Nell's house, dark and gloomy, my apartment in Queens, shabby furniture and loud neighbors, all my possessions stashed away in one closet, leaking pipes, all those places I lived had never been home.

How have I been getting on, he asked. I'm torn between letting him know how lame his question is and owing him an explanation. I don't know what to tell him. Words don't have the adequate power to convey the mass and weight of this moment. The tears I try to keep at bay burn my throat like acid. I raise my hands, palms up. *Look around you, Anthony. How does it look? How does it look like I've been getting on?*

His eyes shift away from me. "I'm sorry," he says again. He looks from the lawn chairs filled with patients to the large building behind us.

"I don't know what to say, Stella. This is all a big mess." He pauses, then again, "Big."

I don't know if he's referring to the building or my life. Or both or none of those things. Big clouds up in the sky, big lumps in our throats.

"I couldn't believe when I heard—"

"You've changed," I interrupt him. I look him up and down. He is wearing slacks, a button-down shirt, and a coat. "You're all grown now."

He tells me about West Point and serving in the army for the past ten years, and that he works for the FBI now. "But it's not as glamorous as people think. Lots of overtime and not enough sleep. Nothing like on TV."

"This place is nothing like TV, either. Not half as much fun as the Cuckoo's Nest, that's for sure."

He tells me about Abby, the woman he married two years ago. How he met her dropping off his dry cleaning. "I asked her out and here we are," he says and pulls out his cell phone. He taps and swipes and then hands me his phone.

A picture of Anthony in a blue uniform. Identification badges, bars on the sleeves, insignia on the shoulder loops, a black beret. I swipe the screen. Anthony in a navy suit and a pretty woman with long brown hair in a white sheath dress, flowers in her hair, on a beach somewhere.

"That's Abby. We got married on a beach in Hawaii when I was stationed there."

I swipe the screen again. Anthony and Abby in a sideways embrace against the backdrop of a mountain ridge. Abby is almost Anthony's height and very athletic. Next to them sits a black dog.

"That's Patton. We got him from the pound. Part shepherd, part Lab. He was hit by a car and had a broken pelvis and was about to be euthanized. We had to have his leg amputated a week after we got him but he has no clue he's got three legs."

I keep swiping through Patton at the dog park, Patton with a cone at the vet, Patton on the couch, sleeping on his back, three legs up in the air.

My brother got up one morning, put on a navy suit, and married a woman named Abby. He loves hiking and he adopted a dog with a shattered pelvis hours before he was to be euthanized. He named him Patton after an army general and war hero. And he has a sister who is in a mental institution, unable to remember what happened to her daughter.

"You're a lucky man," I say.

He smiles and I realize he must have had braces as an adult. I listen to him tell me about his wife, his job, not getting enough sleep, and going to dog parks. There's still an ordinary world out there, something easily forgotten in a place like Creedmoor.

"We should've stayed in touch. I don't know why we didn't." His voice sounds strained, as if the implications weigh him down.

"You called me in the beginning, I remember that," I say and turn my head as if to distract my mind, a physical attempt at moving on. "I guess we just lived our lives and before we knew it years had passed. And I moved a lot, it's just something that happened."

Anthony takes in a deep breath, holds it for a long time. "You've heard about Nell?" he asks. "She had a brain aneurysm, what . . . almost two years ago."

"No, I didn't know." I can't categorize what I'm feeling when

I hear Nell's dead. I don't think I feel any particular way about it. "How did you even find out I was here?"

Anthony looks at me, his eyes wide.

"What?" I say and shake my head. "Who told you?"

"Stella"—he cocks his head to the left like he did when we were children, right before he used to say something he wasn't sure should be said out loud—"people know you're here."

"People?"

"Do you have Internet in here?" he asks.

"Yes," I reply and catch myself scanning my surroundings as if we've decided to climb over the fence and make away. "But it's mostly blocked. No news." That's an understatement; all we really get to do is play solitaire. I swipe my finger over the screen. When I find the browser app, I type in my name.

"No, no, no," he says and reaches for his phone.

When I turn my back to him, he lowers his hands as if there's no use. The first link is a video. All I see is a blank screen with an hourglass. Then a cheery voice sounds.

Cate: "This is Cate Trent from WGBK in New York. Welcome to our viewers and welcome to today's guest. In our studio we have Liza Overton, host of *Current Crimes*.

"Liza, welcome. I'd like to start out with a quote from your show last night: 'It's not like the baby vanished. Come on, people, use your common sense. We have another baby killer on our hands.' Is this another one of your over-the-top comments? Isn't it too early to call this woman a killer? Are you trying to influence the opinion of your viewers for the sake of higher ratings?"

The image of an airbrushed woman with lip gloss and hair that doesn't move fills the screen. The picture stutters for a second, then continues. I recognize her immediately but cannot remember her name. She is a TV legal host, a former defense attorney turned prosecutor, turned victims' rights advocate, turned vengeful and eternally furious television journalist.

I look at Anthony. He looks away and the video continues.

Liza: "Thanks for having me, Cate, glad to be on your show. First of all, no one believes the kidnapper story. Legal experts agree that the circumstances are suspicious, to put it mildly. There are more questions than answers about what happened to the infant. She wasn't reported missing until the mother was found severely injured in a car upstate, roughly three hours from her home in Brooklyn, NY. What mother does not alert the authorities when her child goes missing? Let me answer that for you; a guilty one."

Infant. Mother. Severely injured. Upstate. Missing. Guilty.

Cate: "Authorities say that little evidence has turned up, and according to the police chief there are no indications that the parents had problems with custodial issues, they've been cooperative but the mother needs to answer some questions, and there are questions galore, I have to agree. Liza, give us your take on the fact that the mother didn't report the disappearance."

Liza: "Well, first of all, the more time goes by, the harder it is to remain positive. But the actions of the mother bother me. And no, *eventually* reporting the crime is not the same as screaming bloody murder when your kid's gone. But come on, Cate, let's get real. I'll break it down for you and your viewers."

Cate: "Go ahead, Liza, break it down for us."

Liza: "Let me tell you about mounting evidence that will lead to the killer—that's what this case is about. Evidence. Mom doesn't report her daughter missing. That in itself is suspicious, but there's more. Supposedly she doesn't show up for her daughter's doctor's appointment. Why not? I ask. I believe by the time the appointment came around, the deed had been done. Then there's the convenience store incident. According to my source she goes to a local convenience store and attempts to buy water—"

Cate: "Just to let our viewers know, the tapes have been released to the public in an ongoing effort to find additional witnesses who can account for the mother's actions the days before the disappearance of her daughter. Go ahead, Liza."

Liza: "Thanks for explaining that, Cate. So she goes to a local convenience store to buy water. But she doesn't pay for it, leaves it sitting on the counter! No word, nothing. And mind you, the stroller was covered in a blanket! The clerk never even saw the infant. For a baby that was supposedly colicky she's asleep peacefully in her stroller? So, the mother pretended to buy water but then doesn't, so the clerk remembers her later on, another part of her devilish plan to fool everybody around her into thinking the baby was still alive. And that's not conjecture, the clerk has spoken out publicly. And the store has CCTV, there's proof, I'm not making this up. All this is in evidence, Cate."

Cate: "I'll tell you how a defense attorney will explain that. If I were her defense attorney, I'd say maybe she changed her mind. That's not a crime, right? Maybe she forgot her purse or didn't have any money on her. Covering a stroller with a blanket? Cold weather? Too many people gawking at the kid? The infant was sleeping? There are many logical reasons. Not a crime, Liza, not by a long shot."

Liza: "Let me play devil's advocate, Cate. Let me tell you why I have no doubt that she's the perpetrator. She disregards the appointment because the baby is already dead! And she knows that, because she's killed her! And now she has a body she has to get rid of and she panics, doesn't know what to do with it. Textbook, by the way. She drives around not knowing where to go, and she drives and drives and ends up upstate. That's when she decides it's time to look for a place to dump this little innocent angel. Finally she has the courage to pull over and I'd bet my life on the fact that somewhere between her home and the accident site is a little grave in the woods with the remains of the child. But then, let me not go overboard here."

Cate: "Going overboard? In what way?"

Liza: "I'm giving this mother too much credit. She may not have buried her. Maybe she just dumped her in a river or a lake. I'm not going out on a limb here when I say that we will never recover the body. And days before that, she had walked into a police station, sat around like a bump on a log, threw up, and then left without talking to anybody. Again, on CCTV. Do we really have any doubts who killed the child? I don't!"

Cate: "There are sources, unconfirmed sources, which tell us that the mother suffers from amnesia. What do you make of the amnesia claim? And she did have pretty serious injuries, none of them considered self-inflicted, am I correct?

One could argue that she's a victim, we don't know what occurred, and we have to give her the benefit of the doubt."

Liza: "Let's go back. You asked me what do I make of it? Of course she has amnesia. Wouldn't you? Don't they all? Please! I'm convinced she killed that baby. As to the injuries, as far as I know, there's no proof either way, she was just banged up pretty bad from the accident. Driving in a ravine will leave some marks."

Cate: "But is the media to blame for the fact that people's opinions are swayed when the accused are by law innocent until proven guilty? Especially in a case like this, where a baby is involved, such deep-seated hatred among the public for mothers who hurt their own children. It's just an overall very emotionally charged case and don't we have to be vigilant not to draw unsubstantiated conclusions?"

Liza: "I don't want to speculate on what I don't know about the case, I'd rather stick with what I do know. And I know I don't give much credence to the mother's claims of suffering from amnesia. How convenient, how useful. 'I don't know what happened' is not going to fly when your baby is missing. At least some mothers try to elude authorities. Just ask yourself how many mothers have we seen, in tears, describing some phantom abductor, a black man, a Spanish-speaking hooded man in dark clothing? A carjacking or a masked intruder, whatever they decide to make up. Just check the records, there's more than one case. And in the end we find out they killed their children! But not her. No, ma'am, she just doesn't remember.

"But back to the facts of the case—it gets even better. Supposedly, according to a source close to the case, there are a couple of witnesses who allegedly saw her on the day the baby disappeared."

Cate: "Emphasis on *allegedly*. That's unconfirmed right now, Liza, which is my point exactly. Are you, and the media as a whole, going too far putting this on the air with an array of unconfirmed allegations?"

Liza: "Let me finish first. According to my sources, she was seen discarding a baby seat on a heap of garbage on her street. How do you explain that away, Mrs. Defense Attorney?"

Cate: "I see no need to explain unconfirmed witness reports, so-called witness reports, I might add. And I don't think that—"

Liza: "There's a witness who saw her handing a suitcase to a homeless woman around the time the baby disappeared. A suitcase large enough to contain a small body. Really, what else do we need to know? The evidence keeps mounting against her. What was in that suitcase? Don't we all want to know? And most of all, where is that monster of a mom? I tell you where she is. In a cozy psychiatric ward. How do you explain that, Cate?"

Cate: "Let's talk about that for a moment. She allegedly suffers from amnesia. She's been in a horrible accident, she has the injuries to prove it. She doesn't remember where her daughter is, she's in a psychiatric ward, in treatment, and we—"

Liza: "In hiding is where she is. Because decent mothers and concerned citizens are lining up in front of the city courthouse and demanding justice. How come she's not in jail? This is outrageous!"

Cate: "I was going to say, I don't think we need to rush to judgment here. One could argue that while you are crucifying her, she is trying to figure out what happened to her precious little girl."

Liza: "Wait a minute, wait a minute, Cate, that's not all. A neighbor of hers has spoken out as to her odd behavior. Not wanting anyone in her house, hearing the baby cry all hours of the day and night, even leaving her in the car unattended. Does that sound like a caring mother to you? It will all come out at trial. I'm not sure how a defense lawyer can explain all of that away."

Cate: "But, Liza, babies cry! And they do so all hours of the day and night. And she lived alone, her husband worked out of town. I'd be careful who I let in my house, too. Haven't we all been less than perfect as mothers? All I'm trying to say is that the media plays a huge role in the public's opinion of a defendant, and she is innocent until proven guilty."

Liza: "Even if you don't believe a word I just told you, be honest with yourself, the time frame is all we need. She waited too long to report the disappearance, actually didn't report it at all until she was found and questioned. Something's just not right. That's common sense, not an assumption."

Cate: "But is it right to dub the mother 'Amnesia Mom' in the press? How will she get a fair trial?"

Liza: "That's what she claims, right? She claims to have amnesia and therefore it is an accurate description of her, don't you think? When it comes down to it, Cate, I only say what ninety percent of the people are thinking. And as to the fair trial, a venue change is common practice. I, personally, can't wait for her to go to trial. I wouldn't be surprised if there was a guilty plea before the case was even heard."

Cate: "I don't know about that. I hope not, I hope people use their own judgment or rather withhold judgment until there's definite proof of guilt. I hope the jury is unbiased and of her peers, as the law requires.

"Thanks for being on our show, Liza. Razor-tongued, as always. We have to go to commercial. After the break we'll switch to the local news. Be right back."

The video halts, freezing the host's face in a grimace. There's more video links but I click on the browser's image tab. Photos of me, of Mia. Images of news stations. I recognize North Dandry. I'm everywhere, in every living room, Laundromat, gym, and radio station. At every doctor's office, every car showroom. Farther down, images of women I've never seen, empty eyes staring straight into the camera. Mug shots, orange tops. Some hold up a small board with letters. Name, number, police department.

"Amnesia Mom," I say and fight back the tears. I've been reduced to a mother without a memory, a caretaker guilty of harming her daughter. "I had no idea."

"I'm so sorry, Stella. So sorry." His eyes darken, tear up. Then they turn into slits. "She's nothing but a ratings whore, everyone knows that." Anthony slides the phone back in his pocket. "I'm sorry, I should have taken the phone from you. Every psychologist and psychiatrist is weighing in, everybody has something to say, and suddenly everybody is a subject matter expert. Reporters have called my house for weeks. No one is interested in the facts. These people are relentless and most of what they're saying has nothing to do with the actual truth. People know that, Stella." He pauses. Then he says, "They asked me if I thought you did this."

I want to ask *Do you think I did this?* but I know better. It takes me a moment to make sense of it. *Of course not,* he'd answer, smoothly. So smooth that I'd know he had thought about it before, rehearsed his answer.

Anthony keeps his eyes on me, then he shivers as if shaking off a thought that's making him uncomfortable.

"Before she died, Nell told me you left and she never heard from you again . . ."

"I've never forgotten how she wore Mom's brooch and her dress to the funeral. Who does that? Who wears her dead sister's clothes on the day of her funeral?"

Anthony shakes his head. "I remember the brooch. But it was Nell's brooch, I think. Mom had borrowed it and never returned it. I don't remember all the details, but the dress, I don't know, Stella. Nell was three inches taller than Mom and twenty pounds heavier. I don't think she would've fit in Mom's dress."

I feel anger inside of me. "That's what I remember. Are you telling me I made it all up?"

"I'm not saying you made it up. That's how you remember it."

"You left me, Anthony. There's nothing more to it."

"I couldn't be responsible for you . . . I was eighteen. I was a kid. I couldn't have raised you. I love you, Stella, but I had to leave."

"It was just so hard. I had *nothing* left. I was alone. I—"

"*We* had nothing, Stella. *We* had nothing. It was unfortunate, but what was I supposed to do? It happened to both of us . . . the accident, Mom, Dad, our sister. It happened to both of us, not just you. It was what it was. It wasn't going to be easy."

"I needed you, Anthony."

"I know you did and I should've been there. I was a kid. I wish I could do it all over again."

I don't know what to think. Did I expect too much, or did he give too little? I don't know anything anymore. I've believed so many things for so long. Believing something else now is hard. Maybe he's right. Maybe going down all these roads, of what could have been, is a lost cause. A treacherous path. We get the life we get and that's all.

"I brought you something," he says and reaches inside his coat and retrieves a shabby-looking book with worn edges. I immediately recall a book I used to read obsessively as a child, asking Anthony the meaning of words I didn't know. I finally realized that the words meant nothing and were just made up for a fantasy world on a nonexistent continent. I can't remember the title or the cover of the book, only that it was about a girl pickpocket, a thief.

"Do you remember this?"

It's not the book I long for, but a paperback, familiar, like a toy from my childhood, yet I can't make a connection. Looking at the book feels like seeing a person you know but cannot place. I read the title: *The 365 Funniest Jokes Ever.* I turn the book over and I flip through its pages. There are jokes, riddles, and a collection of funny stories. I see cartoons of elephants sitting on small chairs, men dressed up as women in wigs and aprons, puppies pulling diapers off babies, and the outline of a cat busting through a brick wall. Funny, childlike, silly pictures.

"I bought this book for you when you were about nine. You were always so sad and I wanted to cheer you up. I knew every single joke in this book . . . every single one. Just couldn't make you laugh. Not even the funniest jokes."

I feel as if I've let him down, back then and now.

"I read you one joke a day for an entire year. While I was rolling on the floor, laughing, you never even cracked a smile. Don't you remember?"

I just shake my head. I was nine; I should remember something. I just stare at him and my eyes fill with tears.

"Knock, knock." Anthony's voice is soft now.

When I don't say anything, he repeats it. "Knock, knock," he says, looking at me with anticipation.

"Anthony . . ."

"Knock, knock."

"Anthony, stop . . ."

"Knock, knock."

"Anthony, it wasn't funny then, it's not funny now."

"Just try, Stella. Just once."

I just close my eyes and try to imagine something else. But it's not working. I give up because I know he won't. "Who's there?" I say.

"Boo."

"Boo who?"

"Oh, boo hoo. Don't cry. It's just a joke."

I smile. *Boo hoo, don't cry, it's just a joke.*

"It finally worked." He pauses. "Don't cry, Stella, everything will be all right."

"Right," I say but I know nothing will be all right. Anthony has a wife, a dog, a life. This here is my life. Amnesia Mom. A news cycle amusement. Mothers all over the country are outraged. That's all I am in everybody's eyes. Guilty.

———

That night, as I flip through the pages of the book, I notice a hint of almond hiding in its pages, and like a rush of water, I remember a moment long past. Legs pulled up, I melted into the leather tufted wing chair in my father's study. I was never sure if Dad knew I was in his study or not; he just continued to brood over contracts, building codes, or historic preservation guidelines. I was reading my favorite book, *The King's Thief*, a fantasy novel about a truth-speaking thief and a king's jester so powerful he was able to turn upstanding people into liars. There were corrupt servants, a wicked lord, and guards set on suppressing an uprising. The plot, even though I must have read the book a dozen times, is now elusive. But I remember the map. With almost photographic detail I recall the woodcut-style village cabins, the river merely a black line separating the crowded settlement from the lord's vast estate. A mountain chain behind the castle, separating the flatlands from the rolling hills of the lord's hunting grounds. The village was surrounded by a hedge, adjacent to a pine forest. If you looked really close you could see the wolves lurking under the shrubs and twisted plants below the piney trees. The compass, instead of the four cardinal directions, was made up of the four elements.

Then my head starts spinning and my tongue feels as if it is too big for my mouth. A memory visits me, a map I bought at the newsstand. I close my eyes and hang on, stay in the moment.

Images pile up like heaps of leaves. *Newspapers, magazines. Cigarettes, candy, flowers. A soda dispenser. Chinking coins as a man with a turban dropped the change in an ashtray atop the* New York Times.

The next day, during our session, I curl up on the couch in Dr. Ari's office, a pillow propped under my arm. The file in front of us has no more secrets to give away—it is on me now to solve the rest of the puzzle.

"I remembered something last night," I say.

Dr. Ari sits quietly, his fingers interlaced, elbows propped up on his desk.

"Is there a map?" I ask and point at the folder in front of him.

Dr. Ari pulls out a thick piece of paper, folded numerous times, its edges bent and worn like a favorite childhood book. He shoves it over the desk's glass surface toward me and pushes the button of the digital recorder.

It's time to enter the elevator, to descend. I go down to the first floor, and feel an immense sense of calm. I take the map off the desk and hold it. I rub it between my thumb and index finger, feeling the folds of the thick paper, an origami riddle of creases and pleats that automatically unfold but are awkward to close. I descend farther.

I hear a loud popping sound ringing in my ears. It turns into a sharp pitch, and then my ears ring. I've heard this sound before. Something inside of me shifts; I smell gasoline, metal, and gunpowder.

I open my eyes and I look at Dr. Ari. Everything around me starts to buzz and then the world grows muffled as if I'm underwater. Dr. Ari's lips move but I cannot make out any words. The world around me switches to black-and-white and the silent movie is complete.

Roads, traffic lights. Rain, darkness. Upstate New York. A dot on a map. Dover.

CHAPTER 20

Dover, New York. Nine thousand people on less than sixty square miles. No major highways, just two thorough-fares. Numerous hamlets and rural communities too small to be considered villages were scattered and their inhabitants rooted within its soil like the knobbed and rugged oaks, leaning with the wind. No one lived out here unless they were born here or wanted to disappear. As I drove down Route 434 toward Anna Lieberman's house, I passed miles of dense trees that changed abruptly into open fields dotted with barns. The once-red boxes sagged toward the ground, stood abandoned, bleached and gray, ready to be taken over by nature.

Dover's Main Street was like so many Main Streets in upstate New York. The roads, lacking white center lines, followed along the hilly terrain, flanked by small wooden houses, roads worn, not so much by traffic, but by time. Concrete cracks wove their way along the roads like snail trails. Some of the cracks were filled in with black tar, some left to deepen and lengthen. The narrow sidewalks, distorted by tree roots, were broken up by T-shaped power-poles with their power lines draped from one pole to the next. The poles were ghostly onlookers of a parade canceled decades ago. The houses were covered by drooping roofs and surrounded by chain-link fences keeping old, arthritic dogs at bay.

Anna Lieberman's last known address was off Route 22. Anna and David were originally from Dover, yet the farmhouse they'd grown up in and that burned down back in 1982 was located so close to Oniontown that they might as well have been from there. Oniontown is a Hudson Valley hamlet of Dover, not actually a town, but a collection of run-down trailers and dilapidated farms.

When I arrived at Anna's, the sound of an ax splitting wood echoed down the street. A garbage truck's diesel engine revved on and off. I passed 126 Waterway Circle slowly, taking in the house and the yard. Anna's backyard was fenced in by seven-foot-tall sun-bleached poles.

The first word that came to mind was *warped*. The first of six houses off a cul-de-sac, 126 Waterway Circle appeared unkempt but not uninhabited. The entire neighborhood was dangling lightly off the ledge of being deemed ramshackle. There was a crooked FOR SALE sign posted in front of the neighboring house to the left of Anna's.

I parked the car on the main road instead of in front of the house, got out, passed her home, and continued down the warped sidewalk. I strained to read the sign in the front yard of 128 and I took out my cell phone. I had only 5 percent of battery life left and I wasn't going to use it on a call pretending I was interested in a house. I slid the phone back in my purse.

I turned and went up Anna's pebble walkway, a scraggly, fuzzy mess of stones and weeds cushioning my every step. An old Chevy Caprice with mismatched hubcaps sat under a carport partially covered by a blue tarp. The fence paint was chipped, the posts' concrete anchors gaped open, releasing the posts from their duty of keeping the fence in an upright position. Some fence sections were standing upright, some leaning, and one was flat on the ground. The overgrown yard was covered in knee-high weeds. Whatever shrubs and bushes there were appeared wilted, their dead leaves cracked and bare roots exposed to the elements.

On the front porch wind chimes dangled from the rafters above abandoned chairs. The chimes clinked a wretched song of despair while the strings holding the metal pipes in place were about to give in to gravity. Some of the missing pipe parts had been replaced by forks, their tines bent about randomly. The drooping black roof was patched with brown shingles.

The porch slumped worse than the roof. Two crates formed a makeshift table, with two folding chairs placed on either side of them. The chairs looked as if they had been stolen from a reception; their chipped gold paint alluding to a wedding ceremony long past.

I took a few deep breaths but couldn't keep my hands from shaking. My purse was heavy, weighed down by the loaded gun, more a good luck charm than anything else. I had never fired a gun before and the one in Jack's closet was the first I had ever held in my hand. It was a Taurus 905, a 9 mm, whatever that meant. The gun in my purse was unnerving me, adding to my tension, and the facts I had gathered about its operation started to merge into a ball of yarn; secure engagement, ready to fire disengagement, drop the hammer manually, pull the trigger while lowering the hammer with the thumb. I had spent an entire afternoon online looking up the mechanics and how to fire it, but I had a feeling that if it came down to it, handling it would leave me dumbfounded.

A hollow sound answered when my knuckles rapped the paint-chipped door. I waited what seemed like minutes. Then, like a scene from a Dutch painting, a petite woman stood in the doorframe, in her hands a basket filled with vegetables: carrots with wilted leaves, white bulbous turnips turned purple. There was another green leafy vegetable I couldn't identify, maybe water spinach or Swiss chard.

I recognized her immediately. Anna Lieberman's strawberry hair was tied in a knot at the nape of her neck. Some had escaped and made her look disheveled. She looked wholesome holding the fruit-and-vegetable basket, capable of extracting life from the earth's soil. Her hands were covered in mud, her nails rimmed with dirt. I looked up from the basket and met her eyes.

"Yes?" she asked as she considered me. She was visibly out of breath.

"I don't mean to intrude, I . . . I don't know, I have a question." I swallowed hard and forced my face into a smile. "I . . . I'm sorry to disturb you. You look like you were in the middle of something. I . . ."

She smoothed a strand of hair behind her ears. She then paused as if she had decided there was no use. Her smile exposed white crooked teeth. She put the basket of vegetables on a table in the foyer. The table held a sizable stack of catalogs, the top one a glossy cover of a Greek island, judging by the white houses with blue roofs and the azure ocean in the far background. Threadbare industrial carpet, frayed at the edges, extended over the threshold. She was barefoot.

"I was out back and I wasn't sure if I heard someone knock. How can I help you?" She looked me up and down.

"I wanted to ask you about the house. The one over there." I took a step back and pointed at the little white house next door with the FOR SALE sign in the yard.

She looked puzzled, as if she was unaware it was for sale or surprised that someone wanted to buy it.

"I don't know much about it. Maybe you should call the number on the sign and ask to see it?" She ended the sentence as if it was a question.

"How about the neighborhood, the schools? Is it pretty safe? How about break-ins? Real estate agents never tell you the truth." I added the last sentence to let her know that I valued her opinion.

"I wouldn't know about schools around here. I don't have much contact with the neighbors and I don't read the local papers." She kept holding her soiled hands up like a surgeon ready to make the first cut. "I need to wash my hands. Would you like to come in?"

"Thank you so much. Buying a house is a major investment. I just want to make sure I pick the right one."

She stepped back and I entered Anna Lieberman's house. The threadbare carpet turned out to be a square piece of leftover outdoor carpeting. The rest of the floor was covered in hardwood planks, creaking underfoot.

The house was old and worn, drafty even on this mild autumn day. Straight ahead was the living room, and another hallway to the left. The kitchen, to the right of the living room, led straight into the backyard. The house smelled of mold and musty carpets, traces of furniture polish and Lysol. There was a frayed couch with lifeless throw pillows and a crooked coffee table. Countless travel magazines with glossy covers lay strewn across the coffee table and the couch. Some cover pages were torn, others had rings from sweating glasses, leaving the pages warped. The rugs crunched like straw underneath my feet. The furniture was mismatched. It was the home of a woman who had furnished a house with hand-me-downs and donations, warped and worn, one owner short of ending up in a dump or a landfill. Yet it was as clean as one could clean an old house. The colors were muted, washed out, except for the shiny travel magazines.

Anna Lieberman led me through the hallway and into the kitchen, where she pointed to a chair by a table. She rapidly pumped the soap dispenser while the water was trickling. The soap was unable to cut through the mud, so she washed her hands twice but still didn't seem satisfied. As she applied the third round of soap, she asked, "I was just about to put on a kettle. Would you like a cup of tea?"

"I don't want to impose, really," I said. "You're very kind." I put my hands in my lap and interlaced my fingers to keep them from shaking.

"Tea it is." She opened a cabinet door and pulled out two chipped mugs. She switched on the stove and took two tea bags out of a canister on the counter. She dropped the bags into the mugs and sat across from me on the other side of the kitchen table. Anna Lieberman's demeanor seemed open and friendly, and I felt a sudden tinge of remorse for misleading her.

"I grew up around here and I'm looking to buy a house in the area," I said. My inventiveness surprised me. One believable lie after the other slipped off my lips. "Actually, I'm from Poughkeepsie," I added as I cupped the empty mug, trying again to hide my shaking hands. I had seen a sign by the road and remembered the name of a town just west of Dover. "I really like it here." My mind was racing. I didn't want the conversation to stall, but I couldn't think of anything to say. The silence stretched, became obvious.

Anna jerked ever so slightly when the kettle whistled. She poured boiling water into the mugs, turning it the color of cognac. A fruity aroma drifted toward my nostrils. When the wooden knob of a drawer didn't budge, she wiggled it left and right and then fiercely yanked at it. The drawer opened and she reached for a spoon while turning toward me.

"Poughkeepsie?" she said and nodded. "That's not far from here." She eyed the spoon in her hand, a spoon that seemed small, almost elfin, as if made for a child. New and polished, shiny with a lavender rubber tip, ill-suited somehow.

"About twenty miles west," I said and tried to ignore the image that burst into my mind of yet another spoon. A spoon—wasn't it mere days ago that I had held one just like this in my hand?—Mia's spoon, its lavender rubber tip turning white when food was too hot.

I looked toward the back door, then back at her hand again. Anna now held a regular teaspoon that didn't resemble the one from earlier at all.

Anna returned the kettle to the stove, and while she searched the cabinet for sugar, I took a closer look around the kitchen. The counters were worn and showed deep scratches and knife marks. The table and chairs were old and chipped from use. The buffet— the glass in the doors was missing—had been repainted. The paint, a buttery yellow with a green tinge to it, had been applied in a thick coat and the wood seams appeared caulked with paint. The linoleum floor tiles had risen around the edges and emitted a crunching sound. The fridge and the stove were ancient.

The kitchen counters were cluttered with empty flowerpots, bags of seeds, cookie jars overfilled with odds and ends. Torn pages with colorful pictures of beaches and resorts covered the counters, flowerpots and soil atop, as if I had interrupted her while she was planting, repotting, and pruning right here in the kitchen.

"You have children?" she asked and ran her finger around the top of the mug.

The question caught me by surprise. As she inspected her hands for cleanliness, I took in her shabby floral blouse and the skirt. The colors were faded, yet the blouse was clean and pressed.

"One. I have just one. A daughter." How peculiar it felt to speak of Mia as if she were safe at home with her father or a sitter. What was I even doing here? I asked myself. What did I expect to find? Lieberman wasn't here, his sister seemed to be some meek woman in an old run-down and drafty house, tending to a garden out back. Even more peculiar was the fact that I had no idea how to even steer her in the direction of her brother and my missing child.

As I watched, Anna pulled the tea bag from the steaming mug, never flinching as she squeezed every last bit of hot liquid out of it. She got up and stepped on the foot pedal raising the garbage can lid, dropping the tea bag into the can.

A foul, irritating odor hit my nostrils. The stench was stomach churning, sinister and heavy, permeating my every pore, yet it was sweet, with an undertone of clean in a putrid kind of way, a lemony scent maybe, but not quite as fresh, more chemical, like a potpourri. Like . . . a familiar odor, conjuring images of diapers piling up in the nursery, prompting Jack to shake his head in disapproval.

"Fertilizer," Anna said as she stepped off the foot pedal, closed the lid, and placed a hand on top of it, as if trying to contain the odor. "Smacks you right in the face, doesn't it?"

"Smells like dirty diapers," I replied. I had seen a baby spoon, now I smelled diapers? My anxiety was catching up with me and soon perspiration would begin to soak through my clothes.

"You wanted to know more about the area . . ." Her voice trailed off. She paused every so often and cocked her head as if she were trying to capture a melody coming from the far distance. "Let's see, there is a small park at the end of . . ." I let her go on and on, and smiled every time she looked up at me.

She was no longer the plain girl with the frizzy hair I had seen in the 1982 newspaper article. Sitting across from her, the differences from the older pictures of her became obvious; her face had lengthened; the bone structure was more refined, almost angelic.

I needed to know where her brother was, needed to know if he was capable of what I believed him capable of, and I wanted to hear the story of the fire, the story about her family, her brother's story, something, really anything that would explain what he had done. Was this another one of my thoughts going astray, a thought that started out as *I wish I could talk to his sister* and then ended with me in her kitchen drinking tea?

"You must be doing a lot of gardening," I said. "Just vegetables or flowers or both?" I looked at the floating tea bag inside my mug and reached for the sugar.

"A little bit of everything," Anna said and pushed the sugar bowl toward me. Her hand, free from the mud and dirt, seemed malformed, its movement suggestive of arthritic joints. The edges of the inside of her palms were pulled together by scars, affecting muscles and tendons, restricting the movement of her fingers.

"I didn't mean to bother you, I saw the house for sale as I was driving by, and I want to use some insurance money from my house in Poughkeepsie to buy a home here in Dover." I kept on going as if in a trance, trying to erase baby spoons and foul smells from my memory. I needed to focus and concentrate. "It's not a lot of money and I still have to buy furniture and appliances. Everything I owned"—I paused to make it more dramatic—"burned up in a fire. I have nothing left." I lowered my head, partly to play the role of a victim, partly because I didn't think I looked sincere telling the tale.

Anna didn't answer. I looked up to see the impact. Her eyes darkened and my words rested between us like the sugar cubes in the chipped bowl. She stirred her tea, her hands clasping the spoon, her index finger pointing aimlessly about.

I was good. I was surprised how good I was. I never thought that I'd be able to con my way into her house and then dupe my way into her kitchen. It was easy, surprisingly easy. I wanted her to gently descend into the past and reappear with a story. The story of the 1982 fire and her brother, David Lieberman. And then we'd talk about him being a kidnapper.

"A fire? Your house burned down?" Her voice cracked and her body shifted in the chair. Her spoon dropped with a *clang* back into her mug. "I'm sorry to hear that. Did anybody get hurt?" Her eyes were big, her pupils dark. She hid her hands underneath the table.

"No, it was just an electrical fire, some faulty wiring. I wasn't home when it happened."

My next question would be *So, you live here alone?* Then *Do you have family?* Then I'd say *A brother? Tell me about him*, then *I need to tell you something, I want you to hear me out. It's about your brother . . .*

Suddenly she cocked her head and got up, as if she'd heard something, as if a sound, undetected by me, was tearing at her. I heard a gentle whimper trail toward me. Almost like a baby's whimper the moment right before they wake up.

I'd seen, no, I had imagined Anna handling baby spoons, then I'd smelled diapers. There were bags of fertilizer and clearly she was a gardener; I had smelled odors that weren't there. Now I actually heard a baby whimper. I was afraid of what I was going to imagine next. I felt hot; sweat started to form on my forehead. In a matter of seconds my body was covered in it, forming freely like condensation.

"I think I better leave," I said and got up, knees shaking. "I'll have someone show me the house. You've been very kind, thank you for the tea." I grabbed my purse tighter.

She got up and walked me to the front door.

I reached for the doorknob.

"Wait!" Her voice made me turn around and stop in my tracks. "My name is Anna Lieberman. I didn't get your name?"

She knew nothing about me—so what did it matter?

"Estelle. Estelle Paradise."

I turned back toward the door, reaching for the knob again. She stepped past me and stood between me and it, a barricade.

"You're not looking for a house, Estelle Paradise. Why don't you tell me why you're really here?" Her eyes were piercing, demanding an answer.

I tried to think of something to say, explain myself, but my mind was blank.

"I'm looking for your brother, David."

"You're looking for my brother?" Her eyes flickered as if she was checking her brain for the puzzle pieces she needed to fit together to make sense of everything. I almost felt sorry for her. "Why would you come here asking me about a house and why would you talk about fires when you're really looking for my brother?" Her voice was soft, almost gentle now. "What is it you want?"

"I'm not here to cause you any trouble, I promise. I have questions."

She wore a puzzled expression, one I was unable to interpret. Confusion? Fear even?

Anna repeated, "What is it you want?"

Where to start. *My baby's gone, your brother took her. I found Tinker Bell in his apartment and strange newspaper articles.*

"I think your brother took my daughter."

"My brother took your daughter?" She looked around as if to make sure no one was watching us.

I kept looking at her, undeterred. "I need to talk to him. Tell me where he is," I said.

"I have no idea what you're talking about."

"This is not about you. Where is your brother?"

She was silent for a long time. "David, David, David," she finally said, shaking her head from side to side.

I raised my brows, clutching my purse. "He took my daughter. I have proof. I need—"

Anna shook her head again and gestured with her hand. *Stop making things up*, she seemed to say. "What is he to you? How do you know him?"

"We live in the same house. Do you know where he is?"

"I can't help you, you need to leave."

"I'm not leaving until you tell me where he is."

She put her hands on my shoulders, turned my body away from her, and started pushing me toward the front door. I turned back, pushed her hands off me, and looked her straight in the eyes.

"He took my daughter. Please tell me where he is."

"If you don't leave right now, I—"

"Just answer my questions and I'll leave. Please! He can give her back . . . and I won't tell the police."

We stood in silence for a while, then I heard her voice, childlike.

"Why don't you just go to the police then and tell them?" She stepped closer. I felt her hot breath on my face. She ushered me out the front door. "If you come back, I'll call the police myself," she said and slammed the door shut.

I fought the urge to knock again. I got in my car and sat without moving. The air in the car was sticky and stale, and I rolled down the window. There was a scent of ozone in the air as though a storm was approaching.

I glanced at an open window by the side of the house and watched Anna's silhouette holding an object in her arms. It was small and seemed to shift back and forth. Her silhouette bent over, one arm extended, grabbing something, and whatever it was she held in her arms, it stirred. It moved away from her body and then it broke out into a wail. A wail with a familiar urgency and intensity. The crying stopped as suddenly as it had started.

My hands started shaking with renewed vigor. Another cry sped toward me, making me gasp for air. There was a part of my mind that responded to its familiar frequency, some sort of acoustic cue of recognition, etched deeply into my brain. The baby spoon, the garbage smelling like soiled diapers, the whimper, no longer even close to being a figment of my imagination. My mind burst into a riot of images and questions, none of which I could understand or answer. A tremor took over my body and I felt as if millions of flames were igniting all over my skin. I closed my eyes and allowed the adrenaline to flood my body. This was real, this was a primal response to the wavelength of a baby's cry. Mia's cry.

Lightning exploded. Like two sides of a coin, thunder followed and a booming sound fell from the sky. Then the skies unleashed steady droplets of rain. The drips turned into large drops, then a million spatters covered the pavement. The air was fecund with the scent of soil and earth, and within seconds water ran down Anna's driveway and joined the runoff, disappearing into the storm drains of Waterway Circle.

Through the rain I watched a truck pull into Anna's driveway. The man who got out of the truck was the same man who had taken my child, and he was no more than one hundred feet away from me. David Lieberman opened the trunk, took out a bulky bag of what seemed like clothes or blankets. He walked toward the house and opened the front door, stomped his feet twice on the doormat, turned and scanned the skies, then stepped over the threshold.

All I could think of was to put my foot on the gas and drive, my brain paralyzed by the metronome-like *flip-flop* of the windshield wipers marking every inch of distance I was putting between my daughter and me.

CHAPTER 21

As I slowed the car and turned into a dirt road by a tree line, I passed one of the barns I had seen on my way into town. The unpaved path, rendered awash with mud, seemed as if it could easily bury car tires, and the standing puddles grew larger by the minute. I opened the car door and made my way toward the barn.

Inside, the heavy doors swung shut behind me. I heard the *pitter-patter* of the raindrops surrounding me like calming white noise. The inside greeted me with a scent of hay, manure, and the lingering perspiration of horses. The interior was even more dilapidated than I expected; the wood was cracked and gray, enduring the elements, bearing storms and scorching sun. One strong puff of wind, one more breeze catching the rafters just right, and it would be gone.

I had imagined this moment so many times, the moment I was going to find my daughter, yet I felt empty inside. I'd thought when the time came, I'd scream bloody murder, call 9-1-1. But none of that happened. My back propped up against a post, I sat on the ground, and I pulled my knees to my chest. I remembered the first night Mia had slept between Jack and me. The full moon had spilled through the windows, casting an eerie silver-blue hue on the entire room. Mia looked as if she were made of ice. Images popped in my head like jumpy disjointed pictures from an old reel-to-reel family movie. The hospital, Mia being born. Not sleeping, being hyperalert for days on end, being too tired to function and too tired to go to sleep. How I operated on autopilot, never really told Jack, never told the doctors or nurses, never told anyone. How I waited for it to pass, yet that moment never came. The storm had raged inside this little creature that I loved with all my might and nothing could turn the storm into something gentler. My milk not immediately coming in adding to the guilt I felt of not being able to provide for her. The intrusive thoughts that had begun to seep into my mind were elusive at first, then they had taken shape.

I reached inside my purse and cradled the gun in my hand. Something snuck into my mind and tore at me, this one image, this one thought, this one realization. Within all this darkness, I leaned toward this feeling of primitive attachment: When Mia was born and they put her into my arms, her eyes were covered in medical ointment. They were sleek, roaming, and unable to focus. As she slept, her little fist held on to the tip of my finger, her hand too small to grab it in its entirety. Her need to attach herself to me was ancient, primal, her thin and translucent skin stretching over her skull, her weightless hair, her purple nails, like a message from the universe.

With the gun in my right hand, I forced myself to imagine the future, and I completed the story. I saw flashes of a girl, her life, a succession of milestones—crawling, walking, running—flashes that were branded into my mind.

Mia dancing, twirling, reaching for a hand to keep her from falling.

Reaching for me. Bows in her hair.

Bandannas tied around her head like good luck charms.
Chipped nail polish and crooked tiaras.
Birthday cakes.
Playground games and friends and sand castles.
Good-night stories.

While I sat there, staring at the icy metal of the muzzle, seconds before I'd allow a bullet to rip a hole through my brain, in that very moment, I felt as if some higher power was watching over me, sitting on the dirt floor of the barn next to me.

Rain ran down my back when another lightning burst followed by thunder shook the barn, sending a spark of light through the holes and gaps of the rafters and the worn-out wood. For a second a bright flicker descended onto the ground, dirt particles floating about like magic fairy dust.

I remembered my mother's voice, soft and soothing, telling me that thunder is the sound that lightning makes, how one thing occurs and another follows. I knew it was not too late. Mia was a drop of ink in a glass of water; I was forever changed by her existence and she was right down the road. I left the barn doors gaping open behind me, got in the car, and drove back to Dover to claim my daughter.

When I reached Waterway Circle, the wipers squeaked their way across the windshield, a motion allowing, even if only for a second, an unobstructed view of the world. Suddenly everything was clear. There was no more room for interpretation, just my heart beating in cadence with my daughter's heart in the house in front of me.

The rust red Chevy Caprice still sat under the carport, Lieberman's truck was still parked in front of the house. I got out of the car, walked to the front door, and knocked. There was no answer.

"Anna, I need to talk to you." I knocked again. "Anna, please, open the door."

I knocked again. Nothing.

I stepped away from the house to get a good look at the nursery window and saw that the shades were drawn. Suddenly I heard the front door screech and Anna stood in the doorway.

"Yes?" she asked, her right hand resting casually on the doorframe. Anna now wore a pair of jeans and a T-shirt, and had her hair in a high ponytail. She also wore makeup.

"Anna, I heard her cry. I know you have my baby. I know all about—"

"I think you've got the wrong house." She hesitated for a second, then furrowed her brows. "Are you okay? Are you in some kind of trouble?" Anna looked over my shoulder, scanning the street. "You're soaking wet."

"No, no, no, no, no. Please don't play games with me. I know what I heard, and I smelled diapers, I saw the baby spoon." I reached inside my purse and grabbed my phone. "I'm calling the police."

A shadow appeared next to Anna: David Lieberman, the Prince of Darkness. And together they stood on the front porch, like Grant Wood's image of *American Gothic*, only more sinister and without the pitchfork.

"Is there a problem?" David Lieberman spoke softly, as if not to upset me any further.

"Where's my daughter?"

They both stepped farther out on the porch. I took a step back.

"I told her she's at the wrong house. Maybe a mix-up or something? She's insisting on a baby being here," Anna said, her voice slow and soothing.

"A baby?" Lieberman put his arm around Anna's shoulder. "Like my wife told you, maybe you got the wrong address?"

"Tell him, Anna, tell him I was here. And I know you have a baby upstairs, my daughter, Mia. I heard her cry. Tell him I was here earlier, tell him, Anna."

She remained perfectly still. "I have no idea what you're talking about. I've never seen you before in my life. You're not making any sense."

"We sat in your kitchen, you made tea, and the cups were white, with yellow flowers, you—"

"I've never seen you in my life."

My voice turned into a pleading stream. "You made tea for me, and you told me about the house next door. We talked about the neighborhood." I stopped just long enough to catch my breath. "You plant vegetables in your garden. And flowers. You have my daughter. He"—I pointed at David Lieberman—"lived upstairs from me in Brooklyn and he took her from me. He climbed down into my kitchen, he took her, and I want her back."

David Lieberman's face was blank. "Lady, there's no baby, there are no teacups with yellow flowers, no diapers, none of that. I don't know what to tell you but you're freaking my wife out and I need you to leave." His voice rang false, high-pitched, almost forced in its controlled state.

"I was here earlier. Please, Anna"—I pointed at the chime dangling off the rafters—"all this was here earlier. The chime, the chair on the porch, the house next door for sale, everything."

"You don't take no for an answer, do you? I'm telling you you're at the wrong house and I need you to stop screaming on my porch and leave. We don't know you."

I stuck out my neck, trying to look past them into the house. They mistook my movement as threatening and David Lieberman stepped forward, grabbing Anna's hand. They were closing ranks.

"Don't come any closer. Get off my porch."

I took a step back, decided to play my last trump card. "I'm going to call the police. They'll sort it all out." I held up my cell phone. "I'm not bluffing. I'm calling the police." I pushed a random button and the phone came on just long enough to see the charge indicator blinking. Then it turned off.

"Go ahead—call the police."

"My phone is dead," I said, barely able to control the tremor in my voice.

Lieberman reached in his pants pocket, pulled out a cell phone, and waved it in front of me. "You should always charge your phone. In case of an emergency, you know." Lieberman smiled.

"Is this a joke to you? Is this a game you're playing?" I took a step forward and picked up the chair on the porch. "I will scream so loud the entire neighborhood will hear me."

Their faces remained blank—not so much as discomfort in their demeanor. Anna turned and disappeared into the house.

"Go ahead," Lieberman said and put his hands in his pants pocket. "For someone who goes around knocking on doors and accusing people you're not very convincing. I'm just trying to help you," he said and shook his head.

"Someone help me," I screamed as loud as I could. "They have my baby. They took my daughter from me. Help." I lifted the chair up in the air and pointed its legs toward the window next to the front door.

Lieberman looked at me in disbelief. He stepped forward and grabbed my left wrist and shook it until the chair landed on the porch. I jerked away from him but he held on to my fingers and bent them backward, making me wince.

"HELP. I NEED HELP."

Lieberman grabbed my wrist and pulled me toward the front door. I managed to leave bloody streaks down his forearm when a flashing light made both of us turn around.

A police cruiser came to an abrupt stop and two uniformed officers walked toward us. One of them spoke into the radio attached to his shoulder. Lieberman let go of my wrist.

"What's going on here?" asked the older and heavier of the two officers. "Tell me what's going on here."

"You need to search the house. They have my baby," I said and ignored his hands gesturing me to step back farther.

"I need you to calm down and follow my instructions. Please step off the porch. I need to see some identification."

"You asked what was going on. I'm trying to tell you—"

"Identification?"

I pulled my driver's license out of my wallet and I handed it to him. He glanced back and forth between me and the picture.

"Now tell me what's going on."

"I need you to search the house. They have my daughter. I was here earlier and now they pretend they don't know me."

"I need you to explain the situation to me, I don't need you telling me what to do."

"My baby is in there, I need you to—"

"Please, I can't just conduct a search of a private property, it doesn't work that way."

"How does it work then? How can I get you to search the house?"

"Who called 9-1-1?"

"One of the neighbors must have heard me scream and—"

"I did, I called." Anna stepped back onto the porch and folded her arms in front of her body. Her voice was shaky. "This woman knocked on our door. She's not making any sense and I need her to leave."

"Sir?" The police officer looked at Lieberman. "What's going on there?" he said and pointed at Lieberman's arm. "Your arm's bleeding. Are you hurt?" The second officer gestured for me to follow him and led me to the front lawn, away from the house. "Tell me what's going on."

"He's my neighbor," I said, pointing at Lieberman. "I found a figurine from my daughter's room, and he took my daughter. She's in this house." I pointed at 126. "I heard her cry through the window and I—"

"I'm having trouble comprehending your story."

"No, no, no, you don't understand." I took a deep breath in, hoping it would allow me to sound more coherent. "Look," I said and reached into my purse for the Tinker Bell figurine.

He stepped back and put his hand on the holster of his gun. "Do not reach inside your purse again. Take your hand out and calm down so we can make sense of this."

I jerked my hand back.

The first cop glanced left to the FOR SALE sign in the yard of the house next door. He turned toward David Lieberman. "Is this your residence, sir?"

"That's correct. I live here with my wife."

"Come back over here, Mrs. Paradise. But keep your hands to yourself and follow my instructions." The junior cop and I joined them on the front porch. "You live on"—he studied my driver's license again—"517 North Dandry, in New York City. This gentleman"—he pointed at David Lieberman—"lives at 126 Waterway, Dover. Hours away from your address."

"He's my neighbor, he lives above me. There's a dumbwaiter and I found—"

"Just answer my question. How is he your neighbor if you live hours apart?"

"He's my upstairs neighbor at 517 North Dandry. Why won't you believe anything I'm telling you?"

"Ma'am, let me assure you, I'm not making any assumptions. It's just that you're not making any sense. We received a call about a trespassing violation. You trespassed onto their property and—"

"Why don't you ask them for identification? This is David and Anna Lieberman; they are brother and sister, not husband and wife."

"I don't need to identify myself," Lieberman interjected. "I can't help crazy people coming to my door. I have rights, you know." Lieberman threw the officer an "I told you she was crazy" look.

"This back-and-forth is not helping any. Please step over here with me, and you, sir, ma'am, please stay on the front porch until I'm done questioning the lady."

We moved down the driveway. I realized that my clothes and hair were soaking wet and that, with every step, my feet made a squishing sound. I was afraid he'd ask me to hand him my purse, where he'd find the gun. If he did, I'd be handcuffed and in the back of the cruiser before I could explain anything else.

"Okay, Mrs. Paradise, one thing at a time," the first cop said and took out a small green notepad. "You are reporting that they have your baby and that he's your neighbor. Is he the father of the baby? I'm not sure I'm following you." He closed his notebook. "What I can tell you is that I have no legal cause to search their house. You're hours away from where you live and I can't make sense of your story."

"Why won't you just search the house?"

"Because—"

"Because it doesn't work that way, I remember."

"Officer," Anna called over from the front porch, "this is just a mix-up. I think she's got the wrong address."

"We've been telling her that all along," David Lieberman said and put his arm around Anna.

"I understand, sir, I'll be with you in a minute."

When the officer turned toward me, I continued, "Mix-up? This isn't a mix-up. He took my child. I was here earlier. She told me to leave and I heard my baby cry. I followed him here from Brooklyn."

"You followed him? Why didn't you go to the police where you live?"

"I did, I tried, but . . ." I was going in circles. I knew that if I continued this route, I was going to end up in a psychiatric ward in this godforsaken town.

"Ma'am, is there anyone we can call to pick you up? Your husband, a friend, anyone?"

"I don't need anyone to pick me up."

"I'm doing you a favor here. This can go either way and I'm offering to call someone to pick you up."

"Let me just show you what I found—"

"I told you before not to reach into your purse. Are you on any medication? Are you in treatment for any kind of mental illness? Now would be the time to tell me."

"No, no, no. I'm . . . Why are you asking me this? Why don't you ask him what kind of medication he's on? Ask him if he's crazy. He took my child. He's the one—"

"Mrs. Paradise, honestly . . ." Then his face lit up. "Ah, now I get it." He closed the notepad and turned a dial on the radio attached to his shoulder.

"I'm telling you the truth. If I—"

"Relax, Mrs. Paradise. I know what this is," he interrupted me. "You're the girlfriend and you're trying to keep it a secret from his wife. You probably stood in the rain watching the house. You followed him out here and you realized he has a family. He"—and he pointed at Lieberman—"is pretending he doesn't know you. Which, by the way, is not a crime. You, on the other hand, you could be charged with disturbing the peace and trespassing. And that doesn't include the scratches on his arm, that's an assault charge. You are potentially in a lot of trouble."

I had seen him earlier getting clothes from the backseat and with any luck . . . "His car, can you check his car, just look through the window. If there's anything like baby clothes, diapers, formula, anything, then you'll know I'm telling the truth."

I turned around. Everything about Lieberman was wrong, his smile seemed pasted on and there were two dark wet patches under each armpit.

"Please, just look through the car window, you'll see," I said and watched Lieberman's face change to straight fear. His shoulders were hunched, his movements uncoordinated. He kept moving toward me, yet his body seemed to be going sideways at the same time. His face was paper white. He leaped off the porch, causing the officers to put their hands on their holsters.

"My husband isn't feeling well." Anna Lieberman pulled him back, holding on to his arm while wrapping her other arm around his waist. "We haven't done anything wrong. I think we're done here."

"Sir," the cop called over to the porch, "do you want to file charges for assault against this lady?"

"We're not filing any charges, Officer. This is just a mix-up." Anna Lieberman sounded convincing, and if I didn't know any better, I would have believed her myself.

"Please check their car, you'll see—"

"That's enough." His voice was harsh, his eyes stern. "Either you get in your car and leave or I'm going to put these cuffs on you," he said and pointed at his duty belt.

I wanted to drop to my knees. I felt like a little child whose parents insist that there are no monsters under the bed. No one was going to help me, because they believed me to be a lunatic. I gave him a halfhearted smile and held up my car key.

"You folks are free to go about your business," he called to the front porch, then he turned toward me. "I'm going to consider this issue resolved. I will escort you to 434 and we will forget about all of this. Just a lot of paperwork over nothing and these good folks over there have somewhere to be. Four-thirty-four will take you straight back to New York City," he said and motioned me to get in my car.

We reached exit 434 and the officer in the passenger seat waved to the right. I took the exit and the cruiser disappeared from my view. I had to give it to the Liebermans: discrediting me in front of the cops and getting away with it was bold. My appearance, wet and disheveled, hadn't helped, I was sure. What was I to do? Enter the house, gun in hand, and demand my daughter back? There was only one thing no one would be able to discount: DNA. All I had to do was prove to the police that the baby in Anna's house was mine and science was on my side.

In order to get the DNA I had to return to Anna's house. While I thought about how to proceed—maybe snatching a dirty diaper from the garbage sitting on the curb—I quickly realized I had missed my turn and passed my exit altogether. I pulled over and turned off the ignition. I switched on the overhead light and unfolded the map, struggling with its size. After a few minutes I gave up.

Daylight had faded and traffic had turned from sparse to non-existent as the autumn night became thick with darkness, sticky almost, as if covered in ink. The moon, like a ghostly apparition in flight, appeared and disappeared behind thick clouds.

A set of headlights emerged out of nowhere as if a car had silently approached with the lights off and had just now turned them back on. Slowly the car pulled up behind me but no one got out. It rolled another foot or two forward, then stopped. The car's lights went out and it was dark again. I kept staring in the rear-view mirror. I couldn't make out any movements behind me—it was more a hunch than anything—but suddenly my heartbeat went into overdrive. I reached for the gun in my purse without taking my eyes off the mirror.

Finally, a car door opened. Before my mind realized what was happening, my body reacted. My elbow hit the central locking mechanism and my brain messaged my body to start the car. At that very moment, the back window shattered and shards of glass rained on the rear seat. Then all went quiet.

I sat paralyzed with fear. Out of the corner of my eye, I saw a shadow by the driver's window. I grabbed my purse, scooted into the passenger seat, and reached for the passenger-side door handle. The driver's-side window shattered next and I covered my face with my arms. As I reached to open the passenger door, someone tugged at my hair through the driver's window and yanked me back into the driver's seat. My scalp pounded with pain. I turned my head and a shadowy man stood next to my car.

Fate may visit unannounced, but once it knocks, you know nothing will keep it from entering. Insanity hung in the air, a jumbled scent of sweat and wrath. The Prince of Darkness had come for me. And he was mad.

CHAPTER 22

"Take a deep breath," Dr. Ari says.

I can't contain the panic, it unfurls like a ball of yarn, expanding through my entire body. My breath comes in short spurts as I press the palms of my hands deep into the cold leather of the couch. I try to concentrate but my eyes scamper.

"I need to speak with the detective. They are looking for them, right? What are they doing to find them? All this here, what we're doing, doesn't matter at all. We have to find Mia."

"Let me reassure you that police are doing everything in their power to locate them." He pauses for a moment as if something is irking him. "We haven't reached the end."

"The end?" I ask.

"We have to continue . . . there's just too many questions unanswered," he replies.

I feel the need to retreat for a short while, seek shelter like an animal before birthing her young. "What does Muhammad say about fate, Dr. Ari?"

"Muslims call fate one of the pillars of faith. I know what

befalls me couldn't have missed me, and what misses me could not have befallen me."

Dr. Ari wipes his forehead with the palm of his hand as if to remove invisible pearls of sweat, maybe his way of clearing his mind. Suddenly I realize he is as much afraid of the truth as I am.

Reliving the moment when Lieberman's hand came through the shattered window and unlocked the car door coats my entire body in a layer of sweat. I recall Lieberman's unnaturally long fingers reaching for me, like a sprout of some bloodsucking plant. Suddenly it's all so clear. Bright as daylight, my memories reconcile, gather like oil on top of the ocean surface.

Lieberman's eyes were feverish, dark and intense. The interior overhead light bathed us in a golden glow and the moonlight caught bits and pieces of lunacy in his eyes and reflected them toward me.

"And so we meet again," he said and smiled wickedly.

Having to fight, hurt, or kill him horrified me, but I was determined. Whatever panic took over my body, I would not allow it to reach my mind, and I'd contain it and use it to my advantage. I wasn't shaking, I wasn't crying. I took my fear and hauled it into the darkness. This moment was as inevitable as the black night around me, and wanting Mia back was the only thought I had left.

"You worthless piece of shit." Lieberman's voice was sharp. He no longer was the man who had lied to the cops earlier, the man who had leaped off the porch. His eyes darted about as if voices in his head were tossing him left and right. "Next time you visit my home without an invitation, you should be more careful." His voice had turned into a hiss.

Occupying the same space with him was electrifying. Did he think it was his God-given right to take someone's daughter? What kind of madness ruled his world? Was I supposed to just let it be and let him keep her, walk away without a fight? As I watched his eyes dart about, I realized logic might not be familiar to him anymore.

"Get out of the car."

"Where is my daughter?" My lack of fear was mutinous as he reached for the door and opened it. I didn't move.

"I told you to leave us alone. Why did you come all the way out here and harass my girlfriend?"

We had just begun, but already I was lost. Anna Lieberman was the girl in the paper, his sister. She looked just like the photo in the newspaper.

"What girlfriend? The one you called your wife earlier? You mean your sister, Anna?"

"Who are you to tell me who we are? Why'd you have to come out here? Everything was fine until you came up here." With these words, he waved a gun, motioning me to get out of the car.

The colorless moon covered the world in shades of gray. The clouds had given way to a starry sky, and the moon was bright as if someone had flicked a switch. For the first time I could clearly see my surroundings. We were parked by the side of a cornfield, a dirt road running adjacent to the cornfield. A few gnarled trees obscured the field to the right. I got out of the car, stood in front of him, and I was surprised by how short he was.

Behind him, I made out the silhouettes of cornstalks and sucked in the pungent aroma of wet soil. A dirt road led between the cornfields, cutting them neatly in two halves. The dark night seemed unforgiving, leaving no room for mistakes. A few hundred yards down that dirt road and I'd all but disappear into the darkness.

"You should've left when you had the chance."

"I'm not leaving without my child. You should know that by now."

"Everybody thinks you are incapable. Even the cops."

"You know nothing about me," I said and dug my feet into the gravel.

"Get down on the ground."

His voice was full of anticipation but I stood unwavering. "I'm not going anywhere."

"You go where I tell you to go, sweetheart. And you're going down." He grabbed my arm and twisted it behind my back, forcing me onto my knees.

"The cops are still around making sure I leave town. They'll be here any minute," I said, but we both knew not a single car had passed us since he had pulled up behind me.

"You're just a deranged stalker, remember? No cop is looking for you, trust me." He took a step back and pointed the gun at me. "Stay on your knees," he added, "and don't try anything stupid. Put your hands on your head so I can see 'em."

I interlaced my hands on top of my head. Facing the cornfield, I heard footsteps walking off into the distance. I turned my head and watched him as he leaned through the broken car window, searching my purse. He stuck his hand in, then pulled out the gun. He walked to his car and, through the open window, dropped it on the passenger seat. He looked left and right as if to find a perfect spot to do to me whatever his crazy mind was telling him to do. As he peered down the dirt road, he was confident, so sure of himself, that he was pulling the strings. His smugness forced strength I didn't know I had to boil to the surface.

I darted toward the cornfield and the second I crossed the outer limits and made it through the initial rows of cornstalks, I knew I was in trouble. The rain had soaked the soil and after a few steps the muck sucked at my shoes and made my feet heavy. I felt as if I was stuck in one of those dreams where my legs don't obey and regardless of how hard I try to get away, my feet won't cooperate.

I made my way straight down a path. After about twenty feet, like a rabbit, I made a sharp turn as if avoiding a predator. I took only a couple more steps and collided legs-first with a solid structure. The impact made me drop to the ground with my shins throbbing and my kneecaps pulsating with pain. With the moon high above, I made out a small wooden booth with a partial roof, a swinging side door, and a wooden sign with chipped paint.

CORN MAZE ENTRANCE. PLEASE PURCHASE TICKETS HERE.

Sucking sounds heralded his approach before I could make up my mind which direction to turn. Whatever disadvantages the wet soil had imposed on me also applied to him. I got up and after a few stumbles caught myself and continued down the path. There was one trail leading to the left, one to the right. My knees were in such bad shape that running was no longer an option and I decided to hide between the stalks. I crouched down, sat in the mud, and willed my breathing to slow. I waited, childlike, with closed eyes, hoping that if I didn't see him, he wasn't going to see me, either. My heart beat like a drum in my chest as I waited.

Click. The cocking of a gun coincided with my sucking air into my nostrils.

He came up from behind, forced my hands to my back, almost dislocating my shoulders. He held on to my arms behind my back, pulled me to my feet, and with each step the pain in my knees intensified. When we reached the parked cars by the roadside, he gave me a shove. I fell knees-first on the ground. I tried to stay still but the spiky gravel digging into me made my eyes tear up. The agony in my knees produced colorful eruptions of lights tracing back and forth behind my closed eyelids. I moaned, which made him snicker. He slid something around my wrists. Judging by the *ziiiip* sound of it, he was attaching plastic handcuffs.

When I looked up, he was standing in front of me, his outline framed by the moon. He was slick with sweat and the moonlight caught a shiny object in his right hand; a knife blade flashed a clandestine Morse code spelling deep gashes and blood soaking the already-saturated soil. We locked eyes—three, maybe five seconds or more—and I found it impossible to tear away from him.

"Who's after who now, huh? You aren't cut out for this, you

should've never come after us," he said, taunting me with the knife in short, deliberate surges toward my face.

"Where's my daughter?" My voice was small, puny, not at all how I intended it to be.

" 'Where's my daughter?' " He mocked me, then lunged again, the high sheen of the blade a promise of things to come. "Why are you worried about her now? It's not like you took care of her. All that crying, day and night. Was it so hard for you to take care of such a little thing? Why'd she cry all the time? You probably didn't feed her, didn't change her. Why'd you have her?"

"Mia, where is she? Where is my daughter?" I insisted.

He was so close that I could smell his sweat and his anxiety. He was going to take pleasure in holding the handle of the knife while twisting it into my flesh, the warm blood feeding his frenzy. Then he'd get off coiling fabric and tightening it around my neck while watching my eyes protrude and my face turn blue. The way he was going to kill me was not important; watching me die would make his day.

"How'd you figure it all out? You didn't strike me as the quick-witted kind," he said. He was inches away from me, and when he lifted his right hand, I closed my eyes. He got so close that I could smell his breath.

"You thought you had the perfect plan but you made mistakes."

"All I had to do was get you out of the house. I hid your wallet, I prepared all those baby bottles, and left you a bottle of my special water. Made you sleepy, didn't it?" He snickered and his face switched from normalcy back to lunacy, his eyes piercing, shifting about. "That night, I came in through the dumbwaiter. While you were knocked out in your bed, I stood over you with your crying baby in my arms, and you didn't even wake up. I just walked out the front door with your kid and came back later through the shaft and locked the door. And the only mistake I ever made was that I didn't shut you up sooner."

"You left her blanket in the attic. That was your first slipup."

His eyes darted about. "I must have dropped it when I left the building through the attic. A tiny detail I overlooked, not really important."

"Your second mistake was that you kept the Tinker Bell charm. Like any other sick fuck you kept something so you'd get off on what you did every time you looked at it. And you call *me* crazy?"

He laughed and stepped forward, made more stabbing motions toward my face. "You wanna know where the baby is? In good hands. Better hands than yours, that's for sure. Anna and I, we'll find a nice family for her."

His face was just an inch from mine, his lips parted as if he was trying to kiss me. I closed my eyes. I felt his lips on my cheek, barely touching my skin. I remained still, forced myself not to jerk away from him. Then his lips were on mine, his tongue forcing mine apart. I tried to ignore my bladder, but there was no use. I hated the fact he had this power over me. I turned my head and spit on the ground, wiping my lips on my shoulder.

I felt the knife pressing against my ear.

"She has a family," I said and looked up at him, determined not to show fear.

His eyes darkened and his hand jerked. I felt a sharp pain on the side of my head.

"Why are you doing this to me?" I screamed, feeling blood trickle down my neck, lazily tickling my skin.

"That was for not listening to her crying." He looked at me with his feverish eyes, pleased to have me on my knees. "You can't imagine the fun I had messing with your head. I'd go in your house while you were gone, I sat on your bed, ate your food. And you had no clue. I did you a huge favor. What are you even complaining about?"

"You kidnapped my child!" The last word came out in a howl.

His brow furrowed and he tilted his head to the right. "You're one sick, clueless bitch. *Kidnapped* is what you call that? I was the knight who came along to save the day. I tried to tell you in so many words she was crying too much, that you didn't hold her enough. I was waiting for you to tell me how she was too much for you, how you were overwhelmed, tired, couldn't cope. All you had to do was tell me she was too much and I would have helped you. But you just shut the door in my face."

"I saw the book on your shelf about torturing and killing children. You want to tell me you're some savior when all you are is a lunatic stealing other people's kids. I am not the sick one, you are."

"If you had only bothered to read on you would have discovered the man you think was a monster was a hero. He was destroyed by false testimony, he was not the monster everyone made him out to be."

"I don't care about your books and heroes. This is the real world and you climbed through a dumbwaiter in the middle of the night, stealing my child and taking her to your sister or whoever she is."

"Your baby cried all day and all night. She cried for hours, and you didn't do anything about it. You left her screaming her head off. What kind of mother are you?" I saw revulsion in his eyes and felt droplets of projective saliva on my face. "I did you a favor by taking her."

"If you thought I was a bad mother, you should've called CPS." My voice had gotten louder and louder, the last words made it crack. I decided to plead. If he had any feelings left behind those eyes, he might listen to me. "This is just a misunderstanding and you can end this right now, please, just give her back and I won't tell anybody. I'm begging you, give her back."

His features relaxed and he looked almost normal. He smiled and I wanted to believe that some sanity had returned to him. I felt hope, but then he retreated back into his feverish state. His eyes became dark, as dark as the endless sky above us.

"This is a big misunderstanding. Please give me my daughter back. Please . . ." I was sobbing now, trying to free my hands. The plastic cuffs cut into my wrists.

"What did Anna tell you? No offense, Anna's my girl and all, but she's never told it straight in her life. What did she tell you?"

When I didn't answer right away, he started screaming, "WHAT DID SHE TELL YOU?"

"Nothing. She told me nothing."

He sucked in one deep breath as if he had just emerged from minutes under water. "When I was a kid, I had just one wish. That someone would come and take me from my parents. My mother was just like you."

"You're getting it all wrong."

"Shut up and listen!"

"You got it all wrong, I'm—"

"*I'm* the one getting it wrong? No, you're the one who got it all wrong. You left her in the car. Everyone knows you don't leave a baby in the car."

"You hear a baby cry and you make up this entire story."

"I know what mothers like you are capable of."

"Mothers like me? You know nothing about me."

"I know the likes of you."

The likes of me. To him I'm *one of those mothers.* An abuser. A mother who neglected her child.

Lieberman started pacing back and forth, the blade gleaming in the moonlight. I watched him, hypnotized by his movements.

"Why did you take her? I don't understand—"

"I took her because you didn't want her. I don't care what you're telling me now, you did not want her." He paused for a second, then smiled. "Some mothers are like that."

And then he told his story, the story of the boy he used to be. I listened as he painted a picture of his childhood and he took shape in my mind, a kid growing up in a strange part of rural America inhabited by peculiar people and far removed from romantic notions of wooded hiking trails. Between moments of unintelligible ramblings and pacing in circles, he spoke of his parents, Esther and Gabriel Lieberman. I wanted to ask questions but then I thought otherwise. I decided to allow him to peel back the layers of his madness. He was a little boy, about eight years old, he said, Anna, about five. He spoke of how they trudged around the only neighborhood they knew: dirt paths and dead-end roads. His childhood was spent around a cluster of houses without electricity and running water, just a collections of trailers and shanties, surrounded by lots of garbage and not a glimmer of hope.

At times Lieberman turned and listened to the darkness, his eyes scanning the night as if he was making sure no one else was witnessing his story of living in squalor and misery in an old farmhouse without a foreseeable exit out of a hellish life. Other times his voice would soften unexpectedly, especially when he spoke of his "rescue," his "new family," so full of joy that his eyes lit up like a kid telling you about a new bike. The state intervened, "mercifully" he called it, after he showed up one too many times with bruises on his face and filthy clothes. A large lady with drawstring pants and a clipboard appeared on their doorstep, took him and Anna to live with a foster family.

"We had breakfast that first morning at the foster home, and when they told us it was time for lunch later on, I didn't understand. Didn't we just eat? I asked. Damn, I don't think I ever had more than one meal a day.

"There was running hot water and I had my own room, and what d'ya know, not all families yell at each other all day long and not all dads slap their kids around. I didn't know there was a life without beatings, shooting stray dogs with pellet guns, and disemboweling hogs.

"That foster family, the mom worked in a travel agency. She brought home these catalogs, and Anna and I, we couldn't get enough of the pictures. You could just pick a country, a hotel, and go there. Like it wasn't a big deal and getting away was just a matter of picking a place.

"But the dream didn't last long. The only vacation we ever had was three months in that foster home. That's all we got. And it just wasn't enough. All Anna and I ever talked about after that was getting away.

"The worst day of my life," Lieberman said, "was the day they made us go back. Old Gabe complied, that's what they called it. He was in compliance with the state, he fixed the place up a bit, ran some cables, scrubbed the tub and washed the sheets, bought some groceries, and before we knew it, we were back home. They called it parent-child reunification. What a crock of shit. It was fucking hell."

He spat the word *hell* into the night like some poisonous chewing tobacco. As he continued his story, I wiggled my hands back and forth, trying to loosen the plastic cuffs. I shifted my legs, trying to find a more comfortable position but the move caused him to swipe the knife at me.

"I did a lot of praying but nothing changed after that." His eyes widened and he was far away for a long time. Then his face stiffened. "We started messing around in the backyard shed when Anna was twelve years old," he said, "until they found out."

"So you burned down the house and killed your parents?"

"They smoked a lot and fell asleep with their cigarettes all the time. I just forced the inevitable along."

There it was again. This notion of having a right to do as he pleased, as he saw fit, as he thought the world ought to be.

His eyes focused on me again and he started to wave the knife back and forth. "I was waiting for your baby to stop crying." Lieberman's voice was lower now, almost contemplative. "But you are one of those spoiled rich bitches. House, husband, vacations, car, money. Ever wanted for anything? Tell me, you ever wanted for anything?"

He backed up, started to pace in circles. Then he came toward me again, gravel crunching under his boots. "Some women should not be mothers. Like you." He screamed, his voice carrying into the cornfield, lost among the husks and stalks.

I lowered myself on the ground, sideways, with my legs half tucked under.

"I love Anna. She is *not* my sister. Don't call her my sister." He stepped closer and I turned my head, afraid of what he was going to do, his madness right on the surface.

As if someone had snapped a leash, his eyes stilled and his words started to slur. "You should thank me, is what y . . . y . . . you shou . . . d d . . . Anna told me to do something, but I can't remember. I can't remember. She's gonna be so mad at me." And then insanity owned him like the tide, wavelike it washed over him, and carried him farther away from reason. "What was it, what was it . . . damn . . ." He hit his forehead with his fist, "I can't remember what she told me to do. So much to remember, so much . . . it's so hard to do everything right . . ." He kept checking his watch and wiping his forehead with his arm while holding on to the gun.

Then his face shifted and again he focused on me. His chest rose with primal power. "I'm just gonna kill you."

My bones turned to dust and I felt hope leaving my body. His voice was still there, in the background, yet no longer playing a major role. *I will make him look into my eyes*, I thought, *and I won't whimper or cry or leave him with an image of me curled up in a fetal position in the dirt. I will not allow him to triumph over me.* "Who are you to decide who's worthy and who isn't? And I'm not your mother." I spit those words at him.

"You're a sorry excuse for a mother." He was spraying saliva, and then paused, replacing his angry expression with a revolting smile. "Are you afraid? You think it's gonna hurt? You look afraid."

I could barely sit upright.

"I can't hear you."

"I'm not . . ."

"I can't hear you. Quiet as a mouse, huh?"

He left me no room, no place left to go. "Where is my daughter? Tell me where she is . . . please . . . I'm her mother. Where is she?"

"Safe, bitch, she's safe without you." He laughed. Contrived. Breathless. Diabolical.

And then the Prince of Darkness pointed his gun at me. A bright light exploded. The moonlight faded and everything went dark. My last thought was that no one would ever know what had happened to my daughter. No one.

I felt so much colder than I ever had before. The wind wheezed through the cornstalks and then the crisp autumn night turned to ice.

The next two sessions are eventless. I enter the elevator, I descend, but there's nothing left. Like a dog in hot pursuit, pads raw and branches tearing at me, the shadows are longer, the sun is about to go down, and I've pushed myself beyond all endurance. We sit in silence for a while. Mia is alive, somewhere. Maybe. Maybe not. The Liebermans are gone, nowhere to be found. He shot me, somehow I survived. We have come all this way, yet we still know nothing.

I look up at Dr. Ari and start to cry. "What now?"

Dr. Ari gets up and walks around his desk. "We keep looking."

"Looking for what?"

"We still don't know how you ended up in the ravine. There are still unanswered questions."

"Lieberman shot me. He shot me and pushed my car into the ravine."

"The car drove into the ravine—it wasn't pushed."

I look at him, puzzled.

"The keys were in the ignition. There were also tire marks indicating not only did the car drive into the ravine, but it accelerated." And after a long pause: "The driver accelerated."

"Can I go?"

A long pause. "Go? Where?"

"Home." When I say the word, I pause. North Dandry? I realize I have no home.

"You think this is over?" Dr. Ari covers his forehead with his hand as if to say *You poor fool, what are you thinking?* "Estelle, the police and the DA are not going to be satisfied with this conclusion." He pauses, folds his hands on top of the desk. "This is what we have: A missing baby, a mother who doesn't report the crime, even keeps it from her husband. Yes, we have a missing construction worker and his sister, I give you that, who by the way have been vagrants on and off, and the police have been unable to track their every move before they lived in Dover and before Lieberman accepted the job at North Dandry. Do you know how many people just don't show up for work? Or move and don't leave a forwarding address? Disappearing is not a crime."

I swallow hard. "The blanket. Tinker Bell."

"So what? You could have found that anywhere. There's no proof. Just two people who can't be found and your word."

"Which doesn't count at all."

"You remembered everything else, Estelle. The scent of the blanket, titles of books, flowers on a teacup. But you don't remember how you ended up in that ravine?"

"Do *you* even believe me?"

"What I believe is of no significance. The police and the DA need proof. The truth without proof is meaningless in their world. We'll continue tomorrow."

I get up and start to leave. At the door I turn around. "Short of a miracle, I have nothing."

As I stab at the meat loaf and draw the tines of my fork through the mashed potatoes, the dining room falls silent. Marge drops her spoon and then the sound of knives and forks hitting plates ceases altogether. I look up and see Marge gawking in the direction of the cafeteria entrance.

Dr. Ari rushes toward our table and I detect a slight limp I've never noticed before. I rest my fork on the side of my plate.

Oliver, too, is confused, his hand suspended in midair. "Something's up," he says without taking his eyes off Dr. Ari. "I've never seen him in the cafeteria."

Dr. Ari continues toward me. I push my tray toward Marge. Hope takes shape in the back of my throat. *This is it. They've found her. They've found Mia.* I picture Dr. Ari sitting down, grabbing my hand, smiling at me, saying the words I've been longing to hear.

Dr. Ari doesn't sit down, he doesn't grab my hand. No one can misinterpret his empty facial expression as a smile. One more moment is all I want, one more moment of hope, of believing they've found her. Then I surrender and accept the end.

Later, in his office, Dr. Ari clears his throat. He pushes his glasses way up on the bridge of his nose.

"I received a call regarding a piece of evidence. The lab results have just become available now."

"What evidence?"

"We'll talk about that in a minute. Tell me, do you remember what they found in the car with you?"

"My purse. A map. And Jack's gun."

"Four things. Your purse. A map. The gun. And a piece of paper."

I remember now. My purse, that's how they identified me. A map and the gun. "I don't remember anything about a piece of paper."

"It was soaked in blood. They had to send it to a lab in Florida."

"I don't remember any paper." The air in his office is chilly and I rub my arms to keep warm.

"Tell me about the gun," he says.

"The gun they found in my car? It was the gun from Jack's closet."

"The same gun you took to Anna's house."

"Yes."

We stare at each other.

"What are you saying? What's the point of all this?" I ask, frustrated. "Why don't you ask me what I remember, not what I don't remember?"

"I'm not asking you anything. When you found the gun in the closet, you put one bullet in the chamber. One bullet. I'm telling you the gun had one bullet in the chamber when you went to Anna Lieberman's house. And when they found the gun, there wasn't a single bullet in it. But your fingerprints were all over it. And you had been shot."

"How is that significant?"

"Just a detail I want you to keep in mind. But here's the thing."

The thing. I take a deep breath and look out the window. It's foggy and dark, and I can't make out as much as a tree.

"We need to talk about the note."

"I thought it was a piece of paper."

"It was a piece of paper until the people at the Florida lab managed to take digital photographs after applying different kinds of light sources . . . anyway . . . I'm not familiar with forensic procedures but it turns out they were able to create a decipherable image of the note. I just received a copy an hour ago."

There's a piece of paper in front of him on his desk. I lower my eyes.

"Unfortunately it took the lab this long to decipher the note. This could have been a lot easier." He hands it to me. "Would you read it to me?"

I extend my hand and hold the paper between my thumb and my index finger. The eight-and-a-half-by-eleven piece of paper is a copy of a torn handwritten note with a reddish tint. I skim over it. The letters seem oddly disjointed, I can't tell where one word ends and another one starts. There are no more than twenty words on the page.

"Read it out loud." Dr. Ari's voice is reaching me from afar.

I recognize the handwriting as my own; rushed, hurried, yet mine. I read it in silence. The words wash over me, topple me like waves disintegrating a frail sand castle on a beach. And then I make a mistake. I don't enter the elevator, my place of calm reprieve, instead I go to Stone Harbor, the beach where my family used to spend summers when I was a child.

There were giant rocks above the tide line, butter yellow and blue-green, pink as salmon and mother-of-pearl. The tide caressed the sand, then my toes, just to roll out again into the vast sea. Spitting waves, salty air, and chapped lips. Pink and purple spiny sea urchins, tangled algae around my ankles. Barnacles and seaweed in the dead sand, so serene against the violent waves. *Little water and lots of sand or you destabilize the walls and they will buckle under the weight, just like a landslide*, my dad told me as I scooped the fine grains into a pile. I used the perfect proportions of water and sand but I stood no chance. I made a fist and felt the coarse texture of the grains as I watched a wave demolishing my castle.

"Read it out loud to me," Dr. Ari insists and leans back in his chair.

" 'Everyone, I can't go on like this. I'm sorry for what I've done. I killed my baby. I'm a monster.' "

My mind is hazy and that's where I keep those words, in my mind. Then there's a hard painful lump in the back of my throat and then the tears begin to form. Time stands still and I can't remember any moment of all my life but I see my own bloody hands, my daughter's tearstained cheeks. The story I've been telling was nothing but a sand castle and it was just swept away by an ocean wave. I feel myself breaking. Like a vase falling onto a tile floor, my mind shatters into pieces. I know there is no hope in trying to put anything back together, so I don't even try. I just sit and stare at my hands. I've reached my limit and now I'm just done.

A powerful current strikes a nerve in my head and I hear screaming. The voice is mine, yet it seems so distant. I don't recognize any of the words. And then I crack wide open.

When I wake up, I'm in a daze. Not like waking up from a deep sleep, but having been chemically pacified and strapped down. The nurse sitting next to me gets up and wraps a blood pressure cuff around my arm. This isn't supposed to end this way.

I killed my baby. I'm sorry.

PART 4

How puzzling all these changes are! I'm never sure
what I'm going to be, from one minute to another!

Lewis Carroll, Alice's Adventures in Wonderland

CHAPTER 23

"Call the police," I demand two days later when we resume our sessions. "I'll plead guilty. Let's just end it now."

Dr. Ari and I have been going at this for almost an hour. I've come to accept the truth yet he seems to circle around it without confronting it straight on.

"One thing at a time. Let's—"

"I wrote a note saying I killed my daughter. All this here, what we're doing every day, is just a farce. Call the police."

"But her body, where is her body? What happened and how and when? There are too many questions that haven't been answered yet. I won't allow you to give up." He raises his hands. "This back-and-forth isn't helping. Let's stay focused and talk about the note for now."

"It's not a note, it's a confession."

"Do you remember writing it?"

"Do I remember writing it?" This is getting funnier by the minute. "I'm done with this. I want you to call the police so I can turn myself in. It is what it is and you need to accept it, it's over."

"Do you remember writing it?" he repeats.

"No, I don't remember writing it but it's my handwriting. It looks rushed in a way, but I wrote it."

"I want to show you something."

"There's more? God help me, what's next? A map with a cross where I buried her? Maybe I carved my initials into her skin?"

Dr. Ari hands me a piece of paper. "There's something I've neglected to tell you."

There's no such thing as Dr. Ari neglecting to do anything. Everything he does, he does for a purpose. I grab the piece of paper.

"It's the same note—I don't understand."

"Flip it over," he says.

On the back of the paper there isn't any writing, just random bloody smudges.

"Is this a joke?" I ask.

"Look closer."

I squint my eyes. There's the faintest outline of printed words. "I can't make out the words, but there are some numbers. A phone number maybe? I don't get it." I flip the note over and over again. "I really don't get it."

"It's a receipt from Diane's Diner, a place off 434. A receipt for two cups of coffee and two pieces of pecan pie."

"I had coffee and pie and then jotted down a confession." I shake my head in disbelief. "That's quite a story."

"Thanks to Google I'm a step ahead. I took the liberty to print out a picture of the place." Dr. Ari opens the manila folder and pulls out a photograph.

I try to make sense of the receipt, but it doesn't add up. I don't like pecan pie, the nuts stick to my teeth and the hint of maple is just not my thing.

"I don't even like pecan pie," I say.

Enter the elevator.

I study the photo of Diane's Diner. Diane's is a one-story brick building with a neon sign in the window, a jukebox visible through the front door. I hear a melody from deep within. Strained tunes. Refrains. It tugs at me, gently at first, then it pulls me toward the building's front door. Images rush at me, like a crowd of children waiting to be acknowledged, one by one. Infantile, incomplete. But then they mature, fill out.

A fork scratching against a white china plate.

Pecans shaped like miniature brains.

"A song," I say, "I remember a song."

I need to go back, back to when I saw the flash, when the gun went off. I remember the sound of the gunshot.

Deeper. Go deeper.

Loose rubble under my knees. Raspy breathing. Legs like lead, heavy. My pounding heart, throbbing pain.

Deeper.

Plastic. Blue. Indigo. Or periwinkle. Persian? Royal blue? Navy blue. A tarp. A navy blue tarp.

I sit up straight and uncross my arms.

Deeper.

I consider making the buttons on the elevator disappear. Whatever I find at this diner, maybe I won't want to return to reality.

———

Lieberman stood in front of me, legs parted, his heels digging into the gravel. He pointed the gun at me.

First a flash, then an explosion ripped through my eardrums. My ears went deaf then there was a loud ringing tone. I waited for the pain, the burn, yet nothing happened.

Lieberman's body jolted toward me as if someone had shoved him in my direction. He fell on the ground, face-first. He lay motionless, as if struck by lightning. I watched a dark spot on his back expanding into a large crimson sphere.

I stared into the direction of the sound, the same direction of the flash. A shadow emerged from behind the car. The figure took shape, like a specter gaining strength and coming into focus. A woman. Gun in hand.

"Good-for-nothing bastard," Anna Lieberman said. "Never does what he's told." She stared at his bloody back as if it meant nothing, then disappeared into the dark of the night. I was left to watch Lieberman's body. The crimson that had covered his back had pooled by his side.

I didn't have the strength to get up but I managed to shift my weight away from my knees. Seconds later the Caprice's headlights moved toward me. Anna stopped next to Lieberman's lifeless body.

"Can you get up?" Anna asked and got out of her car.

I shook my head. "I can't feel my legs."

"Try." She grabbed my elbow and pulled me on my feet, reaching around me, cutting the plastic zip ties. She pulled a blue tarp from the trunk. Anna shrouded her brother's body with the tarp, tucked it underneath him on the side, and then rolled him on top of it like a nurse changing the sheets of an immobile patient.

I followed her commands. We pulled Lieberman about fifty feet until we ended up by the entrance of the corn maze. We dragged him inside the booth, dropped the front panel, and closed the side door.

In the car she sat only inches away from the steering wheel. She squinted her eyes as she drove through the night, southbound on 434. Finally she made a turn into a Chevron station and parked by the side door.

GET KEY FROM MANAGEMENT, a sign said.

"Listen closely, Estelle Paradise. We don't need anyone else to get involved, okay? Do I have your word?"

I nodded. I felt hope. For the first time in days I felt something resembling hope.

"I'll get the key." She got out of the car and locked the doors. "Wait right here."

There'd be concessions, there'd be promises not to call the police. I'd assure her I'd never ever tell anyone. David Lieberman was dead and I'd promise to take these days of horror to my grave. I was prepared to give her everything I owned, I'd promise her anything, I'd do anything for Mia. Anything.

Anna returned with a key. "Go clean yourself up," she said and handed me a plastic bag. "There's some wipes in here. Put on the clean clothes and don't leave your bloody clothes in the bathroom. Throw them in the Dumpster over there," she said and nodded toward the side of the building. "They didn't have any shoes, so clean yours the best you can. Hurry up, we don't have all night."

Getting out of the car I could barely straighten my legs and all but hobbled to the restroom. I unlocked the door. Inside, I turned on the water and washed the filth off my hands.

I sat my muddy shoes in the sink and watched the dirt trail down the drain. I put on the gray hoodie and the white T-shirt, and a few minutes later I walked out with the bag of bloody clothes in hand. As instructed, I tossed the bag in the green Dumpster by the side of the building.

We left the gas station parking lot and less than five minutes later Anna pulled by the side of a building with large letters on a neon sign illuminated in a timed sequence.

DIANE'S DINER.

Anna motioned me to get out of the car. "No funny business. Not a word, or you'll regret it." She stood merely inches from my face, reached behind her, and pulled the gun from her waistband and pushed its barrel into my stomach. "I think we just established that I don't warn people before I shoot."

"Why are we here?" I asked.

"To eat," she said and pointed at the front door of the diner.

"I knew you'd do the right thing," I said.

"Don't be silly," she said and pulled a rubber band out of her pocket. She gathered her hair, smoothing the sides with the palms of her hand.

I had hope. I still had hope.

———

Diane's Diner was all stainless steel and red-and-white-checkered vinyl booths. There was a wall-mounted all-day breakfast menu above the counter and specials written on a chalkboard. The diner was empty but for a man in a blue uniform reading the jukebox selection.

Anna directed me to the first booth by the door.

"Diane's famous for her pecan pies."

I put my hands on the table and realized that my fingernails were still rimmed with mud. Then the jukebox came on, a guitar, then a voice. Raspy, shaky. Johnny Cash.

The beast in me
Is caged by frail and fragile bars.

"Coffee and pecan pie?" Anna asked as if it was the most normal thing in the world. She didn't wait for my answer and called the order to the waitress behind the counter, who in turn nodded and took two mugs off a large stack.

"I promise," I said, "I promise I won't tell anyone, I promise. Never will I—"

She looked at me, puzzled, then she laughed out loud. "I promise you that your baby will be okay. Is a promise like that something you need?"

I nodded, feeling hot tears working their way to the surface.

"Just imagine her, in a few years, she'll have nice clothes, a room with a pink canopy bed, more toys than she'll know what to do with. A mom, a dad, maybe a brother or a sister. Someone who cares for her, loves her. All of that. Is that something you want?"

I swallowed hard.

"That's one side of the coin. Would you like to hear the other side?"

"I'll do anything."

"I hope so," she said and reached behind her into her waist-band, retrieving the gun. She stuck it into the front pocket of her hoodie.

"Now let me paint the other picture for you. A little girl living with her daddy. And I use the word *daddy* loosely here. He *loves* her, he cares for her. He buys her pretty things. Jewelry, lipstick, dresses, whatever she wants. But she has to do something for it. Every time she gets something she has to give him something in return. The little girl loves him and she wants her daddy happy. And she does what he asks her to do. Anything."

For a few seconds my brain refused to make the connection, but then hope ruptured. My heartbeat echoed in my ears as her words came into focus.

A middle-aged waitress with wrinkled skin that seemed too large for her elfin frame put coffee and pie in front of us.

"Let's eat and then I'll explain how this is going to work."

I crushed the pecans with my fork, stirring the pieces into the filling. I was parched. The first sip of coffee was tepid and unpleas-ant, some sort of bitterness lingered in the back of my throat. I downed the lukewarm coffee in three gulps, its aftertaste making me shudder. When I put down the empty cup, there was white chalky residue at the bottom. It was too late; I'd swallowed every last drop.

"You're a smart girl, I think you understood what I just told you," Anna said and mashed piecrust with her fork. She put another piece of pie in her mouth and swallowed. "Needless to say that the plan David and I had didn't work out."

I sat still, unable to move. "What plan?" I wrapped my hands around the empty cup. Did the walls just shift or did I imagine that?

"Everything was okay until you showed up. David is . . ." She paused and smiled. "Was a bit on the unstable side."

I tightened my grip around the cup and pushed the plate with the pie away from me.

"Where was I? Oh yeah, my brother. David and I find unwanted babies and sell them to people who want them. *Unwanted* basically means we take babies that are no longer wanted, or neglected. Babies from moms who can't take care of another baby, drug users, even had one from a homeless girl, believe it or not. No agencies, no lawyers, no fees, no court papers. Nothing, just a transfer of responsibilities. Basically we match families, if you will. People pay outrageous sums for a baby. The right gender, the right age.

"And then everything went out of control. David never had sound judgment, if you ask me. All he ever talked about is this island and that beach, this hotel and that trip. Kept bringing me those catalogs with glossy pictures, Paris here and Barbados there. Always talking about where we're going to go, what we're going to do. What a fool."

Fear crept into every bone of my body.

"David told me about you and from what I heard you weren't the mommy type. Letting her cry all the time. I told him a woman like you would never go for this—you've got money, a house, a husband—but he didn't want to listen. I knew it was a bad idea but he was dead set on going through with it. Said your husband was some douche bag trying to flip houses."

"How much money do you want?"

"Money? Who's talking about money?" Anna laughed and then turned to the waitress behind the counter.

"May I have a refill and the check, please?" Anna turned back toward me. "I'm not asking you for any money. I'm willing to offer you something, though. And if you're as good a mother as you claim to be, you'll give it willingly."

The waitress appeared, filled up Anna's coffee cup. I watched her fill my cup, then she put the check on the table.

"Whenever you're ready," the waitress said and scooped up the pie plates.

"We're ready," Anna said and dropped a few bills on the table.

My vision jerked as if I had caught myself falling asleep. My body felt weighed down as if my blood had been replaced by lead.

"I'll pay you whatever you want, Anna. I promise. My husband owns property, how much? Two hundred thousand? Whatever you ask for, I . . ." I thought I heard my words slur, but I couldn't be sure. The world around had turned fuzzy.

"I'm sorry, she's spoken for."

It was getting harder and harder to keep it together, my eyelids were twitching and out of the corner of my eye I saw the waitress pass by our table when I had just seen her behind the counter a second earlier.

Spoken for.

"You want to see her?"

"Yes." My vocal cords created a sound like sandpaper. "Please."

I watched the waitress go to the door, following behind the man who had dropped a coin in the jukebox earlier. Anna got up and motioned me to follow them. My legs obeyed although I didn't know who was giving the orders.

When I heard the door close behind us, the lights in the diner went out. Life unfolded in slow motion. I felt as if up were down and left were right and the world around me was becoming hazier by the second. Suddenly I was in the deserted parking lot. I turned around and watched the waitress lock the diner door. She flipped the OPEN sign to CLOSED.

There was a baby car seat sitting on the table in a booth by the window. Anna motioned through the closed door and the waitress turned the seat around.

There was Mia in her red coat and boots, clothes that had disappeared out of her closet. She held a bottle in hand, feeding in short, intense bursts, pausing every once in a while, allowing the collapsed nipple to fill with air.

Electric sparks traveled through me. I stared at Mia through the window until our faces melted into one. I looked at my reflection and hoped to see Joan of Arc given the gift of courage, yet in the window was a wild-eyed woman with matted hair and a tearstained face.

If hell truly was a place of endless torture and pain, of fire and brimstone, my idea of it was far simpler: hell was here in front of this diner with my daughter behind glass, my drugged and frozen brain in panic, a mental fog of conflicting instructions. It was also heaven somehow, electrifying. She was alive and she looked well, even healthy.

"Don't leave her in there," I cried out and made toward the door.

"Don't touch that door," Anna said and pointed the gun through the window at Mia.

The diner lights faded in and out. I wondered what kind of drug she had put in my coffee and if it was lethal. And if I was strong enough to shatter the glass with my bare hands.

As if she'd read my mind she said, "Don't get any ideas. I'll shoot before you even know the gun went off. Your baby will be fine, but you look a bit green in the face. Better get in the car before you pass out."

"Can I touch her?" I was close to passing out and all I wanted was one touch to take with me.

"Don't be silly. All you're gonna do is make her cry."

"What do you want if you don't want any money?" I asked.

"I need you to make good on a promise," she said. "Get in the car."

I didn't allow myself to feel anything but detachment, for I knew if I pushed my mind any further, I'd never find my way back. The last sound was that of spitting gravel when Anna sent the car bolting into the darkness.

CHAPTER 24

felt foggy. It was like I was there, but not quite. Then the scene outside the diner popped back into my head. I opened my eyes and to my left was Anna with one hand on the steering wheel, the other in her front pocket. I could think of only one reason why I shouldn't reach over and turn the wheel toward a pole, and that was the slight possibility that she was going to come to her senses.

"Why'd you leave her with that woman? Please explain to me what's going on." It was dark and I didn't recognize my surroundings. My speech was slow, but clear. "You brought me here just so I'd look at her through glass while she's with some waitress in a diner?"

"Tell me about it. Nothing went according to plan. David messed up and I had to take you to the diner with me. But don't worry, Diane will take care of the baby until her new mommy picks her up. I told you she was spoken for. And that brings me to the last part of this deal between us. Your promise."

What do you say when you stare crazy straight in the face?

You go along with it and wait for your moment. I took long and deep breaths, realizing that the drugs were wearing off quickly.

The car pulled sharply to the left. I recognized the silhouette of the ticket booth; we were back by the side of the cornfield. Anna stopped the car and killed the engine.

"You're going to help me bury him," she said and pulled a lever under the steering wheel.

The trunk popped open with a loud *thud*.

"Let's get to it," she said, and tossed a pair of stiff working gloves at me. "Six feet long and as deep as we can dig in one hour," she added and thrust a shovel into the wet ground.

We started digging in unison.

One hour later we were exhausted. The soil was soft, yet heavy. As we rested and wiggled our fingers, I felt dead inside. Lieberman could have been a time capsule for all I cared.

"There was only one reason why I sent him after you," Anna said after she caught her breath, "but he started waving that gun before it was time. Plus he wasn't made for this business. He dropped the blanket in the attic, he almost messed up when the cops came to my house. If they'd checked the car, they'd have found clothes and formula. He always forgot to take his meds, and when he didn't, he was losing it by the minute. You can't reason and you can't do business with someone like that."

"But he was your brother."

"Half brother at best. We grew up in the same house, is all."

Anna pointed to the ground, the hole barely two feet deep but long enough for a body. She lit the way with a flashlight and I did everything she told me to do. I dragged the tarp with Lieberman's body to the hole. I rolled him in, filled the hole, and covered it with dirt, compacted the soil by stomping on it. It took me about ten minutes to bury him and get the ground even. When I was finished, the palms of my hands and the webbing between my thumbs and index fingers were burning.

"Now I need you to write a note." She paused for a second and pursed her lips. "Damn him, the paper is probably in his pocket."

"I don't think I can write anything," I said and held my hands up, palms facing Anna. "I can't even bend my fingers."

She stuck her hand in her purse, rummaged, and then pulled out the receipt from the diner.

"You'll manage." Anna pointed to the trunk of her car and shined the light on it. "Word for word. Write: 'Everybody, I can't go on like this. I'm sorry for what . . .'" She paused when she realized I wasn't moving. "'I have done. I killed her. I'm a monster.' Then sign your name."

I shook my head. The pen dropped to the ground.

"I'm not going to write that. You're even crazier than your brother." My mind was moving at warp speed. All I had to figure out was her currency, something that made her tick more than selling Mia to a stranger. "Anna, I'm begging you. I will pay you twice as much. My money is as good as anyone else's."

"I don't need your money, I need the baby. You can't run a business without the merchandise, right?"

"I will pay you more than anyone else, I promise you. I will pay whatever you ask for."

"I don't need *your* money. I need a solid reputation for delivering." Anna looked at her watch, then continued. "When they find you, which could be days or even weeks from now, they will find a woman and a confession that she has killed her baby. Having the confession means they won't be looking for the baby or me or David, for that matter. They'll assume the baby is in a shallow grave in the woods. Or a Dumpster somewhere."

Anna put the receipt on the hood of the car. "You said you'd do anything for her, remember?" Anna cocked her head; her smile would've seemed warm to someone who didn't know the extent of her madness. "If you do this for me, I'll do something for you," she said with a tempting voice as if she were a child proposing a marble exchange.

"There's nothing I want you to do for me but give me back my child."

"You don't understand anything, do you?" Anna shook her head. "You'll be dead, either way. Nothing's going to change that."

I stepped back, which only caused her to raise the gun again.

"I'll be long gone and no one will come looking for us. In return I'm willing to guarantee your daughter"—Anna paused and then straightened her arm with the gun, pointing it between my eyes—"a good family. A backyard to play in and a private school, the whole nine yards."

If Lieberman is the Prince of Darkness, Anna is the Prince's Darkness. "I'm begging you. I will pay you whatever—"

"I promise you no one will break her. Children can be broken easily, you know. And what kind of mother can bear the thought of that, right? What's it going to be? Heaven or hell, both are available. It's your choice, Mommy."

Even if I overpowered her and took the gun, would it really matter? Mia could be, for all I knew, across state lines by now, Canada even, or on her way to Mexico. Even if I got away I'd still spend the rest of my life looking for her.

"Your choice. Do we have a deal?"

I shook my head and whispered, "Please don't do this."

"You'll die one way or another. Do something good for her for a change."

Shaking her head, Anna continued, "A nice home or she'll spend her childhood sitting on some sicko's lap? What's it going to be?"

I kept myself perfectly still. *My life for hers.* My mind and my body detached from each other. I broke away from myself, floated away. *Some sicko's lap.* What one does out of love is untouchable. It looks to mend, to make things right.

I bent over and forced my swollen fingers to pick up the pen.

Anna stepped closer, she was mere inches away from me. "A decent life for your child or a childhood in a basement."

I willed my fingers around the pen, slid them down to the ink tip.

"White baby girls are in high demand, you know. Saudis go crazy over their skin and blond hair. Or I find her nice parents and she'll take ballet lessons and go to summer camp."

Everybody, I wrote.

I can't go on like this, I wrote.

I am sorry for what I have done, I wrote and that part wasn't even a lie.

I killed my baby, I wrote.

I'm a monster.

The ravine was about one hundred yards ahead of me. Mia was with the woman who had served me drugged coffee and pecan pie. Tomorrow morning, people would crowd the diner for breakfast, eggs and bacon would sizzle on the grill, coffee brewing, biscuits rising. And tomorrow they'd find me dead in the ravine with a handwritten confession saying I had killed my daughter—a devilish yet plausible plan.

"There's something I want you to give to her."

I asked her if I could reach into my purse. Tinker Bell's eyes big and blue, as resigned as I was.

Anna put the figure in her pocket. "This is what I want you to do," she said. "You step on the gas while you hold the gun. Right before you reach the ravine, you pull the trigger. Either in your mouth or against your temple, I don't care. I'll keep my promise if you keep yours."

Anna threw the gun on the passenger seat, reached over me, and put the car in drive.

"Step on it," Anna's voice said but it seemed like it took me minutes to process her words.

And then I did as I was told. I stepped on the gas and the car started moving. The tires dragged across the gravel, slowly accelerating. I grabbed the gun with my right hand and held it against my temple.

Fifty yards, at the most. I reached for the seat belt, tempted to unbuckle it, to get out of the car. *Some sicko's lap,* she'd said. I had no argument left, no offer, nothing but my life for Mia's future.

Thirty yards. The Range Rover accelerated, moved faster, much faster.

Ten yards. My entire world was covered in a sticky substance that reeked of metal.

One yard. I pulled the trigger. There were sparks and a loud pop. The back draft was horrendous. It made my hand jerk backward and I was worried if I had really shot myself, but then my ear tingled and my head snapped back. I felt as if someone had injected pepper in my veins. My body lifted off the seat and I felt weightless, like riding a Ferris wheel. It seemed like forever until my stomach dropped and the car landed. Surrounded by the sickening crunch of metal collapsing, I heard glass shattering. My body jerked in all directions. I stopped worrying and then everything went silent and dark.

And, like a death row inmate's last meal, I asked for one last wish. The choices were endless: time travel, a reverse button, the power to become invisible, resurrecting the dead, undoing the chaotic knots of my tangled life. I must make my selection wisely. I must be precise, consider all possibilities, and leave no room for error or misinterpretation.

We were a team, my wish and I. We were immune to the distractions of screaming metal and shattering glass and death. Our creation, my last wish, was a thing of beauty, composed beyond time. It took shape, primal and powerful; Mia, I wish that we'll meet again in another place and time, and when we do, may my body be molded perfectly so you can curl against me.

CHAPTER 25

When Dr. Ari and I enter the 70th Precinct on Lawrence Avenue, I recall the janitor, the urge I had felt to walk out and leave the building. I understand now that I saw the world through a lens, a lens of a brain crammed with hormones and doubts, thoughts jam-packed with contortions, deformation, distortion, and falsifications. The police would have found the dumbwaiter, would have questioned David Lieberman, everything could have been so much easier. Another notch in my belt of shortcomings.

As we pass through the glass doors and wait by the front counter, I can see our reflections in the glass. I'm disheveled and worn; Dr. Ari is pressed, lint-free, and cheerful. One impeccably dressed man, probably passing as a lawyer, and a woman with a strange haircut and a missing ear.

The clerk looks at us and motions us up to the counter. "How can I help you?"

"Detective Wilczek, please."

The clerk picks up the phone and we sit down. After a couple of minutes a detective in slacks and a light blue shirt, his tie tucked into his waistband, walks up to us. The gun in his holster seems too small for his body. His name tag reads DETECTIVE ROBERT WILCZEK.

First the name rings a bell, and then the face. I remember him from the hospital. He was one of the detectives who questioned me. His face is slack, disinterested, assuming we've come to report a minor incident, a stolen purse maybe, or domestic abuse.

He looks us up and down. "I'm Detective Wilczek." Then he straightens his tie. Suddenly he perks up. "I remember you."

"I remember you, too."

Mrs. Paradise, children don't just disappear out of locked apartments.

"What can I do for you?"

I had lost my child, then I found her, then I left her, and when I went back to get her, she was gone. For a while, I couldn't remember, but now I do. And I know who took her. But not where she is now.

"I know what happened to my daughter," I say. "I'm here to report a crime."

He looks at me, then at Dr. Ari, who is determined to allow me to do the talking. He will speak only when I'm not capable of relaying the story. That's how he was when we met and he hasn't faltered since.

"My name is Dr. Ari. I'm psychiatrist in chief at the Creedmoor Psychiatric Clinic. Mrs. Estelle Paradise has been a patient at Creedmoor for the past months."

"I remember, I remember." The detective's eyes light up and he clears his throat. "Let's find a place to talk." Detective Wilczek motions to the clerk behind the counter and asks her to call Detective Riverton and meet us in Room 1.

We walk down the corridor, its blue linoleum polished to perfection. We follow the detective, like ducklings their mother. The interrogation room consists of a table and three chairs, nothing else. The walls are made of plastic panels, the floor covered in industrial carpet.

Dr. Ari and Detective Wilczek leave the room. I can hear them talking in the hallway, but I'm unable to make out any specific words. After a minute or two Dr. Ari pokes his head in. He promises to send someone from Creedmoor to pick me up once the interview concludes. I'm tempted to ask him to send Oliver, but I don't want to press my luck.

Then it's just the two of us. We sit down, Detective Wilczek across from me, and I know this conversation is being videotaped and watched in another room, or at least recorded. Detective Wilczek can't be much more than thirty even though I remember him looking older, yet his dark hair is thinning and I can see his shiny scalp through his buzz cut. There's a white line on his ring finger where a wedding band used to be. His front left tooth is chipped.

I try to avoid my reflection in the mirror. I'm sure it's a two-way mirror and I'm not ready to face more than one person at a time, not even through a wall. The only one who has heard my story is Dr. Ari and I feel as if I'm going to say the wrong thing again. I didn't commit any crime I'm aware of, maybe not reporting the abduction, but that's as far as my legal involvement goes. As a mother, I am guilty of countless crimes.

When I tell him about Creedmoor and Dr. Ari, Detective Wilczek interrupts me, midsentence. "I can't get over the fact that you recovered your memory. When does that ever happen?"

I sense some excitement in his voice. I look down at my purse. "I've been undergoing psychotherapy and memory recall therapy."

"I usually deal with people who intentionally don't remember. You need to tell me more about that. I remember you had a head injury. So what caused your amnesia?"

A female detective walks in then and puts a file in front of him and I wonder if there'll ever be a day when my whole life won't be contained between the covers of a cardboard folder. She introduces herself as Detective Riverton. She's about fifty, but has the lean body of a young woman.

Three hours later I've told them the entire story. For years I've judged myself by the way people looked at me. I'm back at my parents' funeral, people looking at me bewildered, unsure if they should stroke my hair or ignore me altogether. Wilczek and Riverton have seen a lot; I can only imagine how many dead bodies they've come across, how many images are etched into their brains, never to be erased, how many nights they've sat in their cars, in front of their houses, wives and husbands waiting, kids asleep, unable to switch off their minds.

As I told Riverton my story, I tried to decode her, interpret her body language. Did she furrow her brow, did she nod in understanding? She doesn't wear a wedding band, but she may be a mother. A mother who also struggles and empathizes with my story or she might judge me more harshly than any man ever could.

The rest of the night unfolds in stretches of waiting and then more questions, and ultimately I am escorted outside, where there is a van to transport me back to Creedmoor "for the time being." Detective Wilczek tells me he will drop by and have me sign the statements "once everything checks out."

Back at Creedmoor I fall into a deep sleep. Wistful dreams and occasional moments of waking—yet I'm at peace with the chaos of my thoughts. I spend the following days in my room. Between meals and discussions with Dr. Ari about my future, I fill up an entire composition book. I don't leave a single line blank, for its completeness gives me the illusion of also being complete myself. That's the theory anyway. I don't want to spend another minute wondering what I might not remember in the future. I feel as if I've been floating in open water and I've come upon an island that is able to sustain me and I don't ever want to be caught off guard again.

Two days later I get my release papers.

"We checked out your story," Wilczek says.

"Upon entering, the officers . . ." His muffled voice echoes in my head, as if he's speaking down a well. I allow his words to unfold in front of me like a movie: Entering Anna's house, the officers walk with a mission, threadbare carpet underneath their feet. Their eyes glance over the shiny travel catalogs in the living room. They hurry down the hallway, enter the room in which I saw Anna from the street, holding my daughter.

"There were lots of baby clothes and toys," Wilczek says and now he no longer looks me in the eyes, but reads off his notes as if he can't remember the details. "The clothes range from newborn to school-age children. We found photos, ledgers with names and dollar amounts, dates, and even contact information. We're checking into missing children's cases all over the state. There's a couple of promising leads but nothing I can elaborate on at this point. It'll probably take months to sort it all out."

If I'm not the only one whose child they've taken, then there are other mothers out there . . . I can't even allow myself to complete the thought. My own loss is all I can handle, I'm not equipped to take on someone else's burden.

Entering the kitchen, the officers found the yellow floral china I described and the baby spoon. They didn't find any dirty diapers underneath the plastic pots and empty seed packages in the garbage bin.

"There were empty diaper boxes and wipe wrappers. Nothing contained any DNA. The garbage had been collected that day and taken to the landfill."

Officers found the cornfield yet the decrepit barn has not been located. He calls that fact "rather insignificant."

I wonder what "rather insignificant" means. Maybe it's just proof that crazy people get away with holes as long as they are irrelevant and inconsequential to the story itself.

The encounter in front of Anna's house also checks out; no

official report was filed but two Dover police officers confirm an insignificant altercation between three parties on Waterway Circle.

"The diner's had many owners over the years, this year was a seasonal operation. It closed down right after Halloween once the corn maze was shut down. It's the only one in the entire county so there's quite a bit of traffic. An elderly couple leased the diner but hired seasonal waitstaff on a part-time basis and there's no paperwork, no contracts, nothing. And if that wasn't disappointing enough, they hired a professional cleaning company. The entire building has been bleached and wiped clean, no DNA, not even a partial print.

"Forensics dug up Lieberman's body. He died of a gunshot wound to the back. That's preliminary but quite obvious."

I buried a body. I dug a hole and buried the body of the man who abducted my child. I'm not haunted by any of this.

"There's an APB out on Anna Lieberman, but so far we haven't been able to locate her. I don't see how she can get your daughter out of the country—she has no birth certificate, no passport, nothing. Sooner or later her cover will blow. The moment she seeks medical help, tries to enroll her in day care or school, it'll arouse suspicion. Even a traffic violation or her name showing up on a lease will trigger the system. It's only a matter of time. She can hide, but only for so long."

School, day care. "That could be years from now," I say and shake my head. "What do I do in the meantime? Where do I look?"

"I'm not sure if looking for her is the answer. Anna counted on everyone to believe the suicide and the confession story. The fact that you survived makes it almost impossible for her to find, please excuse my choice of words, a taker for your daughter. It'll be easier looking for both of them together than separate. I know it's hard but you have to wait this out."

Hundreds of missing children every day. Their photos in store windows and on milk cartoons. I've scanned the posters before, appalled by the years that have passed since they've been last seen. Teenagers usually, disappeared, never to be seen again. Some thought to have run away. Running away is not a crime. Are they even looking? *Don't fight it*, I tell myself, *there's no end to this. It's a bottomless pit, my daughter just one of many.*

"I want to apologize to you but I know there's nothing I can say to make this better, so I'm not even going to try."

Sorry. The cheapest of all words. It's as if he's trying to cut open the lion and retrieve its victim, expecting life to go on. It doesn't work that way.

"Let us do the looking. All you have to do is be patient," he adds.

"Right," I say and put on my gloves.

Patience. It's starting to wear thin and I haven't even left Creedmoor yet. For every minute Mia's out of my reach, I gain something else. I'm not sure what it is, but it's growing. Resolve maybe? Courage? Hope? Maybe I needed to lose one thing to gain another, for there's a limited number of items I can carry in my hands. If I let go of the pain, I pick up hope. Is that how it works?

The next day, as Creedmoor sits silently overlooking the East River, I say goodbye to Oliver. It's not a traditional farewell—no embrace, no small talk—just me touching his hand ever so slightly as I walk past him, more of a clandestine ritual on my part. For anyone watching this exchange, it'd appear to be a coincidence. The acorn he gave me is in my pocket.

Marge cries as I hug her good-bye. Her body is large and soft, and I feel as if I'm melting into her. We promise to keep in touch but we both know that's not going to happen.

I walk down the pebble walkway on the north side of Creedmoor.

I count five floors down and three up to locate my former room. I find the nest I used to watch through my window. What once was a well-built structure of tightly woven sticks and twigs is now flattened, dilapidated, and abandoned. No worrisome parents nearby to watch the fledglings on their clumsy flying attempts. Life goes on in so many ways.

Dr. Ari sees me in his office one last time. I attempt to take it all in: the diplomas on the walls, the scent of shoe polish, the view of the smokestacks in the distance.

"I wanted to wish you good luck," he says later as he escorts me outside. "And that I hope for a happy ending to the story."

"There's nothing else I can do but wait for Anna to make a mistake. Luck can't be all I've got left," I say and my eyes tear up. I blink them away.

"I'm a great believer in luck," he says and closes my file for the last time.

"Speaking of happy endings, you never told me about the woman with the egg."

Dr. Ari furrows his brow, then his eyes light up. "I forgot I told you about that."

"So, what was it if it wasn't the egg?"

"She's passed since and I guess it's okay if I share her story with you. It was the spoon she ate the egg with."

"The spoon?"

"She ate off a silver spoon. The silver reacted with the sulfur in the egg, created a tarnish on the spoon. The spoon had a foul taste and reminded her of a rather violent experience in her life. The memory emerged and rather than deal with it, she shut down."

"So that's the story of the egg woman."

"That's it," Dr. Ari says.

"Will I ever see you again?" I say after a long silence.

"You have no need for a man like me in your life."

As he extends his hand, I grab it and pull him into an embrace. He's stiff in my arms, but only for a second. Then he softens.

I watch him through the rearview mirror of the cab one last time, straightening his tie and removing invisible specks of lint from his suit.

CHAPTER 26

Months pass and Mia is still missing. Jack and I talk about the possibility of having to identify her ravaged and abused body in unimaginable stages of decomposition—we agree we'll make the identification together—yet we can't quite agree on how to live our lives until then.

In the meantime, I rent a small studio apartment on 58th Street, and even though it's just a short walk off Sutton Place, it's affordable and Jack is surprisingly generous. I enjoy living in walking distance to the 4, 5, 6, N, Q, and R trains, on a quiet, treelined street.

Jack, once his contract in Chicago has ended, finds a position as assistant DA, "entry level, no pay, and long hours." His furnished apartment, the Tribeca Suites, allows him to remain "in transition." We don't mention the word *divorce* quite yet, we allow life, according to Jack, "to play out," whatever that means.

Even though we both hate to admit yet another failure, we've been sitting ducks for a long time. Marriages confronted by tragedy don't break apart because of that fact per se, but it seems as if there's only so much resolve to go around and everything pales in comparison to Mia's disappearance. And so we live separately and wait for the inevitable burial of our union. We know the demise of our marriage is nearing, like a sure winter storm, its icy breath approaching the hairs on the back of our necks.

Once a week Jack and I meet at a coffee shop in a bookstore. There, we are surrounded by a contrived normalcy among people discussing the books they've read, trips they've taken, conversing about normal things that normal people do.

During our time at the coffee shop Jack struggles to wrap his mind around the facts of Mia's disappearance. He makes me recount every minute detail and obsesses over where he was and what he did while it all played out.

"I feel responsible," he says, raising his voice, causing people to turn around and look at us. "I feel it was my fault. I hired this lunatic, I took the job in Chicago, and I told you to move into the brownstone."

My sense of guilt for not having protected my child pales in comparison to Jack's loss of potency. There's nothing he can do and he's not equipped to deal. Jack goes on and on about what he would give if he could go back and take a different path, but he knows it's impossible. He speaks about how guilt eats at him every moment of every day, when he is going to sleep, when he wakes up, during lunch, in the shower, at the gym, watching the news, how these monstrous thoughts pop in his mind and demand to be prioritized, an infinite punishment for a mere momentary oversight. How he is tired of thinking about it, how no amount of analysis is going to turn back the clock.

And during those moments, during those fleeting minutes of remorse, for a split second, I feel something for him that resembles compassion, and I hold his hand. Yet I struggle to find a single word of consolation for him. Since the day he dropped me off at

Creedmoor I haven't been able to cry in front of him. I don't know if I'm gaining strength or if I've lost my soul, but it's easier that way and so I don't analyze it.

As a prosecutor, Jack doesn't invest in the notion that even behind a most wicked and incomprehensible deed is a human being. His world is not so sunny, doesn't allow for any such concessions, his world has only a few rainbows and frolicking puppies. He is quick to see the bad and even quicker to judge, and that's just how Jack is. And Jack judges himself. Because Jack's a logical man.

While I can "claim"—what a choice of words—while I can *claim* to have suffered from a medical condition, he was inept in his task to protect his family. This lasts for mere minutes, then Jack stiffens himself and clears his throat. Composed again, he enters some sort of twisted stage, holding the curtain for all the others to enter: Lieberman, Anna, the police, an array of guilty parties jointly responsible.

Sometimes I don't know what to say and so I just sit there and stare down at my empty coffee cup. Jack's not the man he used to be, he now depends on me for support, and on a certain level I feel annoyed by his emotions. I need him to be strong—not for me, for himself—because I was able to cope, have been coping, but I just can't add any more weight to my Jenga stack of agony.

But all he wants to do is talk, talk, talk. And I let him go on and on and on, listening for what seems like days on end, sometimes tuning him out for long stretches at a time, hours even, his voice without inflection or variation, monotonous and low. Eventually he gets hoarse and we sit among the scent of coffee, the sound of beans dropping into the mill, the grinding noise drowning him out for a few merciful seconds. Finally his voice turns into a raspy whisper and we both go home.

I allow months of these meetings to pass and watch layer after layer of guilt pile on top of him like shovels of soil on a coffin. I tell him about a legacy, *his legacy*, something constructive he can do with the monsters trapped in his head—those were his words, *monsters trapped in his head*—but Jack is Jack and that's all there is to it.

"You could start a foundation in Mia's name. You could speak in front of people, to groups of parents, you could assist in searches for missing children. Jack, there's so much you can do. I think it'd be good for you."

"You know I'm not comfortable around people. That whole speaking thing is just nerve-racking for me. Trust me, if I thought it made any kind of a difference, I would, but . . . once the brownstone sells, I'll put up a reward. Rewards have solved cases before, it's probably the most effective action I can take. That's helpful, right?"

I wonder if Jack has it worse because he was taught to be stoic, to "act like a man." At some point maybe Jack realized he just cannot survive this kind of despair, cannot allow himself to be dragged down, and so he focuses instead on walking away. Maybe his trick is to keep the suffering at a distance.

"I can go for days feeling normal," he says, "and then I think of nothing else and I feel like I'm going crazy."

One day, at the coffee shop, I feel his judging eyes on me while I search through missing children's databases on my laptop. Like a hawk watching a sparrow, he scrutinizes me as I keep track of body parts washing up on shorelines. He frowns, and when I hand him a list of private detectives, he looks away.

And I start getting angry at him. Angry at his inability to fight the monsters, angry at the fact that money is what his solution is, angry that he expected me to grow beyond my limitations, told me to just "snap out of it"—those were his words—yet he's unwilling to do the same.

Eventually everything about Jack strikes me as silly. Those fanged rippers, those elusive little shits he can't get under control when the real monster lived in the same house with me while he was working on foreign exchanges and equity deals.

Fuck you, Jack. Fuck. You.

Eventually the monsters have mercy on Jack and disappear. They seem to just vanish because one day he appears to have gained his strength back, his step is quicker, less restrained, and the bags under his eyes have faded. He even has a tan, as if he's spent the weekend in the sun. And I watch him, after the obligatory display of grief, mentally severing himself from the uncomfortable fact that this crisis will never come to an end. We've held on until there is nothing to hold on to anymore. And then we agree to sign divorce papers.

Jack will go on with his life, someplace else, with hardly a backward glance, no call, no text, no e-mail. He hates complicated relationships and I have no doubt that his emotions, once again, run like a train on steel rails. He's a DA last time I heard, in Boston, I think, I don't remember.

And eventually I realize I'm the only one looking. I request a copy of all documents, of all police files. I read through them, study them, and make mental notes of anything that could possibly shed light on Anna's whereabouts. And when I'm through, I start all over again.

And then there is the media. The amount of time the media spends on a case, any infamous reputation assigned, is directly related to the details they can dig up about your life, neighbors they can interview, and relatives who speak out on *20/20*. I have none of that to offer. At the most there'll eventually be a *Cold Case Files* edition or a *Dateline* legal show. After I decline all interviews, there is nothing else to be had.

Pictures of Mia as an infant were subject to intense media coverage but photos of me were scarce, to say the least. By the time I rent the studio apartment, phone calls from reporters prompt me to change my number for the first time. There are calls regarding book deals and movie opportunities. I hang up the phone and again change my number. Then it quiets down. After all, there is no trial, no gavel-to-gavel coverage dedicated to bringing legal proceedings to the public. There is only so much media fodder and then the primary elections come up, and eventually other headlines take priority.

Anthony now works for the FBI's Joint Terrorism Task Force in Anchorage, Alaska, and heads an Evidence Response Team. The division also runs a Kidnapping and Missing Persons office at the same Alaska office.

Anthony's called me almost every week since I left Creedmoor. I visited him and his wife a year ago. Abby had just given birth to a baby boy and I could only make excuses for so long. The baby's name is William Hadley Paradise and he was two months old when I met him. I never held him, and Anthony didn't ask me to. We rarely speak of our childhood, as if our foundation is shaky, and our conversations mainly revolve around what he calls Mia's *recovery*.

During the visit he suggests I add Mia's case to the nationwide Crime Stoppers website where people can phone in tips, anonymously if they so desire. "More exposure is what you need. Add a reward to it and the chances increase." After I return to New York, he calls me.

"You can stay with us anytime, I mean long-term, not just a visit," he says and I'm not sure how to respond. I've never thought about leaving New York and I just can't imagine turning my back on the city. Something wisp thin has slipped between us, something new, unrelated to the past. We both long to establish a new kind of relationship, a bond that will endure from here on out. He leaves messages on my phone. "Knock knock," he always says, "call me back."

And I catch myself smiling when I hear his voice.

Mia's recovery, Anthony calls it. I try not to think about the fact that Mia knows another woman as her mother and with every passing day I become more disillusioned that a recovery is even possible. I'll never get back what I've lost. There's this hole I feel inside of me that isn't of this world, a sadness that sticks to me like an old faithful dog, stirring when I stir, opening its eyes when I open mine. Never far away, always loyal, steadfast. To be counted on.

Jack offers a twenty-thousand-dollar reward *for tips leading to the whereabouts of Anna Lieberman and the recovery of Mia Connor* as part of the Crime Stoppers website campaign. The statistics are promising; the website has yielded hundreds of thousands of arrests, almost a million cases cleared, and over a hundred million dollars paid out in rewards. The twenty thousand dollars highlight the dark side of the operation; the number of incoming tips is enormous, and while some are obviously phoned in as a joke, others take up valuable resources. The supposed "sightings" of Anna Lieberman are a sculptor in Santa Fe, a Siamese cat breeder in Las Vegas, and a middle school teacher in Oklahoma. There's no attempt to enroll Mia in school, no attempt to access medical coverage, no passport application. It's as if Anna's found the perfect hiding place.

What am I to do? Post flyers all over New York City? What's the point of that? A website makes more sense and so I hire a designer but after a month I realize that for every kind word there are ten comments about my incompetence, my lack of "mother DNA," and those are the kind ones. Some people want to kill me. They don't know they'd be doing me a favor. Regardless of how many nights I stare at the ceiling as I lay in the darkness, I always come to the same conclusion: I can't live like this. And I'm ready to do more.

I call Detective Wilczek daily and he tells me finding Anna will be "a matter of time." A month later I start calling him weekly, and words like *hiding*, *unsuspecting*, and *ingenuity* snake their way into our conversations.

"But we're on it. We're not giving up. We'll have to wait for her to make a mistake, and she will, they all do."

Six months later he tells me he'll call me when something new comes up.

On the one-year anniversary he refers to Anna's trail as having "gone cold." In a matter of months they'll refer to Mia as a "cold case."

Two months after the divorce is final, I return to North Dandry. I'm curious if the place still holds bondage over me. The renovations have been completed, the building has been sold. Hence the reward money Jack put up.

As I get out of the taxi, I deliberately avoid glancing at the building. I pay the cab driver and I finally look up, standing perfectly still. I expect a violent reaction—blacking out, fainting, or even vomiting—yet none of that happens. It lies dormant and spiritless, almost sad. Even the building looks as if it's moved on.

Daily I wonder how Mia looks—she is almost four now—and I know she's changed and has become unrecognizable to me. The fact that I wouldn't recognize my own child if I saw her makes me sick to my stomach.

And so I create her, fill out every inch of her body, stretch her limbs, and elongate her face to fit me just right. I believe she has my fine, wavy hair, Jack's brown eyes, and my love for citrus fruits. Mia's face—the one I have created—lurks everywhere, ready to manifest itself at any given time; in the park, at a store, in the subway, on TV. Blond hair, pale skin, dark eyes. Pink lips, curved like Jack's, full like mine. I reconstruct her features and fill in the blanks as I see fit.

I'm afraid that eventually I'll forget her scent, the feel of her hair against my check. The thought of her existence being completely erased from my mind one day makes me angry. It's a finite kind of anger, the kind that can be endured for only so long until something's got to give.

CHAPTER 27

The Brooklyn Frame & Photo Gallery is only a few blocks from 58th Street. The gallery specializes in custom framing for art pieces and photographs. I love the thought of conserving moments in time. I show our customers catalogs with samples of matting. I dust the frames that cover the wall behind the counter. I proclaim the advantages of classic frames over antique or contemporary looks, I speak on naturally treated hardwoods, finished-corner artisan hardwoods, welded aluminum and steel, unique Plexiglas frames, finished-corner gold-leafed frames, and our large selection of modern and decorative moldings.

For the past five years I have framed other people's memories. It consoles me on so many levels; I'm a bystander, yet I partake in the joy of others since I doubt I will ever again find joy for myself. It is a strange way to live, yet I can function within this limited level of participation, it having been familiar to me all my life.

On a bad day I want to tell them to preserve their memories

because they might be taken from them before they can even imagine a future, before they clip a pink bow in the blond hair of a girl with dark eyes and pale skin.

The look on the customers' faces who pick up their framed photographs, those moments are like the parents of my future; they create the person I want to be one day. Other days, when I hear a crying infant or walk into a restroom where a mother just changed her baby, the smell of baby powder renders me helpless.

The NYPD stopped searching for Mia years ago. They know she is—or was, at one point—with Anna Lieberman. She could be anywhere and nowhere. Mia could be with Anna still, or sold to the highest bidder. Or maybe they live somewhere, in another country or another state. Maybe they went down to Mexico. Maybe Canada.

The other day, on my way to work, I passed a little girl in a school uniform, smiling and skipping along beside her mother. Suddenly fear rose inside me. I actually took a step after the little girl before I forced myself to cut off my thoughts. *Don't be stupid*, I told myself, *that's not Mia*. Except . . . my panic rears up again and again, panic that she might live somewhere close, yet I'll never know.

For five years I've seen babies in strollers and toddlers in buggies and I think: *That's what Mia would look like now*. Those fleeting images of her, images that cause me to stop, bend over, and collect my breath, find me in the most unpredictable places, in the most random forms. A strand of hair, a little finger pointing at something. A wailing baby, a crying toddler, a bawling kid in the park. I see Mia everywhere. Little girls who look like her cross the street beside me, they hold their mothers' hands, they enter school buildings, and they hang off monkey bars in parks. Mia's likeness holds another woman's hand and it tears me up inside.

My therapist, Dr. Langston, who I see twice a week in the afternoons, has a skeleton model in the corner of her office. The day we meet for the first time, I remark that she's not an orthopedic doctor and that the skeleton seems misplaced to me.

"Bones are all we really know about humans. Pretty much everything else is just conjecture. Miracle recoveries, new diseases, the brain, we are basically clueless," she says and squints at the skeleton. "I call him Musterion; it means 'sacred secret' in Greek. A reminder that we know nothing about the human condition."

Her large office window faces the west and during our sessions the room floods with golden light. It makes me smile every time I walk in. I've been keeping a secret from her and today I decide to come clean.

"There was this woman and a little girl, on Delaware and 49th, the girl wore a black down jacket. Her ponytail had come loose under her hat, it sat crooked, and the woman made no attempt to straighten it. One of her pink gloves dangled on a string attached to her coat, her other hand held on to the woman's hand, which I assumed to be her mother.

"I remember her stride, wide and bouncy, had caught my eye. But what alerted me was the red hair she pushed nervously under the hood of her duffel coat. The gesture seemed suspicious, hasty, meant to deceive. I trailed them but after a few minutes I felt heavy and stiff, unable to keep up. They finally slowed down and boarded the B11 bus."

I remember I sat behind them, catching my breath. The bus windows were fogged with the heat and breaths of dozens of people. There was a man in a blue uniform, two teenage girls with purple hair and nose rings, shift workers with empty eyes and lunch boxes on their laps. The rest were old people in orthopedic shoes and drawstring pants on their way back to their senior living facility. The little girl's head rested on the woman's shoulder, then her forearm, eventually her lap.

"Did you think it was your daughter and the woman who kidnapped her?"

"There was a general resemblance to Anna Lieberman as I remember her, but the woman was taller, older, maybe even the girl's grandmother."

I tell Dr. Langston that when the bus reached Sunset Park, the woman gently stroked the girl's cheek. She made eye contact with the girl and placed her hand in front of her right eye and pulled away as if pulling on a string. The girl responded by raising her index finger. Sign language, I thought, and realized what had compelled me to follow them in the first place was the fact that they seemed disconnected from each other. The woman gently slipped the pink glove over her hand and smiled at the girl. The girl bared her miniature teeth back at her. I watched them as they leisurely strolled off to the subway.

"Did you continue to follow them?"

"No, I didn't, but I wondered what I would do if it was her. The pills I take make me tired and I'm out of shape and what if I had to run after someone?"

Dr. Langston looks at me, puzzled. "You're not thinking about stopping your meds, are you?"

"No, I'm not. But on my way home the other day I stopped to buy a pair of running shoes. And I've been running ever since."

Seated on the edge of her chair, Dr. Langston listens to every word I say.

"I feel I have to do something more. I check online, I follow the news, I . . . maybe . . . maybe I will recognize someone, or make out a voice I've heard before. There's still the waitress that the police never found. And I know Anna is still out there. I just can't sit still anymore."

"You run to find clues as to where your daughter is?" Her eyebrows raise and form half-moons of apprehension over her eyes.

"I know it's not very logical and that's why . . . that's why I've been thinking about becoming a crime analyst," I say.

Dr. Langston forgets to blink, then she clears her throat. "A crime analyst?"

"Yes. I'm thinking about it." It had never crossed my mind, but there it is, floating in the air, from hasty comment to a possibility to do something, to a resolve of some sort.

"Maybe we should talk about this before you—"

"I don't think you understand," I interrupt her. "I've been calling the detective for years, the one who worked the case. They don't have a single lead. Nothing. How do you not have a single lead?"

"From what I understand—"

"It drives me crazy that she's somewhere, right now as we sit here, she's doing *something*. Right now, as we speak, she is living somewhere, wearing a dress, having her hair in a ponytail, speaking, playing. I refuse to believe that she's lost. It's not like a stranger grabbed her off the street, we know who she's with. I understand that all the other leads, the diner, the waitress at the diner, turned up nothing. I get that. I may not be able to find my daughter, but Anna, Anna I can find. A needle in a haystack maybe, but hell, there's a haystack and there's a needle in it. All I've to do is take each single blade of hay and remove it. And I'll be left with the needle."

"I just want to make sure that you don't—"

"Become obsessed? You worry that I'll become obsessed with finding my daughter? Listen, Dr. Langston, this is not a healthy life, I know that. But I'm not concerned and neither should you be."

"As your therapist your mental health *is* my primary concern."

"Then tell me what to do, tell me what you would do? Sit around and wait? One more summer, one more Christmas? Another four years?" I laugh out loud, from the gut. Crisp, with a hint of evil.

Dr. Langston remains silent as a broad bar of sunlight bathes her in an angelic glow. She presses down the button of her ceramic pencil. The porcelain shell looks expensive, a Mother's Day present maybe—I've seen photos of her children on her desk—a token of appreciation from people who love her. She aligns the pen with the yellow notepad paper.

When she doesn't answer, I nod with unwavering intensity.

"I'm not managing my grief well, am I?"

"Managing is the important part."

I've read the terminology. Mia is considered "long-term missing." All subject-matter experts from a wide array of disciplines have considered all possible strategies. Nothing else can be done. We've reached the end of the line and I'm the only one standing.

"Sometimes I get up in the morning and I feel that today is the day. Today is the day when the phone rings and there's a lead. A picture. A trace of something." I don't tell her that just last week I went to Anna's house and that it's vacant again. I don't mention the fact that I went back to the cornfield and that I poked the earth with a stick where I buried Lieberman. That I had coffee at the diner, which by now sees a pretty steady influx of customers.

I've done my homework. Dr. Langston is merely a companion on my journey, a spectator of my grief, if you will. Her main mission is to bear witness to my pain. According to her manual she is to emphasize the importance of ongoing support for individuals like me. She is to tell me that I must attend to my own physical and emotional needs. She is to help me prepare for the long term and the fact that my life must go on without my daughter.

She listens attentively and honors the few stories I have of Mia. There isn't much to tell, really, she was born, inflicted by a colic when she was only a few weeks old, a colic that never passed, and then she was gone. No anecdotes of learning to crawl, first steps, or first words. It was all a struggle for both of us. When I run out of stories to tell, and we go in circles for a few sessions, she mentions the support group flyer she gave me a while back.

"Did you ever give the support group I told you about a chance?"

"Not yet," I say and I have no intentions of going at all. The thought of listening to other people's pain is not my idea of finding Mia.

"It can be quite therapeutic and might help you make sense of your new world."

"A world without my child doesn't make sense at all," I tell her.

"Give it a chance," she says, and so I do.

I go that very same day. I give chances, it's the only thing I have to give these days.

Only a handful of cars dot the church parking lot as I pass spindly trees amidst concrete islands and weeds poking through the asphalt. I count eight cars. I scan the flyer taped to the door. *Healing Hearts*, it says. *Weekly meetings. Grief Support after the Loss of a Child.* The group meets at six. At five there's an AA meeting on the schedule. Tai chi for seniors starts promptly at eight.

Grief is universal, the flyer says. *A place where people who have experienced a loss can tell their stories knowing they will be respected and held in confidence.*

I enter the titanic room with intermittent columns holding up the ceiling. It is stuffy and reeks of mold, Freon, and stale coffee. I make my way to the back, where the fluorescent lights shine a merciless blaze on a group of people. I count seven. A man with a folder in his lap. Two couples, one middle-aged and one fairly young woman. I take one of the vacant chairs.

"Hi, my name is Eric," the guy with the folder says and counts heads, then notes the number of people attending on a notepad.

"I'm a licensed grief counselor and the facilitator of this group. Most of us know each other but we have a new face here tonight." Eric makes eye contact with me and strokes his soul patch. "Just so we're on the same sheet of music, let me go over the principles again. Everyone here has experienced a loss of a loved one. We're here to talk about that experience with people who are likely to understand. There'll be words of wisdom, words of support and sometimes"—Eric pauses and glances at a couple holding hands—"sometimes our words cause even more pain. Be patient with each other and remember, we're not a social network, we're not a therapy group. Everything we say is confidential."

I look around. There's a couple with identical T-shirts, the word *Hope* on their chests, the *o* being a butterfly. The woman's pudgy fingers rest in the man's hand, as if he is keeping her from darting for the door. Or off a bridge, I'm not sure. The man introduces himself as Dwight, his wife as Kathryn. "But she goes by Katy," he adds. "We lost our daughter to cancer a year ago."

The middle-aged woman in an outfit that I didn't know still existed—pink stretch pants and a pink shirt with embroidered flowers—is on the verge of tears. "I'm Regina," she says and dabs her eyes with a cloth handkerchief. "My son suffers from a mental disease. I haven't seen him in five years."

The other couple, Kristy and Dave, wear sweatpants, flannel shirts, and crosses around their necks. "Our son was killed in Afghanistan," Kristy says, clutching the cross in her fist.

And then it's my turn to introduce myself. I practiced at home, went over my words dozens of times, expecting the inescapable and obligatory introduction of my loss, and I faltered every time. I haven't lost anyone. At least not yet. I believe Mia is alive but I don't know where. I feel out of place, even more than I imagined when this moment played out in my mind.

"My name's Estelle," I say and take in a deep breath. I'm not sure what to say. My loss is unique, I'm in some elusive limbo state, not quite circle of life, yet all-encompassing.

"Hi, Estelle," Eric says. "Welcome to Healing Hearts. Who have you lost?"

I remain silent. The young very large woman to my left takes pity on me.

"I'm Mary," she says. "The first time can be difficult. This is only my second time here and last week I told the group about my sister Lilly. One day, in third grade, she didn't come home after school."

Mary pauses and I scrutinize her profile, want to see exactly what grief looks like on such a young face. Mary must be close to five hundred pounds, her thighs reach beyond the metal chair's seat. She can't be older than nineteen or so. She wears stretch pants and a large black T-shirt. There's a velvety, light brown ring around her neck, indicating an advanced state of diabetes. I wonder if she knows. Her fingers are stubby knobs, her nails are bitten to the quick. Her face seems unaware of her loss, her porcelain skin is plumb and subtle, her eyes bright, surrounded by long lashes. Nothing about her speaks of pain but her shaky voice. I don't notice any tears but Mary wipes her eyes with the back of her hand nonetheless. Maybe people run out of tears eventually, I think.

"May Christ hold her forever," Kristy chimes in, and crosses herself. "God's love is eternal."

Mary stares at her and, after a brief pause, says, "Amen."

I stick around, watch their chins quiver, hear their voices shake, watch them struggle as they attempt to reach beyond their pain, and I know I have to make a decision. I see myself, weeks from now, accepting invitations for coffee and a cheap King James Bible, partaking in grief retreats where I'll be resting, hiking, and talking my pain away. And I know I can't go there. All I can do is acknowledge the fact that my life has veered off into a direction I never could have imagined and that I can either succumb or withstand. And I choose the latter.

"Excuse me, I think I left my car lights on," I say and get up and leave.

When Dr. Langston asks me about the group, I tell her it's not for me.

"Different priorities, is all."

"I know it's not easy to speak in public about Mia. Each parent's expression of pain is unique," Dr. Langston says.

"I'd rather talk about finding her."

"I'm worried about you, Estelle."

"Why?" I can feel myself getting angry. Dr. Langston watches my emotions intently and she knows she's hit the mark. Challenge is part of the manual.

"We've talked about this before, Estelle."

"Are you telling me to stop looking?"

"No, I'm not. I want you to dedicate a part of each day to finding Mia. And the rest of the day I want dedicated to you. And maybe allow yourself to consider the other possibility."

She's been trying to get me to say it for weeks now but she must know she'll never hear those words from me.

"She might not come back." Dr. Langston's voice trembles ever so slightly.

"You know what?"

"What?" She scoots to the front of her chair and listens intently.

"I think I left my car lights on," I say.

CHAPTER 28

The air is sharp. Liquid ice stings my nostrils and seeps into my lungs. The first ten minutes of running in the cold sucks, but then I get warm and cozy. My legs loosen up, my breath settles into a steady rhythm, and I go on autopilot. Three miles later the cold air has dried out my airways and, after another mile, my lungs start to burn and a hacking cough forces me to stop every few minutes. The cold pavement crawls through the bottom of my running shoes up into my legs. Three layers of clothes, a thermal cap, and tights are no match for New York's arctic air.

I finally give up and surrender to the cough. I spot a Starbucks down the street and decide to stop running for the day. I cut across Second Avenue and pause in front of an electronics store. Hot air blows up a shaft and through a grate, warming my feet. There're numerous flat screens mounted on the walls of the store, all of them tuned to CNN. Silent pictures move across the screens when another coughing fit rips through me. I cup my hands around the coffee cup and the news ticker on the bottom of the screen catches my attention.

Breaking News.

My breath mingles with the steaming coffee and I jerk back as the hot liquid scalds my lips. I watch the headlines pass by.

Fundamentalist church raid under way.

Compound under investigation of child abuse.

84 children taken into custody.

I watch dozens of children in a neat line hold hands as they enter white buses parked by the side of the road. Behind them a group of women emerge from a building, shielding their eyes from the cameras. Some of them step off the porch as if to follow the children being carted off, others remain on the porch, crying, holding on to each other. Their pastel-colored dresses are buttoned up to the neck, reaching all the way to the ground. Their every step kicks up the dress seams, offering a glimpse at stocking-covered legs and dusty orthopedic shoes. Their hair is pinned into tall waves high above their foreheads, their faces are scrubbed clean. Red-rimmed eyes and blotchy cheeks complete the picture of utter despair.

Another news flash creeps over the screen.

Children to remain in state custody while authorities investigate allegations of abuse.

One of the women's braids has loosened and her red hair is reaching all the way to her lower back. She screams at the men escorting the children into the bus while the other women stand in silence, wiping their tears. A state trooper is motioning the woman to get back on the porch. The woman's red hair floods around her as she raises a hand toward him as if to curse his very existence. Then the camera zooms in on her. Her lavender dress and her poufy strawberry hair can't distract me from her hand. Deformed, covered in burn marks.

My intestines turn into a corkscrew, then my body surrenders. A flash, followed by a star falling toward the dark ground, illuminated, shining bright. A recollection, then a memory. Anna, the teenager, the aunt. *Laura Dembry, member of the Church of Appointed Dominion.*

My mind stills and the world around me turns fuzzy.

The haystack. I've found the haystack.

I reach for my phone. "Detective, this is Estelle. Estelle Paradise." I have trouble catching my breath.

There's a long silence on the other end of the line.

"Mrs. Paradise, how are you?"

"I'm calling you because I need your help." I have trouble talking and breathing at the same time.

A pause. Then, "I'm no longer working with the same department. I've been reassigned. I can give you a number to call if you—"

"Are you watching the news?" I interrupt him when I finally catch my breath.

"What?"

"Police raided a compound. They took all the children."

"I'm not watching, but I'm aware."

"This is it."

"I'm sorry, I don't understand."

"Can we meet somewhere?"

A long silence. "Mrs. Paradise, I don't—"

"In one hour. The Starbucks on Second Avenue and 50th."

"There's nothing I can do for you. Like I said, I'm no longer—"

"In one hour. I'll be waiting."

"Hold on a minute, I still don't understand . . . what's the raid got to do with anything?"

"I'll be waiting," I repeat and hang up the phone.

One hour later the words pour out of me. The raid. The children. Anna Lieberman, the woman with red hair is one of the mothers from the Dominion Compound in Plainview, New York. And maybe, just maybe, one of the children I watched on live TV boarding the buses is Mia. And no one at the precinct is willing to hear me out *because any information on the minor children recovered from the compound will not be discussed until DNA analysis has been completed.* And then they hung up the phone.

"One hour, Detective, one hour from here. She's been this close all along."

"How can you be sure the woman is Anna Lieberman?" Wilczek's voice is intense, almost sharp.

"I think I'd recognize the woman who took my daughter. I also understand this is an ongoing investigation, but I need some information from you."

"I checked the official list of names. There's no Anna Lieberman. They won't release any information until the investigation is complete. It's not really out of the ordinary that they don't want to talk about the case."

"That's why I called you."

"I don't think I'm the right man for you, I don't have access to any information. Besides, I don't know what you're looking for." He raises his hands, palms up. There's a change in his demeanor suddenly, like a cloud's shadow overhead. "I can't do anything that's against the law."

"I'm not asking you to do anything illegal," I say, but I don't really know the legalities, and I don't really care, which is just about the same thing to me.

"You don't understand, I've had a lot going on lately, there were some problems at work, and I don't need to get caught up in something . . ." His large thumb presses down on the domed plastic coffee cup lid. "Look"—he says and hesitates ever so slightly—"not that it makes any difference to you, but I'm going through a divorce. New York State maintenance is not exactly cheap. And I have a son. I can't risk my job right now."

I ignore his comment. I have no interest in his problems. I swallow, tell myself this doesn't mean no, it means nothing. There's a way, there's *always* a way.

"One girl, Wilczek." I study the dark circles under his eyes and his wrinkled shirt. His eyes are empty holes, lifeless. But I don't care about any of this. "There's one girl whose DNA doesn't match any of the women from the compound. That girl, five years old, is my daughter. And I need to find her." I imagine nurses with cotton swabs swiping the cheeks of children with large and frightened eyes. "I know there's lengthy backlogs in every crime lab in the state and it could take months to get it all sorted out but—"

"Do you have any idea what kind of circus you're dealing with? There are hundreds of DNA tests to be done. Figuring out who belongs to who will take months. And let's not even take into consideration that they probably gave wrong names and ages. Everybody is someone's mommy, every man's someone's uncle or daddy. It's like untangling hundreds of fucking miles of Christmas lights."

"But if she's one of them, we'll find her." He cringes when I say *we*.

"Yes, I don't doubt that but you'll have to wait. The DNA testing will take some time."

There's too much frozen anger inside of me and I've been waiting for too long. "Hear me out, okay?" I fold my hands as if I'm about to pray. Did he grimace or did I imagine that?

"Five minutes," he says and leans back. He swirls what's left in the bottom of the cup and then downs it. "And I'm not promising anything."

That night, I lie awake. I have kicked off the covers and I'm cold. I must have forgotten to close the blinds because the light of the moon spills into my room, its unforgiving brilliance restraining my breathing like a giant cat sitting on my chest. Reality seeps in slowly. When the pressure becomes unbearable, I sit up.

At night, when my mind drops its guard, the extent of what is my reality becomes too much. My thoughts turn daunting, unscalable. I close my eyes, allow fright to wash over me. I lie still as the panicky wave pounds me, crashes against me, shaking and weakening my foundation like waves eroding the base of a cliff.

I remain silent, patient. My fists are knotted, pushed against my stomach, where the fear originates. I give in, offer myself like a token, and I feel the pain subside. It pearls off me like water off an oily surface, unable to hold on.

Fear is no longer permanent, it passed and so did the doubts. Tomorrow is the day.

I hear a faint chime above the gallery door, its announcement so timid I almost miss it. Detective Wilczek is wearing a suit, a coat on top, and his eyes are wearier than I remember them. He has something to tell me, but I can't read him just yet. He nods and we both stare at each other.

"Do you think you could take a break?" His demeanor lacks urgency. "Maybe we could go for a walk."

I turn toward the framing room behind me. It's filled with sounds of hammering nails, and the shellac wafting toward me is making my temples pound. I grab my coat from the hanger and lead the way.

New York in January is like stepping into a freezer. We stick our hands in our coat pockets as we pass naked winter trees lining the street. Temperatures are in the low twenties, spring is still months away, and warmth is so far removed from people's minds that it almost sounds like a fairy tale no one can believe in. We turn to the right, toward a park. The cast-iron fence near the entrance is covered in ice. Our breaths mingle as we walk.

"She gave the authorities a different name. But it's her. I talked to her aunt." He allows it to sink in and waits patiently. "Anna's gone," he adds.

"When?" I ask, and my heartbeat accelerates rapidly.

"This morning. Her aunt told me she left days after the raid. Took all her belongings and a car from the compound, a blue Pontiac. Aunt wasn't forthcoming with the plates."

"Where are the children?" I ask.

"In state custody."

"Are they all in one place or split up?"

Wilczek cocks his head and his eyes narrow. "I have a feeling you are about to do something really stupid."

"Do you know where they are or don't you?"

"I'm not sure, they usually end up in foster care or shelters, depending on their ages."

"Can you find out?"

"Even if I could, I wouldn't tell you. Don't you get it? All you have to do is wait."

I don't have the patience to wait, I don't even have the patience to respond to the possibility of waiting. "What if Anna takes her again?"

Wilczek inhales sharply. "What are you saying?"

"I'm saying the fact I didn't die in the ravine messed up her plans. No one wanted a baby the entire country is looking for. Anna didn't keep Mia all this time just to leave her behind now."

"*If* Mia is one of the children . . . *if.*"

"*If* she takes her again, it'll be too late. And where will I look then? How likely is it that I find her again?" I've raised my voice and stare back at a couple who're eyeing us, wondering if we're having an insignificant lover's quarrel. "Tell me where the children are and leave the rest to me."

"That's a frightening thought. You can't possibly expect me to do that."

"You can't possibly expect me not to ask." I won't give up—he must know this. "How long do you think until she finds out where Mia is? She'll try to abduct her again. She's smart, she's been under the radar for almost five years and never got caught."

Days, we have merely days to act. And I have no clue how to convince him to help me.

As we walk on, we pass a little girl with sleek hair dancing on her head. She's skipping up and down the sidewalk while her mother rocks a stroller back and forth.

I take in a deep breath, then I slow down my steps, peek at the kid in the stroller. Wrapped up in a pink blanket, hat, and mittens, is a toddler with a round face and rosy cheeks.

"What a beautiful baby," I say. "She looks so happy."

Mom goes on and on about how Emma, that's her name, cries a lot and is difficult overall, "drama queen" she calls her, but calms down when she's being rocked. I just nod when appropriate and manage an occasional smile.

"You have kids?" Mom asks me.

I stare at her for a second. "No," I say and I feel the words vibrate in my throat, as if my body recognizes the lie I just told. It's complicated, nothing you discuss on the street in passing.

Mom looks back and forth between me and Wilczek. I assume she's torn between *Are you trying, Maybe one day*, or some other friendly token of sympathy for a still-childless couple.

I nod and manage a "Stay warm now" comment and Wilczek and I silently continue our walk.

"Do I have kids? That's a hard question to answer, isn't it?"

Wilczek's eyes narrow. Then he looks away. He knows what's coming but he can't escape me.

"You said you had a son?"

"Yes." Hesitantly, his eyes move around as if he wants to make sure no one is watching us.

"You see him a lot?"

"Every Sunday."

"How old is he?"

"Two."

"What does he like?"

"The usual, you know, cars, trucks, that sort of thing. Ice cream. Cookies."

"Let me think . . . two years old, you say." I point to my temple as if I am trying to remember something. "He turns the pages of a book, he can open drawers and cabinets, he feeds himself with a spoon, is easily frustrated, and shy around strangers. Very affectionate, lots of hugs and kisses?"

Wilczek stares straight ahead.

"He can walk up and down the stairs as long as he holds on to your hand, right?"

I step in front of him and stare straight at him.

"Do you know how I know this? Kids' social and emotional development? Physical milestones of toddlers?"

I step forward ever so slightly and put my hand on top of his coat where his heart is. Do I feel a slight tremor underneath? I grab his other hand with mine.

"I read it in a book." I hold his cold hand until it warms up. He's trying to pull back but I squeeze even harder. When I finally allow him to pull his hand away, he steps back and hides it in his coat pocket. He turns and walks off, but his steps are no longer defiant.

I've won.

After I leave work that day I clean my apartment. I obsessively wipe down every surface, vacuum every corner, spray Lysol in every nook and cranny. When the phone rings, I pull the yellow latex gloves off my hands and toss them into the kitchen sink. The oven cleaner fumes linger in the air, making my temples pound. I watch the gloves float on the surface of the murky water. Then they sink. Their cheerful, sunny color swallowed up by the depth of the ceramic farmhouse sink. My pruney fingers struggle to hold on to the pen as I scribble down the address.

———

St. Pancras's Path in Brooklyn is part of the Greater New York Family Services Shelter Care System and has taken in the elementary school–age children from the Plainview compound for the time being. It is an unassuming three-story building covered in beige siding with a screened-off porch. A side door leads onto a spacious playground with a slide, three swings, a sandbox, and a seesaw, all equally spaced behind a cast-iron fence. There's an alcove above the front door with a stained glass window depicting Saint Pancras, the patron saint of children, a man in usual saint garb, baring his hands outward in a welcoming gesture.

I've been sitting in my car for almost twenty-four hours. My back is stiff and the urge to get out and stretch my legs is getting harder and harder to ignore. The Ritz crackers and diet soda are getting old. It's been raining on and off, and the possibility of the children spilling out the side door to go to the playground is waning. I hardly slept last night and it's catching up with me. I close my eyes and imagine a scene I created.

It's a weekday, a comfortable forty degrees, and Prospect Park is deserted except for a few joggers with headphones in their ears, closed off in their own worlds. And a handful of people walking their dogs.

Trees and benches are all around us, squirrels, and a scent of wet soil. There's a playground and a small lake with ducks a short walk from the park entrance.

I imagine a small Ziploc bag filled with stale, cubed bread that I prepared earlier that day. I sit on a nearby bench and a car stops behind me in the parking lot. The crunch of gravel echoes in my ears. Then the ding-ding-ding *of an open car door.*

Out of the corner of my eye I see a child in a purple puffy jacket, jeans, and black boots running toward the playground. Her knitted hat is rainbow-colored with earflaps and a large pompon on top. It bobs as she runs.

A social worker, let's call her Elena Cruz, a kind, tired, and overworked middle-aged woman, is trailing her.

In my vision the playground is surrounded by a fence; the only way in or out is through a small gate. Mia runs straight for the gate, and before I'm able to take her all in, she's swinging off a monkey bar.

Mia's body is stretched as her little hands hold on to the bars. The metal is cold and she's not wearing gloves, but she doesn't mind. Her midriff is exposed as she dangles back and forth, trying to gain some momentum by swinging her legs.

The social worker sees me, smiles, and nods at me encouragingly. I get up off the bench and make my way to the monkey bars. Mia's head is stretched backward, her legs and feet are kicking.

She is beautiful. Not in a way a mother thinks her child is beautiful, but in a saintly way. Curls spill from under the earflaps, her eyes are large and brown and remind me of Jack's. Her eyelashes are sparse yet long and her little miniature teeth smile at me, like perfect Chiclets in a row.

"Hi," she says, her voice strong and confident. "Look what I can do." She swings her legs harder and harder.

"Guess what I have here." I pull out the bread bag and hold it up by its corner and I swing it back and forth.

She looks at me, her eyes questioning, pondering the significance of the bag with its odd contents.

"Bread. Wanna go feed the ducks?"

Her eyes widen and I can see her excitement. Her curiosity is taking over; she jumps off the monkey bars and scans the surroundings.

"Ducks? There's ducks?"

"Yeah, there's ducks. Right around the corner."

She looks at the social worker, and when Elena nods, she jumps off the monkey bars and grabs my hand. I feel chipped paint flakes between our skin and I gently wipe the paint chips off her palm.

"Have you ever fed ducks before?"

She shakes her head and I hand her the Ziploc bag with the cubed bread.

"First time for everything. Ready to go?"

We walk toward the lake, her hand in mine, the bag dangling off her other hand.

I long for someone to take a picture, to capture this very moment as we walk to the lake. In the sunshine, the lake's surface is a perfect looking glass.

As we stand at the lakeshore and throw in the bread, the ducks zoom in on the cubes. Their necks are elongated and their green feathers glimmer in the sun as their heads dip into the water. As soon as their beaks emerge again, they are off searching for the next piece of bread to devour. They search for another cube of sustenance, zoom in, and peck at it all over again.

We watch the ducks trail away from us, rippling the water, disrupting the lake's smooth surface.

"I'm Mia," she says and sounds grown up, her voice still high-pitched, yet mature. She wipes her nose with the back of her hand.

"I know. Mia is a beautiful name."

In the distance, we hear the quacking of the ducks.

The sound of a car door jerks me back into reality. A shadow slides into the passenger seat.

"How long have you been here?" Wilczek seems even more disheveled than yesterday, his eyes are bloodshot and he smells of cigarette smoke.

"Hello to you, too," I say to make this moment seem more mundane. "You look like you've been up for days," I add and look at my wristwatch. It's not as cold as it was earlier but I shiver nevertheless.

He ignores my comment and checks his cell phone. "So . . . what's been going on?"

"Just people coming and going," I say lightheartedly. "So far there was a UPS delivery and the morning paper."

After a moment of silence I ask, "How long do you think until Anna finds out where Mia is?"

"She won't find out at all unless someone, theoretically, tells her aunt, I guess."

Theoretically. I think about the implications of his statement. I study his profile and fight the urge to hug him. I get it, he's a cop, he wants to solve this case. Justice is what he's after. I just want my daughter.

"So what's the overall plan?" Wilczek asks.

"I don't have a plan per se at this very moment," I say and wonder what got to him in the end—his son, my pleading eyes, or the woman with the stroller.

Wilczek puts his hand on top of mine. "I'm going to go talk to them. You stay here and don't move, okay?"

His hand on mine feels awkward and part of me wants to move away—the touch seems almost intimate—yet I also want his hand to remain.

Wilczek gets out of the car and I watch him walk up to the building in his wrinkled coat. He presses the buzzer and I hear a prim female voice through the intercom.

The rain has stopped and the sun is breaking through the seemingly insurmountable layer of clouds. I step out of the car, fearing my legs will end up cramping on me if I sit still any longer. I appease my stiff knee joints by walking up to the cast-iron fence of the shelter playground. The playground is covered in wood chips and an occasional candy wrapper sparkles in the sunlight.

A lonely woolen rain-soaked cap sits abandoned on a red bench by the back door of the building.

I stand by the fence next to an oak tree. The roots have warped the concrete and I step farther toward the property. The trunk's girth hides me perfectly, and while I stare at the back door, I see movement through its glass window.

Then everything slows down and speeds up at the same time. The front door closes and faintly I hear footsteps on the concrete coming toward me. When I turn, I see Wilczek staring at me. The back door opens and children spill into the playground. Wilczek gets in the car and slams the door shut.

Seconds later my cell vibrates in my jacket pocket. I ignore the phone and watch child after child make their way down the steps, toward the playground. The children have taken over the playground equipment. Girls' legs swing like pendulums in unison to gain momentum on the swings while the rest of the kids climb up a ladder to go down the slide. A young woman in a bright red wool coat sits on the bench, shielding her eyes from the sun with her hands. There's so much movement, so much running and chasing, that I can't make out any of the children's faces.

A blue Pontiac stops on the opposite side of the road, facing north. The driver's door opens and a woman in jeans and a black parka emerges, pushing a mass of red hair under her parka hood. As the woman crosses the street she scans the sidewalk, then the playground.

My heart no longer reacts to fateful moments. Maybe I have become accustomed to being tested, maybe I'm so shocked my brain can't conceive the relevance of this moment. Anna and I make eye contact. Before I can move, Anna runs across the street, disappears into the Pontiac. She takes off northbound.

As I stand paralyzed under the oak, I watch my black Jeep trailing the blue Pontiac. Wilczek stares straight ahead while his hands are glued to the steering wheel. He lifts one finger and ever so slightly points toward the Pontiac when I appear in his field of vision. I nod at him.

When both cars have disappeared around the corner, I step out of the shadow of the oak tree and toward the front door of the shelter.

"Excuse me." A woman's voice. The same woman who minutes earlier sat on the bench supervising the children in the playground. Her hands awkwardly clasp her coat in the front as if she didn't find the time to zip it. She smells of coffee.

"I saw you with the detective earlier, outside, in the car. He told us to be on the lookout for a woman but other than a description he didn't tell us anything."

I nod in agreement and pull up my shoulders. "There was an emergency and he had to take off. Would you . . . you mind if I wait inside?"

She hesitates, then points toward the gate.

"I'm Dr. Wallace, staff child psychologist. Please come in."

She unlatches the playground gate and I enter. I just now realize that the children have left the playground. It lies deserted, devoid of laughter and scuffling boots. A couple of mittens are covered in wood chips on the walkway. The gate closes by itself behind me with a *clang*. When we get to the back door, her fingers run over an electronic lock display.

"I see you're prepared," I say and hide my hands in my coat pockets.

"We take in battered women with children sometimes," Dr. Wallace explains, and after the electronic motor sounds she turns the door handle.

We stand in a long narrow hallway with shiny linoleum floors. There's a faint odor of Murphy's soap and something else, sharp and lemony. A cube shelving unit holds coats, bags, and gloves. To the left of us is a large tiled room with miniature sinks and shiny faucets with oversized knobs. A large poster says *Hush, Rush, Flush.*

As we pass by the bathroom, Dr. Wallace turns around. "I didn't get your name," she says and hangs her coat on a hook next to the shelf.

I tell her my name and thank her for allowing me to wait inside.

"We were just about to do our afternoon group activities," she says and points at the reception seating area. "You can wait here if you want."

I nod and take my seat on the couch. Dr. Wallace enters a room across from me, a large round table in the middle surrounded by colorful chairs with a hook for an apron. There's a stack of paper in the middle of the table and a lazy Susan–style revolving tray with an array of paint tubs filled with bright primary colors.

Dr. Wallace claps her hands and from the far side of the room a group of children storm the table and squabble over the chairs.

I count twelve children, seven boys and five girls. I wonder how far I can go, how far I'll be able to intrude without causing suspicion.

Three of the girls have long blond hair and wear identical clothes. They favor one another yet differ in height. Their demeanor is guarded, focused on one another instead of the world around them. They sit close together and seem to wait for a clue from the middle girl, the tallest of the three. When she ties the apron around her waist and reaches for the paper, the other two follow suit.

The two other girls, one with a brown ponytail and bangs covering her eyes, are more subdued, almost aloof. The girl with the ponytail keeps swiping her bangs to one side. The other girl's hair looks like she's had an unfortunate encounter with a pair of scissors. Those two have chosen to sit between the boys.

I walk down the hallway, look at a set of photographs hanging by the door. The photos of people shaking hands at a ribbon-cutting ceremony and a plaque with donor names hardly register.

I watch the children finger painting, and when Dr. Wallace looks up, I check my wristwatch. The children dip their fingers in the paint tubs and I wonder if one of the girls is Mia. I feel no connection, no pull, no recognition. I imagine her baby face elongating, straightening the dip between her nose and her brows. There weren't any birthmarks on her, no scraped knee scar that would help me identify her.

I discount the three blond girls with their cornflower eyes. Mia's eyes were brown, like Jack's. Her hair used to be blond but children's hair darkens over the years.

Two high-pitched voices erupt and two of the boys argue over a tub of paint. One of the boys, his apron has become loose, guides the other boy back to his chair by firmly placing a hand on his back. The boy starts crying and the girl with the ponytail says something to him. I wonder if I'd get away with taking a seat in the far corner of the room when I hear Dr. Wallace tell the children that I'm a police officer. I never told her I was—she must have inferred it when she saw me with Detective Wilczek earlier. *I'm with Detective Wilczek*, I told her.

The children turn and stare at me. The crying boy is inconsolable, and when he realizes that everybody's attention has drifted away from him, he dips his entire hand in the tub with the red finger paint. He is immediately annoyed by his sticky hands and tries to get the paint off by violently shaking his fingers. Then he turns to his left and wipes his hands on the shirt of the boy sitting next to him.

The three blond girls start screaming and attempt to save their pictures from paint spatters by snatching them off the table.

Dr. Wallace's "Everybody listen up" goes unnoticed. Now the other boys also dip their hands into the paint tubs. The doctor's face is visibly tense and she pulls the entire turntable toward her in order to claim the paint. The children are now amused and smear paint over each other's shirts. Someone is laughing uncontrollably, then numerous loud bursts erupt, then turn into giggles.

Dr. Wallace is frantically screwing the lids back on the tubs. "Everybody listen. We are going to wipe our hands and settle down."

She looks at me and gestures me into the room. "Give me a hand, will you?" she says and stuffs a handful of wet wipes into my hands. "I'll handle the boys," she adds and directs them to individual chairs along the wall.

I distribute the wipes and the girls are busy wiping and chatting. I hand the girl with the ponytail and the bangs a wet wipe last. She looks at me, puzzled, and doesn't move. I lean down and gently start wiping the paint globs off her fingertips. She wiggles her hands out of mine and checks for stickiness by rubbing her hands together.

Suddenly her eyes fill with tears. Her painting is covered in paint splashes, torn at the edges. The picture is of a stick figure in a yellow dress with large green dots for the eyes. I stare at the crown of red hair.

"That's my picture." She points at the scribbles. "But now it's all ruined," she adds, her lips pouting. She wipes her eyes with the back of her hand, swiping her bangs to the side.

"Maybe we can fix it," I say. I want to save this picture for her, want to make everything all right. I want to tell her that we can cut out Mommy and glue her to a clean sheet of paper. That sometimes you can start all over and nothing is ruined after all.

When she makes eye contact with me, her eyes swallow my words. Those are Jack's eyes, one raised eyebrow, scrutinizing the world. I fold a wet wipe and encase her hand. Her thumb emerges, clean and shiny. The very tip is covered in round white bumps as if ice is trapped under her skin.

My stomach drops and my hands start shaking. I gently take both of her wrists in my hands. I flip over her hands and wipe one finger at a time with a broad sweep. Countless white lines emerge, covering her fingertips like icicles, remnants of a night a long time ago, a turtle lamp, and a mother who was fallible. I hold on to her hands, want to erase everything that's not right, and I hope her trust won't evaporate.

"All clean," she says and hides her hands behind her back. "What about my picture?"

"The picture," I say and manage a crooked smile, "how about we draw a new one?"

Wilczek appears some time later. Maybe an hour, maybe longer. His eyes are vacant and his jaws are tightly clasped.

I patiently wait for him to go on.

"When she realized she was being followed, she tried to get away, but in the end she couldn't," he says and punches keys on his phone. Finally he gives up. "I called for backup but she had wrapped herself around a pole on Woodside Avenue before they even showed up."

My hands are shaking. "Mia has scars on her hands and she looks like Jack."

"God," he says. Just *God*. Nothing else. His jawline relaxes yet his emotions are confined within a narrow range.

His phone rings. Before I can say anything else, he answers and walks away, leaving behind a trail of cigarette smoke.

"Wait," I call after him.

He turns around, pressing the phone against his chest.

"Tell me everything," I say and step closer.

"I followed her and by the time we got to the first light I could tell she was panicking. She was looking left and right, then just stepped on the—"

"No, not that. Describe her to me."

After a slight pause he says, "She didn't take the time to strap herself in. The pole cut her car in half, the front was basically non-existent. Her knees were touching her chest, the legs were mangled. Her forehead had a long horizontal gash. She must have died before she sustained the injury. The wound wasn't bleeding."

"But I have so many questions." I don't know what I would have asked Anna Lieberman. *Why didn't you just give her back? Why did you keep her? Did you take good care of her? Did my daughter call you Mommy? Does she know she was taken?* The questions humming around in my head are vast in numbers, yet Anna's death has robbed me of any answers, any conclusion, any closure. Therefore any further thought about her is of little consequence.

"I guess I can't have it all," I say, my mind already occupied. There's someone who owes me something.

CHAPTER 29

enter the glass temple of the Donner Broadcasting building, a symbol of its economic power, defining the city of New York as much as the identity of the company itself.

As I sit on the black leather couch with shiny steel legs, I gaze through the horizontal stripes that interrupt the etched-glass doors. I tell her assistant that Amnesia Mom is waiting to speak to her.

When I enter her office, Liza Overton, her cell phone clutched between shoulder and ear, points at a chair in front of her desk. Her facial expression is that of a blank sheet of paper.

"We have to talk," I say and lean back in the leather chair and cross my legs. "I need your help."

"My help?" Now her face moves. Her eyes get smaller, her lips thinner. "What's this all about?"

"You have a way of swaying the public, right?"

"I'd like to think so."

"How about the police?"

"I'm not sure I understand. If you want a public apology from the police, you're in the wrong place."

"There're two things I need from you. One, I want you to do a follow-up show tonight. Two, during that show I want you to put pressure on the cops to initiate an investigation. Call the police chief live on the air if you want."

She throws her head back and laughs. Deeply, from the gut.

"Seriously?"

"I've found my daughter. And I need you to get the police to do a DNA test now. So I can get her back."

"You've found her? Where?"

"First things first. Is that a yes?"

"What's in it for me?"

"Imagine the ratings."

She pushes a button on the phone and tells her assistant to hold all calls.

That same day, as I watch the evening news, I dial Jack's number. We haven't spoken in months but he picks up immediately.

"Are you at home?" I ask.

"Why?" His voice is harsh yet I detect trepidation behind his anger.

"I need you to turn the channel to *Current Crimes*."

"What's going on, Estelle? What the hell is going on?"

"Just do it," I say.

The evening news host fades out and *Current Crimes* fades in.

"*Breaking News Tonight.*" The voice of Liza Overton, her makeup immaculate, her hair stiff as always.

"*Five years ago an infant disappeared from a brownstone in Brooklyn. The mother was the primary suspect in the case, and referred to as Amnesia Mom in the media. In a strange twist of events the child turned out to have been abducted and has never been located. The mother was completely exonerated. Fast-forward, five years later, the child is still missing. And here's the kicker. A cold case at this point, there's reason to believe that the mother has found her daughter but authorities are being less than cooperative in reuniting them. Yes, you heard correctly. The mother has found the child after five years. Don't go anywhere, when we return after the break, we'll get you caught up with the latest developments in the case."*

Current Crimes fades out, a commercial fades in. I switch to CNN and wait.

Jack's flight from Boston to New York is delayed. He tells me not to wait for him and he'll meet me at the New York State Office of Children and Family Services.

A social services agent, a rather large man with a shabby briefcase, oversees our first meeting. There's no park, no playground, and no ducks. He calls it "the exchange," and after he has me sign some paperwork, he tries unsuccessfully to snap his briefcase shut.

"You've been briefed?" he asks and for the first time makes eye contact.

"Yes," I say and think about that little something called "anticipated relationship quality," a term encasing everything that's expected when children are reunited with parents after a long time.

"We don't know if she was abused or even adequately taken care of. She's come to know someone else as her mother, other people as her family. She has no idea who you are."

Makes two of us, I think, but don't say it out loud. My biggest fears are that she won't want to be with me. That she'll hate me when she finds out the truth. And she will never love me.

"After an evaluation, the judge will grant custody. The final transfer won't occur until a judge agrees. The legal term is 'safe-guard for the child's welfare.' "

He turns and opens a heavy metal door. For a second the social worker looks like he wants to shake my hand.

I walk through the door and wait for Mia, and it finally sinks in. No more tracking body parts and children in landfills. No more checking online databases, no more jerking when the phone rings. I've read somewhere that the pain from the loss or death of a child never heals, not until you are reunited, whenever that may be. I'm one of the lucky ones and today is the day.

I sit and fold my hands in my lap. When I hear the door open, I look up.

And then my heart explodes.

KIDNAPPING COLD CASE SOLVED: MIA CONNOR REUNITES WITH PARENTS

Brooklyn, NY—Mia Connor, separated from her family when she was kidnapped five years ago, was reunited with her parents, Estelle Paradise and Jack Connor.

Her mother, Estelle Paradise, was a suspect when she was unable to account for her whereabouts the days after the disappearance of 7-month-old Mia from her crib in Brooklyn.

David Lieberman, a man who lived in the same build-ing, and his sister, Anna Lieberman, were responsible for the kidnapping. The case never picked up speed in the weeks and months after the abduction and went officially cold a couple of years after.

Mrs. Paradise has declined numerous book and movie deals over the years. Liza Overton, host of *Current Crimes* and one of her harshest critics after the abduction, went on TV and broke the story that Estelle Paradise had found her daughter. When all news outlets were flooded with the news, police expedited the DNA test. Mother and daughter were reunited days after the story broke.

"We are happy to report that the family has been reunited," said Joanna Walls, spokesperson for the NYPD. "This is nothing short of a miracle and we couldn't be happier for them."

My mother was a woman rarely seen without her camera. I remember her propped up in bed, among an array of pillows, her camera resting beside her. In her hand a book, a study in light, or angle, or perspective, one of those.

In that memory I climb into my mother's bed and angrily shove a worn and yellowed copy of *Alice's Adventures in Wonderland* at her.

Mom.

She smiles at my accusatory tone and, thinking I want her to read to me, she speaks without looking up. *Not now,* she says, and wraps one arm around me. *How about you read to me?*

I finished it. Did you remember to buy me the other book?

I forgot. I'm sorry.

Do you remember the title?

Through the Looking-Glass, *right? Same author?*

I don't answer, my punishment for her forgetfulness.

What's a looking glass? I ask.

Kind of like a mirror, she says, *it allows you to see yourself the way other people see you.*

Isn't that a mirror?

She doesn't answer and continues flipping the pages of her book. How I hate her books and her camera and her way of being preoccupied with everything but me. What good is a book without words anyway, I wonder, and what good is she anyway, she never talks to me.

She closes the book, puts her other arm around me, and then strokes my hair with her hand. That's how we sit, for a long time. Sometimes I fall asleep, but always she's there when I wake up. Holding me still.

ACKNOWLEDGMENTS

Eternal gratitude to my agent, Laura Longrigg, who gave me a chance when no one else would; my editor, Michelle Vega, who understood my story and, in a very gentle way, helped make it what it is today; and to everybody else who works behind the curtain; talent scouts, production editors, copyeditors; you all rock.

Equal thanks go out to all my fellow writers and early readers who accompanied me on my journey: too many to name and the only appropriate words to express my appreciation: Thank you from the bottom of my heart.

At its heart this book is about mothers and therefore it is only fair that I thank my mother, who shared her beloved books and short life with me; and to my daughter, whose light shines brighter than the brightest star. One day, so I imagine, the two of you shall meet, and I will stand by and watch you be in awe of one another.

Last, but not least, thanks to my husband. You gave me the proverbial room of my own and the money so I could write this book. You are my rock.

Readers Guide for

REMEMBER MIA

DISCUSSION QUESTIONS

1. How would you feel if you woke up and experienced amnesia? Would you rather forget or remember a traumatic event?

2. Throughout the book, Estelle questions her mothering abilities and is consistently judged for how Mia behaves. Do you think if she was offered help or assistance that life would've unfolded differently for them?

3. Jack and Estelle handle their emotions in different ways. How does the scrutiny of outsiders burden the Connor family?

4. There is a heavy emphasis on the choices we make and the people we surround ourselves with. How do the people in your life improve the quality of it and the decisions you make?

5. At what point did you consider Estelle to be responsible for Mia's disappearance? Did you believe she was innocent or guilty? What drove you to this conclusion?

6. How did you feel when Jack took the job in Chicago? Do you believe a relationship can benefit from a temporary separation?

7. Throughout the novel, the reader is privy to Estelle's thoughts. There is a disconnect between what's racing in her mind and her ability to communicate or rationalize her decisions. Have

you ever struggled to speak your mind when you knew that you should speak up?

8. How do you think Estelle handled the assumption that she was responsible for Mia's disappearance? If you were unsure if you did something, would you admit to it or fight to clear your name?

9. When searching through the building, Estelle encounters familiar smells that lead to the immediate recall of memories. When has the sense of smell revived memories of your own?

10. How did your opinion of Estelle change over the course of the novel? How does she change, and how does the author enable us to recognize these changes?

11. How did your perception of the events shift throughout the novel? How does Estelle reconcile Mia's missing status and her newfound freedom?

12. Are all people deserving of a second chance? Is there a time that you received an opportunity to start over?

For more information, or to reach out to the author with questions, please visit her website: alexandraburt.com.